With My Back to the World

Also by Sally Cooper

Love Object
Smells Like Heaven
Tell Everything

With My Back to the World

Sally Cooper

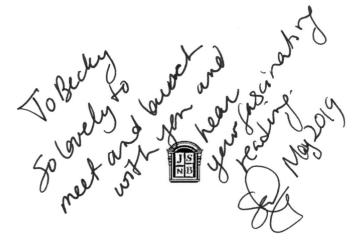

To Becky
So lovely to
meet and brunch
with you and
hear
your fascinating
reading.
May 2019

This is a work of fiction. All characters, organizations, places and events portrayed are either products of the author's imagination or are used fictitiously.

James Street North Books is an imprint of Wolsak and Wynn Publishers.

Cover and interior design: Marijke Friesen
Cover images: (trees) Lanski/Shutterstock.com; (city and sky) 4Max/Shutterstock.com
Author photograph: Melanie Gillis
Typeset in Adobe Garamond
Printed by Ball Media, Brantford, Canada

10 9 8 7 6 5 4 3 2 1

Canada Council for the Arts Conseil des arts du Canada
ONTARIO ARTS COUNCIL CONSEIL DES ARTS DE L'ONTARIO an Ontario government agency un organisme du gouvernement de l'Ontario
Canada

The publisher gratefully acknowledges the support of the Canada Council for the Arts, the Ontario Arts Council and the Government of Canada.

James Street North Books
280 James Street North
Hamilton, ON
Canada L8R 2L3

Library and Archives Canada Cataloguing in Publication

Title: With my back to the world / Sally Cooper.
Names: Cooper, Sally (Sally Elizabeth), author.
Identifiers: Canadiana 20190061537 | ISBN 9781928088806 (softcover)
Classification: LCC PS8555.O59228 W58 2019 | DDC C813/.6—dc23

To my dad, Garry, for giving me the stories and to Isis and Raven for expanding my heart

RUDIE

She was becoming a mother tonight, six months ahead of schedule. January instead of June. Under a dirty dawn sky, Rudie thumped the bundle buggy against the salted, icy steps as she descended to the sidewalk. She could use the car, but her legs needed to move. No skateboarders rolled past today. A white Scottie dog studied her from a bay window. Rudie headed toward the lake – north, not south like when she lived in Toronto. It seemed unreasonable that the world around her hadn't changed.

A pigeon cooed as she turned onto James Street. In a couple of days, she'd walk Roselore here, pointing out the café's mirrored windows and the barbershop's ceramic clowns. They would pass neon stickers plastered on street signs that read Sex Workers are Members of Our Community. *Look at the tomato and meat mincers!* Rudie would say. *What pretty white communion dresses and shiny gold crosses! Look at the bright yellow safety vests!* Cigarette butts and pats of gum littered the snow-dusted sidewalk. Farther down, buildings wearing cupolas and intricate brickwork screamed potential – she thought of Toronto's Queen Street, what it had been and what it was now, wondering if Hamilton's James Street could be the same. She was practised at visually altering what stood in front of her, at seeing restored versions of decrepit structures. A rat ran along the wall, but Rudie's glimpse of the naked street didn't last. Potential could become real. She had proof. And it could happen without any pushing or cajoling. The rat turned a corner. He would run to the lake, swim to the railway yard, some place away from people. He'd do fine. Rudie could distract her daughter when that happened, teach Roselore to see the pleasures that drew her mommy and daddy to this place. Mommy and Daddy! Rudie lingered in the sweet custard scent outside Delicioso, the Portuguese bakery – she'd buy Roselore a tart and they'd sit at the round table in the window – and held her breath past a cluster of smokers outside the Men's Club, packed although it wasn't yet 8:00 a.m. It was too late to cancel Dylan. Her daughter was coming home. She didn't plan to tell him about the adoption, but she didn't want to miss the chance to see him, either. More men stood outside a crowded billiards room. Taran Yang Gallery was showing sculpted cupcakes decorated with beads and satin ribbons. Each hid one flaw, like a worm or mould spot. The fish market smell, with its note of sewage, hit her. Two RCAF corporals in blue serge forage caps and parkas passed as the wind rose, and her eyes teared up. This evening, she'd board a plane bound for Ottawa. The first chance she got, she'd scoop Roselore into her arms and ask her forgiveness for this unrealized street.

—

Rudie had been adding chipotle to a chili almost two weeks ago when the radio reported an earthquake in Haiti. The burner flame crackled with spilled pepper as she fumbled for her phone.

A month earlier, Ann Hepner from Forever Families Agency had called with a match for Leo and Rudie: a daughter, Roselore, who had spent twenty-two of her twenty-eight months in the Angels' Wings Crèche in Port-au-Prince. Ann explained it would take time to push through the Haitian and Canadian paperwork. Leo could finish shooting the season of *Down East Gran* in Nova Scotia, and Rudie could edit her film about abstract painter Agnes Martin. "Plan for June," Ann had said. They'd been planning for June.

Rudie opened up Twitter, heart thudding as she scrolled through reports of the Presidential Palace collapsing, people flooding the streets in distress.

The phone vibrated. Leo.

"Ann left a message," he said. "She's doing everything she can to get through."

"How is Roselore? I can hardly breathe."

"All the power's out. I'll keep phoning."

"What if it happened right where . . ."

"Don't. What about Makenly?"

"Oh God! I wonder how he is?" She hung up and flipped off the gas. She, Leo and Makenly Saintil had all met years ago at an artists' residency. When they decided to adopt from Haiti, she'd contacted Makenly in New York and again before Christmas when the agency matched them with Roselore. He taught in Haiti now, in Pétion-Ville, near Port-au-Prince.

She checked his Facebook page. He'd grown a goatee, trimmed his hair, his smile rakish, his glasses dark-framed. His background photo showed a sunlit, turquoise lagoon fronting a low, treed mountain and storm-rocked sky. He hadn't posted since the weekend.

The next day, Rudie had read all the newspapers, kept the TV on CP24, the kitchen radio tuned to CBC. Images of rubble and reports of devastation rolled over her, often with the same wording repeated. Was Roselore with someone safe, who knew her? Where was Makenly in all the chaos? That evening, Makenly posted a fifty-second video on a global charity's YouTube channel. The camera scanned what appeared to be a collapsed bridge, people in sagging T-shirts and shorts walking in circles, perching on the ruined concrete – children, men, women. Upended trees. Holes. Rubble. Rebar.

Ann had phoned the following morning. Less than forty-eight hours had passed since the quake.

"Sorry I was out of touch," she said. "I lost your number." Did Ann not have call display? "Everyone at Angels' Wings made it, though the building's cracked. The children are sleeping in tents in the driveway but are unharmed. We're planning to go down there, bring aid."

"How is Roselore?" Rudie cleared her throat. "Who's taking care of her?"

Ann's voice softened, slowed. "Reports are good, Rudie. The nannies are with the children. I'll tell you as soon as I know."

Ann flew down on the Saturday, four days after the quake. Rudie studied images of the Presidential Palace crumbled in on itself, its dome askew. She read about dust from collapsed buildings and hoped her daughter and her friend could breathe. When Ann called again last Monday, Rudie's throat tingled and tightened. "Roselore is safe," Ann had said then. "Very safe, you'll be happy to know." Rudie's chest filled with a rush of energy so intense she forgot to ask for more details, instead repeating, "Thank you," over and over.

"I meant to bring down pictures," Ann added. "But I forgot. We can try mailing when things get sorted." She hung up before Rudie could respond.

Makenly posted again: *Helping my buddy Clifford at Muncheez, getting the manje to the people.*

Rudie emailed him: *Do you remember me from Taos? My daughter is at Angels' Wings Crèche. Can you find her for me? Her name is Roselore.* Rudie paused. Ann had never told them Roselore's surname.

From the first night of the earthquake, Leo and Rudie spent hours on the phone when he wasn't shooting. Should they charter a plane? Fly down themselves?

Rudie studied the papers, watched the news. Nine days after the earthquake, the US military airlifted fifty-three Haitian children to Pittsburgh, then offered humanitarian parole to orphans already placed with parents prior to the earthquake. She read that authorities had caught Baptists from Idaho smuggling Haitian children to the Dominican Republic with plans to adopt them out. Many of those children were not orphans.

The missionaries had kidnapped the children. "Roselore isn't an orphan either," Leo pointed out when Rudie told him her worries about losing track of their daughter. He was right. The agency had matched her with Rudie and Leo before the earthquake struck. Still, she worried.

This morning, Makenly had written back:

I do remember you, Rudie.

I am spending my days helping my zanmi, who set up his restaurant as a soup kitchen. My house is intact, most of my street. My parents flew to Fort Myers last week, but I'm sticking it out. Our pantry is stocked with tomato sauce and pasta!

I need more information to find your daughter. All sorts of people down here are coming forward, saying children belong to them, claiming to do God's work. Be wary of this. The offer is still open for you and Leo to stay here when you come.

Fondly,
Makenly

Rudie trembled, but assured herself that Ann would watch out for Roselore. She remembered Makenly's honesty when she'd told him their plan to adopt from Haiti. He'd said he supported them but confessed to wishing all children could stay safe in Haiti with their families. He did agree with them, however, that children thrived in families rather than orphanages.

Rudie replied to his email, telling Makenly that she admired him for staying.

She'd been asleep for only a few hours when Terry Sommerville from Canadian Immigration called. It was five fifteen.

"We've arranged a temporary resident permit and waived the processing fees," he said. "Your child . . ." papers shuffled ". . . *Roselore* is arriving in Ottawa at six o'clock tonight on Air Canada Flight 1252."

Rudie held her breath. She turned on a lamp and sat up against the headboard. The Haitian government was strict about parents coming to Haiti to spend time with their children before adopting them. Yet now they were evacuating matched children and releasing them to Canadians, too. Rudie got out of bed and called Ann, flipping on lights as she walked through the house.

"This is impossible."

"I know! It's a miracle for the children," Ann said. "The Palace of Justice in Port-au-Prince was demolished. You know this. The judge who oversaw adoptions, Judge Cadet, was killed. Now the government is fast-forwarding your case."

"Have you seen her?" Rudie paced the hall, kicking at boots and shoes in her path.

"They were outside playing when the earthquake struck. Luckily, only a few minor scrapes. The nannies are fine, too – Mireille, Lovely, Josette. Yves, the owner. They have tents up now, tarps. We are so blessed."

"Roselore –?"

"She's fine, honey. Don't worry. You will hold her tonight. The military is helping and Air Canada staff. I am pulling together the paperwork. My stuff is everywhere, of course!"

Ann rushed her words. Maybe she feared that Rudie might reject Roselore if the child arrived sooner than planned. As if a birth mother would reject a premature infant! Did others in Rudie's position say, *I won't take the child early, it's June or nothing?* Tears striped her cheeks. She braced herself on the newel post. No, of course Ann didn't think that. She must have other calls to make, was likely highly caffeinated, underslept. It was exciting. Rudie's knees weakened.

Tonight.

"In Ottawa," Ann was saying. "We've booked your flights and reserved two floors at the Sheraton to accommodate the families. Let me just see if I have your flight number." Her keyboard clicked.

"How many families?"

"Twenty-four. Mainly from Quebec and Alberta. And there are military doctors on board the plane from Haiti, with medical supplies to check them out before they land. You can meet her tonight at the hotel. Why don't I email your tickets. You're so lucky your daughter's coming with the first group to Canada."

"Wait," Rudie said.

"Yes?"

"My husband's not here. He's in Antigonish."

Little Roselore. Once they were matched, the agency had sent a picture of a round-eyed toddler sucking her thumb as one hand gripped a crib, her long-lashed eyes the same shiny chestnut brown as Rudie's. Braids tied with red ribbons, a puffy pink dress with a wide, white collar. A heart magnet held the photo fast to the fridge.

She ached to think of Roselore suffering since the earthquake, how confused and scared she must have been feeling. How thirsty.

Rudie's throat opened and pulsed as she remembered the dust in the hills north of Port-au-Prince. Over the March break of grade twelve, her class had travelled to Haiti to help build a school. She doubted she'd contributed much during that short week of hauling cinder blocks. What stayed with her was a day trip to Mirebalais and the waterfall on Saut D'Eau, where the black Madonna was said to have appeared in a palm tree. A boy guided her by the hand so she wouldn't slip while crossing the rocks.

Leo and Rudie had been in the car, driving home from Toronto, when they first decided to adopt. She'd blurted out, "Haiti."

"Why not a child from Hamilton?" Leo had said. "There's such a risk of fraud with international adoption."

"I get that. And it's expensive," she'd said. "But I can't shake it. I think it's a calling."

"Are you sure? Because you haven't mentioned it before and taking on a child from another culture might be harder than anything else." He held her hand and squeezed. She squeezed back, absorbing his misgivings. She searched herself.

"There is every reason not to do it," she said, letting go. "But I still want to."

He rubbed her thigh. "Right. Let's get started."

Rudie loved so much about Leo – how, despite his doubts, he took the risk and committed everything. She took the photo off the fridge, stroked the image of the plump cheek. *I can't believe I get to meet you tonight.*

She had mixed feelings about Roselore's dress in the photo. So unlike the cotton pyjamas and T-shirts children wore on websites promoting international adoption. Surely someone donated it out of kindness or concern, even duty. Roselore must love it. Yet Rudie wouldn't have chosen it. She yearned to dress her girl in the funky chartreuse, fuchsia and turquoise prints she favoured. She slipped Roselore's photo into her wallet. Today she wanted her daughter close.

Rudie leaned lightly on the bundle buggy as she peered into the Armoury's open archway. She went over her list for the day, written in her Moleskine even though she had it memorized:

Meet Dylan for breakfast
Shop for supplies
Check in w. Dad about reno
Meet H.A.S.P. folks at café
Get to airport for 5:30 p.m.

Before she left the house, she'd packed her bag and placed it near the front door. No matter what else happened, she was ready to get on that plane.

She marvelled at the men and women in fatigues and uniforms. What prompted people to choose service, knowing they could, likely would, get sent to Afghanistan? Despite having a successful painting career in New York City, the subject of Rudie's documentary, Agnes Martin, had withdrawn from everything but the self. Military personnel did the opp withdrew from the self and put the body and mind into ser[illegible] of the group. Some people believed adoptive parents were selfless, too. Rudie didn't feel altruistic. Her mother called her selfish. Friends in the know said she was a saint. Rudie just wanted a child, *this* child.

In a few days, she'd push the stroller she had yet to buy along this street. How would people react? Usually people walked past her, like this couple, whose pupils were pinpoints, their eyes glassy even at this early hour. They laughed when they got to the Armoury, making loose gestures. Two men in fatigues and flak jackets loaded stuffed duffel bags onto a truck. Their arms swung with the precision of machines. The couple loped off down the street.

She unzipped her coat and scratched under her collar. Her neck was sticky with perspiration. She raced over the list, hoping the bundle buggy would hold it all. Just the basics, she and Leo had agreed. Bedding, sleepers, bottles, dishes, clothes – who knew what to get for a two-year-old? Did Roselore use a cup? Could she hold a fork? Rudie had forgotten to ask Ann. Haitian children experienced delays in crawling and walking because their mothers kept them off the dirt floors. Did they have eating delays, too? Who decided they were delayed? she wondered. Probably some Ivy League child psychologist comparing them to American children in daycares. Would Roselore fit in a sling? Rudie could only find lists for setting up a newborn. Parents of two-year-olds were supposed to have these details worked out.

She'd have coffee with Dylan first, his idea. She hadn't seen him in five years. They'd had a brief email exchange and were meeting at Swick's on King Street so she could have a fast breakfast before the stores opened.

After Dylan, she'd load up the bundle buggy at Rexall, then go home and get the car for the big items. She wanted Leo here, not in Antigonish. The agency should have given them more notice. Someone must have known before today that the children were coming. What had they told Roselore? Ann said the children had received photographs of their new parents as soon as the agency had matched them. So Roselore would have been looking at Rudie and Leo for over a month if the photo had survived the earthquake. But what would the picture of the pale woman and the grinning man with the wavy red hair mean to a two-year-old? Where was Roselore right now? What was she feeling?

Rudie shivered and clenched her biceps, waiting at the traffic light as cars sped along Cannon Street's four lanes. Snowflakes swirled like blown dandelion spores. She detoured over to John Street so she could pass Stewart Memorial Church, the nearest church with a black congregation. The adoption training course had advised Leo and Rudie to keep Roselore in touch with her culture. Rudie followed black hair care blogs, scouted out black dolls and picture books about black children, and kept a list of Caribbean associations in the city. Leo had suggested church. Since they weren't Catholic like Roselore, Stewart seemed like a safe compromise. As she passed the red brick church with its windows set into lancet arches, Rudie pictured the three of them walking up the steps on a Sunday morning.

A haven for those who'd escaped slavery through the Underground Railway, Stewart Memorial made Rudie's shoulders tense with yearning and fear. The people who worshipped here might provide a beautiful community for Roselore. They also might reject Leo and Rudie. It would take a lot of nerve to bring Roselore to Stewart or to events put on by the Afro Canadian Caribbean Association. She scrunched up and then widened her eyes, feeling awkward and visible, though the streets were empty.

She walked back to James Street, faster now, vowing to wear more colour for Roselore's sake. She crossed Wilson's wind tunnel, then continued south. The buildings here were taller, the sidewalk cast in shadow from Jackson Square's bulk. Rudie paused at the window of the Trundle Bundle Gallery to stare at a blow-up doll sporting a work sock monkey hat and fairy wings. Any community college dropout who threw together kitschy objects with some loose thematic connection could mount an art show on this street. Yet there were exceptions like Taran Yang's cupcakes. Taran made each cupcake more elaborate than the next, bringing beauty and its concurrent destruction into the world, as art could, and should.

Last night, Rudie had edited footage of Agnes Martin sitting in front of her poster of Georgia O'Keeffe's *Black Iris*. *Look at art the way you look at the ocean, just look*, Agnes had said. *Look and look and look*. Now, Rudie did. The work sock monkey hat covered the blow-up doll's face. Knapsack straps fixed the knitted wings to her back. The artist had looped fishing line around the doll's ankles and neck, raising her feet higher than her head so she seemed to plummet. Rudie stuffed her hands in her pockets. The artist wasn't defacing beauty. Blow-up dolls weren't beautiful. What was the point of this piece of "art"? Was it glorifying toys? The work sock monkey wore a manic grin. The doll's teacup breasts puckered at the seams. There were far more sophisticated Real Dolls available now. The blow-up variety was as outmoded as pubic hair and flesh breasts. Was the artist saying something about nostalgia?

She folded back her glove to check the time. Almost eight o'clock. Swick's was a five-minute walk. She wanted to arrive early. Dylan used to make cracks about her weaknesses. As if Dylan knew her now.

Loud chatter reached her, yelling, some screeching, energetic not fearful. A pack – there must be a more effective collective noun: a snarl? an outbreak? a whiff – of teenagers rounded the corner. A boy in a buffalo plaid shirt and jean jacket jumped on the tree planter and swung his body around, one hand cupping the thin tree trunk. Two boys shook the trees in the other planters. Three girls in short, puffy jackets, hoodies and skinny jeans, shrieked, "Stop!" through veils of cigarette smoke.

The boys clustered in front of the blow-up fairy, knees bent, necks craned.

"Sad titties," said one through teeth gripping a cigarette.

"I'd fuck 'em," said another.

Two of the girls walked away. A third lingered, a girl stuffed into a thick hoodie and blotchy, pink vest, standing in the middle of the group, her jokes as filthy as the boys'. Her gaze darted over their faces as she avoided looking directly at the doll. Rudie remembered her from the Rocket Theatre Co-op program where, as a favour, Rudie had stage-managed *Into the*

Woods last winter. Her name was Hannah Merriweather and she'd played the witch.

The others Rudie recognized from the gang who lounged outside Shawn's Place, the youth drop-in centre around the corner, kids who put up with Shawn's praying and goal-setting in exchange for fried eggs and a cold shower.

Rudie caught the eye of the new one, a beanpole with a greasy bang, drainpipe jeans held just above his crotch and a skeleton-patterned hoodie. The beanpole stood beside Hannah, jumping away each time she slapped his shoulder then returning to her side.

"Bomb scare," the boy told Rudie. "Shawn wants a lockdown, but there's no locks. He can't make us stay."

"We're supposed to sit on the floor with our heads on our knees," said Hannah, her glossy hair at odds with her stained clothes and spotty face, her dark, sunken eyes opaque. Rudie caught a trace of patchouli. After the show's run, Hannah's witch cape had reeked of the aromatic oil. Not even dry cleaning could remove the sweet, funky smell.

"So we split," Hannah said.

Hannah talked like a spokesperson. The other boys were now spitting on their hands and smearing the glass. Rudie resisted the urge to say, *Shouldn't you be in school?* Hannah had been in grade ten last year and delivered a passionate, if scene-chewing, performance. Her smoky alto voice had infused the witch with a vital, menacing power.

"They evacuated Jackson Square last month," Rudie said. "La Senza had a bomb threat."

"Who'd want to blow up Hamilton?"

"Blow-up doll. Blow up city. Blow blow blow," the boy said.

"Rude." Hannah indicated Rudie with her thumb. Her smile revealed a shiny set of fuschia braces. She winked, acknowledging Rudie.

"Rudie."

Rudie checked her watch. Ten minutes. Dylan might already be at Swick's. He was driving into town for an appointment. They'd meet as friends. Rudie would update him on her Agnes Martin film. Rudie stepped backward, about to walk away. Hannah pointed at a newspaper box. The headline read PRAY FOR HAITI.

"Look! It's got the same letters as Hamilton. First there's the HA and the I. Letters are powerful. They make words. And words, well, forget about it."

Rudie swallowed. "Imagine what they're going through right now." Her eyes watered, the first time since the earthquake that she'd almost cried. She made herself focus on Hannah, trying to picture her parents but drawing a blank.

The other boys had drifted toward Jackson Square. Beanpole stayed, stared.

"It's about levels, yo." He leaned on the gallery window, wearily, one foot braced on the wall. Rudie shivered, fascinated. "Top level with money. Poor level, like us." He gestured at Hannah.

"*Not* like us." She began to fold the bundle buggy – if she held it under her arm and jogged, she'd make Swick's with a minute to spare.

"Lady, you think we chose this life?"

"It's Rudie." He had a point. Kids who used Shawn's Place for breakfast had good reasons not to live at home.

"Barth," the boy said. "Bart with an H." He faltered, his eyes on Rudie, his face as open and engaged as hers. Roselore's image shimmered in Rudie's mind. Rudie patted her purse, eager to pull out the picture but unwilling to share it. Hannah sneered but said nothing.

Remembering Dylan, Rudie said goodbye, embraced the bundle buggy and left them.

After a few running steps, she slowed. Dylan might drive past and say something charming and unkind from his car window, making her laugh despite herself. Her body thrummed. Her film about a dying abstract painter wasn't turning out the way she'd hoped. She'd shelved it when having a family with Leo turned into her career. Since the match with Roselore a month ago, at Leo's suggestion, Rudie had gone back to tinkering with the footage of Agnes while they waited to meet their daughter.

She practised what she'd tell Dylan, how she wanted to make a film showing Martin talking about simplicity and solitude and the sacred. *Where's the story?* Dylan would ask. Or if he didn't, he'd be thinking it. He'd tease out more than she'd thought to say even to herself. He'd make it sound bigger than it was, fan her enthusiasm, convince her she could pull it off. Underneath his questions would lurk a grinding sense of what the work lacked, what she couldn't do, and what he could, or would, if it were his project. He wouldn't choose a project like hers, though. He made more *significant* films about smog and deforestation. She stopped at the King William light, inhaling the mouldy smell of the rotting Lister Block. Having Roselore would change how Rudie worked. Would Rudie work? She imagined that holding Roselore might feel like falling onto the softest mattress over and over and over, forward and backward.

She doubted she'd finish the film by June. Relief at becoming a mother early brought a new wash of tears. She read posters for events long out of date. Someone had spray-painted red horns and a curved devil's tail on a photograph of Michael Jackson. *Blas-Femme*, someone else had scrawled. The street was dark here and the sidewalk damp, though it hadn't snowed enough to provide a melt. Her feet stuck, throwing her off balance. She speed-walked, hugging the bundle buggy, and made the next two lights, slowing only when she spotted the restaurant.

Meeting anyone made her anxious; it wasn't just Dylan. She admired Agnes Martin. Agnes had shut out the world in New Mexico so she could paint what inspired her without concern for the market. Though the remoteness of her ranch had eventually prompted Agnes to move to Taos, she'd lived all those years alone on the mesa. Before that, she'd travelled all over North America in a pickup truck pulling an Airstream camper. With Leo away, Rudie walked around her James Street North neighbourhood every day, hoping to bump into someone she knew. Agnes-on-film kept Rudie company. The old woman's eyes met the lens, then slid away. Her gestures invited Rudie to lean in and connect. Agnes's pale canvases were more honest and less lonely than Rudie's films, not promising a connection that the artist herself couldn't make. Six years later, Agnes was gone, the words didn't change, and Rudie spent her days mining an old woman's final moments for meaning. Rudie coveted solitude and admired it but felt relief when Leo came home from a television shoot. Tonight, what she had hoped for would come true. Roselore would join their lives. Tonight, she would hold her daughter.

A red awning with curly gold lettering announced Swick's

All-Day Breakfast. Cardboard pictures of faded sunny-side-up eggs and pink crinkled bacon leaned against the windows. Behind them, checkered curtains hung on a rod twisted round with fairy lights. Rudie caught her reflection in the window of the Frugal Loon next door. She ran her fingers through her hair, swiped a line of Crème In Your Coffee over each lip and redistributed her scarf. She opened the door.

The room had a dimness more fitting of a bar. Rudie shrugged out of her coat, arranged it over her arm and squinted into the restaurant. She didn't see Dylan hulking in the corner until she was closing in on him. He stood gingerly, left shoulder hunched as if pulling a punch or protecting a tender fight wound, and eased his way along the low table. He stumbled over and hugged her. Still gripping the bundle buggy, she held up her coat to absorb whatever current might still run between them, especially now that she was so on fire to hold her little girl. She parked the bundle buggy, and they sat.

His grey Gore-Tex hoodie was expensive and fitted, good for cold shooting days, though a far cry from the natty silk shirts of five years ago. He'd cropped his dark hair and gelled it in a few different directions at the front. He looked less conservative, more studied. His blue eyes, saltier than ever, probed her as before, some of their guard replaced by a weariness, almost resignation. The old wariness was there, along with a new emotion that Rudie couldn't quite read.

"Pussycat," he said. She couldn't lie – it felt nice to hear him say it.

He flipped the laminated menu, then flipped it back. A dark-haired girl in a glittery white tank top and black leggings came over.

"Coffee, black. Rye toast, no butter," Dylan said without looking at her.

Embarrassed by her hunger, Rudie ordered the full breakfast. Today, she needed her strength.

"How's the work?"

"My film sucks. The usual."

"That's not up to you to decide," Dylan said. "So? Tell me about it."

Rudie did. She told him about the octagonal room at the Harwood Museum in Taos. She told him that when she was driving through on a solo trip from Boulder to Flagstaff, she met a German filmmaker named Bernadette and spent six weeks on a crew chasing Hispanic death iconography around New Mexico. Yes, the light, the sky and the space had opened her up, but this room of muted paintings and finding out the woman who painted them was in her nineties and lived in Taos in a retirement home had inspired Rudie the most. In a town ripe with fuzzy spirituality lived a woman whose canvases, mouthing truths in pale tongues, had rendered Rudie helpless with the desire to know more.

"I shot Agnes Martin talking about what it took to make those paintings."

Rudie hadn't spoken this much about her film in years.

"When did you interview her?" Dylan asked.

"After our thing – yours and mine – I went on that trip and didn't want to pass up on the opportunity. It sounds shameful to call it that – of course, she was dying – and I met other filmmakers, not just the Germans. And it all worked. Agnes died before we finished."

"She decided when you were finished. Did Leo shoot it?"

Her husband's name clanged on Dylan's tongue.

She widened her eyes, mischievous, proud. "I shot it."

Dylan moved his head into a slightly forward tilt, as if he'd caught her in a lie. "I'd use him if I didn't have somebody," Dylan said. "Word is he's expensive and he won't travel."

"He's in Nova Scotia."

Dylan started as the waitress reached over his shoulder to set down their plates. Rudie unrolled the napkin containing her fork and knife, squirted her eggs with ketchup and took a bite.

With a sideways eye-roll, halfway to a flirt, Dylan peered up at her. "That's only two days' drive. I meant internationally. My films take me all over the world. My man has to be willing to go there, too. We just got back from Pakistan. I'm thinking about Haiti, but getting in after the quake won't be easy. It hasn't been easy for years, but now? I have to consider the angles."

"Not to mention the light," Rudie said. What was it with Haiti? Rudie refused to think of his interest as synchronistic, though her life might be lining up, catching the old feeling that Dylan would make his way back into her world in some way, that they might end up together. Agnes Martin and her visionary revelations about Zen Buddhism and art felt garbled inside Rudie.

"The angles of the story," Dylan said. He removed a jar from his rubber courier bag and spread a chunk of dark nut butter on his rye toast, folding the triangle like a handkerchief and downing it in two bites.

"The story of the earthquake?" Rudie dipped bacon in a puddle of yolk. "Aren't you worried about capitalizing on the disaster? You're turning into a storm chaser."

Dylan crossed his legs and leaned back. The bench seat wobbled. "Are you kidding me? You think I live off victims of climate change? You're better than that, Rudie." He smiled with his lips pressed tight, offended.

Surprised that she'd cracked his guard, Rudie shifted subjects. "I was planning to have a cut by June."

He raised his eyebrows, let out a long breath. "You're close then. You've got five months. What are you doing here?" He dabbed a nugget of almond butter off his chin.

"Do you want to know more about Leo?"

Dylan narrowed his eyes. "The film's a wonderful idea, Rudie. Agnes Martin's a Canadian. You know that. But the Americans have claimed her. It could do well in both countries if you market it right."

"From Saskatchewan, grew up in Vancouver. Since Leo and I shot footage of her right up to her death, this film is about dying, too. That was when we first got together." She wanted to tell Dylan all about Leo. She wanted to hurt Dylan and get his approval, so he'd be more connected to her life now. She needed a reaction from him beyond anger. He hadn't said a word about his wife.

"I bet you got excellent footage. It must be beautiful."

"It will be. I thought of adding other artists, but no one I could find had Agnes Martin's spiritual *cojones*. Not that I do."

Rudie didn't have the energy to explain Dylan's attraction to disaster to him, his desire to help. Compassion on a grand scale. He'd been mean with her when they were seeing each other, withholding his life and, at times, his body. Yet, his films wove together intimate stories in troubled parts of the world. They revealed the corruption driving the regions both forward and into the ground. Dylan's films inspired charity, and he was well funded. He could turn his films into a franchise, a suggestion he'd find insulting. Dylan was made the way his films were. He and Rudie were one story among many, but the whole was unknown, even to him.

"I was supposed to go to Haiti in June," she said. The nerves on her head crackled. Her breath came faster and streams of energy raced around her shoulders. She held her eyes closed for a second and called up Roselore's image. "Leo and I were."

"Yes?" Dylan said, his eyes cautious and greedy. Did he think they'd steal his idea?

"We're adopting a little girl –"

"That's wonderful," Dylan said.

The kitchen door swung open, bringing with it the smell of fried potatoes and onions. Rudie rested her cheeks on her hands, looked down at her plate and smiled, her eyes wet with happiness. A radio played a DJ saying words like *basket weave* and *T-boned.* Then the opening beat of "I Love Rock 'n' Roll." The waitress refreshed their coffees then set their bill on the table.

"But why Haiti?" Dylan said. Rudie snapped her head up. His cheeks had a ragged flush. A forgotten, familiar red dot popped out near his nose.

"It's a calling, I guess. I went there in grade twelve and couldn't shake the idea that I'm meant to do something involving Haiti. Kind of like how we get ideas for films."

"So, there's a story here for you?"

"I'm not explaining it right. It's deeper than that, obviously."

"People have accused me of exploiting people," he said. "Hell, you just laid down that gauntlet. It's a side effect of doing the work we do. But you're taking the exploitation to a new level. It's wrong to do this now, Rudie, wrong for the children and their families. People are jumping to adopt because they want to help, but some of these so-called orphans have parents or grandparents from whom they've become separated. She's not a pet."

Rudie couldn't remember any of the zippy answers she was supposed to give to people's thoughtless comments about her adoption. Nobody had said anything about *pet.*

"We're not exploiting anyone. All avenues have been exhausted. There's no way we'd get a child this fast." Rudie pushed at the table with the heels of her hands.

"Why don't we go to your car," Dylan said. He took out a five, enough for his toast, coffee and a tip. Rudie waited a beat. She used to assume he let her pay for herself so she wouldn't get big ideas about where their relationship was going. Seeing him straighten the edges of his five-dollar bill now made her wonder if he wasn't just cheap.

Rudie stood and put on her coat. The waitress came back. Rudie handed her a twenty and took Dylan's five. He kept his wallet out, one finger inside the fold as if he wanted to ask for the change.

"So you're suggesting that we're using our white privilege to take advantage of a tragic situation? You don't know anything about this."

"I'm going to pretend you didn't say that," Dylan said.

"That's mature," she said. She lifted the bundle buggy and headed for the door. "I'm walking."

"My car then. We can go for a ride. Or back to your house."

"I can't."

Rudie had told only a few people about Roselore: her parents; the friends who'd acted as references; and the people in H.A.S.P., the adoption support group. She didn't want Dylan to know they were meeting Roselore tonight. Claiming she had to work wouldn't fly. They both made their own hours when not shooting. Leo was out of town. She should say goodbye to Dylan now, before she slipped up and gave him the whole story.

Small snowflakes whipped their faces as they crossed King Street. The teenage pack from earlier huddled outside a wig store that was two doors down from the grass café. "There's your Third World," Dylan said. "You could make a movie here, but who'd want to do the work?"

Not much work, Rudie thought, bristling at the term *Third World*. It was about trust and treating kids straight. And looking, really looking, at what they knew you didn't want to see.

"Their hangout had a bomb scare today," Rudie said. Barth and Hannah were watching her. Rudie raised her hand, fingers curved, and Barth walked over. She waited.

Dylan stiffened. "She's not buying, and she sure isn't selling," he said when Barth caught up to where they stood beside a three-foot-tall red cowboy boot outside Leathers.

"Morning, sir," Barth said with a two-finger salute. Dylan scowled.

The measure of a man, thought Rudie, *shows in how he acts around other men.* Dylan took a tight boys' club with him on film shoots. When he was drinking, he dominated, rolling out story after story of set antics, tales of obstacles he'd surmounted last minute. A popular companion, he let others confide in him but said little about his personal life. He was a man who confessed just enough to women he kept unseen.

Rudie revised. Perhaps the measure of a man had to do with how he treated young people. Dylan acted afraid of Barth. Maybe fear got harder to hide.

"I didn't hear anything. Did it blow?" Rudie asked.

"Hardly," said Barth. "But nobody's going back. Shawn'll just make us clean up and share during Circle."

"Do you need spare change?" Rudie asked.

Barth rocked his shoulders side to side. He glanced at Hannah, who rolled her hand to say move it along, cowpoke. "Hannah and me want a room."

"Where do you stay now? I can't –" Rudie said.

"Not at your house. John Wayne here would shit a watermelon."

"He's not my husband," Rudie said. Dylan had walked over to Leathers' doorway where he now huddled, checking his BlackBerry, his face walled up. Rudie's husband would have his wallet out and open, bills displayed, before this boy had even screwed up his courage to ask. *Take what you need, son*, Leo would say, steering Barth to an ATM. In fifteen years, their daughter – her daughter! – could be standing in this very spot asking a stranger for money too. How would Rudie want the stranger to respond? Barth had light brown roots, the rest of his hair dyed black. Dylan must be thinking if he could afford hair dye he could afford a room. It didn't work that way when you were young. Maybe it did for jocks like Dylan.

"Motel room," Barth said. "Not your Holiday Inn – fleas, bedbugs, roaches. But a lock on a door and a bed. Me and Hannah alone. I can take care of her."

Rudie waved at Hannah, who lowered her chin. Dylan was walking west, throwing pointed, baleful glances over his shoulder. Rudie turned her back. She had money set aside for her child, but she didn't need it the way other people did. Melted snow inside her boots had left her tights wet and uncomfortable. This boy's hoodie and jeans had no dirt on them. His face was a pale pink wad. His hair was lank, not matted. She opened her wallet inside her purse and took out a twenty.

"Wish you'd use it for a coat," she said.

"I'll keep that in mind," said Barth.

"Soft touch," Dylan said when she caught up to him. "He'd have robbed you if I hadn't stood there."

"Stood where?"

"I should get going."

Rudie had tried unsuccessfully for years to pinpoint their last goodbye, but now it came to her. On the bed in her apartment. The creak as he turned the corner at the landing. The front door's *huff*. She had booked her flight to Boulder, arranged the car rental and the hotel room. She'd had money in the bank from shooting the reality show *Rock Chick Camp*. Physically, she was the one running. But he was the one holding himself away, refusing to let her come close to him. A tired goodbye.

"Don't go," she said, what she wished he had said then. "Help me shop for Roselore. I didn't tell you before, but she's arriving tonight. I wouldn't mind talking some more."

She walked ahead of him before he could answer, shaking out the bundle buggy and tugging it behind her. She turned to face him, then slowed down so she matched his easy stride.

He smiled, rubbed her back for a moment as they walked. She glimpsed herself in the window of a thrift store. Her face was lit up from beneath the skin as if it were magic hour. Yet it was mid-morning, the sky was pigeon grey, the clouds low, and the buildings cast grim shadows. The only lights were fluorescents, beaming from wig and T-shirt stores. The glow was hers. It must come from the child.

She stopped at the head of Rexall's baby aisle. Back when she hoped to get pregnant, she'd hated the smiling, doughy faces, the hot pink and blue plastic. Dylan gripped her elbow and steered her forward. Her throat grew thick. For a moment at the restaurant, she'd wanted Dylan. Now, she wanted Leo.

"I don't know her size," she said. "I'll go tomorrow." She made a half turn, but he blocked her, his chin tilted and his pupils expanding.

"It won't take long. We're here already," he said.

She sniffed and blotted her nose with her coat sleeve. Who cared if he saw?

"Hey, I could've brought Barth."

"He'll have his own soon enough."

She eased a Super Pack of Pampers off the shelf, then sat on the floor with it between her legs. "I don't even know if she wears diapers. I should know that. And this? What's the difference between a Pull-Up and a diaper? What's a onesie? Are they based on age? Does she need a twosie then? The parenting class should have brought us here on a field trip."

Dylan dropped the diapers into their shopping cart and squatted beside her. "Get whatever you can. Get them all. Send hubby out in the middle of the night if you forget something. Make him feel useful. He'll love it. Do you have a list? I asked you that, didn't I? I'm the least helpful person you know, yet here I am." He stood and helped her to her feet.

Together they filled a cart and her bundle buggy with bibs, bottles, Q-tips, wipes and Toddler Mum-Mums.

"Where are the Man Mum-Mums?" Dylan asked.

"Different store. Someone tried to blow it up, too," Rudie said.

"I'm done," Dylan said. He draped his coat over the shopping cart. Sitting, he wrapped the black vinyl pad of the blood pressure test machine around his bicep.

"I get it. Not your child. Not into kids." She wondered, as she had over the years, how he would have taken news of a pregnancy.

"That, too. My body's falling apart. Stefania and I are too."

Rudie leaned against a shelf of protein bars, replaying the words slowly. "Your wife?" she asked then regretted it. He had avoided referring to Stefania when he and Rudie were together. Rudie thought she'd heard him say Stefania's name only two or three times. Now Dylan's lips stayed pushed out, thoughtful, not sneering as they might have in the past. Near the end of their relationship Rudie would chant *wife wife wife wife* in the streetcar on the way to meeting him.

Dylan pushed the button. The machine puffed.

"Yes, my wife. We're over now. It's as hard as I thought it would be, yet I'm still here! Funny. Blood pressure's low. Must be hibernating."

"Welcome to the wilderness. Do you talk to her?"

"We each have our own place now, but we do still talk."

Dylan caught Rudie's hand. He moved his head from side to side, up, down, trying to catch her gaze, until she looked down at him and they locked eyes. She gripped his hand then released, but he wouldn't let go, so she relaxed and smiled and he smiled back. She moved closer then, and covering his hand with her other hand, she shook herself free and stepped away.

Roselore Roselore Roselore. If she could smell her child, hear her voice, clasp the little body, the plump cheek against her breasts, her thoughts would come clear. She twisted the top of a baby powder container. A puff of white. She coughed. The powder reminded her of nothing. Did any residual feeling she had for Dylan take away from what she felt for Leo? *Ours is a confident, settled love*, she thought, *not requiring obsession and doubt*. She could be right.

"I'm about to open up wider than I ever have," she said.

"That's just cruel."

"I mean my heart. You don't like that kind of talk. I'm expanding myself to bring this child into my life. I have to give her everything."

Dylan flinched as a woman walked by on his left side. He shook his head, an action he'd repeated several times that morning: with the waitress at Swick's, beside the leather store boot while Barth was talking to her.

"Isn't your appointment soon?"

"You're right. I should get going." He stood and put on his coat. They steered down the card aisle.

"Is it something medical?" she asked.

He knocked against a mirrored pillar reflecting red cherubs, roses and hearts. In the lineup, he moved as close to her as he could without touching.

"I've lost peripheral vision in my left eye," he said, "my dominant eye. A mini-stroke to the optic nerve. Some colour blindness, too. Today I have a visual field test with the ophthalmologist to see what I've regained. I can still work with a missing side. The brain adapts."

Rudie waited a beat to respond, sensing a twist to the story, was about to say *I'm sorry* and *I didn't know* when Dylan's arm caught her close and his mouth opened on hers, halting her words, insisting she kiss back, and she did.

AGNES

On a late January day in 1974 on the mesa outside Cuba, New Mexico, six miles from anyone else, Agnes finished installing the threshold to her log studio. For weeks, the Line had refused to leave her. She would honour it, figure it out, let her body recede. She hadn't painted in seven years. First, though, she would walk.

She wore a threadbare peacoat from her New York days, rubber boots over work socks, a peasant blouse and the same pair of overalls she'd slept in. The transition from one state to another should be seamless, she believed. Her daily cycle began when the sun went down. After each evening meal, she cleaned her skin with a pungent blend of olive and castor oils. She shivered more than most at this elevation, though in the past she'd had her share of waking up nights in her Airstream Overlander, covers tossed off, body baking as if in a dry, hot kiva oven even at this late age. She added a knitted cap and a pair of crusty sheepskin mittens and tramped down her long driveway through falling snowflakes the size of pinheads. Her eyes streamed as a cold gust nipped her cheeks. At the road, she turned west toward the horses and Annie and Jesu's farm.

She tried for the last time to shake the Line from her mind. If it stayed, then today she'd paint. The first time it showed up, she'd been framing her log studio's skylight. Liquid yellow broke the horizon now, spilling gold across the upper branches of the trees, the snowflakes turning into spots of spinning pink light. She closed her eyes to warm her lids. Cold air swept over her arms and legs, making her walk faster. The faint nickering of horses came to her ears.

Jesu Sandoval had inserted the glass and sealed the skylight's frame. Agnes had built most of the studio – as well as the other four buildings – herself but called on Jesu when she needed help. She chewed at the salty seam of her mittens, inhaled the oily smell of the wool. In New York, she hadn't known when she would paint. What made her certain she would today? She'd stood on the new threshold in the morning dark with nothing left to build. That didn't mean she had to paint. Gripping her coat collar, she looked over her shoulder, the snow like static on a TV screen now, a corner of the house visible. She'd brew coffee, lay in some supplies, even though in New York she hadn't needed food or drink once she got a brush in her hands. She'd stock up on cheese and walnuts, two-thirds of her diet that winter, food she could rip into and gnaw while her hands moved. Pointing herself toward the blank canvas required work. Even looking at the sky distracted her from her plans.

—

Each moment contained a perceptible change in how the air held light. She'd have to look without seeing, walk back to the house, gathering items in blindness, delaying the brain's urge to name them or make connections. These were what she called her trance states, the catatonia she couldn't quite remember, that had landed her in the hospital, most memorably in India and in New York before she left. She had medicine now and only a few people nearby. *I can control it*, she thought, *use it to jump-start my painting.*

The flag on her mailbox stood at attention. The little door creaked as she lowered it, her hands awkward inside the mittens. A postcard leaned against the mailbox's inner wall. It'd been days since she'd had mail. She refused to install electricity or a telephone, collected rainwater for drinking, pumped the rest from a well. She panted, the back of her neck moist against the wool collar, despite her cold cheeks. Her legs could walk her anywhere with only a pleasant ache when she lay down at night, but her lungs caught her breath if she so much as raised her arms. She'd done no heavy building since the skylight. Her arm strength would return tenfold when she painted. The Line shimmered blue, then pink, expanding and contracting, inviting her closer. First she'd prime the canvas with white acrylic gesso, then mark out the grid with a pencil. Then she'd paint. She'd need a ruler.

The postcard showed a neon-lit Albuquerque strip. She read as she walked, snowflakes wetting the paper. The writer used small spidery caps, wider at the bottoms as if her pen had lingered at the end of each letter. The chatty paragraph told about getting locked out of a room in an Albuquerque hostel, naked except for a slip. Agnes stilled her mind, then held it blank. She wished she didn't recognize the signed name. Marsha Bargrill. How had Marsha found her?

P.S., Marsha had written. *I'm driving up to Cuba Thursday. Hope you're around! Would love to see your work.*

A body had its own intelligence. The arm could swing up, the hand grip the brush, dip it in paint, swirl, wipe, stroke without mental input if the vision was intact. The trick was to tamp down the mind, leaving the Line for her body to pursue and climb inside. Rothko had discarded line for colour. Agnes would drop colour in a heartbeat. Each wanted to reach the unreachable place. Maybe Mark had gotten there after all. If you believed the stories, he'd taken himself there. Agnes didn't buy it. The arrangement disturbed her: the tissue on the razor, the pants on the chair, the rituals of a tidy man – which Rothko was not, at least not with the domestic object. In his mind, yes. You had to be tidy-minded to make the idea real on the canvas. The freer, the more abstract the work, Agnes believed, the more ordered the mind. Her own mind was the product of the voices, which told her what to get rid of, layer after layer stripped away as she sawed the logs and formed the adobe bricks for each new building on her land.

Down the road, a truck rumbled, its tires crunching the snowy dirt. Agnes crossed to the ditch beside a cottonwood, the snow past her ankles here, its chilly damp seeping into her socks. Maybe if Agnes stayed in the studio, and Marsha found Agnes's house empty, Marsha would turn around and drive back to Albuquerque. Unlikely. In New York, Marsha hadn't known to leave what didn't belong to her. Why should she be any different now? The orange truck rolled to a stop at the corner. One wiper shuddered across the window, Jesu's smile a red smear inside the wet glass. Music shook the cab, and the truck bounced on its springs as Jesu accelerated and swung onto the road beside the ditch where Agnes stood. The smell of grease filled Agnes's nostrils.

"I know better than to offer you a ride," Jesu said, rolling down the window. Smoke from his cigarette ribboned and skittered into the wind. Jesu wore a navy parka with orange lining over a denim shirt and black turtleneck. He had big, prominent teeth and an easy smile. Black moles peppered his cheeks.

"Heading back. Apparently, I'm having a guest." Agnes wagged the card. "Is today Thursday?"

Reaching into the passenger seat, he grabbed a *Cuba News* and a *Time* magazine, checked the date and handed her the stack. She studied the image of John Sirica, *Time*'s Man of the Year.

"Think they'll impeach Nixon?" Jesu asked.

"I don't doubt it." Agnes disdained politics, but last spring she'd gotten drawn into watching the Watergate hearings on Jesu's colour TV.

"It must be Thursday," Jesu said after some silence. "Annie's people are coming up today for the weekend. Annie's stockpiling frybread. Had to wait until she turned away to snatch some."

"Brother?"

"Nah. The sister this time. Maybe a cousin or two, I forget. You might not see me. Or I might bring the brother-in-law over, show him the skylight so he can see what we *norteño* builders can do."

"Don't come in the studio if you do. I'm working today." The declaration shook Agnes, but the Line demanded she announce herself.

"You started, yeh?"

"Starting. Or I may just be hiding from my visitor. Never know."

"Who's visiting you?"

"Nobody. An artist from New York."

"Fancy. I'll stay away then." Jesu turned the volume knob. "Tie a Yellow Ribbon" played on the radio as Agnes said, "No, come if you need to, Jesu. Disturb me if she's there, but if I'm painting, pretend I don't exist."

Back at the studio Agnes admired the ash threshold. The Celts believed ash had higher spiritual properties. They used ash for protection and to midwife a new state. Jesu had suggested oak, but Agnes had wanted wood from the land. She'd selected a fine specimen, easily one hundred years old, from the southeastern corner. Her log cabin, the bark-covered vigas, the boards, the windows, the table and chairs and benches – she'd built them all from trees she'd felled with Jesu's help.

Agnes shook off her boots, Marsha's card forgotten, and hung her socks on a rail. She rubbed her bare soles on the sanded wood. Her wet cuffs flapped against her chapped, red ankles. The work would come more easily if she emptied her mind. She stood and stood, her feet growing numb. She willed her leg to lift. Even when alone, she had to push herself through the terror of going through a door, the sense that someone or something in the room didn't want her there. Once she picked up a brush, this anticipation would end and the work, inevitably less than she imagined, would begin.

She bent in front of the kiva oven, ignoring her knees' creaking. Though her joints had cracked since she was a girl, the sounds were becoming more poignant as she aged. She vowed not to give in, but the body's desire to protect itself was unavoidable. She lit the pile of kindling and crumpled paper she'd put in last night. After adding a couple of piñon pine logs, she had a good fire going.

It was early, the sun still low. She parked herself on John Stone. Her friend John had kept such a stone in his studio where she'd sat while he painted, talking with him, thinking, whatever she wanted. Being together in the same room had been enough for both. Whenever she stuck her head into the room and said, *You there?* and he wanted her to stay, he'd reply, *Your stone.* If he didn't speak, she'd leave. They both understood that the body's presence was no indicator of the spirit's.

You won't bring in any outside wood, Jesu had teased, *but you'll cart this stone all the way from California? It's a stone, woman.* This stone she called John Stone had spoken to her one night when she was walking the coast in Monterey, so she'd asked two young surfers to carry it to her camper, paying them with a bag of Oregon grass. John Stone had accompanied her through Salinas and Death Valley, across Nevada and the Painted Desert, along Highway 40 to Albuquerque then north from Bernalillo on the 550 to the Jemez Mountains and Cuba. She'd talked to John Stone then, the way she'd talked to John himself since the day Marsha had called her crying to say John had tied himself to the ceiling pipe in his studio. Marsha had found him swinging above a fallen chair. It was January then, too, 1966. Marsha hadn't let anyone see John's body until the funeral four days later. By then a mortician had prodded his face into a human mask, the thick, dark-framed glasses all that ensured a likeness to the person Agnes had known.

After the funeral, Agnes telephoned Marsha and asked to see John's studio. A week later, Marsha opened it up for her. John's paintings leaned in rows against the walls. Though the smell of linseed and oil paint lingered, the room was otherwise empty except for a chair in the centre. An anvil rose up inside Agnes, slamming everything delicate into a pulp. John's foot had kicked this chair, his final act.

She turned to Marsha, asking, "Why is that here?"

"It was part of his story." Marsha moved past Agnes into the studio.

"I can't bear to look at it," Agnes said from the doorway.

"I treasure everything he touched," Marsha said. She smoothed her hands over the back of the chair and looked up. Agnes turned into the hallway, blinking hard, but not before an involuntary glance at the studio ceiling's exposed pipes. She held her breath then released it slowly. She stepped back into the room.

"What about the rope?" she asked. "Do you treasure that, too?"

Marsha seated herself on the chair and crossed her pale legs. She wore a black-and-white sailor dress, her dark red lips making her auburn freckles pop. She raised her eyebrows and shook her head a tiny bit.

"What do you think?" Agnes snorted. "I'm sure you'll find a use for it," she muttered.

Marsha straightened her back and lifted her chin. "You

don't know me, Agnes Martin. You should be thankful I even let you in here."

Agnes shrugged. She walked the perimeter of the studio once without touching the canvases. Marsha could have them. They meant nothing to Agnes now. The stone wasn't there, but it didn't matter either. What was gone was gone.

Agnes hadn't seen Marsha again. Not long after, someone had found Agnes walking the streets, confused and disoriented, and committed her to Bellevue, where she stayed for several days. When an orderly found a number in Agnes's pocket for a Coenties Slip artist enclave and phoned it, the artists there rallied and had her moved to a less crowded hospital without such violent patients and treatments. After her release, Agnes used the money from a grant to buy a truck and an Airstream Overlander and lit out for the west. That was 1967, seven years ago. The last time she was with John, he'd poured her three fingers of Barbadian rum. She'd ended things with Chryssa by then. She and John took off their clothes and settled onto a pile of coats, her own coat folded and hanging over the chair he would later kick away. He rolled her on top of him. They moved slowly, talking all the while, their gazes linked without effort, and she felt how much they were the same, how they breathed the same air. They'd been naked together only once before, shortly after they'd met. Now, each wanted to know the other's body after years of knowing the other's mind. She stroked his chest hair with her fingertips, then flattened her palms against his solidness to shut out a pang of longing for Chryssa's full breasts. Soon their bodies were pressing together, their union less about detail than about fusion. "My me," he called her.

"Problem is," she'd said, "you don't much like you."

"No. Mostly I don't. But I like you. You're the me I like."

"Backpedalling."

"I mean it. You are the best in me. Better than me, really, because of these." He lifted her breasts.

"That's desire talking," she ventured, remembering the grab and claw of Chryssa's lust.

"In part, yes, but these give you licence that this old fellow doesn't get." His cock stiffened where her thighs met. She parted them slightly, held him there until he softened. He was older than she was. Marsha was more than twenty years younger than both of them. So was Chryssa. "Marsha's worn me out," John claimed. *Down, more like it*, Agnes had been too kind to say. Agnes allowed John everything, perhaps to a fault. "Don't expect much," he had told her as he'd unbuttoned his shirt. He confessed to having to pace himself with Marsha.

"Weak man," Agnes had said. "Afraid she'll leave you."

"Why yes," he said, his brow furrowed and his eyes kind. "Though I suppose it's inevitable."

Agnes shrugged. She was the one who'd left Chryssa after they'd fought over a snub at an opening. Agnes had little energy for an argument.

Her body didn't rise to his the way it had when she'd first arrived in New York, but that was before she'd met Lenore and Chryssa and the others and her desire had shifted where it wanted. Letting their bodies come together now like this, in their decline, gave Agnes a sense of beginning. Agnes saw that John had run out of options, and he was taking her where he thought she wanted to go. Had he hoped for more? Would he have stayed alive if they'd done more than explore each other's bodies that day? If she'd revved herself up, taken over? Had her body disappointed him or was it his own? She wondered if Marsha had a similar last memory, if John had tried to go to a new place with her, too, before he gave up. Perhaps he'd made his decision before that afternoon on the coats, one of them chinchilla, smelling of sweat and stale Rive Gauche. John collected coats, gave weekend-long parties where he hid the ones he liked behind paintings propped against the wall. Guests left tired and delirious, lucky to remember they had clothes, let alone coats.

Less than an hour had passed when Marsha parked the Beetle at the top of the driveway. She tied her fur bonnet and adjusted her large, round-framed sunglasses. The snow had stopped about ten minutes ago, leaving a blue sky with long, high clouds. Marsha surveyed the buildings and walked through the soft snow to where Agnes watched, barefoot, her toque askew, from the studio threshold.

Agnes resisted the stiffening of her will around her muscles, the pull inward. She was close to being unable to move unless Marsha touched her. The light beyond her doorway blanked out Marsha's features, but little about Marsha had changed. The woman walked where she shouldn't, her limbs moving with the boldness of the insecure. Before Marsha could reach the studio, Agnes braced both arms against the door frame and thrust herself into the light.

"Not easy to find you," Marsha said. She studied Agnes without meeting her eyes.

"That's how I like it," Agnes said. She reached for the Line in her mind. As long as she relaxed, it stayed. When she looked at Marsha, she saw John behind her, his white T-shirt, his cigar, his grey-brown hair in tufts over his ears. Marsha's voice carried John's inside it, the way she said, "you." Had Marsha and John spent so much time together that they'd absorbed each other's inflections?

"I found out where you were through Betty, who gave you a reference when you taught at University of New Mexico. I asked around Cuba, too. Someone extolled your bear-skinning abilities. I thought we could talk. Maybe have coffee? I've got a room, shitty hotel, but good price and good material. I have a show coming up in September." Marsha sounded like the little sister, the young artist trying to impress the great mentor.

Agnes rubbed her thumb, cracked the joint, a new trick since the break last summer. Cold air snaked around her bare ankles. She took a deep, comforting breath of piñon smoke and said, "We'll have coffee at the house."

Marsha wrapped her arms around her middle. Agnes had first seen her at a party, standing behind John, who held forth while drinking a Manhattan. A few weeks later, John dropped by Agnes's studio, a privilege she granted only to him, hiding Marsha behind him like a gift. In his mind, she was a gift. He thought bringing another person into their friendship would make it bigger and better. John courted expansion. Agnes, though, was content to be a circle of two; or, really, a circle of one. She had let John into her circle but not any of her lovers. She'd sooner have shoved John out than make space for another. Yet, here was that other. John, with a drippy smile, brought in the sunshine and street dust while Marsha, her black hair long and ironed, played along, peeked out from behind John. She held the grim smile of a child ushered into a living room of aunts and uncles and ordered to dance. Her look said, *I hate this and you, but I'll do as he wants.* Agnes dismissed them, shooed them away wielding a hog bristle brush, then turned back to her work. Marsha clutched her waist then, too, as John swung her into a hug, his happiness palpable. Agnes wished now that she'd shared in it more.

Now Marsha surveyed each building, pausing at the crude, star-shaped opening on the backhouse door. She stood in the studio doorway, waiting for Agnes to pull on her coat, socks and boots, and scoop ashes over the tiny kindling fire. Agnes moved past her, and Marsha followed her across the driveway to the house.

The house had the air of a cottage built for a small, magical race, even with its nine-foot ceilings. Though shorter than Agnes, Marsha ducked when she entered. Agnes had white-washed the walls and left bark on the vigas. A black leather sofa faced a window four panes wide and four panes high. The room had a sweet, smoky smell, with the lemony-tinge of well-polished wood.

Agnes squatted in front of the cast-iron stove, her feet sweaty inside cracked leather slippers. She stuffed in pieces of crumpled newsprint and a few sticks of kindling, which she lit with a match. She placed a tin pot of water on top and set two mugs and a jar of tomatoes on the table next to a kerosene lamp. *Marsha must think I'm a hippie*, she thought. Marsha stood a few steps inside the door, looking from one corner of the room to another, a black-and-white leather clutch tucked into her armpit.

"I hope you like it black," Agnes said.

Marsha shucked off her mukluks and parka. The light through the window cast long, twisted shadows. Marsha chose a rocking chair in full sunshine. She curled both feet up under her.

"I came to talk to you about Lenny," she said.

Agnes set two spoons on the table beside a folded blue cloth. "Who?"

"My son. John's and my son. You knew –" She gazed out the window at the cerulean sky. With a sigh, she heaved out her words, her face in shadow, as she told Agnes about John's son. Because of an earlier miscarriage, Marsha had led everyone to believe that John died not knowing she was pregnant. The doctor had advised her to wait until the third month to go public. Not that telling the baby's father would have been going public, but everything about John, every thought and feeling, every moment she spent with him, got used in his art. He was as likely to stand in the gallery explaining how his angst about his penis size inspired a painting as he was to pull a Rothko and point to the beauty of silence. But a week before his death, Marsha explained now, she'd told John she was expecting his baby. He'd had enough time to plan his method of dying, to fail at talking himself out of it and to paint a final painting. He'd propped that painting in front of their dresser mirror, an azure horizon that could look cheesy if you didn't see it as the last John Patron, painted in the throes of his fatal despair for the child he'd chosen not to meet. Marsha hoarded that painting. She'd planned to give it to Lenny when he came of age. Yet, with her son's current troubles, she was considering cashing in on it herself. Unlike Rothko's work, Patron's paintings hadn't been misused – Marsha had seen to that – and they'd accrued some value. It was a good time to sell.

"I didn't know you had a son," Agnes said. Marsha's story rang true, but then a good lie always did. "Other than Betty, I haven't stayed in touch with New York. You certainly didn't look pregnant when I saw you last, and that was after John died. I'm sure you thought it through." Agnes's own body had told her right away when she was pregnant. Those two months, she'd noted a change every day though nobody else had. She hadn't told her friends, not one of them. Nor had she told the likely culprit, a copywriter who'd already faded from her life. A man she'd met shortly before meeting John. She was new to the art scene, but her newness had nothing to do with keeping her secret. She wanted the child to herself as long as possible. He'd stayed her secret until the end, it turned out.

"He's John's. There is no doubt. He's seven."

"But there is only your word that John knew."

Marsha pushed at her cuticles, then leaned forward on the couch.

"I figured you'd want to meet John's son," she said. "Protect him. Advise him, maybe."

"Like John would? I'm sure you can find plenty of willing father figures in New York." Agnes snorted. "And he's got a mother."

Agnes scooped some coffee into the French press and poured the steaming water. Every couple of months, she hitched a ride to Albuquerque with Jesu to buy these bags of coffee beans, unwilling to give up this concession to civilized life.

"How was he with you in those last days?" Agnes ventured. "I've always wondered." Marsha's cheek looked striated and downy in the sunlight. Motes of dust rose and settled around her as she shifted.

"He wore a beautiful mask," Marsha said.

"I don't believe that," Agnes said. "Maybe others do but, you said it yourself, John would say whatever he felt like, be whomever he chose. He was unpredictable, quixotic, insecure. But I didn't see that darkness in him."

The two events, John's death and his son's conception, snapped together now. Agnes sat in a wooden chair at the end of the table, the French press in front of her, water condensed on its glass sides. She pushed the lid down, heavy with sadness, at the waste if John had not known he had a child coming, the brutal sickness of his death if he had.

"Lenny mustn't think he caused John's death," Marsha said.

Agnes shut her eyes.

"John was a big part of my life," Marsha was saying, "but other things have happened, too, since John. His estate fell to me, so I had to sort through what he had, catalogue the work and make some sales. We held a retrospective in 1970, before the Mark Rothko matter – that business of the executors underselling his paintings, the daughter suing, such a mess – we didn't know where you were then or we would have invited you. It was a success and John's paintings are in seventeen galleries and museums around the country and five in Europe. And my own work – I kept my own name, you see, so my success is not based on being John Patron's widow, though it hasn't hurt. Betty Parsons picked up a show of mine and made my name. I'm bigger than John was in his lifetime. There aren't many women who can say that in our day – you and Georgia being the exceptions."

Agnes blinked and rolled her eyes to look at Marsha, who was chatting away as if nothing had happened. Perhaps Agnes had tuned out for only a few seconds this time. Or Marsha saw her check out and didn't care. She handed a mug of coffee to Marsha, who sipped. Agnes watched her now, her dark eyes wary and assessing beneath puckered lids.

"Success can make us happy," Agnes said. "But it's the work. The work is what matters." She could be talking to herself.

"Yes, I agree. That's why I'm here. In New Mexico, I mean, not at your house. It's not the only reason, but I want to do something with the sky."

Agnes sipped her coffee. The sun had moved higher, leaving the room in shadow. At this time of day, she was usually outside building or walking the roads or her property. She had forgotten how dark the room got. Marsha's face lit up as she talked about her work, but the light was there for Agnes's benefit, the light that sells, not the light that makes and inspires. No wonder Marsha had succeeded – the world fell over and over for that false, concealing light. The light that in Agnes leached her inspiration, leaving her in darkness so absolute she might as well swing from a pipe like John.

"Somebody has to do it," she said.

Marsha squinted. "Do what? Paint the sky?"

"Well, O'Keeffe."

"Yes, O'Keeffe. But I'm different. I bring the New York –" She stopped, maybe remembering O'Keeffe's skyscrapers. Agnes didn't smile.

"What I mean is, my take on the sky will not be Georgia's."

"Yes, you're right. We each have a different perspective. It cannot be helped."

Marsha shifted, crossed one leg and then the other. No matter what Agnes said or how she said it, Marsha would read it as a threat. It was curious. Betty Parsons had wanted Agnes exclusively before Agnes fled New York City, had doubled her gallery's offer, had sketched a grand plan. Marsha's work might be stellar. But what did it matter? Agnes closed her eyes again.

"I came to see you about Lenny," Marsha said. She'd slumped back in her chair when Agnes tuned out again. "Agnes, he's John's son. John's. And you and John, I know you had that special connection, so I want you to meet Lenny. He's talking about dying – a lot. He's seven. I told him everything about his father – a mother must – it's important to be open with them, but now he plays Papa's Hanging all the time, takes one of those black ties John used to wear with his white shirts. Remember? Of course you do. Lenny wraps it around his neck, climbs on a chair, then jumps to the ground where he writhes awhile, gagging and clawing at his throat until he 'dies.' He could hurt himself. Maybe what John had was hereditary. His mother was a sad woman. I need . . . I *want* you to meet Lenny, talk to him, as someone who knew John. He's here, with me, waiting at the hotel. I could get him and bring him back this afternoon."

"What does he do?" Agnes asked, blinking. She kept her features even. Marsha's face was in shadow. A sliver of her hair gleamed in the sun. John's child. He might look like John. Agnes didn't know what to say to children, so she said very little, watching them instead, to see what they saw. And they saw. Since childhood, Agnes had carried image after image stored in her mind: red, peeling paint; pitted green linoleum; Poppa's freckled hands; Mama's shiny red lips; a fringe of fur on a calf's hoof. More interesting was what she saw as a child – the crescent moon following her when she walked, specks floating when she stepped hard in the hay on the barn floor, the lap of brown mud when she jumped into a puddle. This boy, John's boy, would have a way of seeing that Agnes would love to slip onto her own eyes like glasses. John's way, maybe. And here his mother was locking him in a motel room like an animal in a zoo's cage. Agnes did not want to meet him.

"He'll sit for more than an hour at a time and stare at nothing – table, floor – and no matter what I say or do, dance around, clap my hands, shake him, he won't respond until he's ready. Then he'll pick up a book and act as if nothing happened, as if he's just woken up from a nap and has no memory of anything I've done, even though his eyes are open – I'm getting frantic, and he looks confused about why."

"Marsha, I do that too. If anything, John was too aware, too tuned in. It doesn't mean the boy's going to kill himself. I haven't."

Marsha shot her a look, as if Lenny having this madness in common with Agnes was little comfort.

"Other things, too, that I hope you can't relate to," Marsha said. "He hits me. His teachers, too. His art – he'll use one colour and fill a page – and yes, I know, he's not the first – but he's a child. They go through predictable stages and explore, only Leonardo doesn't do that. He's incurious. He's not even one of these boys who destroys things and tortures cats – even that might seem normal to me. He reads and makes his monochrome pictures and slips out of our reality from time to time. But that's not why he wants to meet you –"

"You didn't need to tell him about me."

"I told him I was coming to see a friend of his father's."

"Why didn't you just say a friend?"

"Why would I? He wants to find out about John. He doesn't believe what I tell him."

"Why would he?" Agnes said.

"He thinks you'll explain John's death in some way. I told you, he acts out killing himself. He does it to scare me. He loops a tie around his neck. He takes my razor into the bathtub. He runs around the apartment shaking my diazepam bottle. How does he know this stuff?"

Agnes liked this boy.

"Marsha, I'm painting today," Agnes made herself say. The words filled her with a shaky, dread-filled relief. "I don't have time."

Marsha raised her eyebrows at Agnes's clean hands. Agnes forced herself not to put them under the table.

"I don't like interruptions," Agnes said. Perhaps if she got ruder, Marsha would leave and take her tormented son to Ghost Ranch instead.

"I'll bring him when you're finished."

"That's just it. I like to –" but Agnes didn't know what she liked to do anymore. Seven years ago, she liked to sit alone with her work and a lit candle and drink a bottle of Heineken as she came back into her body after a day of painting. She liked to have a brush in her hand as soon after waking as she could and to end her day with the beer and the candle and the canvases. Days and days in a row the same – that was what Agnes liked. But now? She didn't have the city pressing in here. She only had Marsha, who presented a worse urgency, though a less tempting one.

ELLEN

Ellen dipped a twig in a basin of water and lye and scraped it under her husband's yellow thumbnail. It was January 1870, on the Bobcaygeon Colonization Road. She sat in the chair with the cut-out heart. William lay on the basswood table on top of their bedsheet with his chest split open, dead and delivered to her by three men from the sawmill hours ago in the cold dark. William's body settled her as William himself hadn't done when he was alive. She hadn't thought of a person as *alive* before. Even now, she used the word to contrast what William was not. Life with William had been exciting, whether it was the fear of his leaving her the only black person up here in the settlement around Minden Village or the thrill of his eyes on her and only her. She had learned William's hurt quickly enough and his meanness, which lay not in his hands nor even in his voice, but in words. William did not act roughly, but he did hold himself away from her. Though she expected nothing from William, he did give her their daughter, Safra. Also, William came north by himself two years before, the only black man in the area. He cleared this land and built this cabin, so she thanked him. He was a good man. This thought made her neither sad nor happy. What she felt was calm.

Each day, William had scraped the dirt from under his nails with this twig. Ellen would honour William now by making his body cleaner than he could himself. Out here in the bush, he was Ellen's only connection to their daughter.

Last April, Ellen had been preparing to bring Saf north to be with William. She planned to leave after she helped her mother, May, plant her garden in her Hamilton backyard. Then the fire happened. Then Ellen had travelled north without her child. Who would Ellen talk to about Safra now?

The morning before the fire, Ellen and May were hoeing the garden under an achingly blue late April sky, the sharp smell of chives and turned earth in the air. Safra was napping on a blanket in the grass. When Safra said, "Me wake up," Ellen hurried across the soft dirt, kneeled and scooped her daughter into a hug. She inhaled the warm yeasty smell of Saf's nape and rubbed circles on her back. Saf jollied up quickly, nuzzling into Ellen's armpit. A year earlier, Saf couldn't walk or talk. Now, as Ellen stood, Saf wiggled and struggled so much that Ellen plopped her on the grass. Saf ran straight over to May, who caught her while pretending to be knocked over.

"Mind, child!" Ellen laughed.

"It's okay, honey. It's her first garden. She has to learn sometime."

Saf plunked her bottom down on her grandmother's lap. Ellen kneeled beside them.

"Pat pat," Saf said, bringing her palms together. Ellen raised her hands and spoke the rhyme, Saf's eyes shining into hers every time their hands met.

Ellen clenched her body now, rubbed her thumb across the mountain ridge scar on the back of her hand. The dead skin tugged at her, its ache constant and beseeching. Ellen called up Saf's smoke-exhausted face against her breast and caught her breath. The next day, the last day of April 1869, the fire had claimed the lives of Saf and of Ellen's Daddy. After seeing a medium in the weeks following the fire, Ellen had found a carrier going north and left Hamilton for good. Whether or not that garden had grown ripe, only May would know. Though May had done nothing wrong, she had looked into her daughter's eyes after the fire, and Ellen knew May had seen Ellen's failure to get Saf out of the fire in time to save her life. May had said nothing, but Ellen could see it in her eyes, the exposure of her deficiency. If she went back to May now, she'd have to live with this disgrace between them.

After drying her hands on her apron, Ellen adjusted her stockings. No matter how many layers she wore, she could not get warm. During the day, while William had worked at the sawmill, she'd huddled on her rocking chair near the stove, adding seed stitches to the cardinal design she was embroidering on the front window curtain. Now, her fingers felt swollen, the skin mushy. Her scar gleamed, the golden brown of burnt butter. A metallic smell tainted the air.

She opened the door and blinked against the sunshine, shoulders clenched. Water sloshed in the basin as she prepared to toss its contents. She didn't want a red stain on her threshold's snow, her house marked doubly by blood. She set the bowl down. She pulled on her boots and William's sheepskin coat, then went out into the cold. Snow crunched under her boots. The firewood stacked near the door didn't seem enough to last the day. Her feet sank in the snow for several yards as she tramped up a hill to the edge of the forest. When she was far enough away that she could see the shingles of her cabin roof, she emptied the bowl and kicked snow over the red stain. She filled the bowl, swiped the snow around, then tossed it too, pink now, and filled the bowl again. Her hands smarted and her knitted stockings were wet to the knees, but her body was warm inside the coat. She turned her back to the sun and basked in the light, betrayed by its lack of heat. Branches creaked, although the day was windless. Smoke exited her chimney straight up. Its sweet maple smell filled the clearing.

She headed back along the path, the basin heaped with snow in her arms, touching it with her sleeves only. She bent to set it down at her doorstep, and as she stood, she spotted Micheline's felted red bonnet moving through the trees. Ellen had forgotten that Micheline had planned to come back. Hand on the door handle, Ellen paused. A hat bobbed beside Micheline, a black stovepipe on a taller person. Who could Micheline be bringing? Nobody should see William's body yet, not until Ellen had it ready. One washed hand, no matter how clean the fingernails, was not good enough. She hustled into the house, toed off her boots and set the snow on the stove. She ran to her trunk and took out her summer sheet, the one with the embroidered robin motif. She shook it out. Up it floated, then down over William. She was adjusting the corners when Micheline knocked.

—

Ellen poked at the melting snow with a long spoon. Reverend McCloud filled the doorway behind Micheline, a Chippewa woman who'd married a Scot named Paul McPhail and lived on the next farm down the road. Reverend McCloud removed his stovepipe hat after shutting the door. Micheline helped him off with his coat as if he were elderly, though he was only about ten years older than William, who had just passed thirty. Micheline hung their coats on pegs while Ellen watched from the stove. They had their boots off and were standing by the table before Ellen could will her feet to move.

"Here he is, Reverend McCloud. She's covered him, look. Why have you covered him, Ellen?" Micheline made a pouchy smile, her brow a crease of concern.

Ellen smoothed the corner of the sheet where Micheline's fingers had picked.

"It's more respectful this way, Micheline," she said. "Hello, Mr. McCloud. I saw you were bringing a guest, Micheline, and wanted to do my best by William, who wouldn't have wanted guests to see him until he was fully prepared. You understand, Mr. McCloud."

Ellen and Micheline joined hands and exchanged a glance. Benjamin McCloud stepped back from the table.

"Of course I do, Mrs. Cook. Good morning and please do call me Benjamin. I am sorry for your loss. William was a hard-working husband, and our church tried to be a good friend to him, out here alone as he was without family or others of his kind. Excepting you, naturally, when you arrived, Ellen. I hope I may call you Ellen. We shall miss him. I hope that you will accept us in place of your brothers and sisters and find solace in our arms."

Benjamin McCloud's left foot pointed inward, belying the conviction of his Methodist sermons. Micheline stood straight-backed, chin high. Ellen's gut churned. Religion aside, could they trust this white man? She gripped Micheline's hand more tightly.

Everything about Reverend McCloud worked in contrast. He had close-cropped pewter hair yet wore a brush of a black beard that made his square head seem to loom above his body. His red bottom lip curved full like a spring jack-in-the-pulpit while his pale nose had the sharp edge of a fresh-planed pine board.

He carried himself tall, pausing a moment before moving, his pigeon toes at odds with the lion's voice he'd used the one time Ellen heard him preach in his setting room. He whispered now, his eyes on Ellen, who pictured his lips close to her ear and looked away.

"The spirit will provide comfort where we need it," said Micheline, squeezing Ellen's hand, then letting it go. She flicked the sheet covering William and continued. "I brought Reverend McCloud to take your mind off your loss. We can clean William up later. My brood is fine for the morning, so let's not waste a minute."

Ellen shook her head, rested a hand on William's arm.

"Forgive me, Mr. McCloud. Welcome to my home. Would you like tea? We can sit by the fire since my table's in use."

She held out the hand that had rested on William and raised her eyes.

He hesitated a second, his eyes reflecting the flickering candle flame, then took her hand in both of his.

"Not a concern, my dear. Call me Benjamin, please. I insist. I would like some tea, yes, thank you."

Benjamin McCloud spoke like an Englishman, despite his Scottish name. They all did here, but Benjamin McCloud more so. As a Methodist preacher, he'd read his Bible. Ellen wondered if she, too, sounded English. Like William, Ellen had learned to read alongside her mother at the Sabbath School at St. Paul's African Methodist Episcopal Church in Hamilton. Ellen's parents had come to St. Andrew's Ward in Hamilton the year Ellen turned five, having journeyed north to escape slave owners in Georgia. May had dreamed of reading the Bible and did learn, finally, slowly, to say the words aloud as she traced under them with her finger. Daddy had set up a barbershop on Barton Street and told the Bible stories by heart better than some who preached them, though he did so only behind clouded windows with a razor scraping a man's neck clean of lather. By age nine, Ellen had grown much more skilled with reading than her parents, so the task of reading to Daddy at night had fallen to her. The stories ran through her like sap now. She wondered if it was the same for Benjamin McCloud.

She scattered a handful of velvety red sumac buds in the pot and stirred as the water foamed. Micheline came over beside her, bumped her with her hip, her eyes searching and sad, yet hopeful. Ellen looked down, her lashes wet.

Micheline put an arm around her, a hand on her shoulder, as Ellen ladled the grey brew into each mug, wrapped it in a cloth and brought one to Benjamin who sat with his back to William's body.

"You take the other chair," Ellen said to Micheline. "Please."

"No, you need rest, Ellen." Micheline squatted by the fire. "Besides it's better for a woman in my condition to sit on her haunches."

"You're – are you –?" Ellen stopped herself from saying *again*. Micheline had delivered her latest daughter this past summer, a week after Ellen arrived.

"Congratulations, Micheline," Benjamin said, coming over and crouching beside her, taking her hand. "Every child is a blessing."

"Yes, congratulations," Ellen said. For the first time since she lost Safra, she felt warm wishes toward another pregnant woman. She sat in the chair with the cut-out heart, the one William had made and placed at the table before she arrived here. William had known how to welcome her. Micheline made her feel as if *she* lived in this house, not Ellen. Already, Micheline was up again, getting molasses for Benjamin's tea. Whenever Micheline visited, she would rearrange the dishes and food the way she liked them, and Ellen would return them to their rightful places when Micheline left. Yet, at times, Ellen felt closer to Micheline than William. Micheline's dress bunched around her waist, her large breasts settled on her belly so Ellen couldn't see how pregnant she was. Ellen was happy, not only for Micheline, but because this new life would take Micheline's mind off Ellen.

Micheline settled herself back into a squat.

"I'm here to check in on how you're doing, ensure you are comfortable, so that you know you're not alone," Benjamin said. He had the kind of sugared voice the ear got greedy to hear.

Ellen stayed quiet. When she arrived on Bobcaygeon Road, she'd been content to worship through songs, the spirituals like "In Bright Mansions" and "I'm Gonna Sing Till the Spirit

Moves in My Heart" and the new nameless ones that coursed through her since she'd found her second faith. For William's sake, though, she'd agreed to go to Benjamin McCloud's service one Sunday evening. It wasn't like Hamilton, William told her. Up here in the settlement around Minden Village, nobody else was black. A few Chippewa, like Micheline and some others, lived in the area. Almost everyone was European, mostly English and Scottish. What they did share in common was that everyone had come here from somewhere else. To fit in, William said, they'd need a service to go to on Sundays. The people here sang hymns like "Nearer, My God, to Thee" that Ellen hadn't heard before, every word called out by hearty joined voices, and Benjamin McCloud could spin Bible stories as well as the next fellow. Yet his services didn't express spirit, not as Ellen experienced spirit, not since she'd found her second faith, and she hadn't wanted to return to his house. Seeing Benjamin McCloud now, she knew she'd find it hard to rouse herself to hitch a ride down the road to his setting room service this Sunday and the next and the next for the sake of a honeyed voice and Micheline's baby dreams.

Benjamin stood and brushed off his pants. He helped Micheline to her feet and they approached the table where William's body lay. Ellen stood, too, and backed up so she was leaning against the wall.

Though average-sized, Benjamin McCloud could push his personality into the deepest corners of a room. He rested his hand on William's knee. Ellen jumped, realizing she'd expected William to move.

"He is gone to the Holy Land. The smile of Heaven is upon him. For the will of Him who is invisible is that everyone who believes in Him shall receive his saving grace." Benjamin's dark eyes shone. His smile made him a beacon, yet his energy crowded Ellen. She stepped sideways, brushing her hip against the fireplace.

"Steady, girl," Micheline said as she reached out an arm, her eyes on Benjamin.

Ellen righted herself and leaned against a windowsill. Since she'd learned how to read as a child, the Bible stories had taken on a shifting, watery quality as if they'd happened in the air behind her, leading her to believe that if she turned quickly enough she'd catch sight of Jesus hovering. Several times a day she had to stop herself from checking over her shoulder to see if Saf was running toward her, about to catch her around the knees. The key was to enter each moment so fully that she wiped whatever had happened that morning or even a year ago from her mind. Only then could she turn around and *surprise*! Everyone dear to her might be waiting as if she were the one who'd left, as if she could choose to have it all back.

William liked scripture. Though he could read, like Daddy, William had asked Ellen to read from the Bible every night after supper. Ellen wiped her nose. Trust Micheline to bring a visitor when Ellen wasn't ready. A minister wouldn't concern himself with the odours of the flesh, even a body that had passed, but Ellen didn't like the smell of dried blood in her home, or the idea that Mr. McCloud would see her home as a place of decay.

Benjamin McCloud wiped his hand on his trousers, his movements quick as if he expected her not to notice. His body blocked William's sheet-covered face. She craned her neck, then walked over to the table and rested her hand on the hard chest.

"You'll need somebody to help you with the house," Benjamin McCloud said, turning so he talked straight to her and not Micheline.

Micheline jumped up. "He's right. You can't do it yourself."

William would agree. Yet, hadn't she lived alone with Safra in their rooms on Union Street in Hamilton, those two years while William was up here clearing the land and building their home? Last spring, hadn't she travelled without her husband over roads so bumpy she was often flung from her seat and doused in mud? It was only these last several months alone with William in the woods that she'd had his consistent help. She liked it. She learned to stifle the ready criticisms and say thank you and praise his work. Still, it was hard to know what to do with these thoughts piling up. She loved William. She had grown used to his way of chopping and stacking the wood. She liked Micheline. But she had no feeling for Benjamin.

"I can do what needs doing," Ellen said. She lifted the sheet off William and dropped it on the chair, then tugged his shirt free from where it bunched under his armpit.

"It's too much for one body," Micheline said. "Even without children to care for."

Ellen thought of Safra and closed her eyes, blinking against the grit of tears.

"You're grieving for your husband," Benjamin said. Ellen stood straight, her chin high, eyes turned in his direction, observing without giving anything up. "My son and I, we could help you. Philip can bring you wood. More snow is coming. One of us will clear your path to the road."

"Thank you," Ellen said. People here talked about helping each other out, but where had those people been these past few months? When she first arrived, not a day passed without two or three people rapping on the basswood door, the men offering to mend the roof; the women, to share a pie or an herbal salve. William had no shortage of men to help him roll and burn logs when he'd cleared the land the previous spring. Ellen had invited each visitor in for tea served in her china cups with her silver service. The set, along with the sheets with the embroidered robins, were all she'd brought from home. The talk had been civil, kind, lighthearted, but Ellen hadn't responded to the jokes, hadn't known what was a joke and what wasn't. It had been all she could do not to mention Saf or the spirit body Saf inhabited now. Ellen had asked no questions so neither had they. Yet, their curiosity had hung over the gathering, and her neighbours had left with sagging shoulders and pinched lips. Ellen didn't know how to conduct herself otherwise, and most hadn't returned more than once or twice.

Once the cold descended, no one came to help Ellen as she hauled snow and wood and sticks into the house to heat water to wash clothes, her rooms, her body. *Offer to help them*, William had said. *These are generous people, but they will give up on you.* Yet, they hadn't given up, Ellen felt. No. They were punishing her for not returning to a church service, after her first Sunday at Benjamin's, believing that she had rejected them. Every Saturday night as she'd filled the washtub with pot after pot of warm water for his bath, William had asked her if this week she'd come. In everything else, he'd convinced her to see and do things his way but not this. She would read the Bible but doubted she'd set foot in a church again.

"I can do most things myself," she said now to Benjamin. "And I have Micheline."

"And you have me and my son," Benjamin said. "The people here want to help you, Ellen. You belong to us, now."

Benjamin walked over to the door. Ellen bristled at the thought of belonging to anybody. She was grateful that he didn't touch her. Micheline rubbed Ellen's back as she passed.

"I'll walk out with Reverend McCloud," she said. She reached for his coat, but he stretched past her and got it himself.

"That's appreciated, Micheline, but unnecessary," Benjamin said. "Our friend needs your help preparing William's body. We'll set the funeral ceremony for Sunday."

He folded his scarf over his chest and buttoned his overcoat. After settling his stovepipe hat into place, he left with a wave and no expectation of an answer to what had not been a question. Sunday was three days away, long enough to clean and dress the body and open the house for two days of visits.

"He looks the same," Micheline said.

"What did you expect?"

"You've had all morning to work on him. He should look cleaner than he does. I can still see blood on his neck and look at this hand." She told Ellen she'd helped prepare two bodies before, both since she'd moved to Bobcaygeon Road, but not one that had died in an accident. She viewed blood as dirt and took no issue with it, even when it flowed.

Ellen's eyelids stung. "I did work on him. Are you here to help me? Because if you're here to matchmake, you can head home. I do not need another husband, especially not with this one still in the room."

"What are you talking about, Ellen? Nobody is suggesting Benjamin be your husband. William hasn't even been dead one day. Certainly you can't think that?"

Micheline peered into the basin. A small slush chunk floated in the grey liquid. She broke it up with the spoon, mashing it against the side of the pot until it melted. She scraped some flakes off her lye soap bar and stirred. Ellen's nose tingled at the sharp smell. With a cloth in each hand, Micheline carried the pot over to the chair Ellen had placed next to the body. She handed one of the cloths to Ellen, who rubbed it on William's wrist. Micheline dabbed hers on his neck.

"I will choose to believe you," Ellen said. "And to expect that the subject of marriage will not pass between us again. You must admit, however, that you did ask Mr. McCloud here to ensure it's his church I go to now that William's gone."

Ellen picked up the twig and dug at the dirt under the nails of William's other hand. She should be careful. William would caution her, too. He had explained the way the settlement worked when she'd arrived. Church services in schools and ministers' setting rooms were held Sunday evenings to attract those felled the morning after a Saturday night carouse. Even the most lawless loggers came. Keep on the good side of one and not on the bad side of the others and you were safe. William had attended Benjamin McCloud's Methodist service, but he'd given ends of wood from the sawmill to the Church of Scotland group.

None of that mattered now. Ellen had no illusions about what might happen if she continued not going to church, if she followed her own mind and stayed to herself. She'd lose the community, plain and simple. She might lose Micheline too. Right now she didn't mind the idea of living alone in her cabin, unfettered by others' words and needs, but she wouldn't even be here if other people hadn't helped her parents during their flight north. Attending the church could be a charitable act. She didn't have to believe what they did. She could use the hours on her knees at Benjamin McCloud's service to think about what she did believe. One day she might tell someone else about her second faith and it would make sense. She'd whispered the story to William in the dark the night she'd arrived. He said he understood, although what he saw and felt himself didn't change. It was a miracle that enough people sharing the same faith agreed to meet every week to listen to Benjamin McCloud's ideas. Why didn't each person concoct his own faith? Perhaps each one did. Perhaps people didn't come to Benjamin McCloud's service because they wholeheartedly believed what McCloud had to say, but because they wanted to believe or they wanted everyone else to think they did or they took comfort in the ways McCloud's faith overlapped their own. Surely, if Ellen told enough people what had happened to her and what she felt, she might inspire some who'd had the same experience. She couldn't be the only one. Life didn't work that way. The question, with William gone, was who?

"It's simple. You're obviously not from Scotland. You must come to ours." Micheline had stopped using just the tip of the cloth and now scrubbed William's chest with broad strokes.

Ellen brushed the bits of dirt into a pile on the floor. She would catch them later with her broom.

"I will come to Benjamin McCloud's on Sunday," she said. "You can tell him that he can perform the service and bury William in the churchyard. It is what William would have wanted."

"Ellen, you can tell him yourself. He's coming back today, remember?"

"I don't know how I will pay him."

"That's what William's tithing is for. He'll have one more wage packet coming, which will go to you. The tithe from that and some extra will cover the labour for storing and burying him."

"Storing?"

"Winter, remember? Ground's frozen."

"Benjamin's not coming, his son is."

With a huff, Micheline dipped her cloth back into the water – cool now, the colour of red clay. She held the basin up to Ellen, who set down her twig, pinched the cloth from Micheline and wrung it out. Micheline squatted while Ellen put on her boots and coat and went outside to fetch a fresh basin of snow.

When she returned, Micheline was still squatting. "We should take off his clothing," Micheline said.

Ellen dug at William's thumbnail with the twig. When he was alive, she'd known his hands more by their shape around her waist. His hands moved all the time, carrying or turning or lifting. He had worked from the moment he woke until the moment he slept. What did his life mean then? Had he merely been an ant, born to devote his body to building, to make a union with her, then to die with no issue left to carry his blood and his name?

"I should do that alone."

"Ellen, how can you? He's too heavy for one person to lift."

Ellen's shoulders sank. She set the stick on the floor and stood by Micheline. Micheline's yeasty, salted-milk smell took away William's dried blood scent for a moment. Ellen took a few deep breaths.

"We'll lift together," Micheline said. "Then you can slip off his shirt and put it right into the fire."

"Why?'

"It's unclean now. It's got blood on it. Nobody could wear it without inviting misfortune upon himself."

Ellen couldn't remember the Bible saying anything about a man's clothes becoming unclean after he passed. She did remember people on the farm in Georgia burning a man's clothes after they found him hanging from a scarlet oak tree. May said they wanted to drive out any evil spirits invited by the man's death, that his clothes were part of the farm, that they wanted to burn off that evil, too, so the man's spirit could go to heaven pure. Did Micheline's people share these beliefs? If so, did Benjamin know? Ellen helped Micheline lift William's shoulder and arm. Once Micheline had him braced, Ellen pulled his shirt up his back. Together they bent his elbow and eased the sleeve over his shoulder and free of his arm.

The indigo wool shirt had been his favourite. She wished she could have caught it before he died, so she could save it with the last essence of his life on it. Her job now was to see his body into the earth without contaminating it. The sleeve got stuck on his thumb. His elbow cracked as Ellen tugged at the cuff. Micheline shifted and freed her own arm and yanked the sleeve so it ripped as it came off.

"Micheline!"

"It doesn't matter, Ellen. It's more important that the shirt you put on him is clean."

Micheline lowered William. Ellen set the melted snow on the floor. She leaned her head so her ear met her shoulder. Her jaw popped. She opened it, lips closed. It was stiff and wouldn't open all the way. She pretended to yawn, but it stayed stuck. Her jaw was getting worse. Soon it wouldn't open at all, and she wouldn't be able to talk, though around Micheline, that quality mattered little. Tonight Ellen would climb into bed at first dark. Perhaps they'd finish preparing William earlier, and she could sleep. People wouldn't arrive until tomorrow. She could clean in the morning. Sleep helped her. It had since she was a child.

William's skin felt cold no matter how warm the water. The water slid off the skin the way it did off iron. Ellen hadn't realized how well her own skin absorbed water.

"You don't have to go to McCloud's church," Micheline said. She worked the dried blood off William's neck with the corner of a rag.

"I don't have to do anything," Ellen said. There were things she couldn't do, however. She couldn't go backwards. She couldn't hold Saf. She couldn't walk into Daddy's barbershop. Where could she go if she didn't go back to May or at least back to Hamilton? Toronto? Kingston? Her stomach ached at the thought.

Micheline dipped the rag in the water, swished it around and squeezed it before dabbing it against William's neck.

"But you'd be accepted into the community, finally." Micheline kept her head down as if she hoped Ellen wouldn't notice that last word that had slipped out.

"Haven't they accepted me already?" Ellen retreated to William's boots. The men had deposited him intact on her table, then made a fast exit. The ice that covered the laces before had melted and now the cold, wet strings were stiff. Ellen worked at them with the twig.

"Yes – as William's wife. And that's because every Sunday, there he was in the front row, an empty space beside him as if he expected you to show up mid-service. After that first time, you didn't come, as you know. And every time somebody needed help building a house or fixing a broken wagon, there was William, part of the crew, keeping spirits up, moving the party along. But as Ellen? They don't know you. They haven't seen you. They think you think you're too good for them, as if you've been hiding out from them."

"Nobody thought William was hiding me away?"

"Why would they? We both know that wasn't the case."

"They're the ones who think they're better than me. You'd be a fool to deny it, Micheline."

Ellen had loved her community in Hamilton. Since childhood, she'd had a few favourite friends, all of whom had married and moved off, like Ellen and William, to settle elsewhere. Since she arrived on Bobcaygeon Road, all Ellen had wanted to do was stay in the cabin. Need forced her outside to fetch snow or water or wood, but otherwise, she kept to herself. She had a hard enough time getting up from her heart chair to make a meal for William. The idea of dressing herself and taking the wagon down the road and sitting among a group of people listening to Benjamin McCloud's sermon had overwhelmed her. If Micheline hadn't come to her house every day that she could, the baby and one or two children in tow, Ellen suspected the rest of the settlement would have forgotten she existed, and she'd have faded into town mythology as William the Black Man's hidden wife. Perhaps they'd think she'd died or run off. The possibility of it, the story, would prove more interesting to them than the truth of her ever could.

The wet boot wouldn't budge. Ellen worked the twig down inside and leveraged the boot away from the ankle on all sides until it loosened enough to yank it off William's foot. She cradled the boot in her lap. Tiredness overtook her and she slumped. Oddly she felt less overwhelmed than she had since she arrived on Bobcaygeon Road, yet she had lost her lifeline. Without William, more seemed possible, friends or no friends. She could even go to New York City. Thoughts of all that might happen exhausted her. She yawned and her jaw cracked with a shooting pain.

"His foot?"

"My face."

Ellen wanted to tell people about her faith. And if they laughed or ignored her, she'd move to the next settlement and the next. The worst had happened. She had nothing left that anyone could take from her. It was more important to find someone who would understand her message. She didn't need to exclude the people here. They feared, as they sat on chairs at Sunday services to ensure the help of their neighbours when the worst danger they'd ever encounter lay inside their own minds.

"I don't believe he's gone to Heaven," Ellen said. "I know Jesus is real. He was. Everything in the Good Book happened. But it happened to people like you and me. William's spirit has gone, it's part of a bigger spirit that we all return to. Not God. Not any person, but a spirit so big we cannot name it." Ellen worked the wet sock off the swollen foot and draped it on the boot.

"That's not what William believed," Micheline said. She'd moved William's arms over his head, the elbows bent, hands dangling, and was washing the black curls in his armpits with the lye and lard soap. "William believed he'd be in Heaven right now sitting at God's knee."

Ellen wet her own rag in the lye mixture and started on the foot, its swollen top as pale as its sole. "Along with everybody else?"

"What do you mean?"

"Everyone believes he'll be the one sitting at God's knee. How is that possible when there are so many people in the world?"

"I haven't met that many."

"But it is said that there are. Anyone you meet who has sailed here tells you how many people live on the other side of the water. The way I see it, we are all a part of everything and when we die we go back to what we came from."

"Which is?"

"This," Ellen indicated the air around her with a sweep of the rag. Lye water dripped on the floorboards. Ellen left it. "Everything. The air, the sky, the ground."

"You mean we're breathing William?"

Ellen watched her, a smile ready to fill her face.

"It's a beautiful idea, Ellen," Micheline said.

Before her arrival, Ellen knew William had told his neighbours at church that his wife and daughter would travel up from Hamilton. Ellen imagined their neighbours thinking William's wife would be as warm as he was the way they expected her skin to be as dark. Then she'd shown up, slack-jawed and grey, her hair sticking out of her braided bun, her hand wrapped in iodine-dipped gauze. She'd come to Duffy's Store and asked for William. Duffy's son had run down the road to the sawmill. Several minutes later, along came William in an apron, glowing with relief and anticipation. When he realized Ellen was alone, his face dropped.

He'd enfolded her in his arms and led her out of the store. "There was a fire," she said when they got to the cabin. "It took Daddy and it took Saf. Safra."

The rest of the story she kept inside, how she'd crawled through the stink of smoke with Saf held tightly to her chest, one hand pushing her daughter's face into her breast to keep the smoke from her lungs, that propulsive animal crawl through the hallway and over the threshold and onto the steps and down to the street where she'd rolled into a ball on the dirt sidewalk lined with stands of lilac trees in early bloom, the charred smell drowning the blossoms' sweet, powdery scent. She'd kept her arm's grip on Safra but loosened her hand, her daughter's mouth open against the skin above her breast, her face streaked with a paste of sweat, tears and soot. Motionless. *Good girl,* Ellen chanted, her throat sore and her voice hoarse, *my sweet baby girl,* at the same time as the cold knowing struck all through her, and she prayed and willed herself to believe that the child had gone into a sleep to protect herself. Or because, despite her mother's attempts, she'd breathed the foul smoke, and the sleep was to take the pain away until she could breathe some out again. Ellen held the little head close, cupped with the most tender mother's hand, and prayed for someone to find her as she emptied herself of anything but a love beyond waiting.

The dark thoughts had tumbled in soon after, heralded by the fierce, dire womb-rooted screams she bellowed forth as they prised her arm and finally her hand free of her child. She hadn't witnessed Safra's final removal in fact, as they'd resorted to spirits, and the last memory she had was the cloth pressed against her face as she clung to her child.

Ellen rinsed her rag. Dirt particles filled the water. She squeezed until the rag was damp, then returned to dab the foot. Soon she moved to the other foot, working again on the laces. The work did go faster and easier with Micheline there. She dropped the sock and boot beside the others. "I know you pray to the sun, Micheline. Can I tell you about my second faith?"

RUDIE

Rudie climbed the porch steps. Her cheeks smarted. Dylan had scratched her skin with his whiskers, the way he used to. She hadn't expected Dylan to kiss her and for that kiss to last long enough to mean they still had a connection. Or did she just pity his vision loss? She'd have to give the moment's meaning some thought.

The top step had a worn board. When she and Leo bought the house, their first, it shone in their minds in all its renovated glory. Rudie's films beckoned her this way, too, objects of perfect unreachable light. The first year, they'd ripped the stained grey carpet from the stairs, then pried nail-studded plywood strips using a hammer claw. They'd sanded the wood smooth and stained it. The only imperfections – knots and chips in the wood – were the sort that pleased her. Since that day, the staircase gleamed for her, the afternoon sunshine through the leaded-glass windows bouncing rainbows off its cherry grain.

She could ignore the plaster cracks and chipped glass and picture the whole house finished to the standard of that staircase.

She unlocked the door. A hammer banged upstairs. She unloaded the white plastic bags from the bundle buggy and dropped them on the floor. Next time, she'd bring her own bags to model green behaviour for Roselore. The hammer banged louder. Then came a crack and the clatter of wood landing on a pile. She parked the bundle buggy on the stoop and entered the house.

Rudie unlaced her shoes and set them beside her father's Sorels. Crumbs stuck to her socks as she went upstairs. She should clean the house today too – alone, because Mom wouldn't help her with Dad here, and Rudie needed him to install the new toilet and sink before they brought Roselore home.

The cupboard, the countertop and a neat stack of broken wood sat in the upstairs hallway. Bob crouched in front of the toilet in jeans, a white T-shirt and a pair of paint-splattered Top-Siders. He was unscrewing the base of the toilet. The lid leaned against the wall.

"Dad," she said.

Bob dropped the screws in the pouch of his tool belt. A hole gaped in the wall where the sink had been.

He pulled the dust mask down around his neck, wiped his hands on a fluorescent orange rag.

"I'll stop for a coffee," he said. He stepped over the wood and pipes into the hall.

Downstairs, she brushed at the soles of her socks.

"I didn't buy much," she said, sweeping a hand in the direction of the bags. "Everything was too ugly or expensive or pink. How am I going to do this?"

Bob wore his sandy hair clipped short. He visited a barber every second Saturday, and his hair hadn't changed since Rudie was young, aside from the silvering above the ears that increased every year. He coughed, to show her the air in her kitchen smelled too greasy for his taste. He was a fastidious man. He kept his work site neat and followed every goggle, dust mask and glove precaution ever dreamed up.

He straightened her shoes and carried the shopping bags to the kitchen counter.

"She hasn't met you," he said. "There are plenty of folks lining up to take these kids. Doesn't have to be you."

He poured a coffee, sniffed it and dumped the mug's contents into the sink. He placed the filter in the compost bin, filled a fresh one.

Rudie's head throbbed. She stepped into the living room, grinding her teeth from side to side. This was the last day she'd have the house to herself. Once Roselore came home, she would be part of every conversation, whether she understood it or not.

Rudie went back and leaned on the counter. "If I was about to give birth," she said, close enough to touch her dad's shoulder, "you wouldn't say that."

Bob rooted around under the sink until he produced a container of white vinegar. He nodded at it then at her, approving, then stood, shoulders straight. He poured some into the carafe and swished it around.

"You're not about to give birth," he said, head tilted, expression reasonable.

Rudie's eyes filled. Better than anyone, she knew how adopting Roselore was not the same as carrying her own baby, in every way but the wanting, which might be fiercer, more primal for having had to fight so hard to fulfill itself. Everything about adopting a black Haitian two-year-old into their childless, white Canadian family was different. Rudie was a fool to pretend otherwise, but there was a space where creating a family this way could hold the same resonance as a biological family, a space reached through intention and love. Tension gripped Rudie's shoulders and arms at the awareness that her father wanted no part of this space.

"Dad, I didn't know you felt this way," Rudie made herself say, using one of the responses that H.A.S.P. – the Hamilton Adoption Support for Parents – had taught her to try when confronted with resistance from extended family members.

After rinsing the carafe and filling it with Brita water, Bob gave the coffee maker a careful going-over with a wet sponge, then pushed the on button. He sat, and she did too. He put his hand on her knee, then her shoulder and pulled her into a hug. She stayed seated and soon her arm ached, and she freed herself.

"At Christmas, when you told me," he said, "you said I had six months to get used to it. It's barely been a month and you tell me she's coming today. That wouldn't have happened if you were pregnant."

"Some babies are premature," Rudie said.

"This desire to be a mother comes directly from you, Rudie. And honey, I love this about you, that you want to do this, but I thought I had time to prepare."

"Dad, sometimes pregnancy is not an option." Rudie bit her lip, reminding herself of the raw skin on her cheek. Her mouth flooded with the memory of Dylan's taste of Juicy Fruit and coffee.

Bob took in her words without expression, then said, "You'll have to put gates at your stairs top and bottom. If you pick up a couple, I'll do that up for you when I'm through with the sink."

"I'm going out again anyway," Rudie said through a forced, squinting smile, her lip stinging. Bob wanted to help, but she didn't have his full support. Suddenly she didn't want her daughter to meet anyone who wouldn't shower her with love.

She'd make the coffee first. She set out two turquoise Fiestaware mugs and got the soy milk out of the fridge. She'd have to buy food. Roselore would want to eat Haitian meals for a while before she'd accept Canadian food. Rudie had practised making rice and beans and *legim* using combinations of peppers, garlic and thyme. She'd bought eggplant, yam, cabbage and spinach at the markets on James Street, though she hadn't been able to locate chayote. The food had turned out hot and gummy. In Haiti, Rudie could have learned how to spice the recipes right.

"Do you know any Caribbean grocery stores?" she asked, pouring the coffee.

"Hardly. I like to be able to taste my food."

Rudie set a spoon near the sugar bowl and put a mug in front of Bob, along with a black-and-white-checkered napkin.

"Dad, is it her race? Because to us her race doesn't matter," Rudie said.

"There's where you're wrong, honey. Race always matters. Ask one of those ladies who works for the agency – or are all the agency workers white? Ask one of the cleaning people at the airport. They'll answer your question. Race matters for this girl, and you're a fool if you pretend any different."

"You're right. It does matter. To her, it will really matter, of course, more than we could pretend to know."

"If you have the energy for that, it's your life."

Out of habit, Rudie turned on the water to rinse her mug. The tap coughed and spat a few drops, then hissed. Of course. Bob had turned the water off while he hooked up the new sink. She grabbed the calendar from the top of the microwave, went into the living room and flopped onto the couch. She needed a list. She didn't want to leave Bob here alone now, but couldn't say why. What did she think he'd do, spray-paint racial slurs on Roselore's nursery walls? When Rudie was a child, schoolchildren used the slurs, but even repeating them in her mind gave her a bruised, cringing sensation.

How could her dad have harboured such rigid feelings and not revealed them? She stopped herself. Everybody had complex feelings, even Bob. This certainty had drawn her to documentary filmmaking. Sometimes in a crowd she reminded herself that every person there had a wealth of emotions and thoughts that they couldn't reveal to anyone else. When filming, she could tease out more of the iceberg below the surface than the subject might expect or even be comfortable sharing. The camera captured that surprise and discomfort, that vulnerability. When it went well, Rudie believed the undiscovered territory she was revealing might not see light without her fostering.

Her morning list had one word left:

Diapers?

She jotted down
Baby Gates, 2

The drill's *rzzz* started and stopped. She counted the length of the intervals between drills and the length of the drilling time and matched the times up, searching for patterns. She'd had a fantasy of her dad teaching Roselore how to fix the house. Neither she nor Leo was good with tools. It made no sense that they'd embarked on this renovation. Each found the process from the list-making to the shopping to the planning to the set-up anxiety-inducing. It was only in the middle of the job, in their paint-splattered, too-small work clothes, that they found some pleasure. For Rudie, that pleasure lasted about ten minutes, after which she wanted the project over so she could live with its finished state. Bob helped make the renovation bearable. He expressed his love for her by fixing her house, and he liked feeling superior to Leo who, for all his vigour, had only a loose idea of how to build with wood.

She paced the room, unable to concentrate. Tears gummed her eyes. She punched the couch cushion. Her Strat stood in the corner, beckoning. She hadn't played it with Bob in the same house since she was a teenager. She settled the strap on her shoulder and rocked her hips against the guitar's weight. She flicked the switch on the amp and hit the chords for "Wild Thing." After months without playing, she needed to tackle the easy songs for a while before her fingers could do much else. Dust coated the frets. She hit a few more chords, found the rhythm and thrust her hips into it, eyes closed and face tense, as if she were dancing.

Leo was all for keeping the guitars out when Roselore arrived, letting her pick them up and discover the sounds they make. Rudie wasn't so sure. For her, the guitar was a tune-out method, much like television. She slammed her thumb over the strings.

It was noon. Rudie had to go out and buy the big items – toddler bed, change table, high chair – then bring them home and set them up. Who else could she call for help? Though Rudie and Leo had lived in Hamilton for two years, neither knew anyone here well. Kikka, Rudie's mother, lived in Toronto. Kikka would drive out if Rudie begged, but then she'd have to do whatever Kikka suggested, though Rudie might find Kikka's bossiness a relief right now. She wouldn't have to think as much, be so responsible.

She played "All Day and All of the Night" then put the Strat on its stand and went back upstairs. Behind the bathroom door came the drill's *revs* and *whirs*. She took a copy of Roselore's picture from her bedroom mirror. Curling up on her bed, she drank in the brown eyes and strong, wide smile, the tiny, milk teeth. She hoped her own brown eyes would comfort Roselore. Or would she see only difference? While the guitar had calmed Rudie, Roselore's picture filled her with light.

She dialed Leo's number.

"Where are you now?"

"In the parlour of the bed and breakfast, waiting for a receipt. Excited?"

"Am I! And scared. Leo?"

"Rudie?"

"You'll be there, right? You've got your flight booked? All your arrangements?"

His voice held the same manic triumph as when she'd told

him Roselore was arriving tonight. She estimated he was on his third coffee, aiming his winning smile at everyone in his path, passing out cigars if he had them, though she was more superstitious and wouldn't announce much until she held Roselore in her arms, and maybe not even then. Let people figure it out. Leo's laugh caught her up, and shame coursed through her. She thought of Dylan. Had telling her about his split-up marriage meant he wanted to start seeing her again? Practically, yes, she could make an affair work, if she used daycare or babysitters. Leo went out of town often enough. Roselore would get used to Rudie's absences without understanding the details.

Rudie flushed, appalled at herself. Leo's big-hearted voice drew her toward him, making her lose sight of the details of an affair, of how her mouth might meet Dylan's, how her clothes might come off with him, her skin heat up next to his, or how she'd make any of the many many moves required to take on that intimacy. Here was Leo, and Roselore was on her way. Rudie shouldn't need more.

"You got it. Just finishing up here. My flight's not until five. Arnie's meeting me up on set after lunch and driving me to the bank then to Halifax Airport. How are things on your end?"

"My dad."

"Is Grandpa there fixing up that sink?"

"He doesn't want to be Grandpa."

"Okay. Roselore can call him Bob for all I care."

"I have a question. Am I a mother yet? Or does that happen when she's placed in my arms?"

"Do you think they place her in your arms, ceremonially?"

"All the pictures I held in my mind were of you and I arriving at the orphanage with a group of parents. And yes, I imagine the parents approaching the children one after the other. When it's our turn, someone hands Roselore to me and she snuggles in tight, shows me in some way that she knows I'm her mother. Maybe I read it somewhere?"

"It could happen that way. Just change the setting of your vision to a conference room at the Sheraton with fluorescent lighting. Be sure to include a coffee urn and bottles of orange juice sitting in a bowl of ice cubes."

"Leo."

"Do you think they'll mind if I film it?"

"You mean the other parents?"

"The children?"

"Some people might mind, though there might be media there. Let's just experience this one camera-free, let it become a genuine memory, a story we can tell her."

"Aren't you excited?"

"Are you kidding me? I should be pissed off and hurt about my dad," she lowered her voice, "and I am, believe me, but I'm having a hard time accessing the feeling. Even when I do, I can't hold onto it. It's a problem."

"Sounds like you're doing just fine."

"This is big, Leo. Has my dad ever seemed like a racist to you?"

"Many racists don't seem like they are. That's the thing."

Rudie turned the wand on the blinds. The grey outside depressed her. She pretended she'd shut the slats against the sun. The drilling had stopped.

"Leo, I've hardly bought anything," she whispered. "I have to go out again. It's funny. Maybe he shouldn't help if he's not intending to have a relationship with her."

"It's that serious?"

"How will I explain it to her?"

"By the time you have to, we'll have figured out a way to talk about it."

"It?"

"Racism."

"They mentioned it in H.A.S.P. I think I should ask him to leave."

"He's your father."

"But if he's not going to be a healthy influence, or any influence . . . what will he do, act like some guy who happens to drop by? She will figure it out."

"She's not here yet, Rudie. Let him do what he offers. You need the help. I wish I could come home before Ottawa."

"How can I face him?"

"He's still him. Don't forget you're driving to the airport in rush hour and you have to find parking. Bring the digital camera. We'll take pictures."

Rudie sat on the floor, her back against the bed, facing away from the door. She doubted her father eavesdropped. If anything, he'd make more noise if he suspected he might overhear an unwelcome comment. Her mom leaving him last summer had thrown him off, but now Bob had reached a place of balance. He'd met a woman named Donna at his church. Every Sunday they went to the original Tim Hortons on Ottawa Street for a cruller and coffee after the service. Fridays, he took her out for fish and chips and bowling. He called her his lady friend. Leo thought they'd get married as soon as Rudie's parents had finalized their divorce. Rudie wasn't so sure, but Leo reminded her that statistically, married men lived longer and were happier.

Until she met Leo, all the men Rudie knew wanted to avoid marriage. Even Dylan had married only to satisfy his Polish wife's residency requirements. The quality had seemed a blight on her generation. She couldn't count how many of her girlfriends had lived with a man who couldn't commit, who needed space, all that blahblahblah. Dylan was the worst. If committing were the most important quality to her, she'd stick with Leo. In fact, she had no good reason at all *not* to stick with Leo. What could appeal to her about a secret union with Dylan? She allowed herself a quick memory of his mouth's bitter fruity taste, the heat of it, pressing into him hungrily, the grip of his palm on the back of her head. It made no sense to throw away everything out of greed for another's skin. One kiss with Dylan didn't have to mean discarding what she had with Leo. If she believed that . . . There was more. She wanted more. Yet, the connection she felt to Dylan in his arms didn't negate what she had with Leo. It was different and – if she allowed it for herself – more intense for being illicit. That feeling might have shifted with her married now and him single. Why, on the verge of having what she wanted, was it not enough?

Leo hadn't spoken for a while. Maybe he was thinking about his own private life. The prospect amused her. He was less capable of maintaining one than she was. He had an open nature, one that could seem careless, but what was going on in his world absorbed him so much that he couldn't hide it.

"Is there anything else I need to do?" she asked him. She stroked Roselore's picture. Leo had a copy on his laptop.

"What about that email Ann sent this morning? You said you were going to print it up."

"I did. It's right here on the dresser. Collated and stapled."

"Weren't you planning to chat with the H.A.S.P. types? Maybe they'll help you with your dad."

"I'm one step ahead of you. I've got a 'Café Intervention,' as Gabby calls it, with some H.A.S.P. folks this afternoon, at the Persimmon. Gabby will be there. I've talked to her on the phone but haven't met her in person yet. I'm lucky they could meet on such short notice. They do it all the time apparently."

"They probably love it. What about your mom?"

"I felt slightly ready, and now I'm overwhelmed. And Dad's been silent for a long time for someone installing a sink. I hope he hasn't heard me."

"I can barely hear you. You haven't called her?"

"I'd better check on Dad."

"I love you, Rudie. Do what you can. The important thing is that Roselore's going to have us tonight. She can sleep with us! As if we're going to sleep. We'll talk this afternoon if you want. I'll call you once I've checked my bags."

"You got it. I love you, too, Leo. Woot!"

"Who are you?"

"Woot."

"Bye."

After changing into a black turtleneck, Rudie sat on the bed with the agency's package about Roselore's history. When Roselore was three months old, a woman brought her to Angels' Wings Crèche along with six older children, none of them hers, or so she claimed. She had looked after all seven, but she was sick and nobody else would promise to take them when she died, let alone help her out now. The oldest was an eleven-year-old girl named Danielle. It took Danielle a long time to let the women at the orphanage handle the care of the other six children, especially of Roselore, the youngest. Danielle was fourteen now and worked alongside the nannies. The agency suspected Danielle was the woman's biological daughter, but Danielle hadn't confirmed, if she even knew. The woman had died a few days after dropping off the children. Since nobody knew if or how the children were related, the agency was placing them with separate families unless someone came forward requesting siblings. A family in British Columbia would adopt Danielle. Roselore had continued to have a close relationship with Danielle, preferring her over the nannies. So Roselore had grown up with love. She had been malnourished but had shown no signs of congenital illnesses. As nothing was known about her birth parents, the agency couldn't say for certain, but by all appearances she was healthy. She slept well, laughed often, knew how to walk, talk and feed herself, liked to run and dance and woke up singing most mornings. She should have no difficulty transferring her attachment from Danielle to Rudie.

Rudie resented the connection Danielle had with Roselore, although she was the most important person in Roselore's life. Ann Hepner had hinted back in December that Rudie and Leo could adopt Danielle. Yet if Danielle came with the package, Rudie knew Roselore would continue to think of Danielle as her mother, not Rudie. It saddened her to separate them, but Danielle had a family who wanted her. The agency assured Rudie that Roselore could stay in touch with Danielle, that

Danielle could send her cards and pictures, and Rudie and Leo could send pictures to her, too. When Roselore was older, the agency and the orphanage hoped the families would bring their daughters and sons back to Haiti to visit Angels' Wings. Now such a trip was vital as the earthquake had taken away their chance to visit the country before adopting Roselore. It was important to Haitians that foreign *blans* who adopted their children have a sense of the country and its culture as they began life as a family. Rudie and Leo had assured Ann Hepner that yes, they would travel to Haiti, and they intended to do so as soon as they could. Rudie yearned to see where Roselore had lived – not just the orphanage – and to return to the places she herself had seen as a self-absorbed teenager. She shouldn't resist Danielle, she really shouldn't. The girl was so young. Ann had suggested Roselore spend time with Danielle and her parents together for a few days before everybody went home. They would all be staying at the Sheraton during that time, Rudie read.

Rudie stood up, the papers falling to her feet, her heart galloping. Why hadn't Ann Hepner told her this? She called the agency and started speaking before Ann had time to greet her.

"Do we have to book a room?" Her words came out rapid-fire.

"Hello, Rudie. Are you excited? Do you have your nursery ready?"

"*The hotel.* Do we book the room ourselves or have you booked it? Have you heard anything?"

"The flight from Haiti should be landing at six o'clock as planned. We'll get them off the plane, through Immigration, and settled with a snack and some clean clothes and then they can meet you. I'm sure I sent you the room number and all that?"

"I only have the conference room number. I just figured out that you're expecting us to stay more than one night. I haven't booked a room."

"It's all booked," Ann said. Papers rustled. "When I find it, I'll send you the number. You'll stay there a week, so pack enough clothing. The charge will be reflected in your agency bill. It'll still be less than a trip to Haiti."

Bob was watching her from the doorway as she hung up.

"Didn't you hear me calling?" he asked.

"I was on the phone."

"I need your help here."

"Dad, I've got a million things –"

"Yes, and installing a sink is one of them. Step over here and give me a hand. I can do it, but it's much easier with you."

Rudie braced the sink with her hip as she leaned to adjust her sock.

"Careful there."

She put her hands back in place and steadied the porcelain bowl. They'd splurged on a standing sink. Already the room felt bigger without the vanity. When she and Leo would have time to get a mirror cabinet, Rudie had no idea. She could put it on her list for today, but she had to focus on Roselore's bed, high chair, baby gates, car seat, snowsuit. She wouldn't feel comfortable driving away from the airport without a car seat installed.

Ann should have sent her this information back when they were matched so she'd have had half a chance of getting properly organized. She tapped her foot. Bob squatted, rifled through his tool box. She liked being quiet with another person. She loved Leo for his silence too, and not only when he was filming. It was not unusual for a cinematographer to go quiet behind the camera. When he wanted to, Leo had the biggest personality around, the sunniest, grandest voice and gestures, but he could also take time to think of what he wanted to say and often would sit in a group without saying a word or trance out when the two of them were alone together. Rudie found it harder to stay quiet when they were filming Agnes, as she was the director. In order to interview people well, one should let them say what they needed to say without guiding them in any direction.

Today Bob's silence goaded her.

"It was the agency on the phone. There are new details I just read in the material they sent me. I like it when someone tells me what to do. It shouldn't be in the fine print of some email I have to print myself that nobody reads anyway. Turns out we're staying at the Sheraton until they think Roselore is ready to come home. She's got a nanny – an older girl – she's attached to and the transition to her accepting us as parents takes time. So now I have to pack another suitcase, think this through."

Why she was telling him? She should call Leo back, even Kikka. Bob didn't want to hear it.

"Let that nanny adopt her then." Bob had located a bit and was inserting it into the drill.

"She's fourteen, Dad. She may or may not be related. Besides, they've matched her with another family, from British Columbia." Rudie leaned her head against the wall. Why had she told him that? Now she and Leo would seem extra cruel taking this child not only from her homeland but from her family, someone who loved her like a mother. Maybe she felt guilty for that? Should she?

"You can always send her back," Bob said, "if it doesn't work out."

Rudie dropped her hands. Bob strengthened his grip and lifted his leg to brace the sink with his thigh.

"You can't be serious. Sending her back would be like killing her. To offer her this love and this life, this family and then take it away from her because I didn't like something she did?"

Rudie was crying.

"It happens all the time. You don't know what you're getting. She could be one of those kids who threatens to stab their parents with scissors. I read about one last week. Seven years old. The mother sent the boy back to Russia on a plane. She feared for her life."

"How cruel! Nobody should have a child if they have the capacity to give up on him when he doesn't match their ideal."

"Have you had her checked out?"

"Who?"

"The girl. The *baby*. Isn't that why you were supposed to go down there in the first place, so you could sample the goods? Take her to a doctor and make sure she's what they say she is?"

"The agency wouldn't be allowed to offer her for adoption if she weren't healthy."

She cringed at the word *offer*. Bob was bad enough for saying *goods*. Was she using such terms now because she had a layer of detachment? Or was she falling into Bob's way of seeing the world?

"I've heard stories about people who adopt overseas and the child has an illness they weren't told about like cancer or spina bifida. You should make sure you have an escape clause."

"That's not me, Dad. That's what I'm saying. I'd take care of my child regardless of what illness or condition shows up. You would too. What if I'd had cerebral palsy or a brain injury – you wouldn't have given up on me, I know you wouldn't!"

Bob started the drill. Rudie sank to the floor, sobbing. He turned off the drill and set it down in the bowl of the sink. With one hand propping up the sink, he reached down to pat her knee.

"Honey, I'd hug you, except I have to keep this propped or it'll rip the wall out."

"It's not the ideal we all might have wanted, but it is pretty amazing that Roselore is going to be our daughter. I need you to see Roselore as your grandchild."

"The child will see right through me. You would have."

"Are you serious? You really can't accept her because she's black?"

Bob's fingers twitched and he flexed his hand.

"You can't blame me. Everyone else has grandchildren who look like them in some way. You won't be able to fool anybody."

"Why would we want to?"

"They'll know she's not yours."

"But she is."

"I won't be able to be the same toward her as I would have if –"

"If she were white." Rudie felt hurt by her own words, but was surprised to find she enjoyed the pain.

"It doesn't have to be bad. Just not the same."

"That's not good enough. She's got to feel like she belongs in this family, that we're hers. We can talk about issues as they come up."

Bob finished drilling in the screws and crouched to pack up his tool box.

"I'll clean up here," Bob said. "Leo can finish the job. He'll be on some sort of leave, I presume? Or you can. Or your mother."

"So you're going? Good. I wish you would."

"It's the right thing to do. I can't be the person you want me to be. The child won't know whether I'm here or not. She doesn't know me. I was willing to help but not like this. You let me know how it's going when you get back from Ottawa."

It was ten thirty. Rudie hauled another suitcase down from the attic and flipped it open on her bed. As she added jeans and leggings, she thought about the day ahead. She would have to be at the airport by five thirty to make her six fifty flight to Ottawa. Once there, Leo would meet her at Arrivals, they'd catch a cab, check in and find the conference room where they would meet their daughter for the first time. Her ribs hurt thinking about it. She grabbed six pairs of socks and stuffed them into the suitcase. If she could get the furniture home by two, then spend a couple of hours setting it up, she might stay on track. She considered calling Kikka but didn't think she was ready for the opposite of Bob's rejection – Kikka's brand of closeness. Rudie shook her head sideways, as if she had water in her ear. Her thought processes felt clunky and juvenile. Kikka and Bob weren't unalike. Both were intense, only Kikka was energetic and probing, while Bob held his harshness inside, hiding his emotions so he didn't have to look at them if he didn't want to.

Rudie forced herself to think about children's furniture. The list she had made while talking to Leo sat on her dresser. Roselore could sleep with them. Rudie felt heavy, her head drooping. She sat on the bed, her hips propped by the pillow. She could push the suitcase over to Leo's side and curl up under the duvet, dozing off for a quick nap. She should make more coffee to perk herself up. Her body didn't want to move.

A knock sounded at the door. She sighed, wishing it away. She was almost there, in the sleep that eluded her at night. This time a flurry of knocks came and a heavier sound like feet stamping on the porch. She and Leo didn't mind people coming to their door the way some of their friends did. They lived one street away from James Street on a block of people with No Soliciting signs on their porches, so they got only the most persistent charity workers along with people who took a wrong turn after leaving This Ain't Hollywood or Mission Services. She liked the interruption when she was working, the randomness of the moment, to see what the person had to offer, not that she'd accept. She wondered what motivated a person to go door to door with anything, though she'd done it often enough as a child selling cookies or candles or magazine subscriptions. Maybe there was a documentary film in this idea.

Yawning, she opened the door on Hannah and Barth. She flinched.

"How did you know where I lived? Did you follow me?"

"Not really. Everyone knows you live here."

"Everyone? Who even knows me?"

"We've seen you here before."

Rudie stood in the door, holding it a quarter open, her foot blocking it from opening farther.

"I'm not giving you any more money. And you can't stay here."

Wrapping her sweater more tightly around her waist, she came onto the porch, closing the door behind her. Why, she didn't know. If these two decided to barge in, she would be powerless to stop them. Maybe they had more friends hiding. But their faces were open, hurting, confused. Nobody spoke. Rudie shivered, the air icy against her neck and through the weave of her acrylic top.

"Just a minute," she said.

She went back inside and got her knee-length down coat. She pulled on a toque and fingerless gloves, wound a striped scarf around her neck and came out again, locking the door behind her. Hannah and Barth had returned to the sidewalk. Rudie sat on the bottom step, looking up at them.

"Really, what is it? Why me?"

"We don't know what to do," the boy said.

"Yes, we do," said Hannah. "I'm having a baby and we need somewhere to stay."

Rudie lurched upright, the ice on the step throwing her off balance when she hugged Hannah so that she was leaning on her for a moment. Either out of surprise or welcome, Hannah didn't push her away. Rudie thumped Hannah on the shoulder, then clicked her teeth as she climbed back up a few stairs.

"How do you know?" Rudie asked.

Hannah glared.

"She knows," said Barth.

"I don't have room for you," Rudie said.

The boy hopped from foot to foot. He looked scared and uncertain, though deeply pleased to have someone need him.

The girl stood with her hands on her bum, breasts thrust out, defiant and proud. She had full hips and a bulky vest so Rudie couldn't tell how far along she was, if indeed she was telling the truth. Her face looked pale and sweaty beneath the spots, as if she might throw up. Rudie straightened. For the first time in years, she'd received news of a pregnancy without feeling a clamp of envy. Maybe because she didn't believe Hannah, though clearly Barth did. Nobody moved.

"What can I do?" Rudie said. "My daughter's arriving today so maybe I can help."

"Is she in university?"

Rudie smiled. She must look as old as their mothers. She might even be *older* than their mothers. Why would they trust her?

"She's two, and she's coming from Haiti. We're adopting her."

She felt relief saying what was happening out loud but also felt a pang, as if she were saying too much. Hannah shivered, then swayed, wrapping her arms around her body under her breasts. Barth motioned as if he wanted to hug her. She stood straight and tall and he backed away.

"She's got her own kid coming," Hannah said to Barth. "Forget about her. She doesn't want to help us."

"But she has a car," Barth said. He pointed down the street at Rudie's red Ford Fiesta.

Hannah turned to Rudie. "You're having a kid and that's your car?"

Rudie nodded. Even if the furniture came boxed up with assembly required, Rudie would need to do some creative bungee cording to squeeze her purchases into that trunk. She should buy everything online and have it delivered. When they got home from Ottawa, Leo could entertain Roselore while Rudie assembled.

"We need a ride," the boy was saying. "That's all. We're going to Hannah's parents who live out in the country, too far to reach by bus. Nobody'll rent us a car, not that we have enough coin."

"You could drive us, though it'll be a tight squeeze in that tiny box. It probably barely holds you. Don't you need a car seat?"

"Yes, yes, I do. And a toddler bed and a high chair and god knows what else, none of which I'll be able to fit in there and my husband and my dad are both AWOL. Gates."

"Take us with you. We'll help you stuff everything into the hatch. Then you can take us to Glanbrook, to Hannah's mom's place."

"I won't be able to wait with you. I have to get to the Hamilton Airport."

"Who's asking you to wait?"

Hannah's low brows made her eyes look purpled, sunken and glowering. She threw dark glares at Barth, who mostly looked cowed but underneath showed a determination that Hannah seemed wearily happy to accept.

"I do need help today," Rudie said. "But not in picking up the bed. Why don't you meet me back here at two o'clock. You can help me set up. We'll leave at four and I'll drop you off, then head to the airport. Glanbrook isn't that far out of my way." She wondered if Bob was back at his house now, or if he'd gone for fish and chips. She wished she'd thought to borrow his truck. "How do you think your mom will react?"

"Probably give me the boot. Again."

"You don't know that," Barth said. "And you ran away, you didn't 'get the boot.'"

Hannah shot him another look.

"Whatever. Getting kicked out isn't superior to running away."

"Nobody said it was. She might be good about it. It's her grandchild."

Rudie chewed her lip. This girl's mother was a fool if she rejected the child. If Roselore came to her at this age with the same news, she wouldn't push her away. Not at any age. How could Bob do this to her? Hannah was barely a child herself. Who knew why she had run? Still, Rudie didn't know how any parent could say no to her child's child. It was a profound rejection of your own child because a child, however she comes into your life, takes all your love, everything you offer, and feeds it into her own soul, bringing even more energy and light to your life, to life. What could have happened to make Bob what he was?

As a young father, Bob had kept running shoes and shorts in a gym bag behind the seat of his Ford Explorer, parking at a carpool near the highway and running the five kilometres home, stopping at the fridge to fuel up on pink lemonade then running back. When she was old enough, maybe ten or eleven, she'd wait for him in her Adidas track suit and shoes, stretching to warm up her hamstrings in the driveway while he drank, then jogging off down the gravel hill beside him, their breaths puffs of steam in the crisp air. She kept pace with him and recorded her times and distances meticulously in a notebook stowed in the glovebox the way he did. "What a fast runner you are," he said to her many times, admiring her ability to keep up with him. "You're a natural," he said, and though she caught on in her teens that he was holding himself in check to boost her confidence, she forgave him.

She should stop thinking about him. This Hannah needed a lot of luck. Barth too.

Rudie hadn't driven her car in days. Winter driving agitated her and the match with Roselore before Christmas had made her extra anxious. She could walk or bus most places, but today she needed speed. A pickup truck slowed as she unlocked the door, its steel-haired driver watching her from an open window. She met his gaze and held it until he nodded with a small smile, rolled up his window and drove away. He looked like any of the men who stood on the street outside Downtown Billiards.

The key took some jimmying before it would turn in the lock, her Gumby and Pokey keychain rattling against the door. Then when the door stuck, she yanked it so hard the handle almost came off in her hand, the door opening with a *screech*. She idled the engine until the frost inside the window melted then wiped the window down with a towel. She adjusted the rear-view mirror and tried to imagine a car seat back there. Many women had their monumental labour stories to tell. Would this day be her version of a labour story?

The car shuddered into action as she inched it out of its parking spot and headed south toward the escarpment. She refused to call it a mountain the way the locals did. Next week when she drove down this street, Roselore would sit behind her in a car seat. When the light turned green, she inched forward, pacing herself with the bus ahead of her. In front of the communion dress store, she spotted Hannah and Barth again, perhaps imagining Hannah's baby in such a dress. Rudie privately mocked frilly dresses and religious rituals, her adolescent self having not quite left her. And yet, she yearned to belong to something that offered such rituals. Mostly she wanted the faith – and the simplicity – felt by those who bought the white organza dress and the crucifix necklaces and derived profound meaning from them.

Agnes Martin hadn't talked about God or Christianity, yet Rudie hadn't met a more spiritual person in her life. That included the sand-painting Buddhist monks who'd rolled through town the year Rudie and Leo bought the house and whose garbled presentation had yielded few truths for her, though Leo had found them inspiring and they had both felt better for having been blessed. Agnes was all about inspiration, and had studied Zen Buddhist teachings. Roselore's arrival made it urgent that Rudie figure out the spiritual piece of her life. They would be in Ottawa for a week. Maybe they could start going to Stewart Memorial Church the Sunday after they got back. She had discarded religion in her teens, yet she longed now to have faith. She wanted Roselore to have a spiritual life. She wanted to get it right. She supposed she'd be *that kind of mother.*

She was that way about everything. She sacrificed sleep, food, even hygiene, to get her house clean or her film edited, to get whatever she was working on done properly. The problem was, she rarely finished any of those important tasks. Her film, for instance. She'd completed the interviews with Agnes six years ago but was still editing the film because it didn't match her vision. She struggled to find what it was missing. Should she visit New York City and interview those who'd known Agnes in the day? She didn't have to go to New York, of course, not now, with Skype and instant messaging. She could conduct interviews from here. Speaking to someone without the camera created an uncommon sort of intimacy.

Wellington Street North split off in two. She followed the faster cars to the left, rounded a curve onto the Claremont Access and ascended. Soon she could see the city laid out below her in panorama. She sought out the lake first, its grey-brown like a strip of pavement lining the factories huffing smoke. She stayed in the outside lane as the road curved back on itself and the escarpment rose up beside her, bulging with waterfall icicles. Down on her left, chimneys vented flames. She felt a thrill, along with a resigned anger. What would her child, used to bright greens and yellows and oranges and pinks, think of this dirty, grey place? She focused on the road. At the top, she passed bungalows. With Roselore she would point out the moments of beauty, the greens and blues deep in the ice, the glazed red winter berries. *Love and safety*, she reminded herself. *That's what she's getting from you.* Rudie wouldn't let herself think of Danielle. The love Rudie and Leo would give Roselore contained this life, her education, this place, the food, warmth and shelter and opportunity that life in an orphanage couldn't give her. Danielle had love too, Rudie reminded herself. She did have that.

AGNES

Marsha's hat cast an oblong shadow on the cracked asphalt of the Frontier Motel parking lot. Agnes smelled sage and burning wood and dirty cooking oil. She followed Marsha to the door closest to the road, room 9. Heavy drapes covered the windows. Marsha retrieved a key from her purse, opened the door and entered the gloomy room without a word. Agnes stayed outside, fear percolating. The light out here was harsh and urban, even though Cuba was a town of only a thousand people. The overhead light flickered on.

"Oh God," said a nasally boy's voice. Agnes had come with Marsha out of loyalty to John, though she didn't trust that this boy was even his. All she had, all anybody had, was Marsha's word. Yet, the annoyed, resigned tone of the boy's high voice made her curious. Children inhabited a space Agnes wanted to understand and regain. If she was patient with a child, she might glimpse that place, experience it again and use it as a portal into her work.

Marsha was back at the door.

"Why aren't you coming in? Lenny's wondering what's wrong."

The thought of painting made Agnes want to turn tail and hike back to her studio. She still might dip her brush in paint today. The light here was long-lasting, the day not yet half spent. A walk might set her right.

Marsha pinched at her coat sleeve. "Not now, Agnes. Please not now. This is the last thing Lenny needs. If you don't snap out of it, I'll have to believe you're doing it on purpose, and I'll be forced to not let you see any of John's papers or his things when you come to New York."

Agnes willed her limbs to move.

"I do not intend to come to New York," she said as she stepped onto the pine green carpet. A varnished oak bed with a geometric-patterned brown bedspread dominated the room. A zipped-up, emerald green World Cup Adidas bag sat on the corner. She saw no other luggage. A narrow passage between the foot of the bed and the opposite wall led to a table and two chairs in the corner where a seven-year-old child in flared jeans and a white T-shirt, with shiny, shoulder-length auburn hair, sat eating Honeycomb cereal from a yellow box. He swung his dangling legs, his pallid feet bare.

"You will. You'll have another exhibit sometime," Marsha said, her lip curled. She stood back as if she thought Agnes would approach Lenny. Agnes stayed near the door.

Lenny ignored them. Every time sugar powder dropped on the table, he brushed it away with a grand gesture as if to illustrate his boredom. He yawned widely while watching Agnes beneath studied droopy eyelids.

Marsha slipped into the bathroom and closed the door. Nothing in the boy reminded Agnes of John, who would be seventy now if he had lived. He was in his early fifties when they met. How did one search out the father inside the boy? Marsha claimed to see much that resembled John. Maybe she was looking too hard? Or maybe she was putting those qualities there herself, seeing what didn't exist, a habit many artists – particularly the mediocre ones – possessed.

Lenny placed one Honeycomb in his mouth and sucked on it, his cheeks caving.

Agnes forced herself to speak. "Met any good rocks lately?"

"I got some from the parking lot. I don't like all the deserty ones."

"They are rather dusty."

"They aren't as strong as other rocks. I saw a hare *and* a coyote."

"No wolves?"

"I thought it was a wolf, but Marsha said it was a coyote. Wolfs don't live in the desert, she says."

"I disagree. A pack crosses a corner of my property regularly."

"How do you know?"

"We can tell by the poop. The farmers get skittish, but they've left us alone for the most part. They're more interested in your hares. Your mother does like to take her time." Agnes nodded toward the bathroom door.

"MARSHA!" Lenny popped another Honeycomb into his mouth.

"You call her by her first name?"

"She doesn't like the name Mummy."

Agnes shifted her weight from one leg to another. "Mind if I sit?"

Lenny said nothing, so Agnes seated herself on the empty chair.

"I'm only going to stay a minute or so," Agnes said. "Your mother said you wanted to meet me and now you have. I don't know what else you want from me." She checked in with her thoughts. John's voice spoke full force: *Touch him, touch him. That's my boy, can't you see? The resemblance is uncanny.* The Line hovered in the distance, like a dream whose emotions lingered with her into the day. She fought the urge to spit and stood again.

"Tell your mother I'll be in the parking lot. We can talk when she gets back."

Agnes had the heavy door open and was stepping onto the sidewalk when Marsha came out of the bathroom.

"What's going on?" she asked.

Lenny sucked on another Honeycomb, watched Agnes.

"I'll be outside, Marsha, when you're ready." Leaving the door to shut behind her, Agnes walked across the asphalt to a stretch of earth and sage where the Line coruscated as if it were biding its time. Agnes remembered arriving in Cuba, a random town, on the day the voices insisted she stop running. She had asked the owner of a gas station near here if he knew anyone who had land with a stream running through it and found out his wife did. Six years later, Agnes had built her structures on the rented land. The voice had made it clear she shouldn't own it. The setting waited for her work to begin. The vision had finally arrived, insisting she make it real, and here she was back near the gas station as if none of it had happened. But it had and Marsha was a fresh reminder, even all these years later, of John and what he had taken from her when he chose to tie a rope around the pipe and kick away the chair.

Marsha called Agnes from the doorway. "I'm not avoiding you, Agnes. There's a problem with the toilet. Lenny's looking at it."

Agnes took a deep breath of tar, manure, sage and exhaust. Did Marsha think Lenny really was John? Who let a seven-year-old fix a toilet? She strode across the parking lot, blinking as she left the sunshine for the dim room.

Marsha fluttered her arms as Agnes passed her. The boy kneeled on the closed toilet seat, peering into the open toilet tank, his hands in the water. The lid was propped against the wall. A battery-powered Evel Knievel toothbrush stood on the back of the sink beside a tube of Crest. Nothing of Marsha in here, either.

"Clear out, young man. I'll see to it." Water pooled on the linoleum floor. The boy's bare soles were damp. He fiddled with the chain but didn't leave.

"I mean it. That's no place for you. You might break it further. Leave it to me."

"Yeah, right."

"You can watch, maybe learn something if you like."

"What do you know? You're just an old lady," Lenny said, turning at the hips to stare at her while he jiggled the trip lever.

"That's what I am and why I know better. How many buildings have you built by hand, son?"

Lenny unfolded his legs, the rims of his eyes moist, his face a storm of anger and admiration. "I'm not your son," he said.

But he stayed. He stood beside her as she rolled up her sleeve and reached into the tank to thread the S-hook back into the plug. When she was finished, she soaped her arms up to the elbow like a surgeon and rinsed them under cold water in the sink.

As she dried them with a bleached towel, she said, "You can put the lid back on, Pilot, then flush it. Then we'll see if it worked."

Lenny set the ceramic lid in place and flushed. He studied her.

"What?" she asked.

He lowered his eyes as he went into the main room. Agnes finished blotting her arms with the rough towel. She hung it on the rack and was unrolling her sleeves when the boy came back. He stared from the doorway, fear in his eyes, John's kind of fear, maybe, though more likely a fear bred in response to living with a woman like Marsha. He looked smart and caged, greedy for something new.

"She's not here."

Agnes followed him into the empty room. The Adidas bag was gone. Only the cereal box remained. She opened the door, surveyed the parking lot. The boy scooted past her.

"Look. Her car's not here."

Agnes scanned the road. No cars waited at the gas station. The main drag was empty, but it was midday. Most people were napping or off to some other place. The Line winked from a new spot near the horizon.

"Stay here," she said. She walked up to the sidewalk and searched the street in each direction. No sign of the Beetle.

She went back to Lenny. "Does she do this often?"

"What, leave me with old ladies?"

"My name is Agnes. I was a friend of John's. I'm sure your mother told you."

"No," he said. His eyes widened with interest. He took her hand. She didn't grip his back, but she didn't pull away. Instead, she crouched and looked him in the eye.

"Lenny, right?"

Lenny nodded.

"How long have you and your mother been at this motel?"

"Marsha."

"Okay, Marsha. How long have you and Marsha been staying in Cuba, really."

"One day."

"Does she leave you alone like this often?"

"Yes?"

"Maybe she just went to get gas, or some food or something?"

"She's coming back."

"Okay, good. That's something. In a few minutes, right, maybe half an hour?"

"She waits until I fall asleep then she creeps in step by step. Or she flies."

The boy didn't sound self-pitying and wasn't challenging her. Agnes believed he lived his life this way. He didn't question it because he had no idea he could expect anything different. Agnes ached to be in her studio, the Line having moved to a thrum at the base of her mind. *But Agnes, he's mine*, John's voice said. *You couldn't help me but you can help him.*

It irritated Agnes that for all her solitude and her acute, deliberate connection to her inspiration, she should encounter an inner voice so melodramatic and male and so insistent that she do what would work against what she most wanted to do. But she was loyal, and John was the person closest to her as an adult, and that voice made sense. She couldn't leave this little boy in the darkened motel room and walk back to her farm. Even if his mother could. Especially since his mother had. She would do right and get the boy in the hands of the authorities. Then she could walk the roads home to her studio and paint.

The sun was midday bright. Clouds layered the horizon, but there were none above. Agnes stayed inside at this hour when she could. She shivered in the parking lot, the skin on her hands dry and shrinking cold. She pressed her upper arms against her body. The boy stood in the window, his fingers gathering one curtain. She hadn't worn a hat, hadn't expected the cold to increase. She made herself move across the parking lot, resisting the urge to walk right past room 9 and out to the road. She had no guarantee the boy would follow. She paused, then turned to leave. If he didn't want her . . . but why should he want her? Waiting for his mother, though boring and frightening and abominable, at least had its familiarity. Going with Agnes, this woman he'd met less than an hour ago, promised adventure, perhaps, but also danger. The door swung open.

She felt like an exhibit as the boy examined her from his position in the doorway.

"What are we going to do?" the boy asked.

"You're coming with me," Agnes said. "It's walking weather. I hope she's bought you good shoes."

—

The sidewalks of Cuba were more like shoulders for two scenic highways than streets. Crumbling buildings sat close to the road. The faster Agnes walked, the warmer her body felt and the more her sense of purpose returned. When she looked back, Lenny followed her in his brown duffel coat and desert boots, taking in her face with interest but no emotion. Aside from a one-room schoolhouse and a claim to have housed El Brujo, the wizard outlaw who ran with Pancho Villa, Cuba had little to offer other than a dead logging industry, its ranches and the sky. The town held the desolation of a highway at the top of any town, with the ground around its ochre grasses and dried sagebrush painted with stale snow. Agnes hunched her shoulders, her ears ringing with the cold. She searched for Marsha's Beetle but couldn't remember the colour. The boy walked beside her now, a hand on her sleeve. She slowed.

He pointed at the gas station.

It was Tony Trujillo's. Tony's wife Elena had rented Agnes the land then died the following year, from childbirth, as if they lived in an earlier century out here. The child stayed with Elena's parents in Kansas City, if Agnes recalled correctly. Tony's new wife, Sandra, ran a coffee shop at the back of the store.

"How's my land, Agnes Martin?" Sandra called from the doorway. "I hear you're clearing your neighbour's trees for them too. Some people like to do their own work these days." Sandra spoke through a wide-mouthed laugh that sounded friendly to those who didn't know her.

Agnes nodded. Willed herself to walk. She wished to avoid places where people didn't like her.

"Can we go here?" Lenny said. "I'm thirsty."

"I have no money on me," Agnes said. "And I'm not asking Sandra Trujillo for credit."

"Please? I have my own money! How do you think I got breakfast?" Lenny smiled, revealing big centre teeth with a gap on either side.

Sandra yelled again. Agnes tuned her out, intent on the boy. Up close, she saw the constellations of pinprick freckles dotting his cheeks, nose and forehead. His hair shone dark red in the sunshine. When she met John, he had auburn hair, though it had faded to a rosy blond by the end. She couldn't let Lenny climb back into his hotel room and wait for his mother. Agnes wouldn't worry about offending Marsha. She'd take the boy into town to the police station, not back to her ranch. Then it would be up to the police to deal with Marsha. Sandra walked toward them, an arm sweeping the air in front of her, her smile big.

"Move along then! This gas station's not for sale." Sandra spoke as if her words were one big shared joke, but jokes contain kernels of the teller's true thoughts. Lenny walked toward Sandra while Agnes stood on the sidewalk until Lenny went inside. When Sandra turned to follow him into the store, Agnes shook her face as if to rid it of water. She took herself up to the building and stood in the small patch of shade under a multicoloured 7 Up sign as she convinced herself she'd be safe inside the coffee shop.

Garlands of red chili peppers hung around the door. The floor was swept, the potato chip and chocolate bar racks pushed to the side to allow for two tables with green-and-white-checkered vinyl coverings and glass bud vases, each with a plastic carnation.

"Coming in for a coffee?" Sandra said.

"Cream and sugar, please!" Lenny grinned.

Agnes should tell him he was too young, but he was buying and she was not his mother. The light in here was fluorescent. Sandra had filled the high window along the back wall with red candles in tall glass jars depicting Our Lady of Guadalupe, so the light on that side of the room had a pink tinge. The effect was soothing and medicinal, yet claustrophobic. Shoulders tight with fear, Agnes wished she'd stayed outside.

"I'll wait for you," she said.

His smile fell. "It's a joke! Coffee's grody. I want soda. Really."

He spoke like a boy who was used to getting what he wanted with adults.

Inside this room, Agnes felt like the murky after-sludge of a day spent eating sugar.

"We can stay," Agnes said. "Coffee, please, Sandra." Sandra poured coffee into a glass and brought it to the table. "That'll be twenty-five cents," she said to Agnes.

"Ask him," Agnes said. "He's paying."

Lenny helped himself to a bottle of Orange Crush from the cooler. He took out a stitched brown leather wallet imprinted with the image of a lasso-wielding cowboy and removed a dollar from a decent stack of bills. Agnes sipped her coffee black. It tasted like a burnt crayon.

"We haven't far to go," Agnes said.

"To your house?"

"Somewhere else first." Agnes didn't have it in her to lie to a child, but it was hard to say the truth.

"Don't take me to the police. Marsha will get mad. I can take care of myself."

"Better than I can, I'm sure."

"I could smoke a cigarette if I wanted. You couldn't stop me."

"I doubt Sandra would sell you a cigarette."

"If I found one, I'd do it. I have before."

Agnes walked across the asphalt, avoiding the pits where divots had come up. She wanted to sleep. She struggled to keep her eyelids wide. Lenny followed her, his small shadow nudging her feet. A cloud formation had cast the far-off rocks in shade.

"I have to work today."

"I don't care." The boy's voice sounded muffled. She checked and saw his chin dipped against his chest.

"I can't leave you, so you'll have to come with me first."

"I won't." Lenny shrugged and kicked at the ground.

"Lenny, I won't break the law."

"My mom didn't break the law."

"Yes, she did. Think about how dangerous it is for her to leave you alone."

"No bad guys can get me. I'm super-fast and I can fly and nobody can stop me." He sprinted a few steps then lunged, arms spread.

Agnes stopped. She'd forgotten how much energy children had. She nodded and went blank. When she woke up, the boy stood staring at her on the sunny street.

"Keep walking," she said.

"You just stood there. Your eyes were blinking but you didn't answer me."

"Don't be ridiculous, Lenny." How long had she stayed out this time? The clouds had a new position in relation to the sun. She hadn't moved. And, there was the Line, off beyond the streets below the distant mountains. The Line that curved. She did the math. She'd forgotten about the math, how she'd need to calculate the Line, its width, from where to where on the canvas. She had a yardstick but could use a small ruler, too. The hardware store wasn't far. She doubted Lenny would mind the diversion. Lenny still stood beside her in front of the gas station. She'd hung the canvas, six by six, as big as a person, on the wall, but she had yet to prime it with white gesso. Every act counted. The urge to get back to the studio surged stronger than ever.

Lenny was pushing at her hip. "You did it again!" he said. "I do it too. Just shake your head. That's what the doctor tells me to do."

Agnes did shake her head. Her hair brushed her eyes. She pushed it back. The boy must think she had spells. Well . . . she did. Art wove a spell, and she succumbed. The boy was an inconvenience, unplanned. She shouldn't be here. She had chosen not to have children. *Shake your head again, Agnes. You didn't choose, not really. Your child abandoned you on its own because it was unready for this life.* How did one explain the child that didn't grow long enough to leave the womb intact? The soul that got here then decided, no, I made a mistake? Or was it not a soul yet? Maybe she had to get that close to having a child in order to embrace not having one. And now she'd met this boy. She walked, so he would stop studying her, his concern calculating. He had spells of his own, Marsha had said. Perhaps he hadn't seen anyone else have them. Clearly Marsha didn't enter anything resembling a trance state when she painted. Agnes wasn't surprised.

Walk and walk and walk. Movement was good for the body. The sun shone full and bright but not at the top of the sky.

"My dad was a painter," Lenny said.

"He was."

"His name was John. You knew my dad, right?"

The boy matched her pace, striding beside her now, his hands in his pockets. He was direct, like his mother. Before she even stretched a canvas, Marsha calculated what buyers most wanted by speaking to them directly and painting to order. His father had been the opposite – he hadn't gone to his own exhibitions and didn't want to meet the buyers. Instead he'd kneel before a completed painting and kiss its bottom corners before letting his agent take it out to show, then wept with what he described as reverse homesickness. Once his hands and eyes had done their work, he let the painting go. Any hint of commerce attached to his art made his eyes water. After each painting left, he needed recovery time before turning his light onto another one.

"Yes, I knew John," Agnes said. She stepped up the pace.

They passed a series of new houses, the fresh adobe beige and smooth. They waited on a corner and when a break in traffic came, they crossed the highway and headed to Jorge's Hardware.

"Señora," Jorge said when they entered the dim store. He stood her height, his thick, trim hair lending a young look to his fair skin, which folded pink around his dark eyes.

"*Hola.*"

"Jesu drive you?"

She glanced at Lenny, who ran his hands through a barrel of bolts. "I'm on foot. This young man and I are old friends, and we are walking." Lenny stood straighter. He came up to her shoulder.

"*Si.*"

"Just a ruler, that's all I want. Oh, and my friend here is buying it for me. A gift, for leading him to the next destination on his journey."

Lenny rolled his eyes and shrugged, made a show of patting his pockets and opening up his billfold.

"No charge for you, Señora." Jorge handed her a red plastic twelve-inch ruler, the kind his store gave out to the schoolchildren every September.

Agnes and John had compared childhoods. Not whose was worse or harder but with a sense of wonder at first perceptions. For Agnes, it was the overwhelming heights and angles of the houses on her street in Vancouver where she'd moved from the prairies at four years old with her mother. How she'd counted the triangles, the houses' peaked roofs. For John, it was lying in bed in Queens listening to the rise and fall of his parents' voices in the kitchen and, on warm nights, drifting up from the stoop. What he read in the voices, how he entered them like songs, his pleasure deep at hearing the fear and tension drop away after his mother turned out the light in the room he shared with his brothers. He'd had three. Agnes wondered if Lenny knew.

Agnes and Lenny walked to the end of the strip, then crossed the street and walked back. They'd seen nothing that looked like a police station. It must be outside of town. Lenny wasn't saying much, and Agnes felt no discomfort about the silence.

Knowing his mother had left him made it difficult not to stay with him. Agnes remembered her many years in the Pacific Northwest as a schoolteacher at schools in the deep woods. She hadn't had to say much, especially with boys. If you trusted children, opened yourself to them and worked with them, they would read your body language and know what you were asking, what you wanted them to do or not do and most, if not prodded or nagged, would start doing whatever you'd asked, imperfectly, but with cheer. Agnes did not have the resources to talk much to young Lenny. Her questions could wait.

They stood back in front of Jorge's again. Agnes scratched her palm with the red ruler.

"You can wait here or come with me. Up to you."

Lenny stared at her, dully.

"There's something I forgot to ask Jorge."

"How to find the police station, right?"

Agnes was more obvious than she thought. Her face baked. Perspiration collected around her ears, trickled down her neck. She resisted the urge to swat herself. It wasn't hot, but the sun here was strong even in winter and she'd raised a sweat.

"Right. Just to let them know your mother is missing."

"You mean I can stay with you?"

Agnes looked across the street. The buildings blocked the horizon. What would this boy hanging around mean for her painting? His question faded. She searched her mind. Yes, she still knew what she wanted to do. Without giving an answer, she went into the store.

—

When she emerged a few moments later, the street was empty.

She scratched her head and looked down, shoulders rigid. *Stay calm. He won't have gone far. Cuba is a small place.*

"Lenny?" she said, her voice slightly raised. "Lenny," she called, her voice louder now. No response.

Maybe he'd returned to the motel or to Sandra's. What had they talked about? Smoking, coffee, cereal. Marsha. He'd joked about doing adult things. She sucked cold air into her lungs. No. Either he'd be right close by, watching to see what she'd do, or he'd have made a run for it between buildings down the next street and the next until he reached the fields.

Lenny filled her mind now: what he wanted, what he needed, what he thought. He was John's boy. But John had killed himself. She cleared her throat. She hated those words, but her mind's voices loved to say them. *Killed killed killed.* The voice repeated and repeated the word, underscoring her thoughts more forcefully the more she tried to cruise her mind toward inspiration. She didn't think of suicide every time she thought of John. She didn't think of John. But with Lenny missing, how could she not? Maybe when she'd walked back into Jorge's, she was half-hoping the boy would make his escape. He was a survivor, a warrior; he could fend for himself. If anything happened, she would say it was his mother who had abandoned him, not Agnes, even if Lenny had run away under Agnes's watch. Jorge had told her where to find the police: Burch Street, two streets east of Main. With no photograph and less than an hour spent with Lenny, Agnes wouldn't be much help.

She trotted across the empty street calling his name. Long trucks tended to drive through Cuba in clusters. Seven would pass in a row then none for a while. She searched her way along the street, checking at each shady corner or nook, peering in each store window.

If the boy wanted her to find him, he'd make a sound or leave a track, but she spotted nothing. A transport truck rumbled up the road. Soon it was passing her, followed by a pickup truck pulling a horse trailer. Lenny could have hitchhiked and caught a ride with one of these dudes. Agnes's mouth felt dry. She could inspect every inch of every street of this town, yet she might not even find him.

As she approached Burch Street, two people in shearling coats came out of a grill restaurant and headed toward her. The shorter one, her waist-length hair swinging, talked animatedly as she lengthened her strides to keep up with the taller one, a young Navajo man with black braids and a red windband. Agnes stopped, not wanting to bump into them, but they kept coming, their eyes locked, the dark, limpid eyes of the stoned. Had they been on the street when she'd gone in to Jorge's?

"Excuse me," she said.

They slowed their pace but kept talking, the woman taking the man by the elbow. Agnes drew herself up, invisible old woman that she was. The man kept shaking his head.

Agnes spoke more loudly this time. "I've misplaced a boy. His name is Lenny. *Lenny!*" She craned her neck, scanning the street. "Have you seen him?"

They stopped. The man leaned against a store window, eyebrow raised. His jeans cuffs draping over his white sneakers were bleached and ragged. "Burch Street is the other way," the young woman was saying to the man as if Agnes weren't standing right there. "Does this mean you're ready to tell the police about Rodney?"

The man shook his head at her, and she fell silent. "Ma'am," he said to Agnes.

The young woman, several strands of beads dripping out of her coat, her long, brown boots zipped up to the knees, studied Agnes with surprise, as if she'd just noticed her. "Do we know you?" She looked at the young man. "We know her."

"I don't see how you could," Agnes said. She took a step back and scanned the street. The high sun gave the illusion of warmth, but Agnes's knuckles were throbbing with cold. Lenny could be hiding in a doorway or someplace else nearby. Children loved to squeeze themselves into small spaces. He might even be able to hear her. "*Len-ny!*"

The young man spoke with a low, powerful voice. "You're Agnes Martin, the painter. I recognize you from pictures. I'm Shilah, and this is Julie. We study art at UNM, but we started too late to have you teach us."

"Ah! I'm sure you have far better teachers than I." Embarrassed and worried, Agnes smiled sharply. She tried to think like a seven-year-old. He could be hiding under a car or in a garbage can, waiting for the right moment to jump out and yell "Boo!" to surprise her. She raised her voice and talked slowly as if she were playing a game, hoping Lenny could hear her. "I had this boy, about seven? Imaginative creature, wily, a master of escape. He's up and hidden himself around here. That or made a break for it. I'm very fond of him and I know a lot of interesting stories about his father that I'm sure he'd love to hear. Have you seen him?"

ELLEN

Ellen had told Micheline. She'd told her that she believed she could know God as well as any self-designed minister could. That yes, going to school, performing rituals passed down from one bishop to another to another and handed over to those ministers connects them to God. Telling the story over and over from one mind, one heart, through one set of lips to another's ears from those who knew Jesus, to those who witnessed his undoing to those who claimed to see him resurrect – that being connected to that chain did mean something.

But what she didn't say aloud to Micheline in this moment is that there were other ways to connect to that chain. A story told once alters. Each time spoken, it alters more, and more again with each teller. Secrets and mysteries handed down through the chain to man after man after man were held tight and distilled only as much as the ordinary mind was deemed able to understand. But those mysteries were there for anybody to understand, anybody who strove, who could open his heart and mind and receive them. As Ellen had. And ever since she had, nothing had been the same. Nothing looked the same. Her body did not feel the same. She was conscious of every cell and how it connected with all it touched. Yet she felt made of air. She didn't tell Micheline all this. What she did tell Micheline was that she experienced God the same as – she didn't dare say more than, although she did believe it – a man like Reverend Benjamin McCloud did. Her experiences had led her to this place. What Reverend McCloud was talking about in his church, and what he was holding back, didn't compare to what Ellen knew.

"God is more than Our Father," she said to Micheline, who was preparing a bowl of soap and water for William's hair.

Micheline dipped her hand into the cloudy liquid then held it over William's head. Water ran down his skull. Ellen shivered.

"God is everything," Micheline muttered. "Anyone would agree." She straightened and listened with more care than she usually did.

"God in the Bible. God in the church," Ellen had a hard time saying it. Her voice struggled, a furry animal trapped in her throat, twisting and turning, searching for an escape. It was like yelling in a dream and having only hoarse air come out.

Ellen busied her hands. She and Micheline had cut the legs of William's pants into strips. They would need more people to help lift William's body to take them off. Then they would cover him with a sheet.

Micheline saved her. "Everything is perfect about our world. Take the trees with their roots and their sap. The buds unfolding into leaves, brilliant and then bright green. How they darken and colour, turn and fall off. The light, the air, the sky. They all move together. I see it too."

A rush of warmth poured through Ellen. William's hard muscles resisted her touch, his flesh cold, no matter how much she moved or cleaned it. Micheline could see what she saw. Yet, that one Sunday, when Ellen went to the service in Reverend McCloud's sitting room, there was Micheline sitting on a pressback chair, chin high, not a trace of a smile teasing the corners of her mouth. Her eyes didn't seek out patterns in the flowered wallpaper, imperfections in the design or the dye. She didn't let them shift the room out of focus. She trained her gaze on Reverend McCloud. Ellen imagined she did the same every Sunday. Was it about Reverend McCloud for her? If Micheline wasn't giving him full authority for her spiritual guidance, then why was she there? Or did she hand over that authority for other purposes, even knowing what she knew? Ellen wanted to know what Micheline knew, what she had seen.

"We are women," Micheline said. "We do have our special way of relating to the world. We feel the world course through our bodies. We carry life and deliver it. Men, too, but for them the coursing is powerful, fleshly, pushing them outward. We take in the world and know how much it is a part of us. Denied the authority, denied access to the mysteries, we live in the mysteries."

"Yes," Ellen said, though the last part confused her.

She repeated the word to herself: *Yes.* Over and over. *Yes and yes and yes.*

Micheline bent her head over William's as they talked, her fingertips scratching circles on his scalp. Then she dried him with a strip of linen. By the time she stood to go, they had cleaned his body, save for his private parts. Ellen would bury William in his good worsted pants and wool shirt, the set he had bought last Christmas before she had arrived, the set he wore every Sunday to Reverend McCloud's and sometimes on Saturdays if he took her to Buck's for a dinner out. Hamilton society, where she and William were both raised, would dictate he wear a suit, but such a sartorial choice would seem an affront to these quiet, watchful settlers. What she was burying him in would seem more appropriate to rough loggers and the slightly-less-rough sawyers.

Oddly, after they revealed what they believed to each other, Ellen and Micheline found little else to say. They hadn't clutched each to the other's heart. There was no sense of kindred souls having cleaved. No animated chattering about meeting or organizing or even wondering whether, if two of them existed, they might not find more in the community. What had lived silent for so long in Ellen stayed that way, even after being uttered, as if that well, unused to being uncovered, had pulled the lid right back over itself. Ellen didn't know how Micheline had come to think what she thought: whether, like Ellen, it had struck her in a vision so undeniable that she hadn't been the same since.

Outside: *clunk thud.* Then a rhythmic *thumpa-thump-thump.* An axe on wood, the sound coming from the back shed. Had she slept? She was sitting on the heart chair, chin on her chest, William's boot at her feet, alone. She pieced the morning together. She had told Micheline. She had told! Micheline had smiled, the corners of her mouth pointed, her teeth carved like a wolf's. Micheline had nodded, her eyes on Ellen, then not. Instead she looked out of the corners, around the room. Micheline agreed with her! But Micheline had left, and now this pounding had started up outside. What was her friend doing?

Ellen's knees buckled as she stood. She had been napping for a while. The sun shone bright and clear outside her one window, but no sunlight warmed the floor. Noon. She scolded herself. She had no business sleeping in the middle of the day with so much work to do. How she managed it with her husband lying dead on the table escaped her. Ellen shook her leg, stamped her foot, clenched at the pain of her nerves coming to life, then hobbled to the window to check for wagons, horses or footprints.

She saw nothing different. She scraped a rind of frost from the corner of the glass, stroked it through her hair. She poked at the coals in the stove until they glowed, then stuffed in another log, watching until flames caressed the bottom and then setting the lid back in place.

Back wearing William's coat and boots, her spade raised in front of her, she ventured out into the snow. Flakes glistened in the sun like the white sugar shaved from cones she remembered from her childhood. Her stockings were soon wet past the knees as she rounded the cabin to the back. A wind snuck around the corner, blowing fluffs of snow up her neck, pelting her eyes. The *thwack*s got louder. Though she doubted she'd find an animal this deep into winter, she gripped the spade harder and stepped around the back of the house.

A figure arced and bent, raised an axe, hacked through a log, stuck another in place, arced and bent some more. His body, broad in its wool coat and pants and high, laced leather boots, moved like an animal's, like a black draft horse that worked the logs on a team for Old Davenport, but not so heavy. Young and spirited, like her. Certainly not tired, old Benjamin McCloud.

"Stand back, girlie!" he yelled. He laughed like a horse, too, his mouth all teeth and tongue.

"You shouldn't call me that," she said, amused. She stepped back and laughed, then closed her mouth and tilted her head back.

His eyebrows rose like roof peaks to two black, intelligent points on his smooth, tan forehead. He relaxed his face, his lips in a closed smile now, his aquamarine eyes curious, concerned.

"Mrs. Cook. I'm truly sorry. I thought you were Micheline. She was here a minute ago."

"Good morning, Philip. I expected you later."

"My father sent me to do the man's work. You can go inside."

She scanned the area until she spotted his ponies standing still on the other side of her cabin. The wind must have blown snow across their tracks.

He had added two layers to the woodpile stacked against the house and stood with several chopped pieces littered around his feet. He was working with wood the first time she met him, too.

It was that summer Sunday she'd attended Benjamin McCloud's setting room service. Midway through the sermon, she whispered a fib to William that her monthly bleeding had started. Outdoors, she was standing, eyes closed, soaking up the evening sunlight through the white pine branches when she became aware of a rhythmic scraping along with a tuneful whistle. She strained to catch the melody as she wandered around the back to investigate. It wasn't a hymn, at least not one that she knew. Near the edge of the woods, she found him, sleeves rolled up, hunched over and carving a substantial piece of basswood. Philip was tall, taller than his father, taller than any man Ellen had met with the wide chest and shoulders and shiny black hair of a woodsman. Only he was clean-shaven and wearing a brown linen vest and trousers.

"You must be Reverend McCloud's son," she said.

"And you must be William Cook's wife," he said, his eyes so warm she excused his cheekiness.

"The sermon didn't catch your interest?" she asked. "I'm surprised. One should think you'd want to absorb your father's ideas first-hand, perhaps follow in his footsteps?"

Philip looked down, his forelock covering his eyes, red rising to his cheeks. "I've heard it before," he said. He brushed off a mound of sawdust curls. She followed the path of his hand as he smoothed it along the board and revealed three tulips blooming from a heart.

"I suspect you have," Ellen said. Moving closer, she traced the flowers with the side of her thumb. "I find more spirit out here in the white pines than sitting in a room while a man interprets scripture to me, no matter how pleasant his voice sounds."

"I feel the same way, Mrs. Cook." Philip rested both hands on the board and looked at her, his eyes startling in their crystal clarity. "If I had my way, I'd spend my days up there." He jerked his shoulder and head behind him, indicating the trees and the sky.

"You look like a grown man to me," Ellen said. "Why, you must be my age! I'm nearly twenty-one, and I've already married and had a child." She gasped at her boldness but refused to look away. He held her gaze, his eyes bright and searching, full of understanding.

"My mother died, too," he said. "And my father is afraid I will die if I make my life felling trees. So I humour him and teach school and he humours me and excuses me from his services to build him furniture or chop his wood. I'm making a threshold, by the way. For the church or the school, I haven't decided."

"Perhaps for a home of your own?" she asked.

The sound of voices rising in chorus came to them through the open window. The service was ending.

"I'm nineteen," he said.

Now, Philip watched her for a moment, then set a log on the stump and raised his axe. The log cracked in half. He kicked it aside with his boot, scooped up another. A hard bubble lodged near her heart. She felt it front and back, too. She took off her mitten and placed her palm against her chest. Her stomach burbled. She hadn't eaten today, but the feeling was more lively than hungry.

She stuffed her chilled hand back into her mitten. The wood cracked and thumped as Philip split log after log. When he had an armload, he carried the split logs to the side of the house, where he added them to the stack. She hoped he didn't think William a bad husband for letting the stack get low. She used more wood than she should, and they were running out sooner than William had expected.

Her stomach lurched. The sun dazzled, making her head hot and her eyes fuzzy. She squinted, reeled. She should have eaten something that morning. Every day she made flapjacks for William with a circle of molasses or maple syrup on top, which he ate at the table on a tin plate. He took two wrapped in a towel in his pocket as he walked or snowshoed to work at the sawmill. This morning, with William laid out on the table, she'd had no desire to mix the flour and water and melt the fat in a pan and eat the flapjacks from a plate on her lap. Instead, she had stoked the fire, brewed a kettle of sumac tea and sipped all morning from a china cup.

The cracking and thumping stopped. Philip looked at her from under the brim of his beaver hat. He was a teacher, a preacher's son. He could read, had read the Bible. There was nothing about him that wouldn't recommend his father, too, except that Philip McCloud had those light, crystalline eyes – blue or green she couldn't tell in the sun – and when he walked toward her, as he did now, her knees buckled and she grabbed at air as she fell hard to the ground.

She woke up on her bed in the loft, a tiny triangle of sun across one knee, her wool leggings itchy and close against her skin. Her nose had stuffed up, her jaw so tight it took some wiggling to make it pop, and then the pain moved into her shoulders. Her eyes stung, raw as if she'd been crying, but she hadn't cried a drop since she'd heard a knock on the door and opened it to find Elven Handy from the sawmill standing on the threshold, with his earflap hat in his hand and a shock of hair sticking up, telling her that William had slipped and landed chest first on the saw blade. She hadn't expected such an event, hadn't lived with a constant sense of the danger William was in, as some women out here did, aware of the hardship of living in the forest alone. Those women had children and worried what would become of them. Ellen was Ellen. No child. No more child. The hope of a child was not the same as a child in your arms, she knew that one.

Moments after she opened the door on Elven Handy, two other men – John Otter and Thomas Paste from the sawmill – had hefted a long object from the wagon and carried it, sagging in the middle, up the path. When they stopped to adjust, she saw that Thomas Paste had his arms in William's armpits and John Otter carried William's ankles. They moved slowly, with care, but efficiently, too – they were used to hauling heavy loads as a team. They'd laid William out on the table, adjusting him so his head rested on basswood, his feet dangling off the end, but not taking time to wipe the table or put down a blanket or cloth. She had insisted they lift him again while she smoothed a sheet from her trunk to protect the wood.

"Mr. Horn from the sawmill will come after lunch," Elven said before he followed the other two out the door.

Once William was home, she'd seen no sense in crying. She couldn't think whether he'd want her to or not, but it wasn't that. It was that as long as she could see and touch him, she didn't feel a loss.

Now, from the room below, the fire roared. The stovetop clattered. She started up, liquid sloshing in her stomach. *William*, she thought, with dull expectation.

She opened her mouth to yell but couldn't push the words out, couldn't think of any words, a sure sign she was dreaming. She got up and peered over the edge, bracing herself against a beam.

Philip McCloud stood at the stove, his coat still on, his boots off.

"You fainted," he said. He tilted his head, looked up at her with the soft eyes of a parent even though she was the older one.

"That wasn't my intention," she said. He must have lifted her in his arms like a load of logs, carried her around the house and inside to her bed. Had he lugged her up the ladder? His height would put him at a disadvantage on that front. She climbed down and watched his long arms moving around the stove, stirring the porridge, filling the bowl. Despite his stature, his movements were compact and confident.

He held out a bowl and spoon. She took it with both hands. Heat flared up her arm as his fingers brushed hers. For a moment, their eyes met and he witnessed what she knew and believed and reflected her back to herself. The bowl contained gruel, a rich brown, swirled with molasses. She couldn't make her mouth move. William lay shrouded on the table. Her cabin was small and cozy, these four walls more familiar to her than William's hands. When she crossed the threshold into this room, she could wipe the fire from her memory. Her erasures returned her to herself and honed her beliefs until they gleamed. William hadn't seen this increasing glow. Yet, Philip had, just now. Ellen doubled over with pleasure, followed by a sudden cramp, the bowl bumping to the floor, spinning and landing on its bottom, the sticky gruel intact. Philip got her the chair, his movements unhurried and assured, those of a more mature man. She sat.

"You caught something from the body?" he said.

"No, not that. I have had these feelings for some time." As she made this declaration, she knew its truth, a truth she'd felt once before. She felt faint, her stomach churned, her skin felt tight and her limbs had been weakening for days now. She had written her symptoms off as a response to the cold weather, for she hadn't felt this cold before in her life. In Hamilton, her parents had provided her with a fur coat and a buffalo robe, which she'd left behind when she came north in June. How was she to know this wasn't what deep cold felt like? "Perhaps I have a catarrh."

Philip's small smile told her otherwise. "Perhaps William will live on after all."

Round, cool tears dropped onto her lap, unbidden. She didn't sob, nor did she feel particularly sad. Instead she was admitting he was right. She was carrying a baby.

She steadied herself, checked the wall she'd built around each moment with Safra and vowed that though she would love this baby, it couldn't take away from Safra, whom she would never forget. Falling in love with Safra had made each moment so fresh and immediate that any such moment with another baby might seem less than, not real and not right. And besides, how likely was it that this one would make it to birth, let alone childhood? Grief expelled babies. So did cold and hunger. And death, who knew? She might be the next candidate for a brutal accident.

She picked up the bowl, eyes down, and stirred the gruel. "You made this?" she asked. Philip squatted beside her, an elbow propped on the table, and peered into her face, studying her.

"My mother taught me how," he said. "She made sure that my sister and I learned the same things."

"Your father?"

"He has his own idea about me. I let him think what he

needs to think and then I do what I want. He can't stop me from being who I am."

"A schoolteacher?"

"A helpful man. A man who needs to be among the trees, to use his hands to work with wood. I hold many of my classes outside, did you know that?"

"I didn't. I suppose if my child were in your class –" It was fine to speak with him this way because he understood about Safra. Ellen pictured another child of hers five years from now sitting under the pines, slate pencil in hand.

"I do," he said. "My father doesn't know." He laughed.

She looked him in the eye.

"I amuse myself," he said. "I sound like a little boy sometimes."

She took in his bulky jacket, the loose wool pants covering a union suit, no doubt, the knitted woollen socks, and said, "No, not a little boy."

He jumped up and took a step backward. "Eat! Eat," he said. His hand twitched as if he would spoon-feed her. She ate the sweet mess, her eyes on William's corpse, a penance for enjoying Philip's company. Her stomach stayed quiet, perhaps content that she was taking care of herself finally. She had much to repent with William. Neglecting him even as she took care of his physical needs these past months living together in the bush. Hoarding that dear, shiny place inside her where she'd stored every memory of every moment with Safra. William had died without having heard about her months with Safra before the fire, about Safra learning to talk and to run, about her baby arms around Ellen's shoulders, patting Ellen on the back, her knees tight against the hollow below Ellen's ribs.

She should have shared her daughter's life with her husband. She had meant to but hadn't felt ready. She saw her mistake and her loss. Without William to cherish them with, each dear moment would shrink and crystallize. Making it a story between them would have been the surest way to breathe life back into her firstborn and bind her husband close.

What had started as a slight discomfort in her right side now pushed at her. She stood fast, sending the heavy chair scraping back. She carried the bowl to the wash basin and considered what to do. She needed the backhouse but didn't want to tell Philip.

"Philip, I would like some time alone with my husband." That didn't sound right so before Philip could answer, she said, "What I mean is, that it is time for my husband to be dressed, and I need two men to help me. Would you go and get your father? Mr. Horn from the sawmill is supposed to come by this afternoon."

In her reverie, Ellen had forgotten about Mr. Horn, so warm and comfortable she felt with the extra wood both she and Philip had fed the fire. The cabin almost glowed red at the seams.

Philip looked her up and down, his gaze resting for a moment on her belly, then moving back to her face.

"Are you well?" he asked. "Can I help in some way? I can make a tea."

She cocked her head. His forearms bulged bigger than his father's biceps, curved strong like those of the men who felled trees and even those who fed the trunks into the saws. Arms built for swinging a poleaxe or pulling a crosscut saw, with a nest of dark hairs that glowed mahogany in the sunlight. She felt safe, consoled. Since she'd arrived in the bush, they'd crossed paths several times – near the schoolhouse, on the road – and had often been drawn into conversation, their affinity so easy and natural she'd overlooked its strangeness. She allowed herself the forbidden thought: *would he marry me, would he agree to father William's child, to take us both on*? Not in this bush, not when he still lived with his father, following the path his father had laid for him. He cared too much about what his father thought and Ellen had brown skin and carried her husband's child. Her husband had died today. It was too soon. And besides: affinity and easy conversation did not necessarily a marriage make, though Philip might help her in other ways.

"I am in good spirits." She smiled, demurring, chin tucked tight. Her lessons on manners and etiquette had taught her well. It all came back to her as effortlessly as knitting did when she looped the wool around one needle and nudged the tip through. "I've become unused to company, pleasant though it may be. You could help most by arranging the dressing of my husband so that other visitors won't have to witness him in such disarray."

A flush crept over Philip's cheeks as he looked at her. He had the skin of a boy, skin that told his story before his words could deflect. "I will bring in another stack of wood, then leave you in peace, Mrs. Cook," he said. His hands hung at his sides for a second, then were in motion again. Off he went until soon a few thuds came from outside. A few minutes later, he reappeared with an armload of split maple, which he stacked beside her stove.

He tipped his cap at her and backed out her cabin door. She waited until the crunch of his boots on the snow had faded before she put on her own boots, wrapped herself up in two shawls and ventured out along the well-trod path to her backhouse. People were coming and going so frequently today, she didn't dare pull out her chamber pot lest someone find her squatting in the corner.

Her choice had been a wise one. For no sooner had she adjusted her skirt, straightened her stockings, fastened the backhouse's door latch against animals and turned into the wet wind, but a team of black horses approached through the trees.

The sky had darkened and small wet drops blew through the air. Some local people believed that rain in winter meant evil blowing in. Ellen wondered if they'd consider her husband falling into the saw a bad omen. Of course, here was the omen happening after the accident. There had been full sun when William had stumbled and caught his shirt on the blade. Would something else happen?

The horses stood almost twice as high as Ellen who, even in her boots, wasn't much more than five feet. Their black chests, muscled like tree roots, shone wet and foamy with snow and effort. Sweat darkened their harnesses. One chewed at his bit, lifted his head, shook his ears and snorted. She resisted the urge to put her hands on them. They were working horses, working even now as the wagon had stopped, and they rested in front of her.

Two men sat in the carriage, but only the driver got down. Darius Horn owned one of Minden's four sawmills – though not Sawyer's, where William worked. Ellen had seen Darius Horn in the summer at Duffy's Store. William had taken her to buy fabric for a winter dress. She was looking at a bolt of indigo-dyed wool on the counter at the back when shouting started on the street. The windows at Duffy's sparkled, but the dust from the dirt street rose up, making it hard to see. Two women rushed in saying men were fighting. William ran outside, ignoring Ellen's pleas to stay with her. She couldn't make out the voices outside. Soon the yelling got closer and in walked Darius Horn with William close behind.

"Rotten lickspit –!" he was saying until he saw the room full of women. He clamped his mouth shut. His face was turning purple.

"Yes," said William, his hand on the man's back, his own face swelling around the eye. Ellen resisted her urge to go to him, to touch the wound and upbraid Mr. Horn. She knew William would brush her away for getting in the middle of his moment with the rival sawmill owner so she stayed put.

"Everything okay, boys?" asked Mr. Duffy, cradling the bolt of indigo wool.

After stalking around the store, his vast stomach heaving in and out as he caught his breath, Darius Horn faced Mr. Duffy and ordered a root beer.

"A difference of opinion," said William. He flashed the smile he reserved for people in public settings. Then his face fell serious, and he glanced toward the door. Neither he nor Darius Horn said *whose* opinion. The two ladies who'd entered during the fight made themselves busy in front of the tea display.

Ellen hadn't known of William's acquaintance with Darius Horn until that moment. While Darius waited for his root beer, he had given her a long look, his eyes the slate grey of dirty coins until he glanced away at William, then back at her, eyes now shining. He hadn't asked her name, but it was clear that he had deduced that she was William's wife, though William made no move in her direction, nor did he introduce her. William claimed later that he'd wanted to respect her shyness with the people in the town, that the fight had rattled him and that he didn't know Mr. Darius Horn well enough at that time to introduce him to his wife.

Darius Horn had those same dull eyes as he looked at Ellen now, on the edge of the woods outside her cabin, those eyes as grey as the low winter sky. One eye, like William's that day at Duffy's, receded inside a violet bruise, the shiny skin coated unmistakably in pine tar, the same salve she had given William only yesterday, his last day of life, to rub into the sore knuckles of his right hand.

The horses snorted, the breaths condensing. The trees glowed black and slick. The temperature was rising, though Ellen still shivered. Darius Horn wore a beaver hat and greatcoat, his boots laced and tied through the top grommets. He stamped his feet as if unused to snow clumping on the bottoms. The other man sat still, arms folded across his considerable girth.

"Mrs. Cook." Darius tilted his head and touched the fur covering his forehead as if to tip his hat.

Ellen nodded. She hadn't felt this alone before, not even riding in the carriage over the bumpy roads north from her city home toward her husband waiting in the woods. Not even when she was ash-covered, as two men pried her burnt, silent daughter from her breast. Not even in the church pew waiting to hear God's voice as promised. Her cabin was all that anchored her to this land. It wasn't enough. She would have to find a way to be here or leave. Despite the efforts of men to tie and chop and fell the trees, endless bush surrounded them. God's voice wasn't speaking to her now. Maybe if she sought far inside, she could find the white light that sustained her. If she reached down into the frozen ground and through it to the earth's molten core then up and out of herself through her crown, the white light spilling over and around her like a fountain, she could surround herself with an energy more real than any authoritarian god a man could dream up. She hadn't met Mr. Horn's friend before.

Mr. Horn's upper lip curled in what he might have meant to be a smile.

She squared her shoulders.

"Will you invite me in?" Darius Horn glanced at his friend, whose toque moved as if he were attempting to raise his eyebrows. "Both of us, I mean."

Mr. Horn hadn't regarded her like this in the store, not with William present. At Duffy's, he had appraised her like a toy, a surprising extension of William. William had told her about his friend Mr. Horn, how lucky he was to have a friend who was boss of a rival sawmill, how he appreciated the after-hours work Mr. Horn gave him. At first, Ellen believed people like Darius Horn were responding to William's difference, that his being black brought out a complex mix of others' need to help, to be entertained or even to have a pet. Yet, up here in the bush, much of that business didn't matter. If a man had strong muscles, if his hands could grasp an axe, he could find a place regardless of his colour. William had chosen a slippery route, opting to see the light in every man and missing the shadows in some. Ellen carried the light in herself, but her parents had taught her to think about how another was thinking about her and then behave accordingly. Often Ellen did nothing and said nothing and trusted her silence to keep her invisible to most.

Now Mr. Horn had the colder look of one who's paid for an item whose shine was about to wear off. His assessment relieved her. As long as he felt that way, she posed no threat and could make her plans without undue notice. His broad chest heaved. He was a short man, shorter than William.

"My husband hasn't been arranged," she said. She wished Philip would return with his father soon. "I'm not ready to accept visitors."

"I'm not here to pay my respects," he said. "I'll save that for the funeral. We have other business to discuss." He brushed at his beaver hat, calling attention to his battered eye. She wondered if William had bruised his knuckles making contact with that eye. William wouldn't fight unless something were very wrong. Ellen's aversion to having Darius Horn in her house intensified.

"My husband has yet to be dressed," she said. "It wouldn't be right. The McClouds are on their way to help me suit him up. You could return later, after they're done." The snow had seeped through her boots, packing in around her ankles, dampening her calves. She rocked in the light she held around her. Since that first vision, she had held on to the ability to draw the light inside herself. Whether it protected her or not, she couldn't say.

"Early!" Horn said. "Git down here. We're going into the cabin to dress young William for his visits."

The other man, Early Badger, tilted his chin into his red wool muffler. He held his position like a cow refusing to budge, but then he heaved himself down from the carriage, reins in hand, and led the horses over to a tree. He draped the reins over the nearest horse's shoulder and gave it a few good thumps with his hand.

"She'll stay put. Doesn't like to move when we want her. You doing your Christian duty, Dar?"

"It's only right. Mrs. Cook says William can't receive visitors in his altogether."

"Man's dead, clothes or no clothes," Early said.

"Show respect," Darius said. He nodded at Ellen, his neck blooming into multiple chins.

The men were walking through the mushy snow. Ellen didn't want them in her cabin. A thin stream of smoke wound out of her chimney, much less than earlier when Philip had stoked the fire. The men had her door open and were looking over their shoulders at her.

"Mrs. Cook?" Darius said. "Show us the clothes you want for him and we'll have him dressed in a jiff."

The horses snuffed and nosed the snow as if to turn up a grain or fleck of bark. Ellen followed the men inside, where they shed their coats and boots. Early was at the wood stove before she could reach the logs, poking coals, and stuffing it full.

"Enough, Early," said Darius. "You want to cook this man?"

"I ain't no cannibal," Early said. His voice sounded like it rolled over a plug of gravy.

Darius inspected William. He moved his fingers near William's head, made as if to touch him but didn't.

"He's clean," said Ellen. She stood between the stove and the table, her hand on the back of the heart chair. It was hard to brighten this room. On a cloudy day, the room was as dim as dusk. She turned the wick of the lantern on the sideboard, touched it with a lit match and set the lantern in the window.

"Yes, he is," Darius Horn said. "Very."

"The McClouds are coming," she said again. She thought of Philip asking his father to return to her cabin, of Benjamin McCloud washing his hands, perhaps trimming his beard close. She thought of Philip watching his father do this. Philip wouldn't think to shave, would come back only because the job required two men. Unless he suspected she needed more of him. She would follow him into the woods if he ran. She would have to separate him from his father to talk to him. That was, if she made it out of the cabin intact. She edged closer to the fire.

Darius and Early lifted the sheet at the top, folded it back on itself then back again until it lay across William's feet. They stood on either side.

"You should leave the room, Mrs. Cook, while we remove the undergarment," said Darius, his voice wobbling in and out of an English accent.

"I've seen it before, if you don't mind, Mr. Horn," she said. She resisted the urge to let her voice waver, too.

"Yes, Mrs. Cook. I expect you have."

"Perhaps you might want to be the one who waits outside," she said, "if my cleaning him embarrasses you."

Darius shuffled his feet. Early stood still, hands crossed over his stomach. The two men looked at her, eyes gleaming and expectant, like young boys with a schoolteacher. Philip McCloud could teach their children, though Darius had at least two old enough to work the sawmill.

"Or you could cover him up. The McClouds will be here momentarily."

"Yes. We passed Philip McCloud coming down the road."

Early snickered. Ellen pictured Philip driving his ponies down Bobcaygeon Road. It would take him an hour at least to find his father and return to her. She braced her shoulders.

Darius studied the wound on William's neck. "Did they tell you what happened, if you don't mind, Mrs. Cook?"

"He fell into the saw is what they told me," she said. Yet, William rarely stumbled. A tall and solid man, he moved through the world as if all spaces were his. He was aware of how near objects were, how far apart walls, how high ceilings, tables, counters, window wells, doorways. He had the attention to space of a builder, though other than their small, tight cabin, he hadn't built anything. His talent had made him a valuable worker at the sawmill, his ability to estimate sizes and amounts of wood needed to construct any building or item based on the space. He had only to drive out to a cleared area in the bush where some soul expected to construct his home, and William could tell to a board how much wood was needed. So, yes. A fall into a saw by William sounded suspicious. But Ellen didn't trust Darius Horn, so she hid her concerns.

William was a man ready for the unexpected. He hadn't come north, bought and cleared land, built a house and forged his way into the little community of loggers and settlers, the only one like him, without keeping an eye on objects in his way and smoothly moving around them. If someone had pushed him into a saw, that man must have meant business. Or had help.

"That's what I heard," Early said.

Darius looked at Early until Early looked at him, then away. "You heard nothing, Early, that I didn't tell you."

"That's what you told me, I mean."

"Enough. This look like the wound of a man who fell?" Darius fingered the kerf open to muscle on William's chest, a wound that should have been dressed, and that a doctor ought to have sewn up, if one could be had. Ellen hadn't thought until now that the wound might pose a problem with William's shirt. But his face was unmarked and everything was attached.

"I've never seen such a wound, whether of a man who has fallen or one who has not," she said. William had worked after hours for other people, sometimes staying out all night. Men like Darius Horn hired him to break up fights, catch them before they flared up, divert and keep the peace. William did what others needed to get along, but he was shrewd, too, staying on good terms with everyone. Clearly his objective hadn't worked, not if another pushed him into the saw. Ellen edged closer to the wall, brushing down her dress with one hand. If Darius was suggesting someone had shoved William, could he himself have done the act or arranged to have it done? He could have come here to cover up his handiwork or to gauge what she knew, whether she had information that could hurt him. Ellen estimated the distance to the fire poker.

"Nobody should have to look at this wound," said Darius, his voice a muted rumble. "You get his clothes, Ma'am." He flicked his wrist, and Ellen thought of the switch snapping against the horses' flanks. If these men were here to hurt her, they must think she knew something that could harm them, something William had witnessed and told her. She couldn't imagine what.

Ellen turned her back and headed for the plank ladder. The men stopped talking as she hustled up to the dark loft and patted her way around the bed to the dresser. She should have a lantern with her, but she didn't want to waste time going back down without William's clothes.

She didn't dare peek over the edge, so she stepped lightly and listened, her breath held in a round tight balloon behind her breasts. She opened the drawer too quickly, and it squeaked. Her hand went straight to William's good shirt, made for him in the summer to wear to church through the winter. After each Sunday service, Ellen folded it away, washing it only once a month so the wool wouldn't fade or bunch. She pressed it to her face, her eyes shut, and inhaled. The wool's oils mingled with William's own piney, peppermint scent in a sharp, sudden smell that pricked her eyes with tears. Not tears of grief nor longing nor even loss, but the physical jolt of pain brought on by biting into the bone of a fresh-caught fish.

A thud came from below and a line of muttered curses. She straightened her shoulders and, William's pants and shirt draped over her forearm, dropped down the opening, using the ladder for only the final few steps.

Early dabbed at William's chest. The green knitted rag was not one of her own. They must have brought it. Darius stood in a corner, arms folded across a broad, high stomach. He'd tucked his chin into the flaps of skin skirting his neck.

"Mrs. Cook," he said. "It must be covered up."

She went straight to the stove for the pot, but Mr. Horn was ahead of her there, too, for the cauldron sat on top, its scummy contents swirling, curtains of steam rising.

"Why are you boiling water?" she asked.

"We'll clean him again, and pardon your delicacy, we'll drain him some."

The backs of Ellen's ears tingled. Someone should have called for the doctor. Why hadn't the doctor come? She assumed a doctor had tended to William at the sawmill. She hadn't felt safe questioning the three men who'd shown up at her door, one carrying her dead husband by the armpits, another holding the legs, not even a blanket to keep him warm, pallbearers in advance of a casket. She'd kept her other questions to herself, but it had worried her then, as it worried her now, that she had very little voice with the men in this community. She would have to find a way out.

This draining, it did make sense. They would do the same for a slaughtered pig or hunted deer, but those animals would be gutted and splayed, their hooves knotted with ropes and hoisted high so the ground could catch their offal. She didn't dare ask how the men expected to achieve the same end with her husband here on her table.

Where was Micheline, nosy Micheline, when Ellen needed her most? The men stood at William's neck, blocking her view. She dreaded the knife she'd seen Early slip from an unrolled buckskin pouch. They were hunters, men up here had to be with the land so rocky and the crops so paltry. William, too, had gone into the woods with men from the sawmill, but he'd stood lookout, he'd said. He'd carried a knife not a gun or bow, had whistled low when he spotted the white fur of a surprised tail. William refused to keep a dog the way other men did out here and not just for the hunting. Dogs were unclean, he believed, and Ellen had understood, though she didn't agree. As children, many in their neighbourhood had shared his belief. It had more to do with social position and wealth. Those who had the most money, the biggest houses on the escarpment cliff with a view of Lake Ontario, they kept a pet or two, usually a dog and a cat, and their help cleaned up whatever mess the pet produced. Many in Ellen and William's neighbourhood were the help who cleaned up after the pets of the wealthy. Yet, up here, those who had the least kept an animal or two about, dogs who lived in pens, dogs with noses so discerning they tracked a deer or moose in fresh snow, dogs worth the meat that families portioned off for them and then some. Ellen might like a dog that lived in the cabin with her, if only, now, for that warm body to absorb the pain from her scarred hand laid on its side. A dog might protect her, too, ward off men such as the two in the room.

The men moved efficiently, one towel held about a foot away from the body, the other used to dab up whatever fluids it released. The smell in the room took a turn for the noxious, making Ellen retch. She should leave, but she couldn't abandon her husband now. The men expected her to have no voice so she channelled the strongest one she could find.

"*We would ask that you leave this man in peace*," she said, her chin working side to side, the words harshly accented and rumbling.

Darius Horn started, bumped Early's arm with the towel.

"Mother of –" Early said, his eyes fixed on his work, his hands making delicate, pinching movements.

"No cause to become hysterical, Mrs. Cook," Darius said, averting his eyes. "There isn't need." He leaned in closer to Early and said something Ellen couldn't hear.

"*We would like this man to be left to rest. Clothe him and be on your way.*" Ellen's mouth wrenched open as if in a yawn, her jaw's pops and crackles sending short bolts of pain and relief down her neck. The words filled her mouth as if the voice inhabited her with a larger energy than her own.

Darius dropped the towel over Early's hand working away at William's chest, doing what Ellen still couldn't see. "Now Mrs. Cook," he said, turning to her, holding his hands up at chest level, palms out. "We're performing the necessary work, what a doctor would do, and what Early here, who does veterinary medicine on his farm, has the expertise to finish for you. There's no need to frighten us. You – you can speak in your regular voice. We can hear you."

Ellen couldn't stop the voice now. She had asked for it, and it moved through her, her shoulders and arms thrown back, her chest thrust out.

"*This man's soul is at stake*," she spoke.

Darius moved around to the other side of the body, beside Early, who worked furiously under the sheet.

"*Never cut a dead man's body. It is unsanitary. It is an indignity.*" Ellen's mouth continued to move as if she were talking around a large item she was trying to chew.

"We can see how some might think that way," Darius said, backing up toward the door. "We're just doing what needs to be done, right, Early? This man needs to be prepared for a viewing, and ultimately for his burial."

Early had wrapped the knife in one towel and laid another, folded on William's chest, his hand on top pressing tight. "It's stitching time, Ma'am. If that upsets you, you're best to return to your room."

"You should not have cut him," Ellen said, in a voice midway between her own voice and the firm voice that had spoken through her moments ago. "He was torn by the saw."

Early fussed with his buckskin flap. "Mrs. Cook," Darius said. He took a step forward, hands out. She recoiled, even though her own hands had spent much of the morning in contact with the flesh of her husband's corpse. "It's a trying time for a wife, a woman, for anybody, with your husband dead in an accident. Stitching has to happen, so he don't soil his clothes."

Darius rubbed his hands together.

"Go ahead then. You will anyway, even though I am opposed. His spirit is what matters anyhow. His spirit has gone home."

"Yes. He is back in the bosom of the Lord."

A note in what he said jarred Ellen. Sarcasm or irony, a challenge to the accepted line out on Bobcaygeon Road that God took people into heaven once they passed. Ellen couldn't say she believed anything that much different, only that the bosom or paradise or heaven people talked about was a place of pure energy that grew stronger with each soul regained.

Ellen handed Darius the shirt and pants.

She retreated to the ladder, gripping a rung but not going up. She would force herself to watch even though she couldn't see much in the shadowy cabin.

The men didn't speak for a long time. Early did most of the lifting, his arms swift and strong under his knitted sweater. Darius fed William's arm into the sleeve. His hands moved with the gentle precision of a mother with a child.

Ellen tugged at the hair near her forehead. She scolded herself for thinking of Darius Horn as a mother. She remembered the late summer night when William had stayed out until the sky was pink with the sunrise. The evening before, Micheline had come to the door to tell her the boys were out playing cards because some of them, like her husband, were going into the camp in a few days. That Ellen shouldn't worry because William was a good man who, even if he did play for money, would know when to stop, like Micheline's husband did. But William wasn't playing for money. If Ellen hadn't known it before, she certainly knew it the next morning.

Ellen had stood on the threshold in the coral dawn, the door open behind her, apron wrapped tight and tied twice. She held herself around her middle, eyes on the coral light wrapping the trees. The crunch of William's feet in the leaves and dirt had reached her first and then his body, shadowed with the sun behind him. When his face appeared, his features were empty until he registered her in the doorway and broke into a gap-toothed grin. He was missing two teeth on the left side and small cuts covered his hands and neck. He also had more money and wanted to take her to Duffy's before the cold settled to buy her a new coat.

Early supported William now, arm around his shoulders while Darius worked his second arm into a sleeve.

Ellen hesitated. She did not like these men, nor did she want them touching her husband. If she retreated now, though, they would take over. She wished the voice would return as it had clearly rattled Darius. Even in death, she must do the right thing by her husband. She made herself step forward. She took William's hand and guided the cuff over his wrist. Darius said nothing as he tugged William's shirt at the back and smoothed it near his waist. She reached across William's belly for the other side of his shirt. Early guided William's torso down, then wriggled his hand out from beneath the body. Ellen stretched the shirt into place and fed the buttons into the buttonholes to his neck, the fabric looser over his body than it had been in life. She resisted the urge to lay her face on it, the desire to come close to William suddenly intense. Some believed the spirit stayed in the room until the body was buried. She didn't think she agreed. Shouldn't she sense his spirit if it were here? Anything she intuited about William she believed was the remainder of his physical presence, sitting at this very table in the morning darkness, drinking coffee from a pewter mug while she drank tea brewed from sumac buds.

Both men stood back, hands crossed in front like pallbearers after setting the casket down.

"We'll have to unbutton the top few, Mrs. Cook," Early said.

"Never you mind," Darius said.

"I never do," Early said.

"I meant Mrs. Cook," Darius said. "She's a fine wife. William was lucky to have her." He smiled while sucking in his cheeks, making his mouth into a question mark as Ellen ducked her head.

One side of Early's mouth wrinkled. He stepped around the table, picked up one of the few remaining dry rags, shook it out, then folded it as neatly as any doily her mother had crocheted. Then with fingers as big as kindling sticks, he released the top five buttons from their holes, laid the pad on William's chest, straightening it to align with his shoulders and refastened the shirt. The pad's edges stood out through the shirt but not too conspicuously. Pants on, William looked stern.

"Mr. McCloud, the reverend and his son, both have acted most kindly to me today. They will return to help."

"Whatever you should want, it's me you call," Darius said. "Early will stay here with you until someone else arrives."

She steeled herself, glancing at Early, whose full, bushy beard and hunched, hulking frame added threat to his meandering intellect and his attentiveness. Was he protector or guard? Mr. Horn must consider her a threat. He must think she had some information that could compromise him, something William had told her, or had inadvertently shown her. What if he had helped kill a man or dispose of him, if he had filled that role once or more than once – and Ellen knew the details? Mr. Horn would need her to stay where he could see her. He must know that she would stand up for her husband and protect herself. Especially now, carrying a child. She must be three months along, she estimated. Darius Horn wasn't taking chances, so neither would she. She would stay under his watch until she was safe to leave. To where, she didn't yet know.

"You shouldn't stay alone with a dead man," Mr. Horn said.

Ellen choked at the word *dead*. It sounded like a corner. A sharp, hard, inescapable place. Loss ate through her along with a sharper, more metallic feeling, that rang clear and strong. Envy. Not of Early nor Darius Horn nor the McClouds nor even Micheline nor Mr. Horn's horses – though she had more reason to envy them than anyone. No. She envied William. He had the luck to leave this life and slip around the corner, his light absorbed by the greater light.

"We should wish we were him," she said.

Darius reached out a hand as big as a dinner plate and rested it across her back. She stood still as though pinned by a beam, and willed herself not to tremble. The sharp pain in her jaw returned.

"Mrs. Cook, we might envy the dead their return to the Lord or their sojourn in paradise but we must not. There is much good in this life and you must know it."

"Not his return to the Lord, though you might call it that." Light coated her words so they radiated throughout the room like fireflies, bolder and clearer as they collected. Perhaps her connection to William in life brought her closer to the light that embraced him now. As if, somehow, he'd carried her with him, through their experiences together. She didn't know how to say it. Just as the emptiness carved her clean, the light swooped into every open space inside her, bubbling, hot, eager to shape her words and take flight.

"Yes, we do call it that. William is in heaven now, Mrs. Cook," Early said.

"*William has gone into the light. He has become it, become part of it. Absorbed. Increasing the light we have available in the darkness of our lives*," said the light within Ellen.

Darius backed up, startled. He glanced at Early and frowned, as if to calculate his options then steadied himself. With a deep breath, he stepped forward and took Ellen's hand. She didn't draw away, though she should. She barely registered his rough skin. *Maybe the light might fill him too through this point of contact*, she thought. He would see her in control of her emotions and perhaps as less of a threat.

"Mrs. Cook, I'd like to take you for a meal at Buck's Hotel. You need friends. I can help you consider your options." He lifted his eyes to hers, then looked down at William.

She withdrew her hand. “I’m well aware of my options, Mr. Horn, and I thank you for your kind offer. As I am quite enervated from this morning’s excitement, I plan to rest after you and Mr. Early leave.”

“Mrs. Cook,” Darius said. “There is much you don’t know about your husband – or perhaps you do?” He studied her. “Either way, you do have options, narrow as they might be, and you will need help to accomplish them. Given the scope of my friendship with William and my position in this settlement, it is best that we take a meal together and discuss your future. We need to trust one another, Mrs. Cook, and a meal together is one way to solidify that trust.”

Ellen thought of Philip riding up to the house and finding her gone, having left William fully dressed on the table behind her. Would he come looking for her? Did she want him to?

Yes, yes, she did. Very much.

RUDIE

The delayed bass thump of her "Billie Jean" ringtone jingled in the back seat as Rudie steered her car into a parking spot between a Hummer and a Dodge Caravan. She turned off the ignition and patted the seat behind her for her purse, her chest squeezing as she thought, as she used to when her phone rang, *Dylan*. She had bought the ringtone in the wake of Michael Jackson's death last June, surprised at how teary she'd become when she first read the news on Perez Hilton. She hadn't listened to Michael Jackson when he was at his most popular, had mocked the red leather jacket, the flood pants, the glitter glove, but had grown to love his work beyond reason after pulling all-nighters editing *One Bra* with Dylan, the film where spending all their time together had moved rapidly from colleagues to friends to lovers and, in her mind, though she couldn't be sure about his, more. Dylan was a roots country guy with a secret taste for anything by Michael Jackson or Stevie Wonder.

Listening to *Thriller* in the wake of MJ's bizarre, anesthesia-induced death had inflated the loss she felt as she waited for the adoption placement. Mere months had passed between the end of her affair with Dylan and her marriage to Leo. Once she and Leo had made the decision to adopt, she'd begun missing the textures of her passion for Dylan, though the memories she'd nurtured had eroded. She mourned the loss of him as she grieved the child she wouldn't bear. Her arms ached for relief from the tense longing to hold her baby. Flattened over all lay a blank defeat. At the same time, she and Leo submitted their application to adopt a child from Haiti. They were taking the mandatory parenting course and had paid the agency's fees, though the match hadn't yet been made. Rudie had hope again, and Leo was ecstatic. The other, though, the gaping well of loss, wouldn't leave. MJ's death gave her grief a temporary focus outside of herself, one more acceptable than her sadness for a conceived-of child who'd failed to take form. She used to tell herself Dylan was the only one who'd understand what she felt.

Now she wished she'd mentioned MJ's death over breakfast this morning. She should change her ringtone, stop reminding herself of the obscure sorrow that had crystallized in her when MJ left the world.

Her mother.

"Hello?" Rudie said. With Kikka, she pretended not to have call display on her cellphone.

"Rudie? *Hallo*, it's Mama. *Wie gehts*?" Rudie liked that Kikka felt the need to identify herself by name.

"*Hallo,* Mama. I'm at a store so I can't talk." Rudie started up the car and turned down the heater fan.

"What's that sound?" Even though Kikka's parents had brought her to Canada from Stuttgart when she was eleven, she retained the soft V sound when she said words that began with W.

"Who knows? What's up?"

"Which store?"

"Oh, you wouldn't know it. It's called Thingamees."

"I guess I wouldn't know unless you told me. I'm here, Rudie, in Hamilton. I came to help you get ready. I'm excited."

"I'm on a tight timetable and it's up on the escarpment. How –?" Rudie had told Bob about Roselore's arrival today, but she hadn't called Kikka. She wanted to draw out the moment, go the indirect route.

"Leo thought you'd need me. Your father's no good at shopping, if he's even offered."

"Don't bother. I've got it handled."

"I'm punching it into my GPS now. I will see you in fifteen minutes." Kikka hung up.

Rudie flipped her phone shut, then open. She dialed half of Leo's number and then stopped. She closed her eyes and forced herself to breathe deeply. Leo was Roselore's father. She loved that he was trying to help her even though he wasn't here. But why did that help have to involve Kikka?

Thingamees was the corner store in a strip mall on a road lined with strip malls. Inside, one wall displayed a long row of strollers, many with thick wheels the circumference of mountain bike tires. The one nearest to the door looked like a picnic basket perched on stork-leg bars with giant bouncy tires. The farthest away was a yellow canvas playhouse on wheels with a plastic window and seat belts. She feathered her fingers over a price tag and shut her eyes at all the zeroes. Rudie would have to stuff Roselore into the first one, her legs flopping out, eyes bulging. She thought of the little people who dressed like babies to escape a bank robbery in the black-and-white comedies Bob had shown her as a child.

Stalled inside the door, she rooted around in her purse for her list as a trim, barrel-chested man approached her with long strides.

She forced herself to meet his gaze. Crumpled receipts and a pen tumbled from her purse. The man stooped to pick it up. He had a wide smile with dry teeth and no hint of stubble. His hair was short, with cropped chestnut curls. He handed her the papers, his broad hand ready to sweep outward, encouraging her to take in the store, his domain. The smile widened, his whole face built around it, though the eyes hopped and twitched, not cold, but not smiling either, assessing and suspended as if waiting for her to identify herself and her purpose.

Probably thinks I'm an aging aunt here to buy a gift, she thought. She pictured Roselore's sage nod. *That's right, get used to it*, she said to the Roselore in her mind. *Your mummy is old old old. Almost a crone. Can't be all bad. Wisdom counts, no?*

"Yes, ma'am? What can I do you for?" the man asked, feet planted at shoulder-width, square hands on his hips, as if presenting as part of a cheerleading pyramid.

"I guess most people come in here with children?" she said.

"No, no. Not at all. All kinds," he said, his face perking up with each word. "All kinds."

He would sound condescending if not for the inane shininess of his smile and the sense of mania contained, his eyes squirrel-like, shifting almost imperceptibly as he calculated every detail about her. He looked ready to spring toward whatever she hinted she might want.

She let her words out in a rush, telling him about the adoption, about Roselore's pre-emptive arrival, the flight, Leo's job. He held himself in check, seeming to spin in place, ready to leap the second she stopped speaking.

"You have a list?" he said, nodding at the paper she wound through her fingers.

She patted the list against her chest. "Yes. You sell more than strollers and bicycles? Because we'll need –" A wave passed through her. Her throat felt as though it might close, stopping her breath. She tamped the panic down. "Could I look around?"

"Of course! Call me Pat. I can answer any questions you want. Through this door." With two big steps, he stood at a doorway leading to a second showroom. She followed.

Baby gear lined the room, everything from wraps to bottle washers to diaper bags to blankets, bath toys and dishes. She wanted it all, but today was about a bed and a car seat. She could see from the display that she needed much more. She picked up a silver piggy bank. Pat stood right there, his breath coming in shallow pants, his hands parted and cupped as if to receive a football. She spotted a green, moulded-plastic high chair, zebra print car seats, leather slippers.

A bell rang. "Excuse me," Pat said and disappeared. *Doot-doot. Doot-doot.*

"Billie Jean" again, a Toronto number Rudie didn't recognize. Dylan had this number. The agency did, too. As she opened her phone to answer, Kikka rounded the corner with Pat in close pursuit. Rudie put the phone in her purse.

Kikka's hair stood up all over her head, fine as down feathers, the pink of pickled-ginger. Her lipstick was dark like wet wood, her face blended with colours in the same palette as her hair and lips. She wore a tweed swing coat and black trousers with black leather booties with heels that brought her up to Rudie's height. Her shoulders and chest were broad, her breasts a shelf, but her slim, shapely legs gave the impression, especially in the swing coat, that she might topple. The trousers, which had one crisp pleat, were a rare wardrobe choice, probably in deference to the January freeze. She eschewed clothing with a waistline. Her body went straight from ribs to hips so she often wore blouson dresses or short shifts, with her improbably girlish legs wrapped in tights, her feet in tiny tall heels.

Kikka and Pat closed in on Rudie, cornering her in front of a display of baby wraps and diaper bags. They wore matching smiles that refracted off one another as if in competition.

"I have to check this message," Rudie said. "And hi and thanks for coming, Mom." As she spoke, Kikka's smile lifted, then it flattened, hard and gleaming.

"Pat and I can get started," Kikka said. "Why don't you give me your list?"

Rudie folded the list tight in her fist like a toddler with a coveted toy. "I'd like to keep it. I won't be long."

"How will I know what you need?" Kikka examined a bright blue BPA-free baby bottle.

"I need everything for a two-year-old," Rudie said. "Mom, this could be the agency." She flipped open the phone, stuffed the list in her pocket and stepped behind a crib.

It was Dylan. *I need to see you again today*, he said on the message. As Rudie was flipping the phone shut, Leo called. This time she answered.

"Mother's here," she said. "We're shopping. Thoughts?"

"Oh, I'm happy," he said.

"You're happy because of Roselore or because my mom's here? She told me you sent her."

Across the store, Kikka sank her face into a brown faux-fur baby blanket. Rudie moved over to another display, where she fingered brown slippers shorter than her fingers with cut-outs of a monkey face. She didn't know Roselore's size. Had no way of guessing. One red pair had black dots on it like a ladybug. She turned away. She would come back. She and Leo could buy clothes in Ottawa, bring Roselore with them, buy them together.

"I did," Leo said. "I made a judgment call. If your dad's out of the picture for now, she's who you've got other than your café meeting with the support group and that's not until later, right?"

"Mmhmm." Though Rudie loved that Leo knew her schedule, his attentiveness could be stifling.

"It's your call. We had to tell Kikka sooner or later."

"Yes, but I should have done it. Now I'm at her mercy. At least there's a time limit. I agreed to give some friends a drive, some young people, I mean, street youth, on my way to the airport, so she'll have to leave by then."

Leo's tone softened, grew more caring, involved. "Really? I get why you want to help them, but are you sure you have time?" His lips smacked as if he were chewing gum.

"You're right. I don't have time, but I want to help them the way I would want someone to help Roselore if she were ever in trouble."

Pat and Kikka were approaching, her mother's eyes narrowing behind her dark frames.

"You're a hero," Leo said.

"Mother advancing. Must go."

Kikka strode up, shaking her head, her smile unwavering, one hand out as if to take the cellphone.

"I'm done, Mom," Rudie said. With Leo on his way, she felt buoyant and scared. But why did Dylan want to see her again? "Let's do this thing."

"Everything okay with Rosie?"

"Why are you calling her that?"

"Ma'am?" Pat called from the high chair area. "Your mother has some good ideas of what you could buy."

"I'll bet she does." Rudie dug into her pocket for the list she'd ripped out of her Moleskine but couldn't find it. She scrabbled around in her purse, lifted her feet. "Oh god. Where's the freaking list?"

Kikka turned up the wattage on her smile. "Is this what you're looking for, dear?" She held out the paper. "I've selected some decent items."

Rudie snatched it. "I want to take a look myself, if you don't mind. If you'll give us a minute, Pat? We'll let you know if we need help."

Pat lifted both hands as if doing a push-up on the air.

"Your baby. You do what you need to do. Shout if you need me."

Rudie moved over to the car seat display, the only area

Kikka had neglected. She scanned the rows. She didn't want to touch a seat in case Pat reappeared to grab it and ring it up.

"Leo told you Roselore's coming tonight?" Rudie said.

"Yes!" Kikka said. "I'm so touched. I'm enchanted. I'm going to devour that little grandgirl. Your father must be happy, too. He'd better get moving on your bathroom reno."

Rudie couldn't help herself. She fingered the fabric on a zebra-print seat that looked like a wingback chair. She flinched, expecting Pat to materialize. The door's bells rang again.

"Did Leo explain that you won't meet her for a few weeks?" Rudie asked. "We have to stay in Ottawa at least a week, and afterward we do need time to cocoon with Roselore before she meets anybody other than us."

"Won't you take her outside?"

"Yes, but she needs to bond with us."

"She needs to bond with me, too," Kikka said. "I'm her grandmother."

"And I'm her mother. Her third or fourth mother. Imagine how hard that will be for her. If she doesn't attach to me now, she may have issues all her life." Rudie sounded dramatic, ominous. Could every action she chose have implications on her daughter's emotional well-being for the rest of her life? Had it been the same for her and Kikka? Rudie remembered clinging to Kikka's legs up until she was school age, Kikka peeling her off with a laugh, wiggling her fingers to shoo Rudie away so Kikka could have "girl talk" with some random woman. Had Kikka's reaction to Rudie in those moments influenced who Rudie had become? She should resist picking apart each childhood memory for a parallel cause and effect on the emotional personality in adulthood, especially now.

"I'll take the turquoise leopard one," Rudie said.

Pat bounced over, glanced at Kikka.

"It's a bold choice," Kikka said.

Rudie smiled. Kikka, arms across her ribs, shifted her breasts up, then let them drop. She met Pat's eyes and moved her forefinger and thumb across her closed lips to tell her to zip it.

"Do you want to call your husband?" Pat asked.

Rudie's lips stayed in place, no longer smiling. "I'll take the display toddler bed, too. That's all," she said. "I'll pay with Visa. We'll install the seat ourselves."

"For a handling charge, I can install it for you," Pat said, nodding and smiling at Kikka now.

"You should," Kikka said. "Leo won't have time. Then you'll know it's done correctly."

"Leo can do it fine," Rudie said. "The police can check it out for us if we're concerned, but we won't be."

"Why bother the police when this young gentleman can take care of it right now?"

"Because I don't want to. I've got other things to do."

"What could be more important than your child's safety?"

Rudie's thoughts flew around each other. She put one hand on the counter, her credit card in hand.

"Please," she said to Pat who had leapt to the task, conscious finally that if he didn't ring up the sale, Rudie might leave.

Her face pulsed, her skin hot. Kikka hovered near a display of nursing pillows, her smile unmoving as if it floated on her face.

Rudie put the receipt in her purse and was bending to lift the box when Pat said, "I can help you carry it," his tone conciliatory and helpful. Heat flared across her shoulders. Her neck muscles tightened. Rudie had told Pat she was adopting a toddler, yet he'd called her decisions into question, and so had Kikka. Rudie was most furious at herself. When Pat asked for Roselore's size, Rudie couldn't tell him. Her daughter's life was a mystery. No matter how many stories or photos the agency gave her, Roselore's life in Haiti – and even now, on her journey – would remain unknowable. As Roselore's mother, Rudie should know what Roselore needed and provide it. Yet her shopping list was provisional, and Kikka's help was no help. When Rudie was a baby, Kikka had clutched her on her lap like a purse in the passenger seat of the car, no seat belt on either one.

"I'll take it myself," Rudie said. She paused. "But I forgot about the bed. Do you deliver? The only thing is, I'm going out of town tonight."

"I can receive it," Kikka interjected.

"Just a moment," said Pat. He went through a door behind the cash register and reappeared a few moments later. "My brother is here now. He can take it down, box it up. He could bring it by this afternoon if you like."

Kikka gestured at Pat as if to say, *See?*

"Thank you. Yes," said Rudie. She forced herself to add, "That's kind of you." She shifted her purse to the back of her hip, squatted and hoisted up the car seat box in both arms. Bracing the door with one leg, she stepped out into the dim grey parking lot.

Kikka followed her to her car, so Rudie invited her home for tea to fortify her before the drive back to Toronto. Kikka hovered as Rudie wedged the car seat box into the Fiesta's trunk.

The lid flew up, wouldn't close all the way. She rooted under the box for bungee cords.

"I can stay and take you to the airport," Kikka said.

"We need our car at the airport." Rudie was reluctant to tell Kikka about Hannah and Barth. Would Roselore hold back details from her the way she did with Kikka? She hoped not. "We'll have Roselore when we come back and will want to drive her home."

"I could pick you up, too, make myself available."

"Mom, you've got your clients. We can do it."

"Leo will have to install the car seat at the airport."

"He's prepared to do that. It's a small airport." Rudie found a clear plastic bag with six multicoloured bungee cords. She took one out and hooked it to the clasp on the trunk lid.

"What does the size of the airport have to do with anything?"

"I can stay inside with Roselore and have a snack while he does it."

"With a two-year-old?"

"Mom, you don't know her any more than I do. We'll figure it out. Maybe I'll have time to install it myself."

"I'm just trying to be helpful."

"I know, and you are. Helpful, that is. Thank you for coming to the baby store with me."

"I don't know what good it did. You only bought two things."

"But I got lots of good ideas of what to get when I come back. I don't have time to do more today. I have to get home and get ready." Rudie added a second bungee cord and agitated the trunk lid to test that it was secure.

"Do you have clothes for her?"

"Mom, can we not?"

"What? Can't a mother help? I can make suggestions. You can't have thought of everything, not you."

"Are you being sarcastic?"

Rudie parked halfway down the block so Kikka could have the spot in front of the house. As she parallel parked, she wedged the right rear wheel up on a crusty mound of snow so her door opened on an angle with a shorter drop to the ground. The door bounced back open when she shut it, the clasp not hooking properly. She slammed it a few times, then worked at the clasp with her gloved fingers until it gave and the door connected. She unhooked the bungee cords and slid the car seat box out onto the ground, locked the car, then hefted the box into her arms.

Her mother waited at the top of the stoop. "You should give me a key," she said.

"I'm surprised we haven't," Rudie said, setting the box down. "But you're right." Rudie reached around Kikka and unlocked the door, saying, "The place is a mess."

"Looks the same as usual." Kikka hung her coat on the rack. Dust floated in the air. "Is your father here?"

Rudie stashed the box in the corner. Her sock stuck to the kitchen linoleum, making a sound like tape as she lifted it up. She bent, peeled up something dark and gummy.

"What if he is?" Rudie lifted the coffee mugs out of the sink and piled them on the stove. She sprayed water to loosen crusts of oatmeal. The back of the sponge was black, with bits of hair stuck on it. She laid it on top of the garbage in the can, then opened the door below the sink for a clean sponge. She really should devote her day to cleaning at this point. When she and Leo had done the adoption home study last summer, they had kept their house showroom-ready, but with Leo gone and Rudie working on her film, she had let the cleaning slide. When Bob came over, she didn't care, but with her mother here, the heaps of notes and books, CDs and Sharpies, receipts and bills – you name it – on every surface, spilling onto the floor, assaulted her. She could pick up only one item at a time. Maybe her mother would regress in a helpful way and clean the house for her. Not likely. Rudie squeezed soap into the sink, then aimed the running water at it. She said a silent *Thank you* to Bob for turning it back on.

"That's not the way I do it," Kikka said.

"No. It isn't," Rudie said, her hand on the tap's curve. Kikka would move the faucet back and forth to give the water even bubble coverage. Rudie added every cup she could find to the water, then turned it off and flicked on the kettle.

"It wouldn't matter if your father was here," Kikka said. "I could handle it."

She picked up a stack of VHS cassettes from the pine chair with the cut-out heart on the top rail and set them on the desk. She brushed off the seat, then sat, her ankles together, only her toes touching the floor. The chair had once belonged to Kikka and Bob. Kikka had painted it white back then and set it by the door beside a basket of colourful knitted slippers and a bootjack. When Rudie stripped the paint, she'd found a piece of paper glued to the bottom. Though Kikka had painted over it, Rudie gently scraped the edges and peeled it off, intact.

It was a page from the Bible with the words *Spirit so big we cannot name it* written in pencil along the top margin. Rudie had framed the paper in a shadow box and hung it on the wall above her desk, though she hadn't bothered to find out which page of the Bible it was.

Rudie and Leo often left their shoes on in the house, turning their floors into a breeding ground that made a Celtic knot form in Rudie's chest when she thought of Roselore crawling on it, then putting her hands in her mouth. At least she'd thrown out that festering sponge, though the lid on the stainless-steel garbage can didn't quite shut and a smell of rotting vegetable matter permeated the air. Kikka held her wrist to her nose.

"Dad was here, fixing our bathroom," Rudie said. She dropped two Red Rose tea bags into the stained white teapot.

Kikka stood. "I'm dying to see it. I have to use the bathroom anyway." She headed down the hall, Rudie following behind her, hands dripping and bubble covered.

"He's not finished," Rudie said. She stood at the bottom of the stairs as Kikka went up. She lifted a mitten from the newel post, rested her hand there. Kikka didn't return so Rudie went back to the kitchen. Neither she nor Kikka liked yelling from one room to another, let alone one floor to another. Rudie washed up the mugs and glasses and slid the plates and cutlery into the sink. She set out her turquoise sugar and creamer set.

Her laptop sat open on the table amid piles of books about abstract expressionism and religious experience. She had hung O'Keeffe's *Black Iris* on the far wall, the same print displayed in Agnes Martin's final room. She had ordered in three copies of every book she could find on Martin – there weren't many – and razored out images of her face, of her at work and of her paintings, using them to cover the wall around the O'Keeffe. Her office upstairs was becoming Roselore's room . . . *was* Roselore's room. The dining room would stay her studio. The kitchen had a table they would use for meals with Roselore. Both Pat and her mother had suggested a booster seat. She should remember to put *booster seat* on her list.

Kikka stayed upstairs for a long time. Rudie made neat piles on her table, clearing the floor. She sat on the couch and called Leo.

"Mom's upstairs," she said.

"I've just picked up my cheque," Leo said. "I'm still here in Antigonish, waiting for Arnie to drive me to Halifax."

Rudie's gaze landed on a photo of her and Leo at an Oscars party – he in a tuxedo T-shirt, she in a white cape – arm in arm and smiling.

"What about photos?" she said. "Should we bring some?"

"Sure. Grab some of us, maybe take one of your mom in the nursery."

"What about *your* mom?" Rudie asked.

"We have that eight by eleven studio portrait she sent up last year but that's it."

"Might scare Roselore." Leo's mother wore her dyed black hair yanked back in a shiny, structured bun. Her drawn-in eyebrows accented the cheekbones and chin. In silhouette, with an artful shadow falling behind her do, she resembled a Disney villainess or a crow. His father had died before he was born.

"It's not like my mom will be in her life."

"One never knows." Rudie scraped at some crust on the couch arm with her fingernail. "Children have unpredictable effects on people. I mean, who knew my dad would turn out this way?"

"It may not be permanent."

"It may not, but it's true for now."

Kikka spoke Rudie's name from the top of the stairs.

"She's resurfaced," Rudie said into the phone.

"Here's Arnie now," Leo said. "I'll see you in Ottawa."

"RUDIE!" Kikka called again.

"Something must be wrong, Leo," said Rudie. "She doesn't usually call from another room. I've got to go."

Kikka was standing inside the door to what used to be Rudie's office, one hand on her chest.

"You can't be serious, Rudie," she said.

"I don't know what you're talking about."

"This bathroom. This room. How can you bring the child home to this?"

Rudie stepped past Kikka into the nursery. The old sink that Bob had removed from the bathroom sat in the middle of the floor, tilted, S-pipe in the air with debris stacked up beside it: boards with nails sticking out; chunks of plaster. Emptied of Rudie's work, pushpin holes and tape scars pitted the walls. Grease smeared the window, the curtains tucked up on the rod, their navy cotton grey with dust.

"I know, Mom. They gave me no time to prepare. And Leo's away." Hard, gritty tears spiked Rudie's eyes. She didn't wipe them away. She hated to cry in front of Kikka. "Roselore will sleep with us until we have it ready."

"It doesn't make sense that your father would leave it like this. He doesn't like a mess."

"He left in a hurry. It'll get done." Rudie dabbed her cheeks with her sleeve.

"Are you crying?"

This sort of invasive, obvious question irritated Rudie the most about Kikka. What should she say? *No, I have a runny nose and have wiped it across my face? No, I'm allergic to plaster? No, I spilled a drink all over my cheeks?*

"I want the room finished, too, but it's not. What can I do? My flight leaves at six fifty, and I still have to drive to the airport and do more errands. I have a few more things to pack since I found out we're staying for a week. I can get that done now, while we're talking." Rudie went into her bedroom. "We can get other things tomorrow. The agency will help us."

"So that's why you're crying. You're overwhelmed."

Rudie's eyelids ached and smarted. Her throat craved water. She added a nightgown, a bathing suit and three T-shirts to her suitcase, then zipped it up.

"When's your father coming back to finish up? I'll do what I can to get this place in order."

"Don't worry about it, Mom."

"You need help, *liebchen*. It's what mothers do. You'll know soon enough. You won't let me come to Ottawa. When Wendy's daughter Elsa had the twins, she paid for a cleaning lady for them for a month. New parents need help."

Rudie closed her eyes. She suspected her mother was offering to help to make a good story for her friends about her maternal sacrifice.

"Why don't you get me a cleaning lady then?"

"You know I can't." Kikka's eyes welled up, too.

"Dad's not coming back," Rudie said. She brought her suitcase into the hall then picked up the broom from its spot beside the newly installed pedestal sink. "I forgot to ask Leo what he wanted to do."

"Do you two have to agree on everything?"

"Isn't that how a good marriage works?" Rudie didn't want every word she said to come out as a dig at her mother's failed marriage, but the half-completed bathroom reno had weakened her. "We could carry the sink downstairs, sweep up. That would help."

"You should have hand sanitizer in the bathroom. Lucky for you I carry some on my person."

Kikka took the broom from Rudie's hand and swept the room, moving from corner to corner and swishing tufts of hair and dirt into the centre. Rudie bent for the dustpan and handed it to her. The sink cabinet sat in a corner of Roselore's bedroom. Inside it, Rudie found paper towels, Windex and green garbage bags. She passed a bag to Kikka and squirted the window.

"Is he going on a trip with that woman?"

"Who, Dad?"

"You should take the curtains down first. Yes, your father. You said he isn't coming back." Kikka's voice came out higher than usual, rising up and down as she fought to keep control. With both of them in tears, the conversation seemed unlikely to end well. Though Bob wasn't going to come out in a good light so maybe Kikka would rally. Watching Kikka kneel as she guided small, purposeful sweeps of debris into the plastic dustpan, her high-waisted black trousers firmly belted, her sparkly pale green top with a print of Paris stretched across her wide back, Rudie was filled with a rushing urge to confide. She should get out of the room right now, call Leo, call Dylan back – anything but confess her frustrations with her father to her mother who was divorcing him.

"Dad rejected Roselore," Rudie said. "He already has. I can't believe it. He said he can't love her because she's black."

"He said what? I can't imagine him ever saying that." Kikka stood up and put on the red-framed glasses hanging on a beaded necklace. "You need some light in here." She flicked the switch. She'd reverted to the protective tone she'd favoured when she and Bob were married, one Rudie hadn't heard since, one that understood the complexities of her father, that defended him against their daughter's critiques.

"I'm getting a chair for the curtains," Rudie said. "Yes, he did. He didn't say those words, but what he did say had the same meaning. So. It's done. He doesn't want to be her grandfather." Rudie stopped at the top of the stairs.

"He wanted to be a grandfather, more than anything. He had given up I think, before I left him."

"Are you saying I caused your divorce?" Yet another reason to feel guilty for being unable to conceive. Rudie couldn't wait to see Leo.

"Rudie, you know that is not what I said. And I don't think it, nobody does."

Rudie lifted her suitcase and took a few steps down. She should go to the kitchen and not come back. She descended the rest of the stairs fast, feeling the draw to return to her mother, the lure of her words, what she might say, what she might reveal, the light of her attention. She set the suitcase near her other bag.

Gripping the back legs, Rudie lifted a kitchen chair to shoulder level and headed back to the stairs. She rested a moment on each step before taking the next one, staying closer to the banister so she wouldn't knock any of the family photos she and Leo had covered the wall with before the first home study visit. They'd knocked two down already – correction, *she* had knocked two down with her shoulder while running down the stairs.

"Back up, Mom," she said as she rounded the landing. She lowered the chair so it wouldn't hit the ceiling.

"I'm in Rosie's room, not to worry."

"Not Rosie, Mom. We want to call her Roselore, her full name, so she doesn't lose touch with its beauty, or the mother that gave it to her."

"She should forget that mother," Kikka said. "She probably already has. That mother gave her up."

"That mother couldn't take care of her and then died. We don't know everything. She should think well of that mother, her birth mother, so she can think well of herself."

"Well, you're the one who took the parenting course. What do I know?"

Rudie set the chair in front of the window and stood on it to lift the iron curtain rod out of the holders. She unscrewed one of the fleur-de-lis finials and laid it on the windowsill, the white paint there black with grit from when she'd worked in here with the window open last summer. The curtains slid to the floor. She gathered them in her arms and carried them to the laundry basket in her bedroom. When she came back, Kikka stood on the chair spraying Windex on the window. Rudie wanted to speak more about Bob but preferred to have Kikka's outrage or nostalgia or superiority or whatever it was propel her to stay on the topic and guide the conversation rather than Rudie's own questions. She was considering marvelling again at his desire to be a grandfather when Kikka did it for her.

"You'd think he would have wanted a boy, but he used to talk about another you, another little girl. He could spoil her, maybe be more affectionate with her, show her what he felt for you, I suppose."

"Does that mean he's showing Roselore what he feels for me?" Rudie bent at the knees, wrapped her arms around the sink. Maybe it wasn't as heavy as it looked.

"Anything's possible."

As Rudie lifted, she felt as if a wire were springing free from her spine. She sat.

Kikka continued. "It goes deeper than that with you adopting. You must know that."

"Is it an adoption thing? Because Grandma Virginia was adopted, wasn't she?" Rudie went back into her bedroom for the bags she'd bought at the drugstore with Dylan. She thought of his kiss and felt cold inside her hip bones. The bags rustled, knocking against the door frame. One spilled its contents as she dropped it on the floor in Roselore's nursery. All the activity made the space feel more like a bedroom, if not a child's room.

"An aunt and uncle adopted Virginia after her father fell sick and her mother couldn't take care of her."

"Why couldn't she?" Rudie knew the answer, but she wanted to hear again about her great-grandmother sitting down one day at her sister's table and saying, "Take her. I can't do it anymore." As a child hearing this story, Rudie had thought Virginia must have been a bad, disobedient child. Once a year, when they used to visit Virginia in Port Hope, Rudie studied her grandmother's fluffy white curls and sunken green eyes for signs of wickedness. For a few years Rudie had believed her grandmother was a witch who'd discovered her powers as a girl and had driven her mother away so she herself could grow stronger.

"Who knows these things," Kikka said. "She was an only child. Perhaps her mother wasn't right and nobody knew how to help her. Don't forget they didn't have much money. They seemed unwilling to put her in an institution. The mother disappeared. Virginia never said any different. Perhaps she was following a man."

"Is she the reason, do you think, that Dad doesn't want anything to do with Roselore?"

Kikka climbed down from her stool. She scooped the crumpled paper towels into the bag.

"I doubt it. Why don't you ask him?"

"Why are you protecting him all of a sudden?"

"Why are you talking to me about him?"

Rudie twisted the plastic and tossed the garbage bag into the hallway. "I want to figure this out. I want life to be good for Roselore, not complicated by my issues."

"It's not your issue. You're okay with Roselore being who she is, aren't you? They wouldn't have picked you and Leo as parents if not."

"They only know what we want them to know."

"They're professionals. They can smell a problem. Your father and I didn't talk about race around you much when you were growing up."

"At all."

"That's good, isn't it? We didn't bias you against anybody."

"Who was there to bias me against? Everyone in town was a WASP. It was exciting when the Mahones moved in. You were pretending other races didn't exist. I don't think that is good."

"You do need a man here to help you set up," Kikka offered.

"Mom, he really said it. He said he can't accept Roselore as his granddaughter, that she belongs in Haiti and should stay there with the teenage girl who's been taking care of her. That he might see her from afar or at a group event but not to expect him to interact with her in any way. I really didn't know he was such a racist."

"It's not that simple, Rudie," Kikka held up a three-pack of size two footie pyjamas. "I hope you're keeping the receipts. The size doesn't always match the age. Did they tell you?"

"I don't know if they know even. They have clothes in every size donated by charity groups, and we'll all be able to use what we need until we have time to buy new."

Kikka folded the clothes and put them in the top drawer of the dresser. "Your grandparents, Chester and Virginia, lived next door to each other as children. They were raised like siblings. Virginia told me many times."

"That Dad was the child of incest?" Rudie turned her face away from Kikka. The word tasted like bitter Aspirins. She hadn't uttered it aloud to Kikka before. Why would she have?

"He wasn't." Kikka sounded gleeful, hushed in her confiding. Kikka thrived on moments like these, she drew from them when she crossed her index finger over her middle finger and crowed to her friends that she and her daughter were like *this*. "Grandpa Chester's grandmother, whom Grandma Virginia had met, mind you, so it wasn't a rumour, was black."

"Isn't that a good thing, then?" Rudie asked. She knotted the bag, a trick she'd read about on a Mommy Blog, done to keep the toddler from putting it over her head. The action felt both professional and practical, as if by snapping the plastic through her fingers she was inhabiting her role as mother and protector of her child.

"Not if you're ashamed of it. And Chester raised your father to feel shame. You don't remember him, but when I was pregnant with you, Chester stayed away from your father and I completely until you were born and Virginia could report back that you were 'healthy.'"

"You mean white."

"Yes, and why wouldn't you be?"

"What does *that* mean?"

"Just that your father is white and so am I. This great-great-grandmother was one person. She doesn't define everyone who descended from her."

"Yes, but," Rudie said, "she doesn't *not* define us either. She is part of us."

"Does that mean she is a part of Roselore?"

"Of course."

"And what about her own grandmother? I mean, Roselore's birth grandmother. Everyone whose blood she has in her from way back."

Rudie scratched her eyebrow with her ring finger. "I guess she has more facets then, more ways of being defined because she's got her birth line and the line of those of us who will raise her. Even if Dad doesn't want to see her, I'm still connected to Grandpa Chester and all the way back."

"Chester ended up doting on you, those four years he had with you. Your father is capable of such affection, too."

"If his granddaughter looks the way he wants her to. He's never even said anything racist that I can remember. I don't think I've heard him swear. I haven't heard you say anything either."

"Yes, but I'm not nursing a secret racism. If I do have any prejudices, I speak them, and I'm open to discussing them until I work through them."

Rudie believed her. Kikka had said plenty about harbouring Communists in the 1970s when the "boat people" had come to Ontario from Vietnam. She didn't speak kindly of overweight people or those who collected welfare or employment insurance. She loved the arts, though, and it thrilled her no end that Rudie and Leo made films. As long as they didn't collect "pogey."

"If Chester was so ashamed of himself and his grandmother, how did Virginia meet her?"

"Minden was a small town, remember, fewer than a thousand people. Chester's grandmother lived in the bush, was known as a mystic, a witch even, though she fancied herself a prophet, a spiritual healer, and was somehow left alone, though it doesn't seem likely in those rough times when every second person around Minden was a lumberjack. There were Pennsylvania *Doy-tch* up there, too, Germans, and they were peaceable, a bit radical, settlers trying to hack away at the rocky land."

Rudie thought of Virginia. Maybe Rudie's child-self had been onto something in her witch-projections. Maybe Virginia had picked up on her grandmother-in-law's ways. "Do you know what her name was? Chester's grandmother? My great-great-grandmother?"

"I know she didn't have a common name for that place. Let me see. Not Ruby. Or Cinnamon. It was a spice or a gem or a mix of the two."

"Rosemary? Jade?"

"Sapphire. Saffron. Something like that."

Rudie told Kikka she was running out for milk. It was just after twelve o'clock. "In case you need to leave while I'm gone," Rudie said, "I'll say goodbye now."

She found Bob filling in a sudoku puzzle at the Corner Bar on James North, a beer and a checkered-paper-lined basket of French fries on the table in front of him. Women's curling played on the wall-mounted TV.

He nodded and shooed at her with his left hand. "This is my sanctuary, Rudie. Enter only if you intend to leave me in peace."

A tall woman with pale caramel hair teased high and clasped with a barrette on the top of her head approached, clutching a notepad. Bob shooed her away. "Just get her a beer. If she doesn't want it, I'll drink it."

Rudie sat down in her coat. "I won't keep you long, Dad. I've got things to do, as you know."

Bob nodded, his eyes roaming the sudoku page.

"You don't even have to look at me," Rudie continued. "I would like it if you'd talk to me though. Mom says –" The words turned to chalk on Rudie's tongue. How dare she presume to tell this man what he felt? But here he was, red-faced now, pushing back his chair and staring at her, legs wide, hands on his knees.

"It's not up to your mother to say anything," he said.

"Who else is going to tell me if you won't?" Rudie's beer arrived, and she took a long swallow, licking the foam from her lips, then drinking some more. She pulled her shoulder blades together, sat back and crossed her legs. "She said your –"

Bob gathered himself up and let out a long, heavy breath through his nostrils.

"She said my what? I'm not having this conversation." He swivelled around until he caught the waitress's eye. He nodded at her, then took out his billfold.

Rudie drank more beer, a bubble forming in her stomach. "Dad, don't go. You should be proud of it, Dad. I am proud. It has nothing to do with adopting Roselore because I didn't know this detail when we applied, but it opens up a door for us, don't you think?"

Bob snorted. He dropped a twenty-dollar bill on the table and pulled on his jacket without making eye contact. The waitress eyed him from the bar where she tallied their bill.

Halfway to the door, Bob turned, his face red, his eyes narrowed. "No, it doesn't open any doors. If anything, it shuts the story up further, because that's what it is, a story, because you're right. It's got *nothing* to do with the current situation." Then, without saying goodbye, he opened the door and disappeared into the light.

AGNES

"His name is Lenny. His mother is Marsha Bargrill." Agnes adjusted her hips as she settled into a wooden chair. Across a desk sat Officer Javier Flores, writing Agnes's answers onto a yellow legal pad using a pen designed to look like a navy-blue pencil. The station, a storefront, sat empty. A typewriter behind a counter had a folded sign on it with a picture of a teddy bear carrying a picnic basket that read Out to Lunch. The young woman from the street, Julie, filled out a form at the counter. Shilah leaned against the door, arms crossed. They had their own missing person to report.

"Do you have a picture?" Officer Flores asked Agnes. His thick black hair bristling on his neck and shaved around his ears made him look no more than twenty.

"No."

"How long have you known the boy?"

"An hour or two." Agnes checked the door. Every minute she spent answering these questions, Lenny could be running farther away.

"Can you describe him?"

"Dark red hair. Blue jeans. Checkered shirt and brown duffel coat. Tidy. He's seven but acts older."

"What reasons does the boy have to run away?"

Plenty, thought Agnes. She shrugged and twisted her right shoulder to release a stiffness settling there.

"He's used to his mother leaving him alone, but this time, she left him with me, someone he doesn't know," Agnes said. "Though I did know his mother years ago and his father – granted, I did lose the boy – I had just popped into Jorge's. He was right behind me."

"Then he wasn't. What about these two?" He tilted his head at Shilah and Julie. Shilah jutted his chin and glowered.

"I'm not with them." Agnes shook her head. "They didn't see him either."

"Did you ask anyone else?"

"I did not." Agnes's hips aching, she leaned forward. The more they searched now, the better chance they had of finding Lenny. Unless someone picked him up. She refused to consider a bad result. She slumped. She doubted she'd make it into the studio today. Already she'd forgotten the Line for such long stretches of time – walking here with Shilah and Julie, for example – that she feared she wouldn't get it back. Not once since the weeks following John's death, when paintbrushes had repelled her hands, had she thought that she wouldn't paint again. Yet here she was, with all her inner and outer constellations synchronized, at a rinky-dink police station filing a missing persons report for a child she'd known all of two hours whose father was her dead best friend. She blinked rapidly and made to stand. Enough.

Officer Flores closed up his notepad, then flipped it open.

"I will need your name and phone number, Señora. Then we will type up the description and begin to search the town. You can search, too, it can't hurt, but rest assured we have it covered." He flashed a smile that revealed two front teeth so large his lips had to stretch to cover them.

"Agnes Martin," she said. "I don't have a phone."

"An address? A neighbour? Help me out here."

"The Sandovals," she said, then gave them Jesu's number. Nothing fazed Jesu and Annie.

Julie came over and handed Officer Flores the clipboard. "I wrote down what Rodney looks like," she said. "And everything you asked for. We saw him in town yesterday at Los Bruces House."

"Local boy?" Officer Flores said, with a warning tone, his eyes on Shilah, who stared ahead, unperturbed.

"He went to high school here, but he's moved back to Colorado."

"He's not one of those AIM characters, is he?" Officer Flores cranked a sheet of paper into his typewriter. The Wounded Knee conspiracy trial had just opened in Minnesota. The American Indian Movement was all over the radio, setting up protests, looking for publicity. Agnes raised herself out of the chair. No wonder Shilah hadn't wanted to come in here with Julie.

Julie shook her head.

"Good luck to you both," Agnes said. She stepped around Shilah and opened the door.

"We think he got rolled," Shilah said in an assured voice, his eyes fixed on Officer Flores, a challenge.

"Go look in a canyon then," Officer Flores was saying as Agnes stepped out onto the street. "The missing child takes priority."

The wind blew a milk carton down the street. Agnes strode toward the motel, her hands stuffed into her pockets as she scanned each doorway, calling Lenny's name over and over. The cold air on her face calmed her. The Frontier Motel was Lenny's most likely destination. If she didn't find him there, she would check Sandra's café, then backtrack and ask at every store and cantina, knock on doors, shake up a few garbage cans. She would find this boy if she never did another thing. The street stayed mostly silent, the only sounds the rumble of a passing vehicle. Agnes wished John's voice would speak to her again – she even missed the other voices – but her mind held its tongue, blockaded against any hint of fear.

Agnes was nearing the gas station when a mint green Ford truck turned off the road and stopped, blocking the sidewalk. Shilah rolled down the window and hung his arm out. Agnes craned to see around the truck while considering all of the places a boy could hide at a gas station. "*Lenny!*" she called through cupped hands. Maybe Marsha had picked him up? Agnes had to get to that motel.

"Agnes, climb in with us!" Julie said. "We'll drive you."

Shilah raised his hand and then patted the truck door. He nodded, his dark eyes serious and good-natured. The truck purred and bounced as if on unseen springs.

Julie continued, "We can help you look for Lenny while we look for Rodney."

Agnes came closer to the driver's side door. Olivia Newton-John was singing "Let Me Be There" on the radio. She turned and studied the doorways across the street. "Lenny's a little boy. He could be hiding around here as part of a game. You said your friend got rolled, you think? You mean a thrill-crime joyride situation? It's not really – what I mean to say is –" She stopped herself before she said anything that would hurt them. "That motel, just past the gas station, I'm going there first."

"Agnes, it's no accident we crossed your path," Julie said, leaning so far across Shilah she covered his lap. "We are meant to spend some time with you, especially since we intended to look you up when we came to Cuba. Before Rodney went missing."

Shilah frowned at her then held out his arm. "Come with us in our truck here, Agnes Martin," he said. "We want to help you find Lenny. It's cold. If we find Rodney, too, then great. But the cop was right. The child comes first."

The lost boy and the lost man. Agnes revised. Not hippie rainbow children. But art students. Art fans. And their friend Rodney, recently arrived from Colorado, likely did have some involvement with the government standoff at Wounded Knee. What about these two? Did they carry guns?

In New York, she hadn't thought much about guns. On the farm in Saskatchewan, two rifles had hung on a rack inside the door. Here, in New Mexico, men had guns in their trucks and on their ranches, but people didn't pack pistols in their belts or pockets. She sucked in her upper lip and walked around the front of the truck, exhaling an involuntary *oof* as she hoisted herself up into the cab.

Backing onto the road, Shilah said, "If he's not at the motel, we'll be methodical, drive up and down each street, then head over to the concession roads."

"I was planning to check the stores and restaurants."

"Let the police do that, Agnes. They'll find him if he's here. I mean, if he hasn't gone down a different street. Not much bad will happen to a white child. The major pastimes in this town are mud boggin' and Injun rollin'."

Agnes had heard both terms. Mud boggin' involved driving a souped-up vehicle through a mud pit. The more sinister, less-talked-about recreation, 'Indian rolling,' had white boys picking up homeless alcoholic Navajo men and assaulting them with rocks and eggs and the like. A hot brick of tiredness grew inside her as they pulled past the white fence shaped like waves and into the motel parking lot. Pushing through the lethargy, she opened the door as the truck rolled to a stop.

The motel room was dark behind the closed curtains. Agnes couldn't remember if they'd left them shut. Marsha's car was still not in the parking lot. The room's door was locked. Agnes knocked and knocked, then strained to see around the edges of the curtain. She heard nothing. Nobody answered. She shook her head no at Shilah and Julie then walked around the side of the building. Marsha and Lenny's hotel room was closest to the street.

Behind the motel was a stand of bare trees with untouched snow at their roots. The window was a few inches higher than the top of Agnes's head, positioned right up to the roof overhang.

She went back and motioned for Shilah to come with her. He lit a cigarette as he got out of the truck.

"It's a long shot," Agnes said. "He told me he was used to climbing in and out of windows." Though the window had a high drop, she believed the boy could do it. Shilah followed her behind the motel.

Shilah studied the window. "I can't break in here. We're right by the road. I shouldn't even be back here." He flicked his cigarette toward the trees and strode back around the building. Agnes lingered for a moment, then trundled after him.

"We should speak to the hotel manager," she said, raising her voice.

He turned. "The police will do that. Let's keep moving."

The road was empty, though the vehicles parked at the gas stations and restaurants suggested people were around somewhere. Shilah turned at the first light past the town and drove east. "I'll circle Cuba, come back in at the other end and then turn at the first side street."

Clouds hovered far off, some solid, some stretched. Sandstone and clay dabbed with snow rolled past as Shilah inched along with two wheels on the shoulder. Sitting back, Agnes stretched her neck. Trees clustered around parts of this road, but the rest offered uninterrupted views of sage-dotted land and shadowy mountains. Fast or slow, if Lenny were out here, they'd spot him. Agnes's gaze rested, her mind, too, and when she caught herself grabbing images of the land as greedily as she should have been looking for the boy, she shook her head.

What are you doing, Agnes? John's voice said. *My son deserves better.*

Yes, he does, Agnes thought. She pinched her wrist.

After a quick look in the opposite direction, Shilah turned west onto a new road, the tires crunching. Up ahead trudged a figure, prompting Shilah to say, "Whoa!" and apply the brakes, slowing to five mph and rolling closer. Agnes blinked hard. Even from a distance, the figure was too short to be the man Shilah and Julie were seeking. Sunrays hit the mountain and shone pewter through iced branches on cottonwood trees lining the road. The day had warmed up and the gravel turned pulpy so that when Shilah inched to a stop behind the boy, his back wheels slipped in the mud.

Lenny stood still. The three adults sat in the cab until Shilah leaned across Julie and said, "Agnes? This him?"

Agnes scratched behind her ear and sank her chin into her neck with a ragged breath.

"It's him, sure," she said, but she made no move to exit the truck. She brushed at her pants with her hands.

"Go to him, Agnes," Julie said. "He knows you. If Shilah goes, he might think he's a pervert."

Shilah drummed his fingers on the horn. As he reached for the door handle in a huff, Agnes said, "Huh," and opened her door, too, so they both stepped down from the truck cab at the same time and walked on the frozen dirt toward the boy.

The boy stood his ground. Shilah swaggered, kicking at the odd stone, jerking his neck as if to release kinks. Agnes kept pace, her head angled, forcing herself to meet the boy's dark eyes. She and Shilah stopped in front of him.

Shilah stayed silent, and so did she. Finally, the boy lifted his head and smiled at Agnes, a full, tense smile, the aggressive, fake kind that parents insist their children make for photographs. He was missing two teeth. The tender gaps reminded her of how young he really was. Relief flooded her chest and she approached him. With each step she took, he stepped back. She checked herself.

"Lenny," she said, her voice croaky. "I'm happy to see you, to know you're all right. Your mother –"

"I don't want her. I hate her." He squeezed his eyes shut, then opened them again.

"Is that why you ran away?" Agnes squatted, wobbling, so they could speak eye to eye.

"Yeah, kid," Shilah said. "It's not safe alone out here."

"Lenny, this is Shilah," Agnes said. "His friend ran away, too, and he's looking for him, like I was looking for you. And I've found you – I'm really happy that I have, Lenny."

Lenny shrugged and then hung his thumbs from his belt loops, mirroring Shilah's stance.

"I would have run away too," Agnes said. "Maybe going to the police station was my way of running away. No more police. You can come with us." She didn't dare touch him nor did she want to. Behind her, the truck door slammed. He could sit on Julie's lap. The boy reeked of the need for physical love. Maybe Agnes did, too.

"Would you like that, Lenny?" Shilah asked. "You'd have to ride in that truck there."

Lenny nodded.

"I'm so happy you're coming with us, Lenny," Julie said. As she took Shilah's hand, they both crouched beside Agnes. "We really want you to. Agnes needs your help getting started on her painting, and we need your help looking for our friend. So you'll ride with us until Agnes is tired, then we'll take you to her place and you can help her with whatever she needs."

At Julie's words, the boy melted a little. "Who are you?" he asked.

"I'm Julie, Shilah's girlfriend and Agnes's friend." Julie looked tentatively at Agnes, whose knee cracked as she stood. Agnes nodded. Julie held out her hand and Lenny took it. With Shilah holding Julie's other hand, the four walked back to the truck.

Lenny sat on Julie's lap, his legs draping down between hers and Agnes's into the well of the passenger seat. Agnes held her right arm against her stomach to mask its gurgling as she leaned against the passenger door. Lenny had fished an eight-track tape out of the pile Shilah had shown him behind the seat, and they listened to "Band on the Run," Lenny and Julie singing along. Lenny leaned against Julie, bloomed under her touch. Agnes was glad to be absolved. Agnes had spent few of her days as a younger woman thinking about having children. At sixty-one, she rarely thought about children at all. Lenny's return prompted her to wonder whether having a child was essential. Had she missed out? Agnes pulled down the visor to block the sun bouncing through the streaked window, giving everyone a golden metal cast that made them look grittier than they were, as if they were hurtling down the road in a covered wagon instead of in this 1968 Ford Ranger.

Julie and Shilah were describing Rodney:

"A lanky sort."

"Dark eyes. Black, almond-shaped."

"Brown eyes, actually."

Shilah glanced at Julie. "You would know."

Agnes interjected. "It's not likely we'll be able to detect the pigment of his eyes from a moving truck. Can you sketch in the larger picture?"

"He's average height?" Julie offered. "Skinny overall but broad shoulders. Jeans and cowboy boots and one of these sheep coats, like ours."

"Shearling."

"They know what I mean."

"I say that because he told us all the time it was *shearling*. Corrected us when we called it sheep, remember?"

"Because they sheared the sheep."

"Didn't skin it."

"The distinction was important."

From his vantage point on Julie's lap, Lenny was taller than all of them, his red hair brushing the ceiling unless he ducked or leaned back against Julie. He twisted so he could see Julie. "Was he your boyfriend?"

Julie glanced at Shilah, who looked straight ahead. "Was. Not even. But we're good friends. We all are, the three of us, I mean."

"Julie and I didn't go to Wounded Knee with him so he hasn't hung around us as much. But hey, we're the ones looking for him. You don't see any of the AIM people here."

Lenny studied Julie. His knee pushed against Agnes.

"I think you love him," Lenny said. He twisted forward again, rocked his body so he leaned into Shilah's shoulder. "And you love her."

Agnes cracked the window and a thin stream of cold air wound around their necks like the tip of a filbert brush dipped in oil paint.

"And who Rodney loves," Agnes said, "is anybody's guess."

"I can guess!" Lenny pronounced this last with a sense of play, his voice sounding, if Agnes closed her eyes, like John's. Agnes opened her eyes and the moment had gone.

The eight-track reached the end of the track and made a *clack clack* sound. The song "Bluebird" resumed.

Shilah idled the truck at a STOP sign, patted Julie's hand on Lenny's shoulder. "Those are some deep thoughts, Little Man," he said. "You think you can turn that big brain to finding our friend?"

"If we see anyone out here," Agnes said, angling her head at the empty stretches of land and sky surrounding them, "I'd be surprised." Her sense of desperation had receded since they'd found Lenny. Now, she could invite the Line to thrum low in her brain stem and contemplate how long she should give this futile search. Was she better off out here in the truck where the Line pulsated all around her and expectations of her were low and she couldn't paint so she couldn't feel bad for not starting? Or at home where she could step into the studio and shed these people, let them wander her land, infiltrate her house, make their herbal teas and their sprout sandwiches and settle themselves in around her life?

"Did sumpthing bad happen to Rodney?" Lenny said.

A river of electricity snaked through Agnes. She thought it must have but hadn't felt comfortable saying so.

"What?" Shilah said, his tone frustrated and scared. "I am sure we will find him like we found you, Lenny."

Shilah had turned east, so they drove through shadow, his face puffy and blood-rushed, emptied, as if hit by a plank.

"Something bad might have happened," Julie said, "but we're still hoping Rodney is okay, like you are." She turned to Agnes. "Rodney hasn't lived here since high school. He's from Colorado, and he didn't have much to do with his family. But, Shilah?" She turned her head back the other way. "Maybe we should cruise the canyons, like Flores said."

Shilah drove with his wrists draped over the top of the steering wheel. "I wanted to find him walking."

Agnes raised her eyebrows. "There's Chaco Canyon. It's too far for me. Why don't you go there? But could you take us home first? I have work to do."

Shilah acted as if he didn't hear her. Or maybe he had and didn't care. He stepped hard on the accelerator and swung out into the intersection, looping the truck all over the road until it roared up to highway speed. They passed the familiar wood fence and arching entry of the Circle B girls' camp, closed for the winter, though a cluster of pinto ponies stood in the meadow, steam roiling from their noses, eyes hidden by tawny bangs.

"Little Grand Canyon's up here a piece," he said. "You're right, Julie. We should face facts. Look for Rodney where we have more chance of finding him."

"If you turn at the next road, you can loop back to my place in five minutes." Agnes directed her words at Julie and Lenny now. "You could rest a bit, have a tea. Maybe you need some equipment if you're going to hike around in the canyon. I'm not dressed for it."

Julie didn't respond. She had drifted away, though not into a nap or a trance or a catatonic state. Agnes couldn't place it at first. Her skin sagged and was the colour of mushroom soup, her eyes filmy and unfocused, not like the dark stars they'd been when Agnes had met her on the street, her skin a glowing pearl then. Her body was more a collection of bones than an animated force. Lenny leaned back on her, but gingerly as though he sensed his weight might be too much for Julie to bear. And Shilah. He held himself rigid, his face and shoulders pointed straight ahead, but his eyes roamed the road and his wrists trembled.

The pair were coming down from a high, Agnes realized. Agnes sank back in her seat, defeated.

Ahead, the low, rolling San Pedro mountains rested like so many woolly green napping bears. They were approaching the local badlands, an area full of box canyons. To comb each one would take hours, maybe days. They should return to Cuba and press the police to organize a search party. Anywhere else, maybe anyone else, and the police would look. They were still looking, she supposed, for Lenny, so maybe they would happen on Rodney, too, though she doubted they'd venture out here.

Shilah turned onto a dirt road lined with piñon pine. Out of habit, Agnes filled her lungs with the damp and spice of snow and piñon pine needles.

The police would rely on a rancher or wait until the summer for a hiker to find any bodies that happened to rest in the canyons, out-of-town white children or not. Perhaps they'd look in the canyons if Marsha raised a stink by showing up before Agnes had a chance to tell them she'd found Lenny.

Shilah turned again onto a single-lane, unploughed road. The snow lay about an inch deep here, dry and powdered, unbroken by tracks. Agnes held her body in one position, her energy receding from her hands and feet, creeping up her arms and slowly inward to her chest where it would hold her fast unless someone touched her. She could control herself enough that she wouldn't slip into that catatonic place where her limbs would freeze until someone changed her position. As drug users, Shilah and Julie would accept any altered state she presented, she had no doubt.

Lenny clapped his hand on Agnes's arm for balance as Shilah steered the jostling truck down to the end of the lane. They stopped in a wide area cleared of trees. At Lenny's touch Agnes jolted and a bubbling heat washed down her legs and arms, her face enflamed and around her eyes damp and full as if he'd woken her from a deep sleep. Her eyes had stayed open, but the trees streamed past her like a sped-up movie. If she couldn't stop the world, she could stop herself, hold a moment close, freeze it. Even when she did that, her body hurtled forward into dust, yet she could hang full in a moment when she contained her energy this way. Maybe she'd found the appeal of drugs for these young people. They must be trying to stop their connection to the relentless objects and events around them so they could pause and capture or engage with a moment, any moment before it slipped away.

How lucky for young Lenny here that he'd figured out the trick at such a young age! She met his gaze. Her return alerted him that she'd checked out, and he raised his eyebrows, interested. And now an old woman desperate to get into her studio and paint shared the same affliction – or magic powers, depending on how you looked at it – as he did. Did it make him more special or less? Or did it mean that there were others too? One thing the boy had yet to learn, and Agnes didn't intend to be the one to teach him, was that there were always others.

Not one thing about anyone was singular, and yet that's all they were, if one chose to look at it from another direction. Solitary inside their bags of blood, searching for what was the same, and resigning themselves to the possibility that nothing was. Agnes wasn't sure if it was better to come to this acceptance later in life, as she had, or earlier. That knowledge had brought Agnes to a bleak place with no parameters, no noise or any qualities of the world that Agnes wanted to stop when social connections overwhelmed her. It was a place, Agnes had found, that one could know about, while moving forward moment to moment through life. Looked at a different way, the place didn't have to have the qualities she'd given it. She could remake it as a calm place of light. She thought of John, then, almost a decade older than her, how he had come to that place but had chosen such a final response, perhaps the only answer he could find to the question of what to do in the darkness. Rather than rage against it, he had imposed himself on his light and choked off the air with his own hand.

The road was long and twisting, the houses set farther and farther back and with increasing space between them. They drove by fields until the road curved, and Shilah steered them onto a dusty single-lane dirt road with shallow ditches and no fences, only the occasional tree that gave way to sage bushes and stretches of snow-streaked clay. He wasn't driving them to Little Grand after all but to a place everyone called Box Canyon. Agnes sighed audibly, but nobody reacted. Box Canyon was thirty minutes as the crow flew to Agnes's land. She hoped the boy was up for another walk.

As Shilah rounded a corner, the canyon walls cast them in shadow. Agnes came here in the summer to cool off, the water too shallow for a swim but good for a wade or a soak, luminous with fireflies at dusk. Snow dusted the sage tips and nestled in the curves of the rock face, but otherwise the land here was bare and dry. The truck bounced their bodies around so Agnes's arm pressed against Julie's. Lenny leaned back and sideways so he was bracing himself between Agnes and Julie, using his knee on the dashboard for extra balance. His confidence and trust of her impressed Agnes, but she pulled away an inch so he would accept her acknowledgement in case he'd touched her by accident. But no. He pushed back more firmly, filling the space she'd made between them. Touch grounded her. She hadn't sought much touch in her years down here, though she had borrowed a horse from Jesu or stopped by Circle B for a ride when she found herself floating loose too often. She had even accepted Annie's offers of back massages during months of brick-making when stooping and crouching left her slow to rise from a chair or bed. The boy must crave touch, she thought, or perhaps his mother hadn't failed him in that area. Having the boy rest against her made Agnes feel uncommonly good, but it made the Line fade so that she didn't care about it.

The front left tire hit a crater and all four of them rose off their seats in unison, Shilah and Julie and Lenny shouting, "Yoohoo!" and Agnes echoing with a groan and landing with Lenny half in her lap, the rise and fall bringing the Line singing straight through her surrounded by a white-lit beam. She gasped and placed a hand on Lenny's upper back and one on his wrist. He rubbed his forehead. "I hitted the roof!" He grinned, the gums above his missing teeth pink and shiny.

Shilah wheeled the truck around until the nose came up flush with a section of canyon wall near the entrance. He left the keys dangling in the ignition and jumped out. Lenny clambered after him with Julie sliding out next.

"I'll sit a minute," Agnes said, making a show of brushing off her pants and coat, wishing her ever-strong voice had more of a tremble. "Lenny, stay with me. I have a couple more things to tell you."

"Are you sure? We can wait," Julie said. Shilah was already walking ahead through a patch of sage.

"Go ahead," Agnes said.

Julie ran to catch up to Shilah, their flat hands making visors over their eyes as they scanned the area. Agnes scanned it, too, as Lenny climbed back in Shilah's side, but she couldn't see much, the canyon's high walls casting the area into shadow. There weren't many trees around, though, so if local boys had tossed a person here, it shouldn't be too hard to find. Agnes checked the lip of the canyon for the road that connected to Cuba. Shilah and Julie might want to investigate up there, too, if only to get a sense of whether anyone had left tracks or evidence of festivities.

Lenny sat in Shilah's place, scooching down so his toes met the wide pedals. Ahead of the truck the couple walked in a huddle, advancing methodically through the canyon, unwilling to break apart and risk – what? Losing each other in this demarcated space? Losing focus? They'd willingly left their truck with Agnes, unconcerned with her going or with her loss if one wanted to look at it that way. Unthreatened by her when it would take barely a minute to turn on the engine, throw the truck into reverse and spin out of the canyon back to her land.

But she couldn't leave them without a vehicle. She rubbed the keychain, a fluorescent green rabbit's foot, and lowered herself from the truck, taking care not to move the door in case it squeaked.

"Come along, boy," she said.

"You said you had to tell me sumpthing," he said.

"No. I needed to make sure you stayed with me."

Lenny fingered the keychain. Then he crawled across the bench seat and launched himself. He made to run toward Shilah and Julie, but Agnes caught his shoulder and stopped him.

"This way, Pilot," she said. "I have only one rule. You will not run away from me again. Agreed?"

Lenny looked up at her with wonder and a little bit of fear. "Okay," he said. Agnes turned her back on the couple, walked with one hand on the truck for balance, then headed toward the canyon mouth, her hand on Lenny's shoulder as if steering him. At the canyon's mouth, she slapped a hand on the rock and they stepped off the road and onto the desert stretch.

ELLEN

"She is William Cook's widow."

"William Cook is the –"

"That's right. I reserved a table for dinner, but we've had a change in plans and Mrs. Cook and I will be dining earlier."

The young man wiped his hands on a towel under the bar. The room had gone silent. His round eyes strained with the effort of not looking at Ellen, who stared at him, taking in cheeks so buttery they had yet to feel the scrape of a razor. He looked younger than Philip – perhaps Philip had taught him at school. No, most men stopped attending school up here around the age of twelve; Philip couldn't have been teaching that long. She stepped sideways to accommodate an ache in her hip, and her hand brushed fur. With a cupped palm, she stroked, knuckles expecting to dig into the muscled neck of a dog, and flinched at how coarse the hairs were, how hard the flesh. Ellen reached again for the creature and saw she'd been scratching the head of a stuffed bear cub.

Ellen studied the bear cub, which had teetered but was rocking back into position, its paws up, mouth open as if asking for milk. Perhaps its mother died defending it and the hunter had taken its life as an act of mercy. Could it have lived without a mother? She couldn't tell how young it was and had no thoughts on the survival skills of bears. Maybe the hunter had shot only the cub, and the mother had raged with the pain of having been left behind.

She tightened her stomach, resisted the urge to give it a reassuring pat, unwilling to reveal the secret of William's baby to Darius Horn of all people.

Philip wouldn't tell. But Darius or even Benjamin might turn this hope into a capture – perhaps insisting she find a husband.

"We hadn't realized," the young man was saying.

He wore his chestnut hair long on top and brushed back from his face. The light from the wall lanterns cast a greasy halo around his head. The bar was tidy, and it shone, but even from Ellen's position halfway across the room, she spotted water rings and salt grains. She stood on polished floors awash in slushy chunks like dull sugar slurry. The men's voices began to murmur again.

"Steady," he said to her after he realized she'd jostled the stuffed bear. "Ma'am, you must mind your environment." To Darius he said, "She's not but a girl."

Ellen's hand rose to cover the sobbing laugh that threatened to escape. His tone condescended so, as though he might be talking to Micheline's five-year-old daughter, Thomasina. Did he truly believe young women merited speaking to in that manner because they mightn't understand him otherwise and might stir up trouble? Did he feel superior to her? She was likely older than him. She rubbed at the dips where her fingers joined her hand. The skin under William's wedding band itched, but she refused to relieve it or to take any action that called attention to her status or lack thereof.

"Jimmer was planning to set you up upstairs, but we would need some time to clean it properly."

"We're content to eat downstairs, Joe," Darius said, "in full view of the rabble."

Darius removed his coat and hung it on a peg near the door. He held out his hands to take Ellen's coat but she shook her head.

"I haven't heard of no policy here," a gruff voice spoke behind them, from the door, "as regards who ye'll serve and who ye won't. Seems to me like ye had no compunction about accepting *her* husband's money."

Sweat glistened on the young man's creamy forehead. The silvery white light of the sun on the snowy road outlined Early's frame in the low doorway.

"Of course," said Joe. "Why not choose the seat that suits you, Mr. Horn."

"Sorry," she whispered to William's child as she tightened her stomach.

Austin Barber had his hands on a white man's neck the morning Ellen told him her plans to move north to rejoin her husband.

The white man was Matthew Pittor, a Dutch grocer whose skin pinked at Ellen's declaration though Austin's razor scraping his neck didn't twitch.

"William has sent word," she said. She held an envelope with a folded letter. A sunbeam caught the back of her head where she'd tethered her braids into a bun and covered them with a lace-edged cloth. Her daughter sat at her feet on Austin's clean wood floor amid the fluffs of blond hair and puffs of black rolling around in the sun. Safra patted at a few with her palms, then sat back to gaze up at Ellen.

"I'm to secure passage up to Minden Village where he'll meet us and take me out to the cabin he's built on Bobcaygeon Colonization Road. He's constructed it himself, but men up there have helped him – everyone, even the –"

She stopped suddenly and curtsied at Mr. Pittor. Austin winced, then smiled with forgiveness.

Ellen felt comfortable enough with the white men who frequented Daddy's barbershop – mostly regulars, including Matthew Pittor – but she blushed at the thought of offending one of them by making an uncharitable observation about a white man's willingness to assist a black man, not only for the cost to Daddy's business, but because it hurt her to witness her words causing pain. She bent and swung Safra up to her hip in a movement as easy as sitting.

Austin tucked the bleached towel into Matthew Pittor's collar and brushed at the stubborn pale bristles clinging to his neck. Mr. Pittor leaned his ear to his shoulder. Austin flicked his neck with the shaving brush as he straightened his head. But Austin's attempt at lightness couldn't disguise his disappointment in Ellen. Since William had left two years earlier, before Safra's birth, Austin and May and even Ellen found it easy to dismiss him, to convince themselves of his non-existence or at least hope that he might return to Hamilton instead.

Ellen searched her father's face for a sign of hope or belief in her plan. She didn't expect relief nor excitement, but she wanted something other than the grey defeat that shut down his face at the news she was leaving to build a life with her husband.

She understood. He had no family with him beyond her, May and Safra. Austin had hoped – May had confided – to build a legacy here in Hamilton, a right denied to his parents.

The ale was warm and brown. Her jaw cracked as she sipped. She pressed at it with her fingertips. She hadn't tasted ale since Hamilton with Daddy at the back of the shop, sitting on her special stool, with two steps that folded up and tucked under the seat. He'd made the stool himself, having placed a square of red leather over a cotton pad and hammered it onto the seat with rivets. She hadn't needed the steps to get on it for years, though her legs still dangled so she liked to use the step to rest her feet.

Now, sitting across from Darius Horn, the tingle on her gums felt the same. The yeasty taste made her think of the quince oil and lavender smell of Daddy's shop and of cigar smoke slinking round the back door because Daddy wouldn't let the men light up inside. Not so here. In this hotel, the men could smoke, and the smoke hung like sinewy ghosts lazily stretching in the weak winter sunlight. All the lamps were lit, but still the place looked hazy, giving Ellen the sense of men lurking in shadowy corners beyond her sightlines, though the room had so little space that if she turned her head she could look into the face of each man at the scratched wooden tables. She kept her coat buttoned though her armpits were perspiring.

That they were all men didn't much bother her. She'd sat in Daddy's shop every day for years on her stool, such a fixture that many forgot her presence. The only ones who paid her any mind spoke to her like one of their own as Daddy wouldn't have it any other way; besides they all knew her mama, had sung under their breaths with her as she harmonized in the church choir.

Ellen sipped and trained her eyes on Darius. The men around them were talking again. Somewhere upstairs a hound bayed. Its voice dipped as if to take in a breath, then soared again. The beer calmed Ellen. She welcomed it and accepted its false welcome.

"Mr. Horn, while I appreciate your concern for my well-being," she said. "And I do . . ."

Darius Horn took a long pull from his pint glass. White foam flecked his moustache. Early stood at the bar talking with a man in a knee-length blanket coat.

"That's one way of looking at it, Mrs. Cook. Yes, your well-being matters and so does the well-being of this community. My business contributes to this community and depends on it too. It's a fine balance. Let me tell you a story. When your husband showed up in Minden Village in this pub here – isn't that right, Early?" Darius Horn projected his voice toward the bar, to where his friend stood, while keeping his eyes cast downward on his glass.

"You speak the God's truth, boss," Early bellowed back across the room, his wet, open mouth revealing not a few dark gaps.

Ellen raised her eyes to Darius's face. She sucked her lip in annoyance at the beer foam in his moustache in the hope that he'd take the hint, but he didn't, acting as unconcerned about his appearance as he did about Early's sitting out of hearing range of their conversation.

"When William walked into this bar, a stranger, more heads turned than they did for you, Missus, and that's saying something, don't tell me it offends you. Imagine the first black personage in this county. Strides in here with a paper claiming his right to an acreage of land. After their shock, people up here took to him right away, and he got more help than the pinkest of freshly minted Englishmen showing up at this door with the same piece of paper. 'What street am I on,' he said, William did." At this, Darius laughed a bellowing, liquid wheeze. "'What street am I on.' You recall that, Early?" he called over. "'What street am I on!'

"We thought him a rube, sure, and that's saying something up here, an idiot from the city – though most of us are from somewhere, usually a city – but after knowing William a while, after a few minutes really, witnessing his unfailing generosity and the twinkle he got speaking of you," Ellen was grateful he didn't mention Safra, "I saw that our William was more savvy and skilled than he let on. Unless the front was all there was to William, the man had depths and capabilities that if put to the right purposes could accelerate a business – or even a life."

Accelerate a life. Ellen ran her tongue around the inside of her teeth and pondered. Darius Horn's words had a quicksilver smoothness designed to slide past a body so she might rest content with the flash of his intent and accompanying smile. Ellen couldn't do that and would rather take the time to play the words over in her mind, slow them down and fully hear them. Did he mean add more excitement to a life, speed up the days by packing them full of interesting events and conversations, providing more fodder to think about in the evenings? Ellen doubted it. Despite his slickness and the air of invention and patter he lent his language, Darius Horn was shrewd and proficient with words, more so than many of his neighbours, but he had no centre that Ellen could see. Yes, he had a wife and four sons and land and a business, but all of it spun around him and he spun, too. All of it was growing bigger but never big enough, none of it with any meaning for Darius, who craved and fed the expansion.

Darius busied himself with a hide pouch packed with tobacco and a pipe. Ellen let herself taste the other meaning of *accelerate a life* – speed it toward its end. Hadn't that been what had happened with Safra? Static noise roared through Ellen's mind, and she struggled to beat it back, to empty her brain and fill it with light. She had not caused the fire. Not even her neglect had caused the fire. The fire, some said, had been an Act of God. A freak of nature. His fault. Her fault. Safer, Ellen believed, to live in a place of no blame or rather a place that levelled all blame at forces of darkness that might wend their way into even the most vigilant lives.

Accelerate meant to quicken. Was that what Darius Horn, the man who sat across from her tamping tobacco into the bowl of his pipe, looking up at her from time to time with a cocked demanding eyebrow, meant? Was he making sure she understood his part in her husband's death, or was he suggesting her husband had signed on for something that would lend itself to an early death? Had William known or expected he would die young? Darius Horn wet the pipe end with little sucking motions of his pale purple lips. Ellen decided that yes, Darius Horn had killed William and that William had known he might. If not, then Darius Horn in some way held responsibility for William's death and was assuaging his guilt. Straightening her shoulders, Ellen took the measure of Darius Horn.

She hadn't told William about the smoke, the way it wound its way into her hair, coated it so she could still pull a curl from her bun, stretch it and breathe the smell in deeply if she wanted to remember the day Safra died. The smell also reminded her of another day when the smoke acted like a filter that expanded the world, the sun's rays fatter and warmer, bounding every which way, and the sounds closer and larger and brighter in the smoke's disguise. The voices came, one at first rising above the smoke, turning with it, inviting, calling and then another higher, reaching into the sun and more, some deep enough to thrum into Ellen's chest and then her own, the sound of the sound bigger than a voice reaching and asking so that she lost her own voice within the stronger beat of their community and had to put her hand on her throat to reassure herself that her body was reacting. Their voices raised in prayer and then song until one broke free and the others parted, the words burbling and thrusting as if multiple lips and tongues and throats competed with pressure to escape one woman's body. Then the other voices resumed, enveloping this spirit, joy speeding them up and amplifying, and Ellen blinked in the light, caught sparkling dust motes and beaming hair and blanked out white flashes, though they all wore grey or brown clothing, and she ascended, her throat opening, her tongue making way for the purest note.

She had widened her stance, her body a vessel for Christian perfection, and the minister penetrated the voices with his own call to glory and to God and that was when Ellen separated and that was when she saw. And it wasn't because Garland Mission's sermon stopped her on her path, reminded her that she was separate from the group at that camp, that she wasn't anywhere near Christian perfection (after all, she hadn't even spoken in tongues yet and many of Garland Mission's flock had done so several times already that day). It wasn't any of these things, though they had all happened. In that moment of separation, Ellen saw that the separation was what was false and that it was what Garland Mission banked on at his camp meeting and anywhere he stood at a pulpit bellowing for communion. The goal of Christian perfection depended on everyone present wanting it, not having it, not deserving it, deserving it more than the next person and on it went. In short, Christian perfection relied on Christian imperfection, and the Reverend Mission and hundreds of others like him were in the business of working with imperfection without acknowledging that there was no perfection inside their story. The tents, the people, the long grasses, the stinking bonfire, the wheeling hawks and springing grasshoppers. The moist earth and all that crawled on and in it. Ellen. They were all the same because they were part of one design. Who designed it wasn't even a question. The only question was *how to be.*

Ellen had stopped singing and closed her mouth. She pulled the Earth's radiance into her soles and up her calves and let it shine from her crown. A man threw a green log into the bonfire. It popped and sent a billow of putrid violet smoke her way. She absorbed the sharp sting and resolved not to sneeze; then she sneezed and coughed and let tears coat her face, grateful for this gift.

All of it she whispered into William's ear when he first embraced her outside Buck's Hotel on Minden's dusty Main Street the first time she saw him when she came north. All except the smoke. He'd hear plenty about smoke soon enough.

"Are you talking about marriage?" she asked to break Darius Horn's concentration. He lifted his other eyebrow and offered a smile. His cheeks folded readily, and she caught the appeal he must have to those who'd followed him. To Early.

"Mrs. Cook. I am a married man. Mrs. Horn wouldn't take well to your offer, but I'll spare her the gossip." He glanced across the bar at Early and continued. "Not to mention your own husband, perished this morning, with air in his lungs yet."

His voice lifted at the end to convey shock while he held his smile and raised brows to make it clear they'd entered a negotiation. Pain shot up the side of Ellen's neck. She massaged her jaw. William would have bartered with this same face, perhaps in this same chair at this hotel. Darius sucked on the pipe and blew streams of smoke from his nostrils.

"Naturally a man might see it the way you propose, Mr. Horn, my situation. As a matter of propriety and a concern for reputation and wagging tongues. Another, and perhaps I took you for same, might see my situation as one concerning property and protection, of what's valuable left in the open without shield. A woman without a husband in this part of the world – why, I can't think of an example to draw upon for guidance! Mr. Early, can this be?"

She addressed this last bit to Early, whose surname she knew full well was Badger. Early stood at the table, his hands on the back of a chair until she finished speaking. Then he sat beside her, sliding the chair away from the table to allow room to cross an ankle across a knee.

"Are you suggesting then, Mrs. Cook, that you have an interest in remarrying – that I should have an interest in your remarrying, because I can't fathom why –"

Early crossed his arms and looked from one to another. He opened his mouth, but Ellen spoke before he could say a word. "Think on it. A man confides in his wife, reveals to her what he knows, what he does. When they lie together in the fading light of a fire. What could a wife know? How best to convince her not to believe these secrets to allow them to rest as my husband and my daughter now rest, as if in a grave. My instinct tells me you'd like me to become the next Mrs. Early."

"The *only* Mrs. Early," Early blurted, flushing. "Mrs. Badger." He cuffed Darius's shoulder. "You was right."

A cowbell clanged as the door opened to let two men out, then clanged again as another man entered. Despite the cold air creeping across Ellen's chest and her forehead, she held herself still, willed herself not to glance at the man, the one who'd saved her from her morning faint.

Darius looked unconvinced, his smile having puckered into two punchy indents in the corners of his mouth. Yet he said, "You have it all figured out, Mrs. Cook. William mentioned you were smart, smart enough to know not to bother him with business. Yes, Mr. Badger would enjoy the opportunity to court you – but, isn't it too soon, really? Though if two souls are willing, far be it from me to come between."

Early laid his hands on the table, made to stand up. Darius stayed him with a hand on his arm.

"Let her speak, my friend. We must never assume."

At the bar, Ellen spotted the corner of a black wool coat with the brass buttons she remembered from the morning. Had he seen her when he walked in? Deciding to surprise Darius and Early with a bold, direct approach, she said, "There was a fire and it took Daddy and Safra, my baby."

"I didn't know William had a daughter," Early whispered.

Ellen adjusted her coat across her belly.

Darius frowned. "William spoke of her, yes. He mention a fire?" Darius pinched his bottom lip as if he were pondering a new idea.

"My hair stank of smoke, but I didn't mind. It helped me remember Daddy." Ellen held her smile as she whispered, "And her."

The men straightened. Early's gaze was a mix of admiration and confusion, his cheeks wide and the skin above his beard rubbery for a young man. She let the image of herself arriving in their town, smoke-stained and wild, set with them awhile.

"I saw a medium before I came here. I wasn't going to come, was all set to leave William to the bears and let my mama care for me and me for her until our times mercifully came. The medium though, she saw my daughter around me. She said it's like I've got a little smoke surrounding me and if you look carefully, in that smoke Safra is playing and dancing and singing to me."

She'd stood straight under the piteous rain of William's questions, even as he curled over and wept, sweat darkening his shirt, teardrops soaking the cuffs until she'd begged him to open his eyes and wipe the water away and see her. As long as Ellen held onto the light, as long as she drew it into her from the earth and sky, the vapours around her would remain strong, and her daughter would continue to dance. William had rubbed his eyes and stared, his head moving in little circles as he searched. Her belief didn't extend to him, not then, not ever.

Far from being baffled and put off by her story as Ellen had anticipated, Early watched her with a droopy gaze of satisfaction.

"My experience with the fire and the medium set me on a brave new path as a spiritual woman," she said. "Marriage is a sanctity."

Early nodded.

"Yet, I'm afraid you're too late, Mr. Early," she said. She stood and gestured toward Philip. "I intend to marry this man's father." Philip raised his beer glass but stayed seated. "The Reverend McCloud is a holy man and, as a spiritual woman, I believe my place is at his side."

She spoke at stage volume, though Philip appeared not to hear her even in such a full room, where the men at nearby tables turned their heads away from their friends to listen to her.

"Missus – please sit down and finish having a drink with us. Early and I will promise to put to rest this ridiculous talk of marriage whether to him or Reverend Benjamin or Joe the bartender or whomever on the day of your husband's death. You're distraught as are my man here and me. We know your husband and want to protect his name in his wake."

Darius held his hand behind the small of her back without touching her. Ellen let herself be guided down to her chair but not before she saw Philip's gaze shift to her. For a second she stared back, mutely asking him to stay.

"I'm grateful for your interest in me, I am, but I must say I'm confused. My husband didn't work for you. You had little occasion to get to know him, yet you arrive at our home to prepare his body and here we are at a hotel discussing marriage." Ellen inhaled Darius's smoke and fought back a sneeze.

Darius lowered his pipe and said, "Oh, your husband and I were great friends. I take an interest in your people. Having found it unusual to meet such a . . . a man in these parts, I made it my business to acquaint myself with him and we – I believe he would agree – became quite fond of one another. He was of great use to me and my business."

Ellen inspected his hands as he raised his pipe to his lips; the nail beds were buffed, the moons shone clear white. She thought about William's work at the sawmill, carrying logs, brushing away sawdust, all tasks requiring gloves that he kept in a satchel he hung on a peg at night. How had his nails gotten so dirty? Did Darius have him working after hours?

Ellen listened to Darius talk while sipping her beer as the server brought one more each to Early and Darius but not to her, as if the hotel had a policy of serving women one drink only. A sale was a sale, at least it had been back in Hamilton. William had come to this hotel many times with men from the sawmill, though he hadn't spoken names come to think of it, none except the name of Micheline's husband, who was there only when he came out of the lumber camp. Ellen wasn't familiar with the other men.

She'd smelled drink on William's breath and skin those late nights when he returned as the birds were waking, so he'd gotten the liquor from somewhere. Why was she thinking this way? She hadn't before.

Her faith experience had lifted her from her corrosive thoughts after the fire, and she sought its help in raising her now as she looked at the pouched, shadowy faces of Darius Horn and Early Badger and saw gravediggers or whoremasters or worse – whatever that would be – who'd ensnared her husband into their activities and possibly accelerated his untimely exit from life.

She took a long blink and pulled the white energy into her from the earth's core and sought the stream from the atmosphere above, allowing herself to sit in the spinning flow. In the past, she'd found that speaking her faith gave her the most powerful freedom from the dark matter in her brain. She'd spoken her faith to William and earlier today, Micheline, but the time had come to spread her truths widely, and she might do well to start with two non-believers.

"You go to Reverend McCloud's church, you and Mrs. Horn and your sons. I saw you there the time I attended with William."

Darius straightened in his seat and glanced at Early, who raised his brows and let his chin sink into his neck a tad. Darius nodded. Early echoed his nod and added a couple of extra nods for good measure.

"Yes, Mrs. Cook, William spoke often of his desire to have you with him at the Sunday services. He had a habit of setting his hat on the seat beside him as if he had the impression you might walk in late."

Early lowered his head, no doubt picturing William's spirit haunting the next service. Ellen wouldn't rule it out.

"Yes, well that time is behind us now," Ellen said. "I wouldn't have expected William to explain it, though I'm convinced that as time went on, he did understand my motivations. You see my faith changed before I came here. I've had visions that spoke to me of the true meaning of spirit and it's not what you think." *It's not what Reverend McCloud thinks either*, she thought.

Early scratched beneath his nose with a bent knuckle. Neither man said a word.

"We are all connected and what we call God is everywhere – it is inside us and outside us and we have the ability, the power, to feel its energy. There is no one god. I feel it all the time and I can increase the feeling when I want and I want to share this feeling with everyone, show everyone how to get close to it, where to find it outside and inside yourself. What Reverend McCloud is saying is a story that underneath speaks the same truths I know. The difference is that I now know how to get straight to those truths without the decoration of the story."

Without looking at her or at Early, Darius made a sound like a cross between a chuckle and a groan. "Did William put you up to this, Mrs. Cook? I mean, what an imagination if you've thought of these ideas yourself! Is this his idea of posthumous humour, to have his widow corner me with a slew of obscure magical notions she wants to pass off as religion? I doubt it. In fact, he took pains to speak only soft words for his wife, whose hardening of herself against the community and its house of worship was deliberate and obvious. He needn't have worried. Nobody in these parts will take these fancies seriously. If you're hoping to share this feeling, go ahead, but you'll find yourself even more alone, dancing in the forest with the deer. You've shared these thoughts with Reverend McCloud, and he offered to marry you? Well there's no accounting for taste, and some men do like a challenge."

Ellen hung her head for a second, then raised it, willing Darius to look her in the eye, but he wouldn't. His gaze danced over her face to her shoulders to Early and then to the table and finally into the depths of his amber drink. Ellen broke her stare to sweep the room in search of Philip, and there he was, standing at the bar facing the door. He smiled with the corners of his mouth turning down, a way of smiling that meant fondness and intent. Her breath quickened, the breaths small gusts, her chest rising and falling as she sat on her fingers.

"I appreciate your hearing me out, I do. A woman must freshen up from time to time. I wonder if you might direct me to the privy?" Darius nodded at Early, who turned around and pointed to the lamplit area beyond the stairwell. "Go past the bar and through that room to the door at the end." Early blushed, no doubt at the image of Ellen lifting her skirts to relieve herself.

She stood smoothly, careful not to brush anyone with her skirts, and walked behind the two men at the same time as Philip opened the door and the bone-white glare of sun on the street's packed snow flooded into the room. She slipped her body in front of Philip's and stepped quickly to the side of the door as Philip paused there, his broad-shouldered bulk filling the door in silhouette. He strode forward into the road and let the door fall shut behind him with a boom. He pointed to where his wagon and ponies waited, and she dashed in front of him to the side that faced the houses. His stride was long, and he soon reached her and helped her in, untied the ponies, took up the reins and snapped them. The ponies hesitated at the weight of an extra person, then swerved onto the road with a practised lurch. The door to the hotel stayed closed, the windows shaded by muslin curtains, no faces peeking out. She'd escaped.

RUDIE

Rudie was digging her thumb into the plastic paper towel wrapper when the knock came. They were early. She hadn't told Kikka about Barth and Hannah: she had hoped to bundle her mother out of the house on an errand or back to Toronto before she had to leave for the airport, but here they were. She hustled into the foyer. Her socks slipped and snagged, slowing her down. Kikka stepped on the top stair, asking, "Who is it?"

Rudie replied, "How should I know?" without thinking because she *did* know. She bounded up, held out the paper towel roll and, with a hand on Kikka's arm, urged her to head back to Roselore's room and clean.

Kikka lingered a moment then took the hint. *A first,* thought Rudie.

The door had a leaded-glass window that revealed one shadow, not two. Maybe Barth had come to tell her they didn't need a ride, didn't need her help. Relieved, she turned the key, letting the door swing open.

Dylan propped himself against the house with one arm. A shock ran through Rudie's hips and down her legs, leaving her so tired she wanted to sit down. She shut the door as much as she could while wedging herself against the frame.

"My mother's here," she whispered, jerking her head toward the stairs, though of course Dylan hadn't been inside this house, *hasn't ruined it,* she thought, without charity, though she could blame him for nothing. He pursed his lips, eyebrows raised in a naughty smirk, an expression she hadn't seen on him before, and she was certain of this because there was a time not long ago when she committed each expression of his, each moment he'd given her, to memory for the long years ahead. This conspiratorial move was not in his repertoire before, and it unhinged her. She caught his soapy bubblegum scent and tumbled into a memory from before – her cheek against his chest: their bodies entwined; his fine, firm skin – and of this morning's kiss, her mouth travelling down his neck. She blocked the entrance with her arm and said, "Wait on the street." Then she closed and locked the wooden door, fingers shaking.

"I'm going out again," she yelled, banking on the startle effect on Kikka of a raised voice. She pulled on her Sorels and down coat, wound her long, stripey scarf around her neck and wiggled the keys out of the lock. Kikka didn't answer, likely waiting for her to come upstairs to deliver the message face to face at a genteel volume.

—

Dylan stood on the corner where he studied the gingerbread trim on the last of their row of houses.

"You chose well," he said as she stopped beside him. She reflected on all the ways he might mean that comment. Her house? To meet with him? Leo? All of it, every choice? Her mind threatened fog. She squinted, though the sky was a pale, oyster grey. She followed his gaze down the row to the red house with the blue trim. Hers. Hers and Leo's.

"Yes, I suppose I did," she said. She resisted the urge to link arms with him, what she would have done with Leo.

A pang of weary loneliness for Leo entered her shoulders and made her shrug, then she masked her shrug as a hunch against the cold though she was warm enough. They walked toward James Street.

"She shouldn't see you," Rudie says. "My mother. I know it's not like anything's going on. My mother has a good radar for misadventure. Or at least she thinks she does. She sees it everywhere, even where it might not be. Then she reports it, she accuses, and the drama begins. I already have one parent emotionally AWOL. I need this one stable."

"Your dad's not around?"

"Yes. That too. He's emotionally gone, I mean." Her face grew warm as she stared down James Street toward Bob's pub. She didn't want to think about where Bob had gone. She didn't care if she ever saw him again. He was probably at home watching more curling.

Rudie's body thrummed as she turned south at Mission Services. "*Dylan*," she said, tasting the old thrill of saying his name out loud to his face.

He didn't answer, let his name hang between them.

"I haven't got much time. I have an errand, and then I'm straight to the airport. Why did you show up at my door?"

At the Persimmon Café, Rudie slid into a bench shaped like a pew. Maybe it was a pew. The high backs gave them privacy, though she couldn't see any other customers. Behind her hung burgundy velvet theatre curtains. The sunlight through the window lit up Dylan behind his right side, so she couldn't quite see the shape of his face. He looked as he might have in bed on a winter afternoon with the blinds closed and the slats flipped, and her heart thumped hard, her neck stiffening with fear at the possibility of remembering them together with him close enough to touch, indeed about to touch or having just touched or touching. She strained to make his features clear, then sat back and resigned herself to staring at his unfamiliar Gore-Tex pullover with occasional glances up to his eyes, the space so dark they'd turned as blue-grey as a snow cloud.

Dylan drank his Sleeman from the bottle. Rudie's stomach bubbled corrosively at her first sip of coffee, but then her shoulders relaxed as if into a hug. Her tongue craved the beer, but she'd already had one this afternoon with Bob. Nobody knew she was here yet. The H.A.S.P. people weren't due for another twenty minutes. Not enough time to go wildly off the rails and into a hidden corner clench with Dylan. She flinched, remembering a few of their final encounters after Leo was on the scene, including a mad and risky errand while Dylan's wife was working late, meeting Dylan in his car a block away from his house, two quick whiskeys at a chain steak house complete with free-ranging gropes outside the restroom and a sad, quick handjob in the parking lot. She made herself list out these flat details to remember the inflatedness and the despair, the false whirling and sucking loss that threatened to fling her around and pull her down but went nowhere but inside.

The happy times with Dylan, before the end, tucked away in the corners of their relationship, had felt pure. Rudie had believed in her connection to Dylan, had viewed it first as a sort of love and soon after as a true love that welled up from knowing the other's essence, outside of the social and from wanting and wanting and pointing oneself toward the North Star of that desire and being lit up, often enough, by that brilliance in return. That was Dylan and her at their heated, starlit best and the frantic heaving endings – for they had needed several leave-takings to get it right and to finally separate – had been about recapturing the energy of the middle of the thing before the ending had been spoken about and agreed upon and put into place. It was not accepting the deal. Shooting oneself in the foot. Entitlement. A tantrum, all that primal stuff and more. She'd stayed the course with Leo, though, and it was with Leo that she was adopting Roselore and she was glad for that. Though the mess of Dylan-want beckoned, she shouldered her happiness and bore up. "You know what? I'm getting a beer, too," she said, sliding out of the pew.

When she returned, Dylan squinted up at her. She smoothed her hair, lingering on her eyebrow.

"Your eyes," she said. He stopped her with a hand on the table between them.

"It's one eye. I got it checked out this morning. It's a one-off deal." He paused. She scrunched up her own eyes as if blinking free a dust speck. She didn't understand. He said, "The damage is done, won't get worse, won't get better. But that's not why I wanted to see you again today, though the sympathy is nice." They smiled as if in complicity. He didn't want her attention on his weakness. This conversation would be about her.

"It's something you said earlier. I can't shake it."

There went her heart again and that fear, like cold juice in her neck. She couldn't remember what she'd said. About Roselore? Barth? Had she flirted? She thought she'd kept her critical and her lustful thoughts to herself. She'd had to work at it but assumed she'd succeeded.

"About –" she started but then she shook her head. She didn't want to give him any ideas.

"You called me a storm chaser," he said. His pupils widened, one more than the other, making the blue of his eyes seem to darken. She opened her mouth as if to laugh then caught herself and sipped her beer instead.

"I resent it," he said.

Rudie fought the urge to check her watch. She'd made a point of putting it back on after washing dishes so she wouldn't have to hear Kikka comment on her chronic lateness. Kikka had made mention of it, saying, *Good thing you have that, maybe you won't miss your flight and miss adopting your daughter!* She'd laughed, her dark red lipstick making her gums look dark too. *If you have to say it's just a joke, then it's not*, Rudie imagined herself telling Leo later. Leo liked Kikka, but they did get a lot of mileage out of discussing her missteps.

The Hamilton International Airport was less than twenty kilometres from where she lived, so she could get there in fifteen minutes, though with traffic she'd allow for double the time. Once there, she'd need only half an hour to park, walk inside and check in – it was that small. She'd have to keep the meeting with the H.A.S.P. folks short so she could get home, lock up behind Kikka and pick up her bags, which held her ticket and papers and stood in the hall by the front door, and the car seat. If Barth and Hannah didn't show up by four, she would leave, hit the airport early and enjoy a Tim Hortons' apple cinnamon tea and chocolate dip donut while she waited.

Rudie worried now that the H.A.S.P. people would arrive early and catch her with Dylan. She wasn't sure how she should feel about that possibility. What she was doing shouldn't be wrong, but for some, her sitting in a café with a man who was not her husband was not right. Not to mention, saying she was having a drink – a drink! – with a man who had an affair with her before she met Leo, or *rather she* was having an affair with *him* when she met Leo, and the affair didn't end until after Leo and she had moved in together but before they got married and yes, *of course* before they started trying to have a child. And now they are having – *do have* a child. Roselore wouldn't have landed in Ottawa yet. Her flight had a layover in Atlanta – but she was theirs. But now, at this moment – okay the edge of her and her absent husband becoming parents – the long-held mutual dream coming true . . . here she was sniffing up against another long-held though much ignored and abandoned, but not forsaken, dream.

She didn't remember the names of the H.A.S.P. people. She didn't even remember the name of the leader who might show up today with them. She remembered nothing beyond the flood of what she and Dylan had done together in rooms. But these women – maybe some men? – would come any minute and Dylan wasn't drinking his beer, and she'd better finish hers and . . . storm chaser?

"I said that?"

"You did."

She swigged her beer and resisted the urge to wipe her lips with the back of her hand. Sitting here with Dylan was all about resisting urges, she decided. Though some might say she should have resisted her urges in the first place, saved everyone the pain. With Dylan, she altered her behaviour, mainly to impress him or rather, not invite his disdain. She didn't do that with Leo. And yet the Dylan-want thrummed inside her. Not so much now. In part because he sat across from her, but in part, too, because of Roselore. Rudie's cells raced in circles when she thought of Roselore. Hours. She would hold her hours from now. She wouldn't count. She'd rather engage herself in something else, then look up and realize it was time.

"You meant that I gravitate toward disaster in my work," Dylan was saying, "implying that, although you'll deny it, I'm exploiting those I document in their weak moments. Well, I take offence!"

Rudie hadn't heard anyone say that sentence before, although she got how he felt. She wished she'd had the gumption to say the same thing to her father. She had time yet. She giggled, stopped herself for a minute and then giggled again. Why should she restrain every impulse?

"You don't hear any truth in that?" she asked. She thought of the film he'd made of children amputated by landmines in the Balkans. The subjects, many of them the Roma people, were an itinerant ethnic group who lived outside traditional society in camps and had a reputation for stealing anything: money, valuable objects, children. They accrued children like pets, using them to rack up multiple welfare assistance funds. Dylan's film documented it all, his images often staged, his subjects set up on streets turned to rubble after an explosion as he filmed their unwashed, canny faces while they picked through the detritus, lifted televisions from broken picture windows or wrung the necks of chickens, the children as active in the thievery as the adults, the blond ones gleaming in the late afternoon light like bounty.

"There's a level of opportunism in your work," she said. "I haven't said it because I haven't had anything but praise for your work, but I do see it and others might say it."

"I don't care what other people say," he said, his colour high. "It matters to me what you think."

She set her beer down, the bottle empty except for foam. He hadn't touched his. She wanted his, but he wasn't Leo, who'd share, and she doubted Dylan would let her. He glanced at the bottle, then returned his gaze to her.

"It does?" she said and then regretted it, seeing that maybe it always had mattered to him what she thought. All along she believed that it hadn't, had heaped praise on his work, not just because she liked it and saw its worth, it was undeniable, but because she'd believed her opinion didn't really matter to him so she'd better make it a good one. She'd thought he wouldn't hear her otherwise but also, she'd been afraid of exactly this reaction, this anger at a criticism even from her. Maybe she'd been afraid of her opinion mattering, of the strength and power that it would give her and that it would take from her.

His anger invigorated her.

She soothed: "Who cares if people think you're a storm chaser? Art can provoke discussion – it *should*."

She ventured to compare herself to him, another threshold she hadn't crossed yet, having always taken on the mentee or underling position. Now she couldn't imagine why she had.

"People could criticize me as being opportunistic with Agnes Martin. In fact, you did. This morning. And you were right. But that doesn't mean those conversations and images and the questions they raised weren't worth documenting." Rudie felt freer now. It came to her that his imagined opinion, the silent voice of her own inner critic, had stopped her from finishing her film.

She had found Agnes as a subject by love and chance. Leo was the conduit. They were each at an artists' retreat in New Mexico to work on art forms they'd long since abandoned – she to write poetry, he to compose music. Her casita shared a wall with a saxophone player who picked up gigs at venues all over town, then came back to play his baritone until dawn. Rudie spent her days riding her bicycle, seeking out roads lined with trees, a relief from abundant sky. In New Mexico, she gorged on light but found she needed, daily, to have her face shaded by leaves, the trees reassuring her like parental bodies. She walked, too, her eyes rimmed with a stinging pain as if tiny jar lids were being screwed into her eye sockets. As the weeks accumulated, she acquired wavy lines in her vision and would stand transfixed for long minutes, watching a storm roll over the mountains, the sky lit up with lightning bolts like slices of sun. She refused to confront Manny, the sax player, who at six foot four towered over her, and instead took to wandering. She felt inspired: not to write poetry, her reason for coming to the residency, but to do something visual. The endless walks and rides would accrue moments until she was filled, and then she supposed she'd know how to shape or where to put them. She hoped they spilled out of her, that she could stand back as the poems took shape. As the days went by, she suspected not only that no poems were coming (she was right) but that she might have a bottomless desire for this place, one that no amount of walking and staring and riding and standing in the giant light would fill.

Leo had met her sneaking out her back door on a Sunday morning. Her aversion to confronting Manny had reached such an internal pitch that she'd erased herself as much as she could from her casita, closing the door softly, muting every noise. The louder he got, the quieter she got. The larger he was, the smaller she would be. Where he announced, she would blend. Not being seen became a compulsion, so she wouldn't have to confront the extent of his invasion in her life. She endured, and the more she covered herself and hid, the more sensitive and receptive and porous she became, so that the possibility of Manny's sax-playing threatened to remove her completely. As long as she avoided Manny, she became open to this place in a lovely, startling way. It was this person Leo met: Rudie flowering, Rudie unfolding, Rudie becoming transparent.

Their love had risen quickly and firmly, and they'd taken each other on. They didn't discuss the laying aside of the art forms that had brought them to that residency. Rudie viewed poetry now – the wish of poetry, specifically the collection she'd hoped to write there or shortly after – as her ticket. A ticket that had gained her admission to Leo and the world that followed. Leo had auburn hair and brown eyes. He wasn't tall like Manny and could hold his own with a violin. He considered jazz crass and ridiculous, couldn't listen to it, and insisted she should not only feel invaded but offended, artistically, by Manny's nocturnal efforts. "Nice try, Manny" was a favourite saying of Leo's muttered under the double-sized zebra-print duvet Rudie had bought at a thrift store, as they listened to Manny's aural exertions next door.

After that, Leo's violin stayed in its case, and Rudie's notebook in a drawer. She slept, though, either in a single bed with Leo, under the big duvet, or in his casita, which had a wooden-armed couch that, though narrow, offered more length and more options. Soon enough, they bought camping gear and took to the mountains. Residents weren't supposed to sleep together, but the land held no such restrictions. Rudie received Leo as readily as she did the sky and moved through each moment with the slow wonder of one in a dream, this lover as fleeting and permanent as the clouds and the hills.

Eventually, they got around to talking art. Both loved art and had carved out careers in the arts – Leo's description that Rudie had laughed at, thinking of her piecemeal work on craft tables and location scouts more as jobbing with a unifying theme in the film industry – he in New York City, she in Toronto. Both had painted, both played music, both wrote poetry. Leo, though, was a photographer and a cinematographer. When Rudie saw the pictures he'd taken since arriving at the residency, skies lit in Technicolor with clouds so rich they appeared pixelated or as if superimposed with a screen, she'd said, "Oh, Leo." He'd told her later that was when he chose cinematography – he didn't think photography could offer him anything more after the joy of her response. She liked to think he'd fallen in love at that moment, but knew there was no moment for them, there was no fall, just enough time between them to see that they were in love.

Her mention of the screens she saw overlaying his landscape photos (shouldn't he have been composing music? Like her poems, his songs had remained in his head) prompted a conversation about grids and the structures underlying art and even the notion of planning a work before beginning. They were walking along an unlit street, their voices meeting in pure darkness when he'd said, "There's a woman you need to know."

"You could say you've been a storm chaser with me," Rudie said. Her remark felt smart. She loved the term *whip smart* though she wouldn't call herself that. Nobody would. Too many emotions under the surface, their currents holding her back.

Dylan blinked. His silence and the blinking felt aggressive.

"I'm the storm," she said.

"I get it," Dylan said. He rested his head on the straight back of the bench at an awkward angle. He touched his right cheek. A scar arced from the corner of his right eye across his temple. Yet his left one had lost the vision, she remembered. Or did she? This morning felt like a vacation she'd taken several seasons ago.

"I mean, you have the image of an intelligent, creative, groundbreaking artist who plays within the elite structure," she said. "You're drawn to chaos. You have insurrection in your heart but you like to maintain the status quo. Like with your wife – when I wanted you to leave her, you wouldn't, even though we had such an intense connection. Obviously, you guys broke up eventually, for whatever reason."

"*You* left *me*," he said.

"You're right," Rudie said. She had been thinking of Agnes, of how finding her and asking to film her was a distinct sort of chase. Agnes had been dying. Rudie saw it after she returned to Toronto, but she should have seen it at the time. Wasn't dying a quiet spectacle?

She met Dylan's eyes and they stared, he into her, she as if at the ocean. He touched his cheek again. It was Roselore she thought about. She wanted to ask him what he knew about Haiti. A band of excitement tightened around her hips. Dylan bumped his head in reaction to the change in her body language.

"Don't you have –" he said.

She shifted, cracking her knee on the underside of the plywood table.

"H.A.S.P.!" she said.

"Bless you," he said, the way she imagined he would say, I love you.

"It's the adoption support group," she said. "I went a few weeks ago, once we knew about the match, and they've agreed to an emergency meeting – adoption triage, they call it. They're good at it, so they say. But maybe you should . . . I should be alone when they get here." She checked her watch. It was two minutes to one. "Which is now," she said, her voice rising. "They'll get here now, or soon."

Dylan had his coat on and was easing a glove over his wrist. "You'll do fine," he said, his words resonant with care. "You will make a beautiful life."

She stopped rummaging and slid herself to the edge.

"Don't get up," he said. "We'll see each other soon."

"Yes, we will," she said, only now aware of the panic she felt at his leaving the coffee shop. She *had* left him, but she hadn't wanted to go. Now his walking out the door into his life with the broken eye and busted marriage without her or any hope of her – she suspected he wanted to have hope of her, and she hadn't given it to him – felt like a push out the door of a flying airplane and all she had to do was pull the release pin on the parachute. Minutes from now she'd tell the group about Roselore, then she'd be off up the escarpment – possibly with Hannah and Barth in tow – and then to the plane. He was erasing himself, and he'd gotten to her. She did stand up to give him a long, friendly hug, but when she raised her head, her eyes had tears and his right eye was wet and she said, "Oh all right. Let's finish this conversation later. Ride up to the airport with me if you can spare the time. We'll work out what it will take to stay friends."

Rudie stared at a lemon whoopie pie in the display case as she waited in line for a toasted marshmallow hot chocolate. One day soon, she would make hot chocolate and popcorn for Roselore, and they would watch Disney movies. Her pulse pounded around her ears. She should order chili or a bagel with cream cheese, feed herself protein, but she wanted sugar. She wanted to be the kind of mom her daughter found fun. Yet from what she'd learned in the adoption course and from what she and Leo had talked about over the years, their goal with Roselore was safety and attachment. They would weave entertainment and treats into their daily lives but not for the sake of fun. *Ugh.* She hated thinking this way. She suspected so did Leo, who had called dibs on being good cop if they went the good cop, bad cop style of parenting. It didn't mean she couldn't indulge herself. She'd gone in and out of indulging herself her whole life. She blamed stress. She couldn't even fathom ordering chili right now – the thought of cheese or kidney beans turned her stomach. She liked to think she was having the adoptive parent's version of birthing pains, only more private and internal. Cravings too. People encouraged an expectant mother (well, she was expecting, wasn't she?) to give in to her cravings. Why shouldn't Rudie? She ordered a mocha brownie and returned to her seat to await its delivery.

As soon as she sat down, two women in shapeless down coats with polar fleece toques walked over to her. She hadn't seen them before, but then she was terrible at noticing her surroundings and remembering faces, had told herself that she'd chosen poetry and then film to counteract exactly that tendency. One of the many aspects of her Agnes film that she loved was the specificity of Agnes's language and art despite its surface vagueness and opacity. The harmony of her grids, the way the pencilled line made itself known in even her most sensual work, spoke to an impulse to tame or regulate or communicate, the way a musical score endeavours to capture a symphony.

"Hi!" said one of the women, who'd tucked her hair inside a white hat. When Rudie didn't answer right away, she said, "I'm Gabby. We spoke on the phone." Rudie tended to love what toques did to people's faces, reducing them to nobs and pouches, their eyes holding full meaning.

Rudie didn't recognize the other woman, who smiled, her

lavender cheeks enormous: round, high and wide. The two women looked at one another then sat, pulling off their coats and hats and scarves and pushing them ahead of them as they slid along the bench seat across from Rudie. With her hat off, Gabby looked familiar.

"Did we meet at the H.A.S.P. meeting? It's coming clear," Rudie said.

Gabby nodded. "I think we did."

Rudie made to stand, then stayed there, knees bent, bum against the back of the bench seat until both women were sitting. Her hot chocolate and the brownie, which was the size and density of a thick leather wallet, appeared. Rudie said, "Thank you," in the direction of the waitperson who'd slipped away before Rudie could register her. A moment later two black coffees arrived. Gabby and the other woman eyed Rudie's brownie.

"You didn't get a fork."

"Or three forks!"

"Oh, I shouldn't," said the one with the cheeks. Her black shoulder-length hair softened her face, giving her an intense overripe prettiness.

"Just this once. It doesn't count if you share."

Rudie lifted the brownie and bit off a corner. "You should get one," she added, her mouth full. "They're organic."

Gabby laughed, and the other woman looked down. Cheered by the sugar, Rudie extended her clean hand. "Rudie," she said. "I haven't met you yet."

"Kaycee, and you *have* met me. I was at the last meeting. But there were so many of us. It's exciting when a new little one is coming." Kaycee took Rudie's hand and clasped it in both of her own. She had tears in her eyes. Rudie flushed, moved. No stranger had reacted this way to her news, certainly her family hadn't, not even Kikka. She wondered how it would feel if both her parents had embraced her decision with this level of love and care. The tears she'd felt coming stopped, and she withdrew her hand.

"We know you haven't much time," said Gabby. "How can we help?"

Rudie forgot all of the ways in which she and Leo had agreed H.A.S.P. could help. Leo had suggested she ask for this meeting. She'd rather be running around the city right now, Dylan in tow, picking up items for Roselore in a waking dream of the first days of motherhood. She remembered Bob.

"How did your families react to your adopting?" she asked. "Because mine –"

Gabby and Kaycee looked at each other, smirking.

Kaycee said, "Mine was fantastic. We're close and we're religious so adoption is considered a blessing. My son's feet barely touched the floor from everyone holding him for months after I came home."

"What about bonding?" Rudie asked. She didn't like the idea of her mom and dad carrying Roselore everywhere. Not to mention Leo's mother, who, thankfully, was unlikely to set foot outside of Manhattan at her late age.

"Oscar was a newborn. Bonding is different then," Gabby said. "Your daughter is four?"

"Two." Rudie was thrilled to hear someone say "your daughter." She wanted Gabby to say it again.

"Attachment will be a big deal then. Not impossible, by any means, but important."

Rudie nodded. She didn't want to tell them about Bob. What he'd said was so unforgivable, she squirmed at the thought of others noting his shame. They didn't know him. Complaining about him here, though safe, felt like a betrayal. She looked at Gabby.

"My family, it didn't matter," Gabby said. "They're in New Brunswick. It's a big family. They'd come by, if they made it out here, pinch our daughter's cheeks, give her a toy and head home. There are so many grandchildren, nobody can keep track. Adopted or not, didn't matter. We're not close. How they react could make a difference in a closer family. Is it a problem in your family?"

Rudie wasn't a fan of direct questions. She often blurted out an answer, conditioned by politeness, then crawled with regret later, having revealed what she'd rather not. Yet, she was the one who'd invited Gabby and Kaycee to come here. She'd intended to ask for child care tips, but maybe she needed to resolve this issue more.

"My dad doesn't want to be her grandfather because she's black."

Neither woman spoke so Rudie continued in a rush. "And now my mom is telling me we have a black relative or my dad does way back and that he has internalized racism or self-rejection and he won't even talk to me and all I can think of is she's a little girl and she doesn't deserve this and I wonder, am I really up to the task of being her mother if I can't confront this stuff with my dad?"

Rudie shivered and twisted with revulsion and longing, two emotions linked surprisingly often for her. She thought of Dylan. Why hadn't she told him any of these feelings? She had put them away while they were together. What was true about him, then, was true about her, too. She did use compartments to manage the different parts of her life. She wasn't integrated. It hit her that *integrated* was how she would describe Agnes at the end and part of what had drawn her to Agnes's work in the first place, the possibility of wholeness and spirit. Rudie had lived a fragmented life, Dylan in her back pocket, Leo on her arm. Writing poetry then filming a documentary, her work itself in pieces, segments of the interview and shots of the desert and Agnes's paintings waiting for Rudie to edit them together into a unified story. Could the child be the key to making her life whole? She anticipated a falling away of everything that wasn't Roselore.

"Hersh and I did come up against a similar problem with Oscar. His birth mother had no declared religion."

Rudie scratched her head. "Your family didn't reject him?"

"Oh no! He's as Jewish as the rest of us. We took both boys to Israel last year. But Oscar had to do a conversion ceremony. In a couple of years he'll have his bar mitzvah and he can choose."

Both women looked at Kaycee, who leafed through a set of papers. "You must have talked about this with your adoption worker. We all had to take a training course. There was a section on adopting a child of another race," she said without looking up.

"We're mindful of the challenges," Rudie said. "As we all are." She raised an eyebrow at Gabby. "It's how to best take care of her in those early weeks that worries us."

"There's nothing here about grandparents. They're not the most important. You're the mother. *You're* the one."

"If I'm estranged from my father – though I'm not, he's the one who's estranged, estranged from his granddaughter – won't it be harder to attach to her with that between us? Knowing she's not fully accepted into the family? We have to make him see. He's seen her photo. What more can I do?"

"Don't worry about it," Kaycee said.

"That's easy for you to say when it's not your problem." Rudie rubbed the skin behind her ear. "I'm sorry. I don't mean to be mean. I wanted you to talk me down from my disorganized, freaked-out state. It's all happening so quickly. I've got nothing ready for her."

"Nobody does! It's normal."

"Not for me. I mean, yeah sure I'm often not prepared for things, but I had it planned how ready I'd be for when she came and I thought I had until June. There's no furniture and we're in the middle of renovating our bathroom. My husband is away working. He'll probably have to go back soon after we get home."

"We could, you know, we could maybe . . ." Kaycee said.

Gabby frowned and swiped her cellphone.

Rudie took her own out, swiped it, too. Her mind flashed names at her: Roselore, Leo, Dylan. She searched for the names of the street kids. The girl was Hannah. The boy had a literary name. Salinger? Kerouac? Huckleberry? She had her plane ticket tucked into the side pocket of her rolling suitcase, zipper closed. She couldn't see the sky from where she sat, but a line of shadow from a hydro wire bisected a corner of the lit-up street. Somewhere in the sky the sun had come out.

Rudie patted the bench and lifted her coat until she found her hat. She lined up the seam and lifted it over her forehead, settling it so it covered her ears.

"You haven't shown us a picture," Kaycee said. Gabby had her wallet out and flipped open before Rudie could answer.

"Here are my two. Get used to it, Rudie. It's what we moms do."

Kaycee moved her head sideways slightly, but she smiled without looking at Gabby's wallet. "You must carry it," Kaycee said. "When the worker sent me a picture of Destinee in a pair of red corduroy overalls and a Winnie the Pooh turtleneck, Pete couldn't tear me away from it. The printout is still in my purse!"

Rudie wanted to see that printout of Destinee in her overalls more than she wanted to admire the snaggle-toothed, long-necked boys in Gabby's ordered wallet. She yearned to take out her own photo of Roselore but hesitated to put her daughter on display. Keeping the image to herself held Roselore inside Rudie and Leo's dream for a few hours longer. After her dad's rejection, Rudie couldn't bear even a raised eyebrow or worse, a sugary exclaim of *How cute!*

Kaycee handed over a printout as loved and worn as Rudie's photo of Roselore. Baby Destinee had tiny sprays of reddish gold hair caught in a ponytail in the middle of her head. Rudie's eyes brimmed with tears. She clutched her purse to her side.

"It's okay to be scared," Kaycee said. "I had this photo for two weeks before I met Destinee and I kept it folded in my bra. I wouldn't show anyone at work; I don't know, maybe I thought they'd recognize her and take her away or ruin it somehow. I get it. It's so fresh and all you want to do is get on that airplane and find that baby and hold her tight."

—

Rudie buttoned her collar to the top and tugged her toque down over her ears. She usually didn't mind the cold, but this afternoon it nipped at her ears and neck. She moved quickly along the street, sidestepping ice slicks and snow heaps, turning her hips sideways and ducking into doorways to let others pass. She held her smile wide, nodded at familiar vendors, the men in the Portuguese café, two elderly women shuffling along arm in arm, rubber boots zipped over their shoes, their cheeks pale even in this cold. She regretted, mildly, not having stroked Agnes's cheek or even held her hand. Her camera had loved the gleaming pine-toned skin. Agnes had worked outside in the desert for decades and had spent as many of her final days in the sunlight as she could.

Seeing Dylan reminded Rudie of a place inside her she had long forgotten. She wasn't sure if it was there anymore. She used to long for him; marrying Leo had tempered that longing. It must have stopped sometime because she was remembering it now, not feeling it. She supposed she could call it up, yet she'd still be aware that she was trying too hard. Even the songs that used to throw her into that stream (The Cure's "Pictures of You"; Bob Dylan's "Not Dark Yet") no longer affected her. When had the change come? She'd met Agnes in the throes of that pining (Leo, too) and had thrown herself into her film from that place of sad desire and loss. Was she trying to release the pain? Prolong it? Run from it or into it? Or was Agnes another facet of it? Her longings found a different sort of home in Agnes: to immerse herself in creating as Agnes had done, to live alone and free under the desert sky, to have a life driven by purpose and to have made a great life. To find faith. Though she didn't wish for old age – in fact, though Rudie wanted to live a long life, the deterioration shocked her so much she denied it – she yearned to grasp its wisdom. But why? What did she need to know? How to live better now? Something like that.

She stopped at Cannon, the toes of her sneakers bending over the edge of the curb as a bus sped past. West of her, a black woman shook out a bundle buggy, patted a plaid bag into place and approached James Street. Rudie remembered a roti shop around the corner. Though not specifically Haitian, roti was Caribbean and maybe she could discover a local restaurant where she could take Roselore. She turned on her heel, knocking the bundle buggy with her foot as the woman passed behind her on the tight corner.

"Sorry!" Rudie said. She tapped the woman's coat sleeve and reached to adjust the buggy. The woman nodded and said, "Don't worry about it," her voice hushed and friendly. Rudie stepped back, resisting the urge to keep helping, wondering if her actions revealed a hidden bias. The woman was smiling, and Rudie had caught the hint of a Jamaican lilt in her words. Rudie let out a deep breath and smiled back. Sometimes a human exchange was merely that. Nevertheless, Rudie did squirm a bit inside her jacket, the fabric feeling suddenly uncomfortably tight as the woman continued on her way.

The red and black stripes of Rudie's scarf swam across the glass of each store she passed, the sun low and weak but showing itself. She trotted now, halfway to the roti shop. She didn't have time for detours. Ann Hepner had stressed the importance of traditional food for Roselore. Rudie had expected to learn more about Haitian cooking on their trip in June, so she hadn't devoted as much time as she could have to learning about what Roselore was used to eating. With the sun out, the pavement had turned wet and dark. Rudie watched for a break in traffic, then dashed across the street. At the next corner, she turned. The shop was there. She hesitated; she tended to avoid small, new places without Leo around. Today, she could bump into a black woman on the street and breeze away with a light "Sorry," but what about tomorrow, with Roselore in her stroller? What sorts of comments would the woman have? They might start a friendship. Rudie opened the door and walked into a room ripe with roast meat and curry smells. Rudie's stomach gurgled. Dubstep played on a small radio and fluorescent lights made the room seem warm. Two men worked in the kitchen a few feet away; a short woman with beaded braids that brushed her shoulders worked the cash. Everyone wore a red T-shirt.

"Do you sell Haitian food?" Rudie asked.

"It's all roti," a man said. He came forward, wiping his hands on a towel tucked into his waistband.

"Is there a Haitian roti?"

She was about to explain further when the man asked, "What, you having Haitians for dinner?" Both men laughed and Rudie joined in too.

"Something like that," she said.

"She's got a Haitian boyfriend then," the front man said to the one in the kitchen. The woman leaned on her hand, looking down with a smile.

"Oh, nothing like that! Think what you want," Rudie said. "I'm interested in Haitian food. I'd love some roti, though. What's your best?"

"It's all best, but since you ask, take the chicken. Next time try goat, then oxtail and you see what you like."

The woman raised her eyes, and Rudie nodded. "Get working then, Sammy," she said, and Sammy headed back to the kitchen. "Might as well have a seat," the woman said. "He makes it from scratch."

Rudie swiped her phone but had no messages. The H.A.S.P. people would question why she hesitated to tell these strangers in the roti shop about her daughter. She wondered herself, too. After today, she doubted she'd reach out to H.A.S.P. again. Even though Kaycee's words had comforted her, they were dealing with very different issues. The meeting she'd gone to had featured a speaker who specialized in international adoptions and though he'd had some fine suggestions, the parents in the audience had all adopted girls from China. They had formed a tight local network and took their children to Saturday Mandarin classes and Chinese New Year celebrations in Toronto's Chinatown. Rudie had asked how local Chinese people responded to their families. One woman said they'd taught their daughter to greet them in Mandarin, and all had been very respectful. If she was alone with her daughter, people assumed that she was married to an Asian man. Another woman had said it was the white people she needed to worry about more. They were the ones with the nosy questions and judgments and worries. Rudie had her list of responses folded in her wallet. Roselore would go to a French immersion school, but they would have to connect with Haitian culture. Rudie studied the woman's braids and saw they weren't braids at all but evenly rolled dreadlocks. Rudie would have to learn what to do with Roselore's hair. The picture had her hair twisted with bright red ribbons all over her head. Someone must have tied them. Danielle, probably. They were tight and beaded and prettily done. Rudie hoped Roselore liked having her hair touched. She herself had screamed whenever Kikka came within a foot of her with a brush and had earned herself a pixie cut for most of her childhood.

When the man came out with a roti the size of a dinner plate wrapped in foil, Rudie lifted the soft, warm package. "It's for my daughter," she said. "She's going to love this."

Two men stood on the sidewalk, their mouths closed. One looked at the ground. At the top of the stairs, Kikka leaned with her hand propped against a box in front of the porch window. She nodded at Rudie, who was chewing her final bite of roti, and kept talking. When Rudie got closer, the shorter man stepped over to her with a clipboard.

"Don't sign it," Kikka said. "By law they're expected to carry the item into the designated room."

The man met his partner's gaze and shook his head. "Not our instructions, Ma'am," he said.

"It is a regulation. I should know," Kikka said. In Leo's khaki parka, she resembled a kitten dressed by a child.

"This must be the bed from Thingamees," Rudie said. "I have people to move it. I don't mind."

"What people? Your father's not here, not to mention your husband."

"Snap. Like you have to broadcast it?"

"Your neighbours have eyes. They know you're home alone. Except when you're having visitors."

Rudie thought of Hannah and Barth knowing she had a car, then remembered Dylan. She took the clipboard.

"The pen's attached," said the shorter man.

Kikka trotted down the stairs, her burgundy nails hovering above the icy railing. "Rudie, think a minute. If you sign for it and don't have help to take it inside, the bed could get ruined out here and you'd have no recourse. Or stolen. You won't be here to protect it."

"So now you're telling the world I'm going on a trip?"

Kikka's face pinked.

"In case you are thieves," Rudie said to the short man, "you know my solitary and wayward habits. Why don't you just take the bed away?"

The taller man, who was young and wore ironed jeans, said, "You want we should return them? You don't want buy?"

"I'm joking, for my mother's benefit." Rudie signed the form, shaking as if to rid herself of Kikka, who held her hands out as if she were surfing to balance in her heels on the ice.

"Aaah," both men said in unison. "Funny lady," said the young one.

"Always one with the jokes," Kikka said. "My daughter grows on people."

"My mom was just leaving. Thank you," Rudie added, looking each man in the eyes. "I appreciate you hauling the box up the steps."

The men smiled as Rudie took Kikka's arm and led her back into the house. "I thought you had to get back to Toronto."

"I wanted to make sure you were on track."

"I am. It's, what, after two o'clock. I have some private movers coming and it'll be easier if you're not here."

"Do you mean that?" Kikka stood inside the door, eyes dampening.

"It's not a rejection of you. You know I work better alone.

I'm a loner."

"You said you have movers. Do you mean that man who came here earlier?"

"Not him. Well, maybe him. He offered to help. But no, some young people. Full of energy."

"Not like me," Kikka said.

"What are you talking about? You have more energy than anyone I know."

Kikka unzipped Leo's coat, and it slid to the floor. Both reached for the hood, and they struggled until Kikka let go, saying, "Fine."

"I'd like a bit of time to straighten out my office, pack up the car."

"You're working? When you have no time left?"

"I have time. Mom, I'd like to do the things I need to do without you questioning me."

"Is this about your father, about what I told you?"

"What? No. I wasn't thinking about that just now." In truth, her father's rejection of Roselore and the information about her great-great-grandmother had rumbled through Rudie's thoughts all afternoon. On the way home from the roti shop, she had passed another black woman putting a loonie in the parking meter and wanted to embrace her, weeping.

"You met her once, you know. She was almost one hundred years old. Your father's grandparents, Beryl and Jonas, took care of her. Do you remember?"

"I suspect I was a baby? So, no."

"Powerful woman, like a stone in the middle of a family of wildfires. And she loved you. You had that dark straight hair even as a baby. She loved how it shone. She thought you were an old soul, that you would change the world with your power. And here you are."

Kikka stared at her, eyes bulging, her mouth slightly open, as if surprised at her own words. She'd given Rudie such gifts all her life, statements from other people about her powers and her strengths but she'd tended to stop the flow of any information that came from Bob's side of the family, leaving it to him.

Rudie concentrated on undoing her laces. She had the vaguest memory of Beryl and Jonas and didn't remember her dad's great-grandmother at all. She wished she did. She'd liked to have filmed her, to have blended her story with Agnes's. If Rudie made it to that age someday, Roselore would be older than Rudie was now. They wouldn't get to know one another into old and middle age, the way Kikka and Rudie likely would. Was her dad's great-grandmother Rudie's connection to Roselore? She yearned to touch base with her film one last time before the journey began. Hannah and Barth would arrive in less than an hour. Rudie took her mother's coat down from the hook, nudged her boot with her own toe.

"I'll kick you out if I have to, Mama. Let me call you tomorrow. Maybe you can talk to Roselore on the phone."

Rudie surveyed the house. Dust motes hung in sunbeams muted by streaked windows. Piles of extension cords, papers and file folders fell over in corners. Balled socks and crumpled wrappers littered the kitchen floor along with broccoli chunks, toast crumbs and the great, expanding, sticky spilled-coffee patch. She squatted to imagine how the room would look to a toddler. She and Leo should hire a cleaner – or Kikka! – to prepare the house before they returned. She loved a clean house, but the daily actions required to have one escaped her. They'd cleaned for the home inspection in the fall and tidied for Christmas but had done nothing since then, especially since Leo, the neater of the two, had left on his shoot three weeks ago. She needed to turn her mind to it, find a system. Put away five items in each room, then move onto the next until all were completed and then start again, set everything in its place and then clean, top to bottom, left to right. Systems worked for her; she used them in her film, too, her version of Agnes's grid. She'd broken the film down into ten segments, roughly five minutes each, so it would come in under an hour. An organization called W.A.A. (Women in the Abstract Arts) was funding the film and had suggested strong interest from American public television, not to mention the possibility of licensing it to various art galleries as part of exhibitions involving Martin's work.

She'd made other rules for herself too. Before shooting, she'd shaved her head, a move that delighted Agnes and may have resulted in some of the more candid moments in the interview. Leo hadn't minded either, though under the intense New Mexican sun, she had to cover her scalp with pretty crocheted hats. She'd talked as little as possible, going against her instincts, waiting long minutes sometimes for Agnes to link one thought to the next. And she'd refused to interview Agnes sitting down. They'd walked through Taos and through Agnes's apartment; they'd walked along a field-lined road and on the banks of the Rio Grande. They'd followed Agnes up the stairs to the octagonal room at the Harwood Museum designed to hold her work and filmed Agnes moving from one painting to the next, musing.

In a favourite sequence, Rudie had captured Agnes preparing a canvas for a painting she'd ended up not finishing. There, Agnes's focus had changed; she pulled the energy of the room into herself and gave nothing out, like a machine stretching the canvas, then dividing it into tiny perfect squares. Rudie disliked the word *machine* and had sought others that might serve as thematic links. She'd settled on *spirit.* In relation to her work, Agnes had distilled herself down to her essence, an essence that needed only its materials to communicate itself. Minutes after Agnes died, Rudie had yearned for that final canvas, to study its grid as if, perhaps, to inhale the source of that essence, as if it lingered in the thing Agnes had most recently made, as if it were consumable. When she'd later watched the footage of Agnes that day, she'd wept at the light angling into the room and making a square on the floor close enough to Agnes that it bleached one of Agnes's shoes and the cuff of her jeans. The rest of her stood in relative shadow, even her white hair reading as sand-coloured without the sunlight directly on it.

Rudie put the lunch plates in the sink and tossed a handful of socks down to the basement. She swept the kitchen floor, then moved into the living room where she picked up an armload of file folders before drifting over to her desk. She'd backed the film up on a key and had multiple versions stored in her Mac, one for each day she'd worked on it. She hadn't filled in some of her grids yet. Away from the film, ideas rushed her, but in its presence, she floated, unable to speed up her process. It took as long as it took. Leo had even given up asking how far along she was. W.A.A. hadn't contacted her in months either. She didn't have to pay them back if she didn't finish, though she doubted she'd get the chance to make another film. Maybe with Dylan, but Leo wouldn't go for that.

She drifted her hand over the keyboard, piled the papers on the floor and patted around her desk for a static-free cloth. Messy as she was, she was ritualistic about cleaning her screen and keyboard before using them. She had no time to look at her film. Besides, sometimes when she watched it, she fell asleep; other times, like today, it absorbed her, making her brain zing. Putting a camera into her daughter's hand; showing her this film; taking her on a shoot, hers or Leo's; holding her holding her holding her. Rudie had many chores to do, but nothing would make the time between now and leaving to meet her daughter sweeter than showing herself this film. She shook the cloth out and folded it back into its case. She pushed the H key. Her screen glowed with the image of a sapphire blue square shot through with cornflower cloud wisps demarcated by a dotted-line grid, the effect like a tiny quilt of the sky: Agnes Martin's *Starlight*.

AGNES

Agnes and Lenny were half a mile from the canyon and had been walking along the main road only a few minutes when the first eighteen-wheeler blew past them. They stood their ground. The speed and movement of the truck thrilled Agnes, who liked to stand close to train tracks for the same reason. Another truck came and then another. They stopped for the first few, the cold blast of wind, the rush of sound. The boy smiled sideways at her, and she smiled back with a shrug.

"Let's try it backwards," he said. He turned to face the fields, then tugged her sleeve until she followed suit. Snow and dirt stretched in rippled waves to treed hills. As the truck approached, Lenny closed his eyes so Agnes did too. When the truck drew near, Agnes opened her eyes and took in everything – the ditch, the fence, the field, hill and sky. When the wind blast came along with the roar of engine and wheels, she said, "Pretend it's an ocean," as if what lay before them pulsed with movement, energy and sound. Hearing her, the boy dashed forward, knees high and arms wide as if the frozen ditch were a white, sandy beach. Clouds covered the sun, then drifted away, making parts of the field sparkle like gems.

He's so innocent, John's voice said. Agnes's sinuses prickled, and tears warmed the rims of her eyelids. She closed her eyes into slits, so all she could see was the black rubber of her boot. She didn't feel stuck. The trucks sounded like far-off combines working the frozen earth. Then she opened her eyes again, expanded. This was joy, this looking at nothing spectacular, and nothing more than what it was, even the boy. Especially him. Everything else fell away, and she could stare for hours with interest, the way she'd long hoped for people to engage with her work.

She wouldn't call herself a nature lover, though she felt best when outdoors. This joy came from inside her, lived inside her. This snowy desert field could be anyplace, that was the point, and this joy would persist – or not. It was a moment, like everything else, and it would pass, like the trucks, like her time with Lenny. "Come along, boy," she called. She turned to walk again, stopping the moment as it began to wane. The boy ran alongside her in the ditch. Six magpies that were perched on the wire ahead of them lifted in unison and flew over the field.

The walking came smoothly to Agnes now, not in a laboured onslaught as it had when they first left the canyon. Agnes walked the way she breathed as if to move was to rest. She heard her footsteps, the pulpy crush of mud and frozen dirt, the crows calling high up and far off, the occasional whoop from the boy, and she carried the shine of joy from a moment ago.

They didn't have many landmarks to go on, but they had passed the Circle Ranch in the truck, so Agnes's land was down the next line, not a far walk at all, if only Jesu would happen to drive past. She pictured his orange truck, wondered if it would sound distinctive to her.

She wished for sunglasses, squinted to see if she could spot anything coming the other way. Which birds were wheeling in patterns high up across the field? she wondered.

The Line had disappeared for a while and now, here it was again. Had it been waiting all along or had she conjured it? It pulsed stronger than ever – a vision, a certainty, a map – confirming what she'd long believed: that one needed to stay alone to paint. The people rampaging through her day only broke the Line and Agnes's connection to it. First, Jesu, then Marsha, then Julie and Shilah. And the cop.

But not Lenny. At least, not anymore.

Remembering how she'd painted when she was younger wasn't easy to do. She'd had a routine. She'd said no to many rooftop parties and gallery openings and all-night carouses so she could stay in shape to paint. She didn't regret having done so, not then and not now. The parties were appealing only if one threw oneself into the stream full-throttle. Agnes didn't enjoy the wreck of a body (not to mention mind) she woke up with after drinking wine. The men around her, and many of the women, didn't care, but Agnes needed a steady course to live, let alone paint.

The routine had changed but had carried its rituals forward, the lighting of a candle, the playing of a Chet Baker LP, the empty stomach. How had she decided what to paint? Visions had come to her then as well, but the Line itself was recent.

It hadn't plagued nor tempted her until today. Agnes's chest and shoulders tightened with joy at the thought of following that line to its natural end, which she would, and soon. She didn't know what she would paint, but *she would paint* and that knowledge felt like enough. Perhaps she'd paint joy.

Her last show had opened ten years ago. In the nights leading up to the opening, paintings had streamed from her brush. She was living in Manhattan in her studio on Coenties Slip at the time, five storeys above the river, the long windows so close she could see the expressions on the sailors' faces. That week, though, she'd stopped looking out or in and had purely acted, her body in constant motion, engaged with the canvas, brush and paints. She remembered the flow, but there had to have been more to it than the making – a thought or a plan? – and she couldn't remember the vision. Had she always acted purely on intuition? Was that all the Line was? She'd slept in that studio, on a loft bed she'd built in the centre, a ship on the sea of her coloured canvases, the oils both intoxicant and soporific.

Their gaits steady, Agnes and Lenny reached the corner of her road, Agnes's body eagerly throwing itself forward in the rhythm of walking. She'd walked everywhere in New York, her body at its best immersed in slow movement. Lenny had found a stick that he ran along the fence wires and posts as he kept pace with her several feet away in the ditch. At the gas station that morning, Lenny left Sandra's café before Agnes. Coming outside, she'd screwed up her eyes, taking in the sunlight reflecting off car mirrors and bumpers, the gas tanks, strips of snow on the road's edge. After a moment, she'd located him beside a Captain America chopper motorcycle, his hand on the sissy bar. Her instinct told her to stop him – the owner could belong to a biker gang – but she didn't. As a child, she hadn't been stopped from doing anything. She'd used saws and axes, ridden horses, walked as far as she wanted when she wanted. John's child should have that same agency. As he bent to look at the dials, Lenny's tongue poked out between his lips. Agnes sighed with relief at this evidence of concentration in John's boy. John's hand used to go to his hair when a machine absorbed him, fingers turning his forelock into knots. This boy had his own tells. A pang of the love she'd felt for his father clapped Agnes. If Marsha didn't show up soon, she might keep Lenny after all.

Jesu had been one of Agnes's first students in her UNM Arts Foundations class when she landed in New Mexico after a year and a half of living out of the Airstream Overlander. He had shown a gift for three-dimensional art and an attraction to clay. Ecology-minded installations were the rage, using found objects, but Jesu had revealed a traditional mind, a classical mind, and a talent for capturing studied beautiful movement, such as that of a dancer or an athlete first in clay, then as he neared the end of his degree, bronze. Miss Gringo, he'd called her, once he'd gotten to know her. She'd chuckled, pleased he'd said it, knowing that an insult told to the face bred a familiarity or bond. She liked Jesu and when she figured out that the ranch he lived on with his parents bordered the land she'd rented from the doomed Elena Trujillo, she'd struck up a friendship with him.

His father, Arturo, was the *mayordomo* of the local *acequia*. Jesu introduced them and leveraged her prestige as a New York City artist and college professor to secure her an invitation to become a member. Jesu and Arturo showed her the best spot to build near the *acequia*'s waters so she wouldn't need a well. In the spring, when the community gathered to clean and repair the mother ditch, Jesu volunteered to represent Agnes, but every year, she showed up herself. Jesu's talent with structure made him valuable to her when she built her cabin and studio. During that period, he'd met and married Annie, his father had severed thirty acres off his land to transfer to Jesu, and he'd built a house of his own, much bigger than Agnes's, but then most houses were.

The bright blue trim of Jesu's wraparound porch stood out against the snow. Several trucks were parked scattershot across the front of his property. Jesu's orange Dodge sat up tight to the outbuilding closest to the house. Agnes and Lenny followed the tracks up to the door.

The idea of the porch, Agnes remembered Jesu telling her, was to keep it clear so the children could ride their tricycles around the house, picking up speed before a corner as he had at his parents' when he was a boy. Yet, the space was packed with car seats, boxes, stuffed garbage bags, tools, piñon logs – some chopped, some not – and a heap of round stones for an unbuilt fireplace. A rubber mat created a path from the step to the door. Agnes paused, her hand on the porch rail. Lenny hung back.

Jesu wasn't expecting her. She didn't drop by often, though when she did, nobody acted surprised; quite the opposite. She didn't need to go inside, not really. Her house was the next down the road, a six-mile walk, a long walk, especially for the boy.

The sun lit her face without warming it. She thought of the real reason she'd come here. Walking away from the canyon with Lenny, she'd felt borne along by a current, as if guided by the Line. So why hadn't she walked straight home and let it steer her right to her canvas? It came down to a moment, as it so often did. Her challenge: could she remember the instant she first turned on to art? Julie had asked her that question as they had walked to the police station. Agnes had ignored the question, but the answer had come to her again about an hour ago. She'd repurposed the moment for so many situations, sticking mostly to the story that New York City in her thirties had convinced her she could do it. She could trace the *real* moment back to one of her first visions, around the time the voices, which had nothing to do with art, started up. The vision showed a stranger's face, a woman's, and in it Agnes knew just how to work her brush and which colours to choose to capture the light on her brow.

She revised: she didn't have one moment or vision but rather an idea of what she could do or make and of who she was and could be. It was evolving, and it was an energy, and it was a choice to try a thing because it matched a sense of what felt right to do and what she longed to do too. On one level, the doing of it wasn't easy and filled her with disappointment. On another level, one that ripped her open every time she reached it, she felt joyous, distinct and wise when she painted – and even more when she finished. She craved another's eyes on her work soon after, but there was that split second – that she suspected she'd value more and more as she returned to painting now, alone in this desert – after she'd first finished the painting, like the moment after gulping water from a tall glass, when she lifted her head, gasping, sated but still with the memory of the parched tongue.

It all frightened her, even as she craved it, and as they'd neared Jesu's on her way home, she'd seized on the idea that she should dip her oar into New York again, call Betty to see if anyone was waiting to see her work. Doing so did feel wrong, as if she'd been asked to protect an egg and instead had rolled it in front of an eighteen-wheeler yet she'd convinced herself that another layer of belief in her work would make her feel secure.

Random snowflakes swirled in the sunlight. Icicles dripped behind them. The screen door led to a storage room. Jesu and Annie kept the inside door open so family and friends would feel welcomed. Both had urged Agnes many times to walk in and say hello, but even today – especially today – she felt uncomfortable doing so. The house looked dark. She couldn't spot anyone, but she could hear pipes running and voices, maybe in the kitchen, and laughter. The porch was shaded, too, making her shiver. She didn't have to stay. It was foolish to call New York after what – seven years? – and only because of a remark from Marsha that her old agent was curious about what she was doing. She hadn't painted in all that time. Why admit it? Why call from a point of weakness and not in six months, say, when she had a body of work to display? The Line blurred, making her feel muddled, as if she'd just eaten a handful of candy – but she hadn't eaten, not since the diner with Lenny . . . which meant he hadn't eaten either. She'd have to feed him when they got to her house. Or maybe Annie would. Agnes would let the Line blur. Shilah and Julie – or even Marsha, for heaven's sake – could show up at her place any time. It would be good to know the word from New York. Questions would be answered. Even if she were to find out they'd forgotten her, or worse, dismissed her. She shuddered. At least she'd know. The break, the point of erasure – she'd make that the place from which she would paint. Calling made more sense when she looked at it that way. If one quality had marked her life since John died, it was that she didn't deny herself. What she wanted, she got. The only delay she'd experienced, albeit unwillingly, in those seven years, was today. This phone call would send her back to the studio threshold, readier than ever to approach the canvas. Besides, Jesu and Annie had family visiting (when didn't they?) – they would have food.

The hinges creaked as she opened the screen door. She cringed, expecting someone to appear around the corner, but nobody did. She leaned back out and craned her neck for one last look around. Lenny leaned against the wall, eyes on his shoes. She stepped back inside, motioned for him to follow. The voices continued, unabated. On the pine floor, she bent to pull off her boots. When pain shot through both knees, she eased back up and found a bench where she sat with a quiet *huff*.

The place had low tin ceilings painted white and pine boards everywhere except the kitchen, which had a brown linoleum floor. The effect was tunnel-like. The porch blocked the sunlight. Standing lamps with six cones pointing in different directions created blobs of light that only accentuated the relative duskiness of the rooms. Agnes entered in sock feet. She walked with a hand on a wall for comfort and balance, though once she took a few steps her knee lubricated itself and moved fine.

"Hola!" Jesu said when she reached the kitchen. She nodded, eyes down. She wouldn't characterize herself as shy. She was comfortable under a spotlight. Yet, in the presence of Jesu's family (and what other family did she know?), she felt humbled and grateful, almost effaced. What was it about families like Jesu's that made them hard for her to look at? She experienced their groupings as lustrous and bright – especially when there were so many of them together at once as there were today. As a result, she often averted her eyes and blinked a lot. When she walked into the room, she counted eight or ten sitting at the table, leaning against the wall, standing at the counters and sink. She had no time to identify male or female or even where Jesu and Annie were in relation to everyone else before casting her eyes downward, though she expected it was Annie at the stove pouring dough into a pot full of hot oil.

She nodded again, let her smile twist her face. She was happy to be here but waiting out the moment for the family to go back to talking. Jesu came over, stopping only to grab a nephew around the shoulders and cuff his head. "You wish!" the nephew said.

"*Es Agnes*," he said as if they'd all met her before, and maybe they had. Agnes refused invitations to join Annie and Jesu for holiday dinners, but many times Jesu had shown up at her place with a nephew or brother-in-law in tow. Annie was the youngest of nine and even had great-nephews and great-nieces. A chorus of *hola*s and *yo Agnes*'s rose up around her, and she waved.

"Who is this?" Annie said. She gestured at Lenny, squatted near him with a warm smile.

"The son of an old friend," Agnes said.

"Lenny," said Lenny.

"Come with me, Lenny. I'll make you a plate," Annie said, putting an arm around his shoulder and standing. "You, too, Agnes." Agnes nodded again, knowing better than to refuse.

"Everything okay?" Jesu said, his forehead layered with concern.

"Yes, of course," Agnes said. The others had returned to their conversations, laughing at something Annie had said.

"But you're here because –"

"I'd like to make a phone call."

Jesu studied her. He wasn't much taller than her, but he was wearing workboots and she was in her sock feet, so he loomed over her slightly. He wore a loose red-and-orange flannel shirt over a white undershirt with green workpants with a gold cross on a chain. Even when concerned, his eyes flashed with fun. He'd devoted himself to her since UNM. No doubt her antics, such as they were, provided the source of much discussion and amusement on the home front. Annie was a sweet girl, the sweetest. Agnes couldn't have hoped for a better match for Jesu. She was smart, too, shrewd, didn't miss a trick. She saw to it that Jesu was a good neighbour who gave Agnes what she needed, nothing more nor less, but that she and their home came first. Agnes had run out of funds to pay him since she stopped teaching so Jesu's help came more sparingly, a result of Annie's insistence that he fill his own well first. Still, Agnes had a hold on Jesu, held a fascination for him, if only because he, too, was waiting to see what would happen when she picked up a paintbrush.

"It'll be long distance, Jesu, and I can pay you. I will hang up when the call is over, then pick up again and call the operator to ask how much the call cost and I will give you that amount in cash. You won't be put out one cent."

"You don't have to pay us, Agnes. You can use this phone any time, long distance or short, doesn't matter." Jesu hesitated for a moment then glanced at the kitchen. Annie's laughter rang loudly. He leaned in. "I'm happy to help, especially if you've got a need, if you've got to reach out to someone. Your family, maybe?"

"No. My career. I need to call New York." Agnes leaned against the wall, her head banging a framed photograph. She didn't explain further, let Jesu invent a sense of necessity. She was the *gringo* from the city but he gave her a pass because of her age and gender and because she was an artist. She didn't stop others from building up a mystique around her that she didn't feel. It came in handy, though, and she watched as Jesu linked her need to call with this morning's *gringo* visitor and computed that her business with New York was actual business. Maybe it was. She wouldn't know until she called.

Like many people, Jesu and Annie kept their telephone in the kitchen, but theirs had a long cord so it could be dragged into bedrooms with the door shut. Jesu said he'd set it up this way so he wouldn't have to hear Annie's hours-long calls to her mother and sisters. He himself rarely used a telephone. When he did, he got in and out of the conversation adroitly.

Agnes stayed where she was midway down the hall while Jesu headed back to the kitchen. The volume of the conversation dipped for a moment. Agnes pictured Annie's round brown eyes opening wide with questions and Jesu telling her to make sure the boy got lots to eat. Soon enough, Jesu was back, cradling the black telephone in one arm, the other stringing out the cord behind him so it wouldn't get tangled. He led her into the first room, which held a washer and dryer. He set the telephone on the washer, reached behind the machine and produced a folding chair, which he opened for Agnes. She sat with some difficulty and accepted the telephone from him. He tugged the cord taut and tossed it to the floor inside the room. Then he backed out. "Take your time," he said, winking.

Once he'd left, she stood and backed the chair up to the wall, where thankfully the phone extended with cord to spare. Then she composed her thoughts. First, she'd need a number.

She slumped and took a breath. Let her mind drift along with the rhythm of the old in and out. Inhale and exhale. The waves that kept her here. She shooed the air near her head. Thoughts like these were diverting. The brain needed clearing, not ideas to fool itself that it had smarts. She took a deep breath, held it, then let it out slowly, her chest tight near the end. As her mind emptied, she thought of the last time she would have called Betty Parsons. She would have seen Betty at John's funeral, perhaps her last responsible act as a member of that circle. It might have been a year or two earlier, in the days leading up to her show or even in the days that followed its success, to talk about who had bought what and where the work would go. She had paintings out in the world, hanging in houses and offices and galleries and stored in basements and attics and who knew where. Destroyed, she hoped. Other painters used the analogy of having grown children who'd left home. Though Agnes could recall those paintings if she wanted, she'd mostly let them go. Whatever she painted next would connect to those earlier paintings in one way, sure, because they'd have come from the same mind, but beyond that, they'd likely annihilate what had come before, as they should.

Betty Parsons might have some of those older paintings. She might show them from time to time in hopes of selling them or as a way of affiliating herself with the best of New York's most recent old guard. Marsha implied Betty had moved on, was more intrigued by the likes of Marsha than an artist like Agnes, who'd fled the city seven years ago without a word. No matter. The word was coming now, the phone number was not. Agnes picked up the receiver, dialed 411 and got connected. Within a minute, she was saying hello to Betty herself.

"It's Agnes Martin," she said.

"A pleasant surprise!" said Betty, her New York accent evoking a fond pleasure in Agnes, who leaned forward, head tilted, eager now for this conversation. "I thought I might hear from you soon."

"That's funny," Agnes said. She questioned whether she'd understood Marsha's meaning earlier when she'd brought up Betty. "I thought you might have moved on."

"Oh! We've been concerned that *you're* the one who's moved on! Are you coming back? How is your painting?"

Betty was smooth, seeming to keep the door open just enough when it was clear that she'd shut it years ago. Marsha was right.

"I guess you know Marsha is down here. In New Mexico."

"I – I suppose she is. Have you seen her?"

"Yes, and now she's disappeared and left her son with me."

"Her son? Lenny? Is it because he's –" Betty lowered her voice. Agnes pictured her brushed chin-length hair, parted on the side, a look she'd kept since the 1930s when they were young. "She says he's John's. Did she tell you?"

"She told me a lot of things about the boy," Agnes said, "and then she left us together. We don't know where she is. Has she been in touch with you?" Any lies Betty told now might give insight into Marsha's thinking. Agnes waited to hear them.

"Agnes, I did know she was coming to New Mexico, I did. The gallery represents her. Naturally we're all curious about how you're doing. We represent you still. That contract hasn't terminated, not officially, so if you're stockpiling some tremendous paintings down there, I'd love to hear about them. You could invite me down to see them even."

"Has Marsha called you today?" Agnes said. Lenny's safety, it turned out, meant more to her than Betty's reassurances, whether they were false or not.

Betty gave a little sigh. Agnes pictured pleats edging her thin lips with their impeccable red lipstick.

"No, she hasn't. I haven't had my report if that's what you mean."

Agnes paused. Marsha had come to spy on her. Her visit made more sense now.

"I meant do you know where she is, so I can return the boy to her."

"She has disappeared then. That really is concerning."

"Tell her he's with me now," Agnes said. She hung up. The call had given her nothing new, but she felt keyed up and thrown over, buried even. At least she knew where she stood with Lenny. She would keep him. And then? If she could just get him to her home, get herself started. She set the telephone on the washing machine and left the room to look for Jesu and ask for a ride.

—

"The boy," Agnes said. She and Jesu stood on the porch while Lenny did jumping jacks on the driveway. "Marsha. The woman? At my house, this morning. Her boy. She's left him with me and –"

"Annie thinks he should stay here."

"I need to bring Lenny to my place in case his mother shows up to claim him."

"We're about to eat, but when aren't we? I'm sure they won't miss me." Jesu looked over his shoulder into the house, jingled the keys in his pocket. "Let's go then."

Jesu dropped them off at the end of Agnes's driveway. Agnes stood there beside the boy and surveyed her property. The brick post at the end with the peeling sign that read Martin. The snaking drive, ploughed and sanded by a local rancher with a backhoe after the last snow. The flat-roofed adobe buildings and shelters like a giant's blocks under miles and miles of chunky rolling cloud. She'd built each one with Jesu's help and the help of other students, and could claim them as her own. Rarely had making art satisfied her in the same way as building these – but still it had, and more. She knocked the sign twice with her knuckles. "You still hungry?" she said to Lenny, who nodded, eyes wide and glassy.

"Are you okay?" she added.

At the question, he pepped up and walked toward the house. "I'm cool," he said. She followed him, not believing him but unsure what else to do.

The first time she'd stood in front of her studio window in Coenties Slip, she'd had the not-unpleasant sensation of tumbling forward, pitching into the harbour. She could see the texture of the sailcloth on the boats, the sailors' gestures. She mashed her body against the glass and ended up with a shirt covered in dust. If she turned just so, there was the corner of the Seaman's Institute, its roof lined with terracotta bears and eagles to protect the sailors it housed. The studio room, with its fourteen-foot-high ceilings, seemed to roar with the winds coming north off the harbour. Sunshine through two skylights beat the room into a hotbed of coals. Agnes cleaned the entire wall of windows from top to bottom and made it a morning ritual to touch up the dirty spots so the space where she painted had the clarity of outside light, was even more pure for being diluted by the clean glass. She had long discussions with her friends Robert, John and Ell on the roof, figuring out how to rig a contraption so she could wash the window from the outside. Nobody had the money to hire a window washer. The building was a factory. They were lucky to have the space. Not to mention the upkeep – once they cleaned it, the city's dirt would cover it up again within hours.

Although Agnes wouldn't have said so at the time, she'd relished those talks with the men who painted in the studios around her. The grappling and jockeying and scheming and competing, filling the space between paintings. Agnes had rejected most social life, a natural loner from the start. She'd gotten worked up at men like Robert, who banged on her door when she was painting, demanding she join them at this party or that. She'd hidden behind her coat rack or stormed into the hall, dressing him down, not that it stopped him. She missed it all now and wondered what she would have lost if she'd participated more.

That studio had witnessed her defining moment as an artist, one she hoped to surpass in her new studio if she could ever get into it. As she and Lenny walked by it on her way to the house, she petted the door like an old dog for comfort and luck. Inside the house, she went straight for the cast-iron stove and stirred the coals. She stacked some kindling, lit a piece of newspaper and threw that in, too. She shook the kettle and, finding it nearly empty after having made coffee for Marsha that morning, she filled it to the brim and set it on the plate burner. Lenny stayed by the door, eyes leaping from object to corner, all over the room. Only when she sat herself on the bench and bent to untie her boots did he do the same. "Make yourself at home," she said. She opened a jar of tomatoes and spooned some onto a plate on her round, oak table. All her cells seemed to be in motion, yet she didn't feel tired, surprisingly. The Line had returned, and for that she sighed, eyes closed with a smile. But for how long? Long enough to drink a tea and have enough of a rest to get her out the door again and into her studio with a brush in her hand? Long enough to feed Lenny and find an activity to amuse him? Even to stand inside the doors would feel like an accomplishment at this late point in the day, the winter sun beginning its descent, though it wasn't setting yet.

Tea made, pottery mug in hand, she settled herself on the sofa while Lenny dipped saltines into a small dish of preserved tomatoes. If sleep came, she would let it. In New York, she'd been blessed with the gift of afternoon naps, but then she hadn't kept regular hours and she'd sleep when she was tired, whatever the time of day. She didn't sleep any more now than she ever had, though she confined her sleeping to the nighttime, having seen 3:00 a.m. too often with nothing to do with herself. She closed her eyes and set her mind free. The Line, the Line. It unfurled like a highway, like wires joining telephone poles, like fishing line, spooling, unspooling, an infinite source. She shifted so she felt the sunlight on her face and let herself ride this vision.

Soon enough the vision shifted, and she saw the canvases in her NYC studio, canvases that, if nobody had rescued them, would have gotten demolished along with the building, but their fate was their own. Agnes had shut the door on them when she left. In the vision though, there they sat, lining the room, leaning against one another, some up on easels, some up on walls, some on the floor, their colours more vivid in the beginning but muting as she refined her style, the shapes and spaces more textured and meaningful. From the moment she took on the studio space, she'd plagued herself with the question of belonging: where did she belong? Did she belong here? Was she good enough? What did she have to say? To show for herself? She had painted and worked hard, harder, she observed, than the men around her, the ones banging on her door most days and nights to join them at a party or for a diner breakfast or even up on the roof for a confab. She put in more hours, accumulated more paintings, some she even showed, but usually once she was done, she was on to the next one. Then one day when Robert came for his nightly door pound, she slid the doors open and said, *Yes. Let's do something.*

She'd followed him to his studio while he got his coat and ended up spending hours there. Every inch of wall space in his studio was covered, but not with his paintings. Ship wheels, steering wheels, fox lights, chains, block pulleys, lifeboat oars – iron and wire and wood and leather – gears, clocks, lanterns, sextants, brass portholes, deadlights. His walls spoke of an obsession with circles and a history that reached some greater truth inside him making its way into the world whatever way it could. Some considered that Robert was selling out with paintings that were concerned with advertisements and design; others thought he was a brilliant vanguard for his embrace of pop. Agnes didn't judge the artists around her – indeed, she mostly didn't see them – because her muse operated best with her critical faculties turned off.

Agnes didn't go out with Robert that night. When she returned to her own studio, she didn't see an artist's body of work, which she'd fooled herself into thinking she was building, but a child's collection of scribbles. *See, teacher*, her paintings seemed to say, *I did more than everyone else! I must be better!* If she could have taken a bulldozer and rammed them out of the room, she would have. Instead, she shut the doors, rolled up her sleeves and heaved the paintings into a heap in an unlit corner with no concern for their wetness. The next day, she would stuff them in giant bags and haul them to the street for the garbage collectors. She set up one clean canvas in the middle of the room and waited for a vision. She felt like a Delphic priestess, inhaling vapours as she gazed into a bowl of water for guidance. She wouldn't paint for six weeks – an unheard-of break for her at that point – during which time she removed every other previous painting from her studio, dragging each one outside after midnight and distributing the bags in front of other buildings so nobody would connect them to her. The first painting created after that purge wasn't momentous in any way nor memorable, but it was the first that was hers and the first that sold, as did every one she painted after that, except those she left behind when she ran.

There it was. No big mystery. She had set the stage. Now she had to walk the boards. The call to Betty told her exactly nothing but everything she needed to know. She didn't care whether her work mattered to Betty anymore. Her work did matter to Betty only as much as it mattered to buyers. If she could sell it, she would. Simple equation. Agnes didn't need it to sell. She shuddered at the word and set down her mug. The boy had laid his head down on his arms and might have dozed off.

Let him be. You're doing fine, John's voice said.

She closed her own eyes and let her mind bathe in the light of the Line. She felt a syrupy happiness in this place of all potential. All she had to do was breathe and absorb. Maybe that was the key. Maybe breathing was the key. The Zen masters she liked to read wrote about breath. Her own breath was wide and hoarse, especially after all that time walking in the cold, dry air. *Stay attuned to the breath and the rest will come.* She stood, knees pinging. Maybe she'd write that one down.

Ten minutes later, the boy still sleeping, she piled two piñon logs with kindling and a crumpled *Pennysaver* in the studio stove. She lit one corner and sat on her haunches while it flared and crackled, catching the bark. She crossed her arms and rocked back and forth. She wasn't cold yet. She had her coat. She was tired. She was taking advantage of the boy's sleeping – it might not last long – had trekked over to this studio, crossed the threshold and selected her materials and here she was lighting the fire, everything she needed to work. She'd even brought a thermos of tea and a jar of tomatoes. She had to stand or her knees would ache from having been bent too long. When the fire burst with a rush as the logs caught, she shut the door and adjusted the flue. It was time. She was warm. The canvas stood stretched and ready. Her pencils and pens, her brushes and cloths and oils, all sat on a table under the window. She pulled the ruler from the pocket of her overalls. The sun hadn't set, the light was clear. She'd made it past more obstacles than she'd had in years: Marsha, Lenny, Julie and Shilah, even Betty and Jesu. The Line was pulsing.

She was here.

ELLEN

Philip's ponies were slower than Darius's black workhorses, with a light smell of hay that blew back over Ellen. Snow lined the branches of the trees they passed, filled the dips, hunched on the pine boughs. Some trees shuddered, shook off heaps of snow that dumped on Ellen's head. She brushed it off her nose with her coat sleeve, which smelled like boiled greens. Her face was wet from specks of snow pelting sideways.

"I didn't find you at your cabin," Philip said. "So I stopped at Duffy's to ask if anyone had seen you. Then I poked my head in at Buck's Hotel. It surprised me to find you with Darius Horn and Early Badger."

"They want me to marry Early," Ellen said. "I told them I planned to marry your father." Melted snow trickled down her neck, and she blotted it with her collar. She shivered even though her boiled wool coat normally kept her warm but resisted the urge to lean her arm against Philip's.

"Does my father know about this plan of yours?" Philip cracked his whip, making the ponies speed up.

"I have a better plan now," she said.

"Darius Horn won't take lightly to you leaving with me then." Philip's ponies matched in an intriguing way. The pale grey one had black speckles on her haunches while the black one had grey freckles on its neck. Salt and pepper. Her wet neck and the increasing wind caused her to shiver again. She tucked her hands into her armpits.

They headed west down Bobcaygeon Road in the direction of her cabin. A few miles out of Minden Village they met another other wagon, its horses driven by a man Ellen didn't recognize and carrying a long plywood box, resembling a coffin. Her hands flew up to her mouth. Then she grasped the front of the wagon, lifted herself as if to stand, reeled so her hip swung out then sat again with a thud. Both ponies looked back, their manes like white and black flames, their nostrils pumping plumes of air. Philip tossed the reins from his right hand to his left. He patted her back, and she swooned. He pulled back on the reins until the ponies stopped. She wanted to keep going, but there she was with her head on Philip's shoulder looking up at him looking down at her. She could only laugh.

"Are you overcome?" Philip asked.

He was smiling, the reins loose, his hand hanging in his lap, but his eyelids twitched and he watched the wagon as it disappeared around a bend. From another man, that question might hold amusement or superiority, an expectation that she might succumb to emotion. From a different man, it might signify great empathy. But Philip was neither of these men. From him, the words came as a suggestion, a helpful stick for her to clasp if she wished to explain her excitement. She was young, but he was younger and she felt the difference.

She thought of the hollow she'd felt burned into her chest since the fire in Hamilton, of the raspy throat she'd had since she'd crawled from the building clutching Safra, of the light that shone through her, her only guidance, aside from the spirits and of little Safra drifting around her still. Did this bundle of beliefs define her? She met Philip's gaze under his beaver hat and reached up to brush off the snow. He blinked and sneezed and they both laughed.

"Overcome, I wouldn't say so. Adjusting to the chaos and change. We mustn't stop at my cabin. All that meant anything to me there has gone. Anywhere but that hotel."

Philip snapped the reins, and the wagon lurched as the ponies soon got up to speed. They travelled several miles in silence, their arms pressed against each other – *For warmth,* Ellen told herself, *for balance* – but neither pulled away.

Her cabin lurked behind the white pines, its logs dark where they were not patched with snow. A smoke stream wound from the chimney, its smell sharp, arousing, its thinness the sign of a fire dying down, embers winking, asking for more fuel. Ellen closed her eyes and prayed as they passed her house and headed through the woods.

There was no sign of Darius Horn in pursuit but that didn't mean he wouldn't follow. Nevertheless, Ellen felt a tug inside. If she and Philip were running away – though neither had said so, it did seem as though they were – she wanted to see her friend one last time.

"Micheline's," she said. "It's up ahead, down a long driveway. Do you mind if we stop at her cabin? Before we –"

"Run away together?" Philip said, one eyebrow raised.

"Are we doing that?"

"Escaping the scenario, more accurately."

Ellen thought of all the objections she'd given Darius Horn to the idea of marrying right away, but none applied here. Philip excited her. Younger than her, he exuded the urge to work hard and make a life for himself. He had no ties to the underhanded sawmill business. Could she swerve in such a new direction?

"We don't know each other. Not really, other than our few conversations. I didn't know William much either. He moved up here right after we married and I didn't see him for over two years. We could –"

He stopped her with his warm lips on hers, their mouths closed at first, then opening so their tongues met and his arms brought her close against him. She ignored the pain spiking her jaw and soon forgot it. Snow dropped around them, his cheeks cold and glowing red in the golden light.

"Go somewhere new together? Somewhere I could log and not have to live under my father's eye and you could –"

Talking with Philip this way made her lungs fill with enthusiasm. Spirit moved around them in these woods, the low sun strobing through the snow-coated trees. Spirit had brought them together, was twining them close.

Philip snapped the reins and the ponies turned into the long, wooded driveway.

Micheline and Paul and their four children lived in a cabin

not much bigger than Ellen's. The children slept in the loft while Mich and Paul had a curtained bedroom off the main room. Whenever Ellen visited, she settled herself into a chair and didn't move, much as she had done at the barbershop, letting the children run and play around her.

Philip drove the ponies over to the barn where Paul kept their two draft horses through the summer. In October, at first snowfall, he'd driven them north to a logging camp where he stayed with them through the winter. Micheline didn't expect to see him until after first thaw. Philip stepped down from the wagon, holding up a palm so she'd wait. Two faces appeared at the cabin window with two behind them pushing to see. Would she stay still inside Micheline's this time, she wondered?

She doubted it. She was running again, had been the minute she set foot in Darius Horn's wagon, though she hadn't known it then. She was fleeing William and all that he stood for, for the life she couldn't make with him before he died. Philip let the shafts drop to the snowy ground and unhooked the pole linking the ponies. He led them into the stable. This kind of running excited her. Before, one could say she'd been escaping the fire, the pain of what it had taken from her, and she would agree, but she had been grappling with time. She'd wanted to hold time in one place, back it up even. By staying with William and making a family, maybe she could have returned to what it felt like when she'd first held Safra and make up – if only in one small way – for letting her go.

Micheline held the door open, then, and the children tore forth across the snow, coats open, their mother behind them, arms wide as if Philip and Ellen were long-awaited fugitives. Ellen stayed put, waiting for Philip to come back from the stable, cringing at the thought of sitting so out in the open. When Philip emerged from the barn, he nodded at her, and she let David, Micheline's eldest, help her down. The children seemed to read her mood and settled. Micheline must have told them about William.

Philip and David lifted the wagon's stays and pulled it over behind the barn out of the line of sight should Darius and Early arrive.

Ellen waited, her legs calf-deep in snow. Together, she and Philip crossed over the threshold. Micheline gave David a push in the chest and said, "You and your brother and sisters can stay outside. We have things to discuss."

David thrust his shoulders back, his black eyes fierce. "Papa lets me stay when adults are talking."

"Papa also likes you outside," Micheline said. Her face relaxed. "And I count on you to watch the others."

David spun around and tore outside to the woods, where his siblings climbed a tree.

Micheline's skin had flushed and bits of her hair stuck out like juniper needles around her face. She offered Philip and Ellen a concerned look, hugged them each in turn and looked into their eyes as they answered her offer of tea. She whirled over to the stove, lifted the kettle and poured three cups of the steaming brew. Ellen moved to help, ignoring Micheline's *No*'s and carrying a mug with two hands to Philip.

"My friend, you are like a river," Ellen said.

Micheline was at the stove again for the third mug.

"I do what needs doing," she said.

"Mich," Ellen said, "please sit with us. It's important. It's my hope that you can advise us."

Philip stood at the window, his eyes on the trees. Ellen surged with excitement and fear and the desire to stand close to him, to inhale his smoky scent. Most of the women up here in these woods, and there were few enough of them, Ellen included, did not contribute to the work of building and growing and journeying and making a mark except only to tend the house to which the man could return and sup and nourish himself. That didn't mean that they weren't skilled; quite the opposite. There wasn't much a woman living in this bush couldn't do, but what she did, she did almost exclusively within a small radius of her cabin. Micheline was little different in that respect, though she did spend large swaths of time at Ellen's cabin and indeed camping with her mother's family, especially in the summer with Paul. In this family, however, Micheline's work and her wisdom held as much value as Paul's – according to Paul, even more. Perhaps visiting Micheline reminded Ellen of what she believed she should have and couldn't accept that she didn't. Perhaps a home that was run by such a shining woman reminded Ellen how much she wasn't a shining woman. But Ellen was, she knew she was. A light burned inside her so intense, it didn't surprise her that others blinked and looked away. Since coming here, she'd blamed her brown skin. Here, her heart opening up to Micheline and her family, she got that it could be much more than that; it could be her faith, a woman's faith so strong it made people afraid. This morning she'd found out that Micheline shared that faith too. It would hurt to leave her.

"Let me guess why you are here," Micheline said. Ellen put her face in the steam rising off the tea, inhaled its lemony sumac smell. Cedar needles floated here, too, and sweetgrass. The steam moistened her skin.

The fire crackled. "I doubt that you could," Philip said. "Ellen needs you, Micheline. I'll stick right here, if you don't mind."

Micheline looked at him sharply and sat back, arms folded over her stomach.

"I do need you, Mich. Philip and I have spoken and we have decided to go into the woods where he can log as he wishes to do and I can be by his side when he's home. I need you to hear it because you are smart and wise and you can help us know what we need to do to make this escape."

"Escape from what? From being a widow? True, you have a hard road ahead, but you have me and Paul and this community to help you make it to planting season. You two have time enough to sort out a life together if you want that. You have other options. You will have other options, don't you see?"

Micheline rubbed her belly with both hands, making Ellen think about the babies, Micheline's and hers. Yet, only Philip knew about hers. She shouldn't reveal it now. Ellen resisted the urge to stroke her own belly. She estimated she was a few months along. She hadn't started to show, but a few weeks ago a frantic radiance had shown up just out of her field of vision, which she believed was Safra's fear at being replaced. *Not replaced. Never replaced*, Ellen said in her thoughts. *Love increases, expands, and you're always a part of it.*

"I have run out of options. Darius Horn made that situation clear this afternoon."

Philip looked back from the window, his face in shadow.

Micheline stood up, shaking her head. "What does Darius

Horn have to do with any of it?" she said, as she reached and adjusted both plates displayed on her plate rail; then she bent to lower the flame on the oil lamp. "William doesn't – didn't – work for Horn's Mill. Why would Darius Horn have any say in what you do or even concern himself at all?" From one item to the next her hands moved, straightening this, flicking that, brushing another until most items in the room had received the benefit of her touch and what had appeared tidy on first entering now had the feeling of a well-loved exhibit.

"Darius Horn has other business interests, it turns out," Ellen said. "I didn't know, but William did."

As she spoke, Philip came and sat, his face revealed in the lamplight. Ellen pushed aside the instinct to shutter herself and met his gaze. His eyes sparkled like shards of snow crusts under a mazarine sky. But they weren't cold. They held the mystery and warm potential of waterfall ice, of power contained, for the moment. She could swoon again but she kept looking, letting him drink in the river-mud warmth of her own brown eyes.

Micheline came over to the table. She knocked it twice, peeked into each mug then fetched the kettle and refilled them all. "Micheline, please sit," Philip said. Ellen saw, in his kindness, that he knew of Micheline's baby, too. This man should be a doctor. He had a sensibility attuned to other's needs beyond what most people had. Ellen didn't doubt then, if he'd chosen her, that he'd chosen right too.

Micheline sat. "Ellen, I don't know what to say to you. William died this morning. He must be mourned and you must wait a proper period. That is what people will expect."

"Yes, people in Hamilton would expect that. My mother would. I stayed with her for some weeks after my father died.

Every morning she rose, took off the black-dyed linen nightdress and encased herself in black silk and net to shield herself against the world. Her mourning period became her life. I mourned, too, and I had more to grieve than she, but I had a husband still, as she pointed out, so I ran to him. What does William have for me to sell? Who would buy this free-granted land with its patch of cleared brush and one-room cabin? Could Philip live with me there, in this community of wags and gossips? Isn't it better, if I've found the man I want to be with, to drop everything and follow him wherever he wants to go? The heart, like faith, knows no calendar, wouldn't you agree?"

"Were you involved before? How could you make this decision out of the blue? You said Darius Horn has something to do with it, that he is the reason you are running. Was William in trouble?"

"Yes. Darius Horn has other businesses, the gambling for one, and William was likely involved in a violent way." Ellen glanced out the window and lowered her voice, though the children had gone into the woods. "Darius Horn thinks William might have shared secrets with me and he's concocted this scheme to have me marry Early Badger, so I have to do something and sitting pretty in my community and covering myself in black won't be good enough."

No one spoke for a moment, then Philip pushed his chair back. It caught on the rag rug behind him. Micheline made a move to adjust it.

"Micheline," he said, "people came up here for the land grants and to live by their own rules. A widow who marries the day she becomes one is looked at askance only if she is suspected in her husband's death, which Ellen is not. Ellen is being smart and practical but also she is not wrong in suggesting that we have found a trust in each other – rapidly, I'll admit – and a truth that I have never felt elsewhere."

Ellen's shoulders tightened. The edges of her vision flashed. *Yes, you, too*, she thought with a glance sideways for Safra, but love for a child was different. The love that flowed was infinite and expansive, freely given and joyous. What came back didn't matter with a child, but with Philip it did. They were together in life now, both had declared it. Micheline was their witness.

"You forget that some people here came from the United States – Europeans and British – and they like their world just so. Despite the wildness of the landscape, you go into their homes and you won't find a stick out of place." Micheline's cabin was the same way, though many in her family, Micheline included, spent much of the year living in tents.

Philip leaned toward Micheline, who crossed her arms. "Isn't it better that Ellen go with the man she chooses than make an unholy union with a criminal under threat of even worse deeds? Besides, there are always those in a community, people like my father, who would inflict their views on others. Those people often situate themselves in a position of small power, drawing others toward them who wish to be told what to do. It is about keeping that power, not the truth." He drummed his nails against the table. He turned to her. "I think Ellen knows truths we don't."

"Oh, I know she does," Micheline said. She frowned, cocked her head. Ellen turned too. The room filled with the hiss of the lamp, the crackle of the fire and then another noise from the outside like alarmed hens. Micheline's children.

"We aren't done talking," Micheline said, standing. "I will ask the children to take your ponies out and hitch them. If

Darius Horn has you in his sights, you haven't got much time. May David and the girls take them for a short run to Ellen's cabin and back? Ellen, you will need blankets and warm clothing, sugar and flour. I will ask the girls to gather whatever they think a person would need for winter camp. They are smart and will know what to bring."

Philip and Ellen stared at her. The children came closer, their jumbled voices sounding like coyotes several hills away. Micheline said, "The ponies?"

"Yes, of course. You are very sensible," said Philip. He leaned over toward Ellen, his face in shadow with the oil lamp behind him.

"They must hurry," said Micheline. "I'm afraid we may have less time than we think."

As Micheline pulled on her coat and went outside to call instructions to David, Ellen turned to Philip and said, "Early does expect me to marry him because I didn't turn him down when he proposed."

"But you didn't accept him either," said Philip.

"I didn't have much chance. Moments later, I spotted you and the rest fell away." She looked up at him, his head seeming to stretch right to the top of the eaves. She'd forgotten how tall he was.

"We'll have to beat him to it." Philip strode over to the entryway, shrugged into his coat and went outside. Following him out into the snow, Ellen shut the door to Micheline's behind her, possibly for the last time. Philip approached the ponies, which stood half-hitched by David to the wagon in front of the barn. He pointed at David, waved him away.

Micheline scowled. “Keep hitching them, David. They don’t have much time.” David grasped a harness in one hand and rested the other on the grey pony’s neck. He looked from his mother to his teacher and back again, unsure what to do. The other children had scattered.

Micheline fixed her gaze on Philip, feet planted wide in the snow. “We haven’t talked about your plan,” she was saying. “Let David do this. We still have things to discuss. Ellen!”

Philip seized the reins, and David backed away. “It’s fine, son,” Philip said. “It’s good that you listen to your mother. She is a wise woman, wiser than me.”

The glaze on the snow made Ellen blink. The skin around her eyes felt sticky as if she’d been crying, but it was her reaction to living in a house heated by fire. Even in the best ventilated cabins like Paul and Micheline’s, the air had a tinge of ash to which Ellen’s skin and eyes and nostrils couldn’t quite become accustomed. She was forever dabbing her nose and eyes with a handkerchief and took any excuse to stick her head out the door and breathe in the snowy air. Summer wasn’t much better, the air filled with insects and seeds, but at least it was warm.

Thomasina tore around the corner of the house, a brother in pursuit, her black hair flying loose of a braid like black vines. She raced across the snow as smoothly as if it were water and stopped short of the ponies. Ellen said a prayer for her, that one day she would marry a man as young and joyful as herself, as Ellen had when she’d chosen William. The rest of it – the separation, the deaths – they could pray to avoid all they wanted but those events happened even to the luckiest of souls. One could pray only for the strength to go forward after each loss without breaking.

Philip attached the horses to the wagon, then led them in a circle so they were facing the road. David had hitched them as though he were driving them back into the barn.

Philip wasn't answering Micheline, who followed him, saying, "You came to me, you and Ellen, because of my wisdom, yet you leave without hearing it? Why? Have I offended you?" She came around the back of the wagon, letting her skirts drop and drag through the snow.

Philip checked all the buckles and attachments for secureness and ran his hand along the ponies' warm backs, a sign he was readying himself to climb onto the wagon and move. Ellen reached for Micheline and embraced her. Micheline's body was thick and firm. Ellen wound her arms around her lower back and pulled her in tight so their bellies touched, Ellen's face mashed into her shoulder. Ellen wanted their children to meet, if only in the womb. One day, perhaps, in person, but for now she wanted some of the faith and love that had intertwined their mothers to enliven them both. "I'm having a baby too," she whispered through Micheline's hair. "Nobody must know." Micheline gripped her more tightly so her face tingled and she thought she wouldn't ever let go.

"I will see you at church," she said.

"At William's funeral," Micheline said.

Ellen nodded, unable to speak this lie to her friend. Philip meant to marry her and to do so would have to break with his teaching job and even his father. While Ellen's and William's cabin would be an ideal location for them to settle if he intended to find work logging, the proximity to his father, his father's church, all the families of the children he'd taught and the men he'd grown up with – not to mention Early and even Darius

– rendered her cabin an impossible home. They would seek out another community where one could find free parcels of land. They could move there and be the new ones together, as she and William had not. There were always trees. The farther north one went, the more there were. Some men went west, too, she knew. Anywhere but here. Or Hamilton.

"I want this, Micheline," Ellen said in her friend's ear.

Micheline squeezed her even harder, then relaxed. "I trust you," Micheline said, stepping back, her face wet. Then she turned and ran for the door, calling over her shoulder, her voice breaking, "Don't leave yet! I want to give you folks a gift!"

Philip sat in the wagon now, reins held high. He patted the seat beside him. Ellen boosted herself up, then paused. "Will you wait? It's important to her."

Micheline appeared at the door, beaming. The item she held close to her chest made her run duck-like, spraying snow behind her.

She stepped onto the wagon and handed the bundle to Ellen. "Don't look at it until I'm gone. It's to remind you to travel lightly, carry only what makes you feel boundless." She jumped down, raised her arm straight up and turned away. The children watched from various perches on rocks and branches. Philip tapped the ponies' haunches with the whip and they were moving. Ellen clutched the item on her lap, willing herself not to look down. As soon as they passed David, who waved from the end of the lane, she could resist no longer. She unwrapped the embroidered cloth to find a blue beaded bag, decorated with geometric designs of birds and flowers, the beads made of glass and seeds, the background blue wool, the tassels along the bottom as long as her fingers and black. The bag was stunning, more elaborate and beautiful than any item Ellen had owned. She felt struck down her centre at the affection of the gesture. What had she given her friend besides the truth about the child she was carrying? Ellen turned to look back just as Philip's hand settled on top of the purse.

"You must steady yourself, Ellen. We are about to turn back onto Bobcaygeon Road."

It wasn't until they were rounding the corner that she registered the significance of the word *back*.

RUDIE

Rudie's tucked right heel prickled and sparked as it fell asleep. She should get up, throw out some magazines, scoop up balls of dust, brush her teeth – take any productive action that would move her forward to getting ready to receive Roselore in this house – and leave for the airport. Despite Leo showing up one day with a wheeled office chair from IKEA, she had persisted in using the small pine chair with the cut-out heart that she'd taken from her parents' house when she left for university. She'd hung onto that chair ever since, refusing to sit in anything else when she worked. Leo had tolerated her passion for the chair; it was a beautiful chair. The wood glowed golden inside sunbeams, but it was uncomfortable. She kept it so polished with beeswax that those who sat in it had to apply pressure with their thighs to keep from sliding to the floor. That was, when she let anyone sit in it. Just then she decided to give the chair to Roselore, to place it in her bedroom.

Rudie clicked on chapter seven of her film, Leo's chapter, then pushed Enter. She hadn't seen Leo for over a week and wouldn't have much time with him before they walked through the doors to Roselore and their lives changed forever. She loved such pronouncements, though she didn't love the suspended feeling of adjusting.

A younger Leo walked across the frame from the left toward Agnes, who sat in a chair in her studio, the camera pulling back as Leo approached her to give a sense of the empty space mirroring the artist's mind as palette. His jeans looked new, darker along the seams though not from sweat. He leaned toward Agnes and adjusted her microphone, and she reached a practised hand up to his neck. His skin had flared red, Rudie remembered, from some strawberries he'd eaten, not from the sun, for he'd worn his cowboy hat constantly, the one he'd bought at the Albuquerque Sunport, the one that Agnes now snatched off and tossed into the middle of the room as if into a boxing ring. Whatever he'd said before that moment, if anything, the microphone hadn't captured, having sputtered on as Agnes flung the hat, recording him saying, loud and clear, *Bull's-eye!* And he was right. The black leather cowboy hat sailing through the air, then sliding lightly across the swept wood floor to land in the centre of the frame, was documentary gold.

Rudie backed up and watched the scene again. The eye went to the hat, but this time the energy between Leo and Agnes struck her more. Their heads and bodies shaped a heart as people of great affinity often did when positioned together. Neither watched the hat fly. Agnes's hand cradled Leo's head like a small boy's, and she was speaking at the same time as Leo said *Bull's-eye*. Rudie hadn't noticed these details before.

She'd focused on the perfection of the shot at the expense of its subtext, the secret Agnes had been whispering all along.

Rudie pulled up her controls, slid the bass down and the treble up, played with the channels, closed her eyes and strained her ears to parse out her husband's loved voice and to contain Agnes's rich one. She heard "Lightning Lens" or "Lighting Len" or "Light Something Lenny." Leo met her gaze with his strong-eyed smile, the one that kept the world thinking well of him even as he drifted through it on his own terms. He regarded the camera, Rudie standing a few feet behind it, with that same look, the smile even brighter, and hooked his thumbs in his jeans as he bent a knee as if to wipe his boot.

The next shot framed Agnes up close speaking about the importance of perceiving one's self in the work. Lenny? Rudie had heard the name, heard Agnes say it somewhere else, perhaps in the rest of the microphone segment. She took out her shot list, grateful for her compulsive notes that ninety percent of the time didn't get reread. She adjusted her legs so she was sitting on her left ankle. She remembered the day and even the time of the shot. It didn't take long to find. The rest of it involved a short conversation about the volume of the microphone, Rudie exclaiming about how inspired the cowboy hat throw had been. Leo walked back toward the camera, leaning down to swoop the hat up and onto his head, his hair shorn like hers. And then Agnes had said it again, "Looking good, Lenny!"

Rudie had heard the name many times, in person and on this film, and perhaps others, but she hadn't registered it as a name that Agnes was calling Leo, and that he was accepting as his own as readily as if she were calling him the hated Leonardo that only his pretentious mother used. Of course. Leo had met Agnes before he'd introduced her to Rudie. She was a friend of the father who'd committed suicide. It wasn't like Agnes to dub people with nicknames, not as Rudie knew her or even from what others had said. *She'd known him as a child.* Here was a story, perhaps *the* story, and it contained her husband, of all people . . . or perhaps it was *he* who contained the story.

What did it mean that Leo wasn't who she'd thought he was? His father, who had died before he was born, was a minor art celebrity who'd killed himself. Leo's mother had sold all of his paintings, so Leo had none. He was close to Agnes, who despised his mother. He'd told stories of Agnes's visits to New York City and seeing her in New Mexico. Rudie had forgotten about his father and considered Leo an acolyte, intrigued by Agnes Martin the Artist, wanting the brush with fame that proximity to Agnes in Taos might offer. Also, Leo grew up in Manhattan. It wasn't too difficult in Toronto for those who wanted to meet the older generation of artists to follow the connections through art and film openings and book launches that might lead to an introduction. She'd supposed the process was the same in New York and that any kind of meeting they'd had had been lighthearted and not very deep, that he hadn't really known her. But Agnes calling him Lenny, that was intimate, that was his childhood name, it was a name he wouldn't allow Rudie to use even as a joke. While having sex, she could have called him Dylan and it would bother him less than if she were to call him Lenny. But Agnes? Leo's eyes shone in the film footage when she'd used the pet name, as they had with affection and care any time the two were close and speaking – much more fondness than he ever showed his mother.

Leo's mother painted. He downplayed it, but the oil painting of hers that they'd hung over their mantel showed poise and vigour, even if the colours were a little too slick and jewel-toned for Rudie's taste. His mother made a lot of money selling them, Leo had told Rudie, his tone dismissive, bordering on disdainful. He didn't visit her in New York, and she didn't visit them in Hamilton. He spoke with her from the road, not from home. Rudie hadn't met her and had seen only one photograph of a woman with a teased black flip in a belted cashmere coat and fur bonnet. It was snowing, and she stood before a steep set of stairs, head tilted and smiling. Rudie commented that she looked like a television star and Leo just laughed and laughed. "Oh she would *love* you," he'd said, shaking his head. Rudie got the sense that his mother would not love her and that Leo would love that she wouldn't. The burden of being Roselore's extended family was turning out to rest heavily on Kikka's shoulders. Kikka was up to the task, but Rudie's mouth dried out at the prospect. She had to figure out a way to pull Bob into the fold, or to entice Leo's mother.

She flipped screens to the still of Leo stepping away from the camera, his face shadowed by the infernal cowboy hat, and was about to back up the segment when a banging came on the door.

"Didn't know you made movies," Hannah said. She plopped herself on Rudie's pine chair. Rudie swallowed, thinking of all the times she'd admonished Leo to be careful with that chair because of its age. But the chair didn't creak or wobble. Whoever made it had known what he was doing, had made it to last.

Barth leaned on the door frame. He'd kept his boots on while Hannah had not. Hannah had walked in, assessed that Rudie was nowhere near ready to leave for the airport, removed her combat boots and headed for Rudie's chair. Rudie lifted a stack of scripts from the sway-backed brown leather couch under the window to clear space for Barth. She should take the pile straight to the garbage can. Would she even look at this stuff once Roselore came home?

"You could probably chuck all that paper crap and not even miss it," Barth said, his voice more of a baritone than she remembered. The two of them at her doorstep seemed to have aged – no, matured – by half a decade since the morning. They stood straighter, as if steeling themselves against the defeat of having to return to their parents and shed some of their romantic notions of street life in the process. She'd said nothing and held the door and here they were. Small clouds of dust rose off a few of the piles as she relocated them to the floor.

She swiped at the couch with her hand. Barth waved her away. "I'm okay standing. Really."

"Are you, like, famous? Should we know you?"

Rudie grimaced. "Some of it's my husband's." Rudie's throat closed for a moment. She fought off panic and made herself swallow. "I'm meeting him," she added. "Listen, we're waiting for a friend of mine who's coming to the airport with me."

Barth shrugged. Hannah inspected the area around Rudie's computer, her fingers moving near but not touching each photograph, book or Post-it Note she found, reading everything. Rudie wondered how much they could interpret about her film from the detritus surrounding her computer. Would Rudie find a similar tangle of notes in Dylan's office? And through reading those, how much would she find out about the filmmaker himself? How much of herself was revealed in these notes, in this film? Would it expose that faith fascinated her, that she yearned for it, even prayed for it, but that she had found herself wanting at her core? That she could believe only in her ability to make her own results? Yet, although she could conjure what she wanted – a relationship, a work of art, a child – once she had it, she couldn't let go: not of people, not of ideas. In some cases, that trait was a positive one. She shouldn't let go of her parents, much as they might annoy her, nor Leo, nor, especially, Roselore.

Would she ever have hold of her daughter? Maybe it wasn't about that, not for Roselore or her husband, nor even Dylan or the film. Perhaps she had hold of nothing in her life and it was all streaming through her fingers. There was no end. Well, there was one end, and that was pretty much out of her control. But why couldn't she say a final goodbye to Dylan? Have one last run at her film and polish it up?

Maybe ending projects or relationships felt too much like death. Or maybe she was afraid of the rush of life that might follow.

She realized Hannah was still staring at her. What had the girl asked?

"I doubt anybody's heard of me. I've worked on other people's films but this is the first one I'm making myself. It's not finished, though it's close. Once we get our daughter settled into our lives, I'll get there."

"I get that," Hannah said. She lowered her voice to a whisper. Eyes on the floor, she said, "When my baby is born, I'm going to start being a poet. It's what I've always wanted to do." She rushed her words as she said this last part. She looked at

Barth, then at Rudie. "What?" she said to Barth. "I showed you my stuff."

"It's pretty good," Barth said. "She's got talent."

He said this word with reverence, offering the assessment up to Rudie like a treasured gift.

"You should show her, Han," he said. "I bet she could help you with it. I mean, she's an artist."

Who used to think she could write poetry, Rudie thought.

Hannah rummaged around in her army-issue backpack.

"I'm going upstairs to get the rest of my things," Rudie said. "We've run out of time to set up the furniture. I want to be right ready to go when my friend comes." She considered her desk. Her silver laptop sat like a large, clean lozenge in the middle. She leaned over and flicked its power, printer and speaker cords away and scooped it under her arm. She didn't trust these two.

"I'll need this on the plane," she said as she headed up the stairs.

She set the laptop on her pillow. She hadn't intended to pack it but saw the value, if only for downloading pictures or communicating with Kikka while she was away. Other adoptive parents set up blogs and had groups of friends and family waiting for updates as they met their children. She admired the openness of some social worlds while secretly judging them. Here, really, the only one on her end waiting to hear how it went was her mother. It was Kikka who would want the photos and diary updates. Kikka would love, indeed *did* love, Roselore as much as Rudie and Leo did and for that, Rudie felt grateful for her mother and vowed to treat her with more kindness. She couldn't say the same for how she would treat anyone else.

She took the laptop case out of the closet and stuffed her camera in the side pouch. She'd grab the cords downstairs. Leo should be at the Halifax Airport, waiting to board. They wouldn't have any communication until they saw each other unless he found a way to squeeze in a text or two. She thought about texting *Yo, Lenny,* but decided against it, opting instead for his in-person reaction to her discovery. She sat on the edge of her bed then lay back, eyes closed. Her body pulsed, and she sprang up. Things with Dylan had almost ended for good, but then she'd backpedalled. She wished he wasn't coming. She wished he would ring the doorbell, take one look at Barth and Hannah and split. She moved into the bathroom and surveyed the mess of toiletries in a basket on the floor. When she said goodbye to Dylan this time, she wouldn't burden the word with layers and nuances and interpretations; she would simply mean goodbye, and she would let him go.

A knock came and then silence. Hannah and Barth had been chatting all this time, their voices murmuring a soundtrack to Rudie's thoughts. Now neither spoke, probably glaring, each daring the other to open the door. She stood in the hall, a panicked, fatiguing circle rising up around her chest. What if Roselore rejected her the way Leo had rejected his mother? His mother couldn't have been that bad, though he had run away many times. Rudie could screw up so easily, any parent could. Much of her work would be in attaching Roselore to her, not only so the child wouldn't flee as soon as she could, but so the child could attach to others in her life. Rudie wrapped her scarf around her neck until it bunched around her chin.

Downstairs, the door opened. Dylan called out, "Rudie? Are you here? Should we get go – Oh, hello."

Rudie tucked the laptop case under her arm and came downstairs.

"Come in, Dylan," she said. "That reminds me. I need to turn the furnace down while we're away. I should have asked somebody to come by and collect the mail. Maybe I should leave a tap running in case there's a melt. We had flooding last year." She moved instinctively to kiss him, then glanced at Barth in the living room doorway a few feet away and thought better of it. As a teen, she'd possessed a volatile blend of intuition and innocence, tending to have a read on all the undercurrents in a room while often missing the plays others made right before her eyes. She took Barth for a similar cocktail, with a heavier dose of the intuition needed to help him survive on the streets. Little got past him, she suspected.

"Hubby's back!" Hannah grinned, her fuchsia braces flashing.

Dylan tilted his head and raised his eyebrows at Rudie. "You know you're not required to bring home every stray."

"Whoa," said Hannah, standing. Barth sneered, rubbing the knuckles of one hand into the other. He wore leather gloves with the fingers cut out. Hannah had a pair of fuzzy pink cat mittens attached to the ends of a string. Rudie pegged her as the tougher of the two. She wanted to call Dylan on the word *strays* now that they were calling each other on things. Though it was probably his retaliation for *storm chaser*, the word irked her, reminding her of his earlier use of *pet*. She stopped herself. She had her dad to worry about, maybe Leo's mom. Not Dylan.

Rudie patted his arm. “Come in,” she said, “and I’ll explain.”

Dylan slid off his Blundstones and walked past Rudie to the kitchen. Barth held his arm across the door frame, blocking Hannah. “Who gives a shit,” Rudie heard him say as she followed Dylan.

Dylan stopped at the counter, touched it in a few places, then turned to face her. “Coffee?”

Rudie shook her head. “It’s this morning’s,” she said.

“They’re not your house sitters, are they?” His voice sounded kinder. Maybe he suspected her of imminent panic or wrong decisions.

Rudie peered down the dark hall. She stepped closer. “God, no. I’m taking them to her parents. She’s pregnant. It’s not far from the airport.”

“Poor kid,” Dylan said. “At least she’s got you.”

“This car is a shoe, Rudie,” said Dylan, “the too-small shoe of a boy whose penny-pinching mother insists he wear it because it’s good quality.”

Hannah chuckled. She and Barth sat on either side of the turquoise leopard-print car seat, still in its bag.

Barth flexed his hands inside their fingerless gloves. “I think I sprained my thumb moving that bed.”

Rudie inched up the escarpment behind an SUV with a *Share the Road* sticker. She drummed her gloved fingers on the dash and fought the urge to accelerate. Barth twisted around to scrape at the frost on the side window.

“There’s frost on this front window, too,” Dylan said. “This car’s so small I can rub off the frost with my knees.” The wisecracks hadn't stopped since they'd left the house. He was as bad as the kids.

"Whatever works," Rudie said. "It's not like there's much to see."

"The red lights will shine through the frost. You wouldn't be able to see out the back past those two and that supersized car seat anyway."

"You're here, because . . . ?" Hannah asked. "You're not her hubby. He's on a plane to meet her in Ottawa."

"You don't have a driver's licence?" Barth said.

"Like that matters," Hannah said to him.

"Can't you see they're friends?" Barth said.

"Like *we* are?" said Hannah. Barth banged the scraper on the floor. Rudie glanced at him in the mirror. He pursed his lips and studied Hannah with one eye. The car lurched and Rudie depressed the clutch. The traffic snaked up the escarpment, the road dropping off to the left.

"I doubt that," Barth said.

Hannah chuckled.

"What are your plans, Dylan?" Rudie asked.

Misunderstanding her, he launched into a description of the questions he was raising in his next documentary. She couldn't remember the subject of his film, so she turned her mind to watching for the road Hannah had told her to take so she wouldn't miss it and end up late for her flight.

When she first met Dylan, she had loved spurring him into a monologue about whatever project he was developing. He'd been more close-mouthed then, and she'd found joy in circling him, coming at him from all directions in the hope of teasing out a detail here or there. Likely he shared most of his creative process with his wife, but Rudie had found him pathologically private even about his career, where she didn't see why it mattered how much he shared. She wouldn't use what he told her. Did he consider her competition? She'd had no problem talking about her work, back when poetry and being a poet was all she wanted. It embarrassed her now to think about it.

She had been standing at a bar listening to a post-grunge blues band, a glass of Creemore in her hand, surveying the crowd, when she spotted him on the other side of the room. She'd caught his eye (or he'd caught hers) and the room had fallen away as if melting into an impressionistic painting. She'd turned back to the bar and played with a coaster, enjoying the thrill in her chest, more certain than she'd ever been about a man's pursuit. He had presented himself in front of her within moments, his white shirt and black suit endearingly pristine in the sticky-floored rock club, his slight panting even more winning. She'd succumbed to a kiss later that night, then had stretched their courtship out through weeks of phone calls and café meetups once he'd revealed he was attached. Getting involved with a married man was wrong, yet their connection intoxicated her so she justified each little slip, telling herself he was the one hurting his wife, not her. Their second kiss had hit her with the force of a dream train as they'd walked down an alley off Queen Street, his mouth devouring first her tongue, then her lips. She'd surrendered. The solo walk to her apartment was drunken. He took his car so nobody would see them together in public. She got there first. She waited inside, and he entered her there, against the wall, after slamming the door shut with his boot.

They were on the escarpment now, on Upper James, the street lined with car dealerships and mattress warehouses and shoe outlets. It was brighter here, the trees younger, the buildings shorter. Hannah and Barth grew quiet, each staring out the window as if they hadn't seen a retail strip before. Perhaps each had lived on the downtown streets long enough that this stretch would look strange. Rudie, when she returned from her months in New Mexico, had found sitting in rooms for extended periods of time difficult. Movie theatres, especially. When the lights went down, she'd gulp for air as she fought the urge to leap over the seats and flee, the feeling a symptom of months of having all her time to herself to choose to do whatever she wanted, whenever she wanted, a lifestyle that – though life on the streets was hard – Hannah and Barth did have. Every building they passed on the way to Hannah's family's house wiped away some of that freedom.

"The radio!" Rudie said. "What is it you kids listen to these days?" She turned up the volume on Rush's "Lakeside Park."

Barth looked over at Hannah, who didn't move. "Not much. Whatever you like. We're pretty open."

"This is fine," said Hannah, rousing, her voice sounding defeated. The colour had drained from her face.

Rudie turned forward again and struggled to decipher road signs with so much other information whizzing past. A minute later Hannah thumped her shoulder. "That's it. Turn left there," she said. She slumped back.

Dylan sat erect, his head against the headrest, the tops of his hair brushing the ceiling. Rudie wondered if his gel would leave a mark, not that it mattered. A section of fabric drooped low over Barth's head. When she'd suggested to Leo that duct tape would hold it, he'd laughed. She only noticed it when she had a backseat passenger. She made the left turn. Within a minute or two, the stores fell away. They were driving on a country road with houses set far back and far apart. If Hannah had grown up in one of these, surely her family couldn't have been that bad. Rudie caught herself. Providing shelter didn't meet all of a child's needs. Yet Hannah seemed fine with returning. Maybe going back was a sign of how far she had fallen.

"Hannah." Rudie made her voice sweet.

When Hannah didn't answer, Dylan turned around. "Didn't anyone teach you it's rude not to answer someone who asks you a question?"

"She didn't ask me anything," Hannah said. "She just said my name."

Rudie rested her hand on Dylan's wrist. "It's fine. You're right, I didn't ask you a question, Hannah, but I'd like to ask one now. It's very important to me. Could you tell us why you ran away?"

"Is that any business of yours?" Hannah said. Now it was Barth's arm reaching behind the car seat to cup Hannah's shoulder.

"She's just asking, man. She said she has her reasons."

"What are they?"

Rudie sighed. "It'll sound selfish maybe –"

"What else is new?"

"I'm becoming a mother tonight. I don't want my daughter to ever feel like she has to run away. I'd love it if you could tell me why you ran away, if it might help me know what not to do so she won't ever feel unsafe in her home."

"Are you saying it was bad that I ran away?" Hannah adjusted her shoulders, jutted out her chin.

"I'm saying, as a mother, I – *I* want my child to feel safe and loved so she won't need to, I mean. This isn't sounding right."

"Maybe I wanted my freedom. You're wrong if you think I'm not loved."

"We're all different," Barth said. "I left to go somewhere where I could be myself."

"You'd rather live on the street?" Dylan said. "You did your parents a favour, as far as I'm concerned."

"Dylan!" Rudie said at the same time as Hannah squeezed past the car seat and pushed herself between the front seats, jostling Rudie's arm and making her jump.

"Jesus Christ!" Hannah said, inadvertently cuffing Rudie in the shoulder and shaking Dylan's seat. "Why is it your business, asshole?"

"Is it about trust?" Rudie said. "When parents don't trust their teenagers enough, the teenagers rebel and leave. The ones whose parents trust them, the rich tourists, they come downtown for the weekend and go home." She thought of the fights she'd had with Bob in high school, fights that had all but ended when she got accepted at the University of Toronto and moved out. She'd belittled him, everything from his choice of clothes to the way he cut his meat at dinner, and he'd taken it. But he had his rules, against which she'd chafed over and over. When she left, the pressure had eased, and they'd been able to build the respectful friendship they had today – that was until he'd brought up that garbage about Roselore.

"You're simplifying it," Hannah said. "There are parents who are down on their kids and yell about all the things in their little lives that piss them off, and they take their misery out on their kids. And worse. Parents who fuck around and even worse, parents who mess with their own kids." Hannah shot a cryptic look at Barth, then grinned as if to say, *You're next.* But she was on a roll. "Parents who are mean as shit, who insult their kids, who say they're never good enough even if they get A's and join teams and clubs and shit. Two-faced parents. You name it. Think of whatever kind of asshole you can, and there is a parent like that."

"Then try telling *that* parent you're in love with the quarterback," Barth said. He met Rudie's eyes in the rear-view mirror. He wasn't joking. It took Rudie a moment to get his message. He was telling them he was gay, that he wasn't the father of Hannah's child, just a concerned friend. Barth rapped on the window, the frost melted now. They were passing fields of bent, yellow cornstalks poking out of a foot of snow. The grey sky exposed pockets of blue like bruises. Barth continued, "And yes, the street is cold and hopeless and we're treated like crap when we're seen, but mostly we're not seen. To the world, we might as well not be there and it's very depressing and you think, like, what was the point of being born, of all those soccer games and the home videos and the Ninja Turtles and shit? Why do they give us all that and then take it all away when we grow up and can think for ourselves?"

Rudie looked in the rear-view mirror until her eye's met Barth's, who kept his expression peaceful.

"Thank you for telling us," she said. "We've both seen a lot of the bad in this world and we know the depths to which the human character can sink."

Dylan crossed his arms and stared at the road.

"And we respect your choices," Rudie said. At the sight of a pair of horses standing in a field, her chest expanded.

"You realize what your problem is, Rudie?" Hannah said.

"Do we really need to go there?" Dylan asked. "She's giving you a ride, after all."

"No, Dylan. It's fine. I want to hear it. Go on," Rudie said, if only to distract herself. She checked the clock, calculated how much time she had to spare. The drive seemed to be taking longer now that they were away from the stores.

"It's that you can't leave anything, or let go."

"That's not true. I've let a lot of things go," Rudie said, though she couldn't think of anything. "Books! I donated a box to the diabetes people last week. A bathroom sink."

"You're like a person who doesn't want to finish things and move on."

"Like what? How can you say that? I got a degree."

"Like your film. Like this asshole. Aren't you married and here you are carting this douche around with you? You can't finish things or you wouldn't be asking a knocked-up teenager for motherhood advice." Hannah cackled.

"You hardly know me," Rudie said, yet she turned over Hannah's words in her mind. Walking away could be powerful, especially if where it took you was unknown and hard.

Dylan had his BlackBerry out and was scrolling through the messages. "Turn here," said Hannah. "It's the second one on the left."

At the end of a driveway lined with oblong shrubs sat a ranch-style house with a garage the size of a small barn, and a Dodge Caravan parked in the driveway. The nearest house was at least an acre away. Around the side and back grew trees, too, not old growth, but a fairly substantial size – maple, chestnut, oak. An icy nervousness filled Rudie's shoulders. She hoped this stop wouldn't take long. She had less than two hours to get to the airport, about fifteen minutes away. Dylan typed a message into his phone. Hannah and Barth shifted around in the back seat and whispered in each other's ears. Rudie glanced at the time.

Hannah was right. Her house was another example of her not completing things, not to mention the poetry manuscript about Hispanic death iconography she'd meant to work on in New Mexico. Unfinished. Hannah had nailed her. Had it started with Dylan? A project she knew she could never finish. She pulled into the driveway as Hannah and Barth gathered their few things on their laps.

"You don't need to stay," Hannah said, her hand on Rudie's shoulder again. "In fact, we really don't want you to. It would freak my mother out, us arriving with adult strangers and we don't need that. Right, Barth?"

Barth laughed a fake hearty laugh. "No, Ma'am," he said. "At least from what I've heard," he added. Of course. He hadn't met Hannah's parents but would know the real story, or at least a version closer to the truth than what Hannah had fed Rudie.

"Listen to them," Dylan said, as Rudie reached for her seat belt, her wrists shaking. "You need to get to the airport."

They were right, all of them. Rudie didn't have much time left, yet she had a strong pull to go inside. She waited as Hannah got her duffel bag out of the trunk.

"I'll give you my number. I will stay until you text me that you're okay," Rudie said. Despite the van in the driveway, the house looked dark and empty. A straw wreath wrapped in red ribbon hung on the front door. Hannah waved as though she'd spotted someone, took Rudie's business card and she and Barth trudged up to the door. They both turned and waved vigorously, then Hannah made little shooing motions.

—

Riding in the car with Dylan in the early days. All the knee-grabbing, the stick-shift jokes, the half-lidded lip-licking and swerve-driving, desire bouncing and bounding between them. She'd crushed all thoughts of those times so that they felt unreal to her now. Nothing had developed in any kind of straightforward way between them. What they had was as overblown, like tigers let out of their cages, as it was contained, colleagues acting on the set as if they barely knew one another. If she had to study her desire, she'd say she allowed it to rise to meet his, to both bloom and rot a beat behind what he felt. Though she wanted him all the time – *all* the time then – she only showed him once he'd shown her first. That buffer kept a key part of who she was in check and paved the way for various forms of deflation – regret, disgust, indifference – so that now, when she hesitated, her fingers playing with her Gumby and Pokey keychain, Dylan's hand on her thigh caused her to recoil. She couldn't drag her gaze away from Hannah and Barth standing between two porch columns arguing about who was going to carry the duffel bag.

Hannah moved to lift it. In her stained puffy vest, with her hair spread over her shoulders, she appeared to outmuscle him, but Barth, though skinny, was a head taller and moved with the coiled, hunched posture of someone who'd survived a scrape or two. Now they were having a tug-of-war with the handles. Rudie wanted to get out of the car to settle them down before Hannah's mother opened the door, but then Dylan's thumb was rubbing her hamstring and, undiscouraged, promising to travel up her thigh. She turned and caught him biting his lip, forehead wrinkled as he watched his hand in its slow progress as if he were helpless to halt it. Did he think he had to make this move? That it was required, that she expected it? She doubted it, though maybe she'd hoped.

She caught his eye, and the lip bite became more pronounced. The bite had roused her into action before, causing her to launch herself at him, wanting her lip to be the one bitten and sucked into his mouth. Back then, she had liked everything he did to her. She'd been a supplicant on demand and here he was demanding.

A shadow moved over the car, but when she turned she saw only the sun's white beam hitting the brown shingles of the ranch house at a hard angle, speeding clouds flashing light and shade across the roof. The front door, recessed beneath an overhang, sat in darkness. Hannah and Barth had gone inside. Rudie shivered and checked her phone for Hannah's text.

She shoved Dylan's hand away.

Dylan returned to smoothing her jeans as if they needed ironing. In his mind, they probably did. She brushed at his hand, flicked his fingers. She fought the urge to get out of the car. Instead she succumbed to a stronger urge to connect. Not in the old way, though. She had left that behind.

"If we're going to wait here," Dylan said, leaning in for a kiss. "Might as well make ourselves useful."

"Useful?" Rudie asked. "Is that how you see yourself? Like what? A power tool or a personal support worker?"

"You know what I mean," Dylan said.

"Sure. What the hell," Rudie said. "Time's running out. When the opportunity strikes. I'm on the verge of running late for the airport but sure, let's make out."

"No need to get snippy," Dylan said. "I wasn't thinking that. I miss you and want to connect with you before everything changes."

The door to Hannah's house opened, the inside as grim, despite shining floors, as the outside. Barth stepped out then glanced back over his shoulder as if someone had called. The storm door shut behind him. He paused, made a decision, and with his fingertips in his pockets, slowly approached the car.

Rudie shifted her weight, hand on the door handle, then turned to him. "But everything already has changed, Dylan, and you know that. And that's why you are here. Why we are here."

She paused in case he answered, but he didn't. Barth was halfway across the driveway when she opened the door and got out.

"They kicked me out," Barth said as Rudie approached him.

"She okay?" Rudie asked. "I mean, should I –?" She could spare ten minutes if it would help smooth over the situation.

Barth shrugged. "I'm not going back in there," he said.

Cold wind fingered Rudie's belly. She tugged her coat over her hips, hiked up her jeans, then walked up to the door and gave it a sharp knock. If she were Hannah's mother, she didn't think she'd want such interference. Hannah must want it or she wouldn't have let Rudie drive her here. Unless she thought Rudie was just going to drop her off. Hannah didn't know Rudie. She didn't. The low sun gave the sky a shell-pink tinge.

Rudie heard voices through the screen door, then a woman stepped out from a hallway. She was wide on top with tight jeans that made her body look like the letter Y. Her face had broad, high cheeks, rosy as if recently burned, freckles and coarse, clipped brown hair. She'd tucked in her white blouse and secured her jeans with a belt. Her white runners had pink swirls on the sides like cupcake frosting. Hannah's mom.

"And you are –?" She pushed the door open causing Rudie to take a step back. The woman stood with her feet in ballet third position.

"Rudie." She made no move to enter.

"She didn't mention a Rudie," said Hannah's mom. "You didn't tell me about no Rudie," she yelled over her shoulder. A *crash* came in response.

"That guy she brought," Hannah's mom said to Rudie, "the Bart Simpson kid, I told him to get the hell out. If she's back, she's back on *my* terms and they do not include a druggie faggot or – who did you say you were?"

"Ru –"

"Not your name. How does Hannah know ya? You're not on the street, I can tell that much." She looked Rudie up and down with a sniff as if she actually couldn't tell but was giving Rudie the gift of not insulting her.

"It's hard to explain," Rudie said, possessed suddenly of a strong urge to run, what Barth had likely felt ten minutes ago. Kudos to Hannah for hanging around as long as she had. The woman backed up and swept her arm. Rudie came inside as the door swung shut behind her.

"What you mean is you can't be bothered, that my daughter doesn't mean that much to you."

Rudie was struck by the sparse, institutional feel of the room, the spotless ceramic tiles, the pleated grey leather sectional and armchairs with white throw cushions. The white walls held a few pastel paintings, though no photographs, rugs or plants.

"I brought your daughter here, didn't I?" Rudie said, though until a moment ago she would have agreed with the woman that no, in fact, she didn't care about Hannah. In the face of this sparse, sterile home brimming with the mother's anger, Rudie did empathize with bold, expressive Hannah and her need to escape. The woman might have a right to her rage. Rudie had no idea what she'd suffered, but that didn't change the sheer unpleasantness of her life force. Something Rudie could say for certain: she would not end up in a bleached ranch house with her tough-ass daughter scared to come to her for help.

"You can go now," Hannah's mom said.

"Hannah?" called Rudie. "I'm leaving. Are you staying?"

"That's enough." The woman walked toward Rudie.

Rudie backed up to the door. "You haven't told me your name, by the way."

The woman snorted. "She didn't tell ya? It's Tora."

"Like a bull," Hannah said behind her, raising her index fingers and pointing them out from her temples. Hannah laughed. "Right, Mom?" she said.

Tora crossed her arms, squishing her breasts.

"What is it, Hannah? Your woman friend Rudie here claims she cares all about you. You going back with her or staying with me? Or did you just come to get money because that is not happening, girl, not until I see the pregnancy test and maybe not even then."

"She can stay, right?" Rudie asked. "You'll support her."

"She'll have to help out."

"Hannah?" said Rudie.

Hannah shook her head with a scowl that cast her eyes into darkness.

The peace felt fragile, but Rudie had to walk away. As she turned to leave, Tora clutched Hannah's arm.

"Thank the lady," she said. Rudie heard only a spring-loaded clang as she went out. It was easy to get in the car and drive away.

"She just wanted a reason to come home," Barth said.

"That's what everybody wants," said Rudie, thinking about how to make herself into a new home for a child broken away from hers. *Value the child*, she thought. *Value the child and maybe everything else falls into place.*

Barth slouched in the back seat with one arm up along the door window, awkwardly. His bottom lip protruded and his gaze held the nihilism of a rampaging toddler.

"You'll see her again," Rudie said. The engine coughed and caught. Dylan raised his eyes at her and shook his head slightly. Rudie realized what she'd implied.

"I mean she can visit you. It wouldn't be that hard."

She looked over to Dylan shaking his head. Stubble peppered his cheeks and chin with what he used to call his two o'clock shadow though it was now – she checked the clock and made the mental adjustment for daylight saving time – five o'clock. Her flight left at six fifty. She thrust the car into reverse and sailed backward down the driveway and swooped onto the road.

"You can't help some people," Dylan said. Whether he was speaking to Rudie or Barth or himself, Rudie couldn't tell.

"You can help yourself," Rudie said.

Barth scratched his eyebrow. He looked close to tears.

"I had no proof she was pregnant," Barth blurted as Rudie waited for the light on Upper James. The radiator squealed but otherwise the car was silent.

"But I trusted her. It's not my baby, of course. But I would've been a dad to it. As soon as we got there, she went to her room and started being Tora's little kid again. It was weird. I mean, I don't do that at my mom's. I'm nobody's little kid." He straightened as he said this. Rudie pulled to a stop in front of a Tim Hortons on a busy corner of Upper James Street. Barth had high, sharp cheekbones that shadowed his cheeks. With his black hair and eyes and his contained, focused look, he resembled Rudie. He looked at peace with his lot, and she wanted to hug him.

She got out of the car and waited, hands stuffed in her coat pockets. Neither Barth nor Dylan moved. She leaned back in her open door and said, "I'm going on alone from here."

The air smelled of sweet, fried dough and exhaust. Her stomach flipped. Hours had passed since she'd had the roti. She would hold out for the airport, where she could pick up a donut and tea if she had time.

In the end, she did hug Barth after giving him another twenty and her cell phone number. "Call first," she said, "if you need me – or if Hannah does, for that matter, though let's trust that she's safe." His shoulders and elbows were pointy, his body was lean and hard. A survivor.

"What the hell," Dylan whispered as she surrendered to his arms around her. "I thought I was coming to the airport, driving your car back for you. Fond farewell and all that."

Rudie inhaled the delicious soapy smell of him, lingered with her cheek against the warm softness of his pullover inside his open coat.

"That was never the plan," she said. "We had our farewell a long time ago. Now we're just ghosts. We're as lost as he is." They both watched Barth trudge across the parking lot. "But I'm going. The car needs to be at the airport so we can install the car seat when we get back. My plane leaves in less than two hours, and I'm not going to miss it."

She released him. When he wouldn't step away, she gave him a little push. Then when he wouldn't move, she slipped out of his arms and into her car, leaning across to close his door before she drove away.

She reached the airport under a dark, starless sky speckled with drifting snowflakes, though the weather report hadn't predicted snow. Clear skies until Tuesday. It was Thursday now. She got her ticket from the dispenser then parked her car in a cluster of other cars near the building. It was almost five forty-five. She slung her laptop bag over her shoulder and, pulling one rolling suitcase on either side, she trotted over to the airport door, a rectangle of light in the dim parking lot, beyond which lay dark open spaces with only the odd pinprick beam to indicate any life.

As she got closer to the door, she became aware of a man waving at her. She hadn't seen anyone in the parking lot, but she checked behind her anyway. All the cars were empty. An airplane sat at the end the building. Perhaps everyone had loaded onto the plane, and this man was waving her in, kind enough at this small airport to ensure he took care of everyone.

As she got closer she could tell by his shape. It was Bob.

The cold air had revived her, made the skin on her face zing.

She rushed through the door he held open for her, careful not to touch him. Her suitcases bumped on the step.

"Your plane loads in thirty minutes," he said. "I've been here an hour. I won't ask where you were." He handed her a manila nine by eleven envelope.

"Don't," Rudie said. She stuffed the envelope under her armpit, then stopped, head swivelling, scanning the signs for information. She'd used this airport before, but Bob's presence rattled her. He'd given up on her this morning, walked away. Uncharacteristically. She couldn't decipher the pictograms on the signs.

"Over there," her dad said, one hand on her elbow, the other pointing to a counter. "Look there's no lineup. You'll be fine."

He smelled of cherries, tobacco and sawdust. She felt a conflicted pleasure at having him here. He wore a leather car coat and a black toque with a badge that said Raise the Roof! His jeans had creases pressed into the front and fell to the ankles of his smooth workboots, well-worn but clean as new. She wasn't going to let him go easily.

"Mom says you, we, have a black ancestor," she said. She turned to him, to see herself in his brown eyes, his trim hair not hiding the deeply lined skin. She continued. "She said you're ashamed and that's why you pretend race doesn't exist, but it does and with a black granddaughter, you won't be able to pretend anymore. And what if I had been black? How would you have felt then?"

She squatted to unzip the side pouch of her smaller suitcase and took out a Ziploc bag containing her e-ticket.

"It was a rumour," he said, taking the ticket and studying it. "Everyone up north treated it like a big joke. People don't have to know everything. And believe me, you don't want that kind of teasing." He pointed. "Over there," he added, taking the handle of the larger suitcase and rolling it toward a counter.

"What kind?"

"A rumour about something you can't change. At least you have a choice. I had a choice, too, when you were born. We didn't say anything. Nobody needed to, once we were away from the place where everyone suspected. Just because I don't talk about it doesn't mean I'm a bad person."

"No," said Rudie, taking her ticket back. "But it doesn't mean you're right, either."

Their hug was dutiful. There was no reconciliation, no request for forgiveness. It was dutiful, but no less consoling for Rudie, who had worked herself up into thinking she wouldn't have the chance to hug him ever again.

Mama's on the wing, she texted Leo once she was in her seat. Then her phone died. She kept her bag tucked by her legs, her exhilaration rising higher and higher as the airplane backed up, then slowly rolled forward along the runway. She forgot until the last minute to look for her father down below, then couldn't see him when she did. Her ears popped as the airplane lifted, gravity pulling at her tightening hips, and the machine climbed into the air, the pain in her ears like fireworks, love exploding in her heart.

AGNES

Agnes hadn't moved a muscle in over an hour. The heat from the fire was waning, but the sunlight still beamed a warm parallelogram beside her easel. She didn't believe in rising from bed just because the body woke up. Even in New York, she'd liked to lie prone, preserving her sleeping position to let the dream state gel into her consciousness. Lingering in the physical sleep-position while awake had once led to many good paintings.

Now she wasn't in her bed. She was sitting in a chair in her studio. It was afternoon, late afternoon, judging by the angle of the sun. The room smelled of piñon smoke mixed with fresh sawdust and turpentine.

She closed her eyes and saw the Line. Opened them and held it there, too. But the Line wasn't a structure she understood. It wasn't a spine or a foundation or even a horizon; or, at least, not in the way that the logical mind understood those definitions.

The Line was space. A space. It took up space. It represented space, referenced it, contained and explained space. The Line wasn't the point at all. The point was her. She was the point. She was the one who provided the necessary conditions for the painting to emerge, the emotional homeostasis, the pleasant equilibrium. If the conditions inside her were empty, pure and joyous, the painting would emerge. The Line was the vehicle because at its heart, the visual medium required movement from its creator. If that movement sprang from a place without complication or grievance or concern, then what was created had the utmost chance of achieving perfection.

Agnes hadn't known these truths about painting before. She'd conceived of emotions as random occurrences that she needed to control and hadn't considered their influence on her painting. Emotions used to be hindrances, if anything, but really, they acted as catalysts for art, especially joy. She'd landed into joy on her walk back from the canyon, the confluence of having recognized her connection to the boy, Lenny – a blessing! – and the freedom of walking home under a clear, cold sky. Sleep and warmth didn't hurt either. Her happiness emerged from the freedom of figuring out an idea that had puzzled her for a long time. She shrugged off the red-and-black wool blanket. Her knees creaked as she stood and shook the pins and needles out of her calf. Sparks rose and settled as she poked and stirred the fire. After setting two more logs in, she shuffled over to the easel. She carried it to the wall, then lifted the stretched canvas and laid it on the floor directly under the skylight, where it caught the full light on her back table. She selected a 2B pencil and a kneaded eraser along with a yardstick, the plastic ruler from Jorge and a measuring tape, which she flung around her neck. Joy was cumulative. It didn't scuttle away when spotted. It shyly danced into view, spilling over itself like fireworks.

She didn't hear the car until it pulled up right outside.

She raised her face to the skylight, let her skin bake for a minute in the warm sunbeam. Her scalp had heated, leaving the hair around her neck damp after only a short time at the easel. She turned for the door, careful not to look at the work she'd done. It would wait for her. Now that she knew the best state from which to approach it, she was free to make whatever she wanted. The universal pleasure.

It was not Jesu's orange pickup truck in her driveway, but a black-and-white police car. A woman sat in the back as a police officer approached the door to Agnes's house. He knocked, then peered in the window.

The woman was Marsha, slumped and biting her painted nails like a sulking teenager. Had they arrested her?

Without bothering to get her parka, Agnes came outside.

"José? Officer Gutierrez? I'm over here. I was working. Is everything okay?"

Gutierrez turned and squinted. He took a pair of mirrored sunglasses from his chest pocket and put them on, tucking the arms over his ears with a smooth, practised flick.

She knew him better than the Officer Flores she'd spoken with earlier. José was a friend of Jesu's who lived on some land two lines over with his young wife and two little boys. *Good hombre to have around*, Jesu liked to say, though Jesu wasn't one to get in trouble with the law.

Gutierrez took off his cap, smoothed his brush cut, then put the cap back on. He wore a leather bomber jacket and walked slightly bowlegged, as if he would rather be straddling a motorbike – as indeed he might have been had he not brought a passenger.

Marsha banged on the window, her red lips distorted by the glass as she shouted.

"José?" Agnes said. "I'm going to let her out if you don't tell me what's going on." Alarm was rising into her shoulders, threatening to unseat the joy she'd recently claimed.

"*Señora*, I will let her out if it makes you feel better."

José removed the glasses. He stood in front of her now, his eyes round and concerned. How long had she been unconscious?

"Why is she here?" Agnes asked, stalling.

He frowned, sighed. Had he told her already? Never mind. She was allowed her lapses.

"Right. This lady, the mother, she showed up at the police station." He leaned in, whispering, though Marsha couldn't hear and had gone back to watching them sullenly. "We were going to put a charge on her, child abandonment, but then she told us this story about needing to pick up a package in Albuquerque. She said you agreed to watch the boy for a few hours. Her story checks out. The package was in the trunk. Did you say you'd look after the boy?"

Agnes was very sure she hadn't, though she couldn't account for a request she hadn't heard or that had been spoken during a gap-out.

"No, I did not," Agnes said. "That is why I came to you."

Gutierrez's eyebrows made a tent on his forehead. He raised

his shoulders forward, his hands on his hips as if to say, *What do you want to do?*

"I suppose you have a mystery on your hands," Agnes said. Then out of pity, she said, "He's in the house." *His mother's here now*, she told herself. *Let her take him.*

Agnes walked around the other side of the police car. She doubted they'd pull in the Child Protection Services of New Mexico now, not with Marsha here. From behind, Marsha looked like a mannequin poised as if she stood in a boutique window. She'd changed into a poncho fashioned from a Navajo blanket and wore a long, woven skirt and flat brimmed hat. Agnes assumed she'd considered the effect of this look, was making a statement with it. Marsha's skill at projecting an identity might outweigh her ability to paint. Whether or not Marsha had asked Agnes to look after Lenny was not the point. The point was Agnes hadn't understood, and Marsha hadn't made sure that she had.

You took care of him, John's voice said. *She didn't. That is the point.*

Agnes wore her boots but only a shirt, no jacket, and the lowering late afternoon sun had chilled the air considerably. Never mind. Let her body fat heat her up. Agnes wasn't going back inside. She steadied herself on the trunk of the police car so she wouldn't slip. Marsha turned her head.

"How do I open this door?" Agnes called. Gutierrez walked back over.

"I'd like you to go get him," Gutierrez said.

Marsha had blown air on the window, then wiped away a circle in the centre. Her mouth behind the glass made a smeary

O as she spoke words nobody could hear. Agnes held up a finger. "One minute," she said. Agnes had found her starting block, but she had yet to begin. And now the light was sinking.

"You can take Marsha inside," Agnes said. Gutierrez nodded. "But I'd like to talk to her first. Do you mind opening the door?"

The changing angle of the sun had shaded the snow blue in places. Gutierrez stood inside a triangular shadow made by the shed's corner. The car smelled of ingrained cigarette smoke. Marsha looked forward, her position unchanging as if Agnes hadn't just opened the door and blasted her with freezing air.

"Where is he?" Marsha said. She sniffled, tears brimming in her eyes.

"He's safe, Marsha," Agnes said. Though she believed the tears were at least partly manufactured, they might not be and now was not the time to remind Marsha of her failing as a parent. Gutierrez was ruminating by the front driver's-side wheel, perhaps looking for a reason to take Lenny from her. And Marsha wanted him back.

A moment later came the squishy, snapping sound of wheels on snowy dirt.

Shilah and Julie's mint green truck flashed through the trees. It had a driver and no passenger.

The sun painted a mauve strip that turned parts of the sky orange. The earth was a grid. What Agnes saw, heard and felt around her grew from that grid. Happiness and fear rocketed inside Agnes, each lifting her as the other dropped her. Art wasn't more or less than creation and response. Dried flies from last fall stuck to the truck's windshield. The R had fallen off so the grill read FO D. Rusted holes peppered the hood. It wouldn't surprise Agnes if they came from bullets. Julie's head sat level with the steering wheel. Agnes hadn't registered how tiny she was, but then Agnes herself was no beanpole. Julie pulled up by the house, both hands in knitted mittens at the top of the steering wheel, eyes straight ahead like someone not used to driving. She rolled to a stop, then got out of the truck, smiling weakly, her arms around the waist of her olive army parka with its fur-lined hood.

"What happened to Shilah?" Agnes asked.

"I left him at the canyon. I wanted to come back and make sure Lenny was okay."

The door to the house opened and out stepped Lenny, his longish hair in shining auburn clumps, much of which covered his eyes. He walked as if dazed, as if they'd woken him up.

My beautiful boy, said John's voice.

As Agnes approached him, Lenny furrowed his brow. He had his fists on his hips as if about to stamp his feet. Then he did stamp his foot and she laughed into her hand as if coughing. Mustn't let the boy see she took him anything but seriously. Children knew what was authentic, though. Lenny could trust Agnes.

"Marsha showed up," Agnes said. "And Julie." At that moment, the Line came up out of nowhere. She allowed herself a nasty thought: what if the Line were a cord made of thick rubber, a sinister object capable of whipping or hanging? She shook her head and closed her eyes to send this horrible, evil image away. She resented Marsha, that she would take the boy and Agnes wouldn't see him again.

It's all right, she addressed the Line. *I will paint you. I'm coming. Don't forsake me.*

"Maybe I don't want to see her," Lenny said. Agnes opened her eyes. His face was a wrinkled nut of disgust and hope.

"She told the police officers she asked me to take care of you. But she didn't. I'm quite sure of that."

"I didn't hear her ask you. She leaves me a lot, you know."

"I know, Pilot. But she really wants to see you, and I think she's sorry."

"Will you come with me?" he said, his voice frantic and hopeful.

Agnes checked her studio over her shoulder. The windows glowed with warm, shifting firelight. No matter what fantasies Agnes held about him staying with her, Marsha was his mother.

"I'm all yours," Agnes said.

Gutierrez smiled as Lenny and Agnes approached. They stopped about ten feet away from the police car. "Lenny, you can come back and see me any time," Agnes said in his ear. He nodded fast. She couldn't tell if he was listening. She raised her hand to his neck and was surprised at how strong it was. This boy was all self-protective muscle, he had to be, no matter how much he yearned for his mother to stay still long enough for his love to pin her down.

"I mean to say," she said. "You can stay with me. Doesn't matter how long it's been – when you're a teenager you might want it."

Julie came over then and stood with them, rubbing Lenny's back with her free hand.

"Lenny, you can look me and Shilah up too. You're always welcome."

Lenny nodded, his chin touching his chest as if he were ashamed. Agnes supposed he would be of this unstable mother whose abandonment of him prompted relative strangers to offer him a home. Agnes took her hand away and made a light sideways nod to Gutierrez, who opened the police car door and leaned inside. Lenny rushed around to the other side, and there was Marsha, squatting to greet him, throwing her arms open wide after flicking her eyes up at Agnes, and embracing him.

"I wish you hadn't run away," Marsha said. "I was coming right back – I said so."

"I didn't hear it! And neither did she!" Lenny said, pulling back. "Agnes," he added as an afterthought.

"That doesn't mean I didn't say it," Marsha said with practised one-upmanship as if she were his sibling, not his mother. "Agnes, you must admit, you're getting older –" Marsha's eyes flashed like hubcaps in the mauve light of the setting sun.

"Think what you want, Marsha," Agnes said. "You're his mother and you love him. Today, you might have lost him but luckily for you, he made sure that you didn't. He knows what he needs to survive. I told him and I'll tell you: the boy is welcome in my house any time." Agnes screwed up one eye and stared at Lenny with the other, bending with exaggeration so he'd get both the depth and the lightness of her meaning.

Lenny had pressed himself against the vehicle, half his body inside, the other half out in the light. He had lavender circles around his eyes, his lips pursed inward and up near his nose. The sun hung above the trees casting a foot of light into the car, illuminating the metallic blue seat leather and not much more.

He nodded once, solemnly, like a soldier receiving orders. His life with his mother was his mission, and he would perform it flawlessly. Agnes saluted him and scowled at Marsha, who was pushing her bangs above her eyebrows.

After Gutierrez left to drive Marsha and Lenny back to the hotel, Julie hung back, leaning against the truck bed with her fists stuffed in her pockets, eyes to the sky.

"Thank you for coming to check on Lenny," Agnes said.

"I needed to make sure he was all right," Julie said. "Now I have to do what I can to find my friend." She got into her truck.

The sun was almost behind the roof. Agnes might make a mark or two before she lost the light. She sagged. Yet, starting was everything. Julie leaned forward, one arm outstretched along the green seat. Agnes reached in, took her hand.

"The way I see it, your friend," Agnes said, "like the boy, Lenny, has moved out of your circle and you need to let that be. You might not know, you might not ever know, what happened or where he went, but every moment you spend caught in that question is a moment you don't spend in your life. You want to be an artist?" Julie nodded. "Walk out into that world and let joy find you. I promise. It's waiting."

Before Julie could object, Agnes shoved the door, which closed with a shriek, and walked around the back of the truck to her studio. With any luck, the fire would have embers she could stir into sparks. She would throw in a lit match followed by a piece of crumpled-up paper dipped in turpentine and turn to face her canvas while behind her the fire popped and flared.

—

Thirty years later, she saw Lenny again, in her final year of life, when he showed up at her door in Taos. She'd been sitting in her leather armchair with the wide wooden arms, the only piece of furniture she'd brought to the retirement home. Her room had a south-facing and a west-facing window, both of which she kept open year-round. Since the day in 1974 when she'd begun painting again, she'd become partial to the evening sun and liked to sit for long stretches, bathing her eyes in the light.

Though the man who entered looked nothing like the boy, she recognized him. The pinkish skin, the red-gold goatee, the flashing depths inside the brown eyes, this was almost John. He was younger than John when she and John were friends, but the resemblance was strong. If she didn't have to position her feet and steady herself for a good push before standing, she might have leapt up and thrown her arms around him. After all this time, life had brought her this: joy.

"It's Leo," he'd said. Then he'd cupped his chin and looked down and sideways before coming over and squatting in front of her. "Lenny," he whispered. "I came back. I wanted to before, but I felt like you'd want your privacy. But I'm in town for a while, and I've met this woman. She's the one, I think, though she doesn't know it yet, doesn't know I think it, but I'd like you to meet her. She hasn't even met Marsha."

Agnes stroked his head. He wore his hair shorn. The room smelled like Noxzema and Ivory soap. Agnes washed her hands as often as she could. A boiled chicken smell came from the hallway, and the scent of warm clay and sage wafted through the window. It was August. The sole cottonwood on this side of the building meant she'd soon be in shade.

They strolled around the yard for an hour as he filled her in on his life and his plans. He came back every day, soon bringing his girlfriend and their cameras. Though Agnes had decided she didn't want others to film her anymore, when Lenny asked, she said, "Yes." What did it matter? She'd be gone before they were finished. They'd even filmed her on her last day. It wouldn't surprise her, she thought near the end, if they captured her dying. She left drawing joy from each single breath.

ELLEN

The barbershop stretched long, with a wooden counter along one side. Mounted high on the wall beside a cabinet, a rail held a white cotton cloth hanging down. Customers sat in the tall, pink velvet chair with the curlicue wooden armrest and the high footstool while Ellen's father stood behind them and shaved and snipped their hair. When the customer was tall, like Owen Loftus or Justify Philpott, Daddy would stand on his own stool with his collar up and his white apron hanging below his knees. Daddy kept the wood stove red-hot, with a kettle on top and various jars and cups with creams and tonics on the shelf. Beside his stool he kept a pot into which he tossed lengths of hair. In 1850, he was one of the first in Hamilton to install a factory-made barber chair. He kept his tall chair as a keepsake, but when William came around, eager to marry her, Ellen watched Daddy set it up beside the new one, hanging all his razors and strops on the wall for them both to share so he could set about teaching him everything he knew about cutting hair. William didn't need a stool. The new chair had a pedal on the side so Daddy could adjust it to his height, so Daddy didn't need a stool then either.

Ellen took to visiting Daddy more when William was there. She'd stopped while she went to school, but William made the shop more interesting. He talked all the time, making the men laugh and bringing in customers. He didn't cut the men's hair much at all, but they kept coming back so Daddy held his tongue. William also liked to try out all the razors and might make what he called "a mistake," like slicing off a man's sideburn when he hadn't been asked to. William could charm the customer into thinking the new style was what he'd had in mind all along, but he made Daddy nervous. Daddy protested little when William came to him and said he'd like a change. "Like what?" Daddy asked. "We haven't much more space in here." Daddy thought he meant to add in a side business such as polishing shoes. But no. William wanted to find a new profession, a feat he'd performed twice before in the past year alone. Daddy agreed that William should do the work that made him most comfortable. Daddy loved barbering, and it showed. Relieved, William had folded up his apron, swept off his chair and hung his razor on the wall. He walked out into the sunlight, happy. He was going to be a butcher.

Philip and Ellen were travelling back the way they came because the road past Micheline's tapered off into the woods, and the sun was low. Philip planned to veer off at the crossroads before town and head north. They were taking a small chance that nobody would be returning this direction, let alone looking for them. As they approached her cabin, Ellen steadied herself with a hand on Philip's forearm. Her jaw ached as the wagon bounced along the rutted road. She held tight to the beaded bag.

"I'd like to have my chair," she said.

"We have to go quickly if we're going to find someplace to stay tonight."

"It won't take a minute. William made it for me and my daughter and I'd like to have it to remember the family I couldn't keep. Do you understand?"

He looked down at her and let the reins relax in his hand. The ponies slowed to a walk. "Yes, I do understand. My father has many items that belonged to my mother, but there is one that I hold close to me everywhere I go." He reached into his coat and produced a scallop-edged handkerchief of fine, crisp linen, folded in four. "Though I don't ever use it, I wear it tucked inside my waistcoat close to my heart. Take what you must to remember William. We can spare a moment. You might bring your clothing, too, and some staples, as Micheline suggested, but we mustn't linger."

Her house was dim inside, the fire reduced to a few glowing coals and a heap of ashes. The men had disposed of the sheet on which William had lain. They'd arranged the chairs and table such that one wouldn't know a dead man had rested there much of the afternoon. Philip waited outside while Ellen lifted the heart-carved chair to the door and lay her one folded dress on top. She moved quickly, adding a can of sugar, a bag of flour and two cups and two plates that she wrapped in a blanket.

She stood staring at the kitchen tools, considering which ones she might need most when Philip cried out, "Hey ho!" She ran to the door. He stood in his seat waving an arm back and forth above his head, facing away from her, holding the reins in the other hand as the ponies strained to move. He must have spotted somebody. She picked up the items on the chair and dashed to the wagon, tumbling them into the back; then she ran back to the house without looking at Philip. She slipped near the door, landing on one knee, then bounced back up and inside without wiping her skirt. She lifted the chair under one arm and walked with deliberate long strides back to the wagon. By now she could see the dark bodies moving like shadowy water through the trees as horses approached. Philip held a hand down to her as she turned back to the house.

"The door!" she cried, convinced that an open door would leave an important clue to whoever was about to find them that they were running away. She ran back once more and slammed it shut. Just as she slipped onto the bench beside Philip, the huge black horses trotted up huffing and snorting, Early at the reins, Darius beside him, arms crossed, lips tight together.

They stopped in front of Philip's team, Early guiding the horses so they stood at right angles to the ponies, which looked like miniatures in comparison. Darius clasped his gloved hands together, the steam from his breath forming ice beads on his moustache. Early dropped the reins, wrapped his arms around his body and looked down at his lap. He appeared to be talking, but Ellen couldn't hear him. Darius glanced at him, then stepped down from the wagon, brushing off his greatcoat as he moved to a rut in the road where there was less snow.

Philip made no move to leave the wagon or to speak on

her – their – behalf. Did Mr. Horn scare him? Aside from his father sometimes, Ellen had reckoned that Philip was afraid of no one. A man like Darius Horn couldn't touch a man like Philip, she didn't think. Philip had his own money from his job as a teacher and from his father, too, possibly. He logged, sometimes – at least he had done once – and he would again. Besides, logging was not Darius's business – it was sawmills and money, gambling and loans, she remembered William saying. If they ever needed money, Darius Horn was the last person she and Philip would go to even though others in Minden, such as Butch Cowper, who had the Stoney Crop Hotel down the road from Buck's, had taken loans from Darius and their businesses were thriving. At least it looked that way. Had Philip gotten into Darius for some money? Ellen doubted it. Philip had enough, but that wasn't much and there was no sign that he had any more than that. His face was empty except for his bottom lip, which bulged out, worried within by his tongue.

"Hello, folks," Darius said, approaching Philip's side of the wagon. Ellen pushed her hand against Philip's leg. Still he didn't move. His hand, however, the one not holding the reins, trembled lightly against his thigh.

Ellen rubbed her jaw, gathered her skirts and climbed down from the wagon. She went around the front, one hand on the darker horse's haunch, her neck, her muzzle, then on the other horse's in reverse, muzzle, neck, haunch until she stood to the left and slightly behind Darius Horn. Darius's dull coin eyes flicked from her to Philip and back again.

"Are you hitched yet?" Darius threw his question out into the air with a barking laugh. "She was planning to marry your father, last I heard. Reckon you'll have to call her *Mother*."

When Philip's shoulders raised slightly and his chin lowered, seeming to grow more pointy, and when he sighed and closed his eyes after a light flick toward her, Ellen read that he felt shame. For what? It hadn't been many hours since they left Buck's. Most people announced their intention to marry in church for three weeks in a row before they got married. There were procedures and rules to follow. They had to find someone to marry them. She supposed he was reacting to Darius's mention of his father, the reverend, or maybe his late mother. By the thin twist of his lips, she guessed that Darius knew full well they hadn't married.

"We're enjoying our engagement," Ellen said. "You don't think we're too fast, do you? After all, you were ready to set me up with Early Badger and don't think I don't know you probably had a Justice of the Peace in the backroom at Buck's."

Darius laughed, his voice tinny and mean. "Oh, many people frequent that backroom at Buck's, but I doubt you'd find a Justice of the Peace. Though there was that one time. Remember, Early?" he called, without taking his eyes off Ellen. "That Justice of the Peace from Kingston who came up to see what we had on offer? He left satisfied, but we didn't see him again. Maybe he preferred heavier fare."

Ellen squinted at him in the dirty grey light. Behind Buck's Hotel, men who came to gamble would pay for women, too. Women like her, maybe, widowed and alone, preyed upon by men like Darius Horn.

Early didn't answer. Maybe he hadn't heard. He'd hung back, shoulders hunched, one hand rubbing a horse's neck under the bridle. The horse leaned into him, ears flicking. Early met

Ellen's gaze long enough to show her the want in his hooded blue eyes.

She trusted Early but not Darius. Darius had a hold over Early. Or else Early liked being Darius's employee enough to do whatever Darius wanted. Like William. Early had skill with horses. William's skill had been blades: razors, knives, saws. He'd excelled at butchering meat, and though he'd been lax with the customers in her father's barbershop, he'd maintained control. He'd chosen saws in the end but he might have agreed to share his talent in other ways, on the side. Trimming sideburns here; skinning a deer there. If Darius had needed a man to help him cut what needed cutting, it made sense that he would have turned to William. William had held morals. He had believed in doing good acts and atoning for his sins. He went to church on Sundays; people saw him every week. He read the Bible in the evenings, and so did Darius Horn, yet he did deal in illegal gambling and more and he held debts over other men's heads.

She thought of Mickey Halston, a man who'd lost an arm at Darius Horn's sawmill while William worked his regular shift. That night William hadn't come home until the birds were calling in the dawn. He had lit the fire to roaring to heat the kettle for a bath. She'd lain in bed, dangling her leg free of the quilt until the heat got to her, and she'd risen and gone to the kitchen to find him sitting in the tub, his skin smeared with soap from the hard bar he was rubbing on his left foot. He'd smiled at her, his fool's grin to remind her he was no fool and that she shouldn't ask whatever she was fixing to ask. And she didn't. She wrapped a tea towel around the kettle handle and poured the contents into the tub, careful not to let the steaming water touch William's skin.

The air had been getting lighter though the sun hadn't risen. Already it was warm and with the fire, the room felt hot enough that Ellen had broken a sweat on her neck. It didn't matter much if the bath was cool, so she didn't refill the kettle. She bunched up a flannel, dipped it in the water and squeezed it over William's soapy calf. The less she said, the more William would. He'd fallen in love with her vivacious personality but had gotten used to the quieter self that emerged once she moved north. She stirred in some balsam needles and the room grew fragrant as William told her about a horsefly biting a chunk out of Mickey Halston's neck as he'd fed logs into the saw and distracting him enough that it had cost him his hand. Ellen listened to the details while rinsing William clean of soap as she imagined doctors' wives must do as their husbands recounted their day's surgeries. One of her duties as William's wife was to bear witness to him as a man. This thought had come to her as she'd swirled the cloth around his cock. He'd reached for her then, yanked her shift over her head and lowered her onto him, the water splashing across the pine floorboards, his thighs soapy and firm against her hips. Soon he'd flipped her onto the wet floor, shedding the tub like a carapace, the water spraying his back as he heaved into her, her body sore and grateful in its depths.

They hadn't spoken of Mickey Halston again, but she had seen him, once, at Duffy's. It was early autumn when men wore their sleeves short. Below his elbow protruded a nub with a little bow of skin at the end. It wasn't a hand Mickey had lost, but half an arm. The nearest doctor was a surgeon who hung out a sign in Lindsay, a day's ride away. William might have ridden down with Mickey, but then he wouldn't have returned in time. Had William's skill with a saw extended to surgery? What other human butchery had Darius Horn required of him?

"As to whether or not you're moving too quickly, you don't want me to answer that, Mrs. Cook. We must respect the dead. Right, Mr. McCloud?" Darius said. Before Ellen could say anything else, he tapped his knuckles on Philip's thigh.

Philip said nothing, his Adam's apple working up and down.

"Why don't we go for a short walk, Philip? I'd like to congratulate you. I won't keep him long, Mrs. Cook. Early would love to show you the horses while you wait." Early shrugged. Philip stood without looking at Ellen, who put her hand on his arm.

"Philip, what's going on?"

He shook off her hand and stepped down from the wagon, head down. A few strides away, he looked at her finally, not with anger or affection as she might have expected, but with sorrow and resignation. She felt those same emotions roll through her as he turned and trudged behind Darius Horn to the house where they stood talking. She'd felt tall and powerful when she first stood in the wagon; now she sat down, drained. Early stayed by the horses and she made no move. Around them trees cracked and groaned with the cold as the light dwindled blue, lined with faint orange. She shivered and told herself that whatever Darius had on Philip, Philip could face it with her help.

She rubbed her upper arms and rolled her shoulders. Her jaw sparked with pain. Maybe it didn't matter whom she married. Early was staying close by the horses. His shyness might mean he felt something for her or that he didn't but was too kind to force his presence upon her. Either way, a man like Early could make a good husband. He worked hard, was deft with horses; with a man like Early, tall and heavyset, with puckish eyebrows and brown woolly hair, if she were willing to turn a blind eye to his doings with Darius and keep up public appearances, she might have a fine enough life. Nobody would question the baby she was carrying. She was a widow, and it was natural she'd be close to her first husband's child. With Early, though, she imagined herself protecting the child, coddling it and pouring into it the stories of the life she'd lived that had brought her to this point. With Philip, she'd raise the child differently, in a glow of feeling that grew between the three of them. The child would represent the new, the spark flaming from the ashes with all that had happened before falling away. With Early, Ellen would be positioning herself, choosing a certain life, rising to the occasion. Philip had been a surprise but not a choice.

Had God made her as she was and guided her through the worst hardships, pummelling her with one loss after another – and she standing, taking it, oak-strong – only to ask her to wake up and think smart and choose a life that might keep her safe, raising her child, male or female, in the world of these forest-taming men? Or had God, as she'd come to believe, ignited faith in her so that she might move through her life moment by moment in love and joy? What mattered more than Philip and more than Early – each man at his heart a moral man, though

Early's association with Darius marked him a questionable follower – was Ellen's purpose of preaching what filled her up, spreading what she knew, and what Micheline knew, to anyone who'd listen.

She was sitting on her heart-carved chair beside Philip's ponies when Philip and Darius walked back across the snow. When she'd climbed into the back of the wagon to pull the chair back out, Early had left his horse's side, finally. She held the chair out to him, and he lifted it to the ground. After a few minutes of watching her sit, his palm cupping his chin, he lumbered back over to his horses, which hadn't moved.

"No need to let me down easy, Philip," she said, when he was in earshot. "It's clear that Mr. Horn is accustomed to getting what he wants and that he's determined that I engage myself to Early here." Early's cheeks flared red.

Darius held up his hand. "It isn't like that, Mrs. Cook," he said. "I came to see Mr. McCloud about another matter, which he can explain to you as he sees fit. Although I will acknowledge, and so should you, that you have sorely injured my man Early's heart by making a promise to him, then escaping out of Buck's front door in broad daylight to run who knows where with another man!"

"You know where. We came here, to my house. And Philip is the reverend's son. He's hardly –"

"Yes, we know who Philip is." He rested his hand on Philip's back between the shoulder blades. Philip's expression, until now the scowl of a misunderstood son, had shifted into one of canny determination, even shrewdness. Ellen stood.

"Philip?" she said. He looked at her with kind eyes, the rest of his face expressionless.

"Understand, Mrs. Cook," Darius said, "that the distinguished course of action, what any lady such as yourself would do, would be to apologize to Mr. Badger here and release him from his obligation to you. Unless your madcap hijinks with this young man are through and you do intend to marry Early, then I wish you both well."

Ellen swallowed. She wanted to talk to Philip before she spoke to Early. More than that, she wanted to be alone. She picked up the heart-carved chair and clutched it to her chest and said nothing.

Darius inhaled a wave of cold air. He nodded at Philip, then waggled his fingers at Early. "Good day, Mrs. Cook," he said, climbing up on the wagon.

Early stayed put, shoulders slumped, head hanging low. He said something that nobody could hear.

"Pardon me, Early?" Darius said from his seat.

Early looked up. "I ain't going until I speak to her myself. You're arranging all these wheels and deals and I ain't even know what you said to the reverend's young son here. Am I marrying her or not? It ain't up to you, Mr. Horn. It's up to me and her. Mrs. Cook, I –" He cast his eyes down again and swallowed deeply. The horse closest to Early raised a hoof and stamped it impatiently. Early sucked in a breath and looked up again. He leaned against the horse as though if she weren't there, he'd slump to the ground. He opened his mouth and whatever feelings he was having played into a knot on his face. His forehead shone red, and the brown curls peeking out from his hat were plastered against his head with sweat. In a rush of pity, Ellen came over to him.

"I am all for Darius's idea of us marrying," Early said. "And have been playing along with it all afternoon since he put it into my head. I would make a decent husband and father –" He blushed further. "But I will not marry you as part of a deal made by Mr. Horn or because you feel you haven't any other options." He was breathing heavily. The horse chucked him under the chin with her nose.

Ellen backed away from Early. "We don't know each other. We met today under such unfortunate circumstances." As she spoke, she looked at Darius, who sat, arms crossed, in his wagon. "I release you both from any obligation toward me, and we will have no further business together." Her voice shook.

Early's features hardened. Ellen sank against the side of Philip's wagon, grateful that Philip stood nearby.

"Let's hope it stays that way," Darius said. "For both your sakes." Darius leaned into Early, who'd heaved himself up onto the wagon bench beside him, and said something Ellen couldn't hear. Early nodded, then tightened the reins, cracked the whip and the horses heaved forward. They turned the wagon around and soon it had faded into the trees.

The sun had dropped out of sight, but it wasn't full dark yet. The sky had a faint tinge of orange in it as dusk approached.

Philip hung his head and was fiddling with the ponies' halters. Unlike Early, though, Philip wasn't shy. Though she did wonder if he'd capitulated to Darius Horn in some way. She'd rather he had, as long as it meant staying far away from Horn's business interests.

"Darius offered me work at his mill," Philip said. "I turned him down."

"Should we have torches? William keeps some black tin ones in the barn."

"I know these roads like the palm of my hand," Philip said. "There are benefits to riding without light, but we can light one if you feel safer."

She stood in front of him once he held the lit torch, letting his features reveal themselves to her in the light. Inside her cabin, fetching her chair and her clothing, she had thought little of William, hadn't noted his absence or even a feeling of grief or sadness. The men who'd picked him up had discarded the pails and cloths used to clean him. Earlier in the day, Philip had replenished the woodpile and the water. Philip carried the smell of balsam and mushrooms and lamp oil that marked a man who divided his time between outside and in.

"You mean for us to run, then?" she asked.

Philip stayed silent, letting her emerge through the twilight for him too. Some stars blinked now in the purpled sky.

"Philip," she said, "I must know what else you and Darius spoke about before I agree to run with you. If he has a way to impede us, I should know about it."

"It's nothing like that, Ellen. Actually, it is something like that. He suspects you know information about his backroom dealings and was hoping that if you married Early, he'd have control over what you would or wouldn't say. Early Badger is a good man and you wouldn't have a half-bad life if it were Early you chose. Mr. Horn let me know that Early would have you despite your running away from the hotel with me, that Early would consider your actions those of a grief-stricken widow and forgivable."

Philip took her hand. They walked around the wagon, the snow crunchy under their feet as the air grew colder without the sun.

"With Early, though, you'd be agreeing to turn a blind eye to his and Mr. Horn's dealings. As, presumably, you've been doing all along with William's dealings. Do you see where he's going with this?"

"I really didn't conjecture William's involvement in any dirty business. Only today when Darius showed up to help me clean up his body did I have an inkling."

"Darius Horn's gambling and loaning businesses are no secret up here, Ellen. My father knows all about it and has made it one of his missions in life to help men like Darius Horn see the wickedness of their ways and come into the fold and be forgiven."

"Might your father not feel about me that way then? That I might join his flock through union with his son and be forgiven for my association by marriage with these . . . these crimes?" Whatever crimes William had committed, she had been unwilling to ask the questions or read the signs. Each day up here, grief for Safra had walloped her and when she'd had a moment to breathe, she'd sought out her remembered faith. William's comings and goings had mattered to her only as they provided relief from her emotions and safety and sustenance for her body. If she were willing to attend Benjamin's sermons as a price for marriage to his son, she could change people's faith from within, exert her influence on the man himself and perhaps the people as well. She could stay close to Micheline then, explore their faith, raise their babies together.

"My father is a man of startling vigour and capacities of love for those willing to follow his path. I'm not convinced you are that way inclined but then you have caught me by surprise yourself today."

"It is true I have not been inclined to follow your father's path, nor that of any other church up here or anywhere. My faith is my own. It could be yours, too. I hope it will be, but I see now that listening to Reverend McCloud doesn't detract from what I feel and know."

It was full dark now. Wind was blowing snow around their faces. The torch flame bobbed and flickered.

"We don't have a plan. I don't. I thought we might make it to one of the hotels east of here. I have some money saved up from my teaching. Then tomorrow we'd ride to Peterborough and find a man to marry us. People will accept us, you, given time. We might come back here even, keep the claim."

"When my child comes? I have some money, too. William kept it in a box under the bed. And there are his final wages."

"We'll have our own child, too, later on." He looked down. "I'll sign on as a logger north of here, trade my ponies for a good-sized team of workhorses. With you I can do anything, it doesn't matter what my father thinks."

"Would you say that to him?"

"I won't have to say a word. My actions will speak for me."

Philip smoothed the fur on his beaver hat. He had wavy black sideburns and skin like a tallow candle, dense and shiny. The collar of his white shirt drooped open under his greatcoat. He had long straight black eyelashes and light blue eyes, his lids so pale they looked blue, too. She told herself it didn't matter if she married Philip or Early but the way her gaze sank into his told her that it did. Philip had grown quiet, but she didn't feel uncomfortable.

It would be up to her to fill her life, to build the next level. For what reason? For this coming child who would soon stretch against her dress and the next one and the next one. Tomorrow they would ride to Peterborough; on Sunday, she would mourn William from afar as Benjamin McCloud performed his funeral rites in Minden Village; and then for three Sundays following, a minister in Peterborough would read the banns. On the Sunday after that, if nobody objected – and short of the slim chance of Early Badger, who might follow and plead that she was first betrothed to him, nobody would – she and Philip McCloud would be married the following month.

Torchlight danced over them as he cupped her face and kissed her.

When they parted, he took up the reins in his left hand, and with his right arm around her shoulders, drove the ponies to the end of the lane, where they turned north on Bobcaygeon Road.

The first boy will be named after Daddy. The next I will call William. But if she's a girl, my dove, to bind you closer, we'll call her Safra, after you.

RUDIE

They had flown over Toronto. Below lay snow-covered fields hinted at through the dark. Rudie struggled to open a tiny packet of peanuts then gave up. She had the window seat. She had no earbuds, no iPod. Her phone had died after the last text she'd sent to Leo. She hadn't eaten dinner. She wasn't hungry. She rummaged through her laptop bag for the picture of Roselore. Bob's manila envelope took up most of the space. It kept falling out and making an irritating crackling sound. If she could open the window, she'd chuck the envelope into the skies. Whatever was in it, he could have told her in person. Bob had a mysterious side, hiding humbugs in his shirt pocket, mini chocolate bars under her pillow, pulling coins from behind her ear. Giving her anything, including a straightforward answer, outright embarrassed him. He hid cards, comic books, notepads, each with an inscription, his way of communicating with her. The conversation about Roselore must have felt like getting caught in the shower for such a shy (or was it private?) man.

Finally, Rudie had her hands on the image of Roselore, her eyes raw and wet with love at the sight of her daughter, who might look in person nothing like she did here. Children changed and the shot was from a few months ago. It wouldn't matter. This photograph was the dream emerging into reality. Her thumb itched to text Leo. She hoped he was looking at it too. The bald man sitting beside her was all belly. He wore foam headphones and read *The Walrus* while watching *He's Just Not That into You* on the tiny screen. She held the picture up and turned to invite him to look, but his focus was entirely on his entertainment. At least she didn't have to explain the whole situation to a stranger, especially not one in a navy suit with a red wool tie. She was done with the buildup, despite all the preparations she'd failed to make and the relationships she'd left hanging. She was ready to be in the moment with her daughter and Leo.

She slipped the photograph back into the envelope and bent to put it in her bag. Bob's envelope crackled again as it toppled under her foot. She stopped herself from punting it under the seat in front of her. It probably had her name on it and would get returned to her no doubt. No escaping it. She yanked it onto her lap, its pointy corners poking her legs in the process.

The envelope was blank and sealed. The contents could be his way of making amends or he might have sent her to Ottawa to meet her daughter with a handful of clippings of adoptions gone wrong – one never knew with him. She tore the top open. Inside she found a handful of mimeographs of typewritten pages, the first of which held two grainy photographs, one of three lines of people, their clothing and the trees around so dark their features were indecipherable. The second photograph was a man holding a team of horses on a muddy road strewn with logs, his boot resting on a rock. On the second page was a family tree, names typed in with birth and death dates in brackets below them, hand-drawn lines connecting names to their spouses, their children and their siblings. On the third page, Rudie found her father's and mother's names, Robert and Kikka (née Vogel) Bell and below it, connected by a Y-shaped line, Rudie (née Bell) Patron and Leonardo Patron. Someone, probably her father, had written *Divorced* below the line joining his and Kikka's names, though nothing was finalized yet. Rudie fumbled in her purse for her own pen, a Sharpie. Below her and Leo's names, she drew a Y-shaped line and wrote: *Roselore Agnes Patron.* Leo didn't know her decision – she'd just made it and would text him if she could – but she wanted Roselore to have one name, at least, chosen by her parents. If he had his heart set on another, they would add it.

Rudie turned back to the first page. If her father could take the time to write *Divorced* why not write *Roselore*, too? Rudie knew why not. She studied the group photograph. By the clothing, she judged it to be early twentieth century if not late nineteenth. The copy was so degraded she couldn't make out any faces, but she supposed these people were her family. She studied the first page of the family tree. The first name was Anson Bell, with a line connecting him to his wife, Safra née McCloud. At the bottom of the page, she found her grandfather Chester Bell and her grandmother Virginia. Her mother had said Sapphire but she'd also said spice, like saffron. Rudie flipped back to the group photo. It showed three lines of people, the women in front. One man had his sleeves rolled up to his elbows, though the rest wore dark jackets. The woman in the centre was smaller than the others, her face darker, too, though the bad copy blurred everyone's features.

The man beside Rudie had closed his eyes. On the screen attached to the seat in front of him, Jennifer Aniston sat at a bar. Her mother had told her that, as a baby, Rudie had met Safra. According to the dates on the family tree, Safra had lived to be ninety-nine, older than Agnes even. If Kikka had impressed anything on Rudie, it was a fascination for women who lived into their nineties. Here her father was owning up to a part of himself he'd concealed from the world for most of his life. She felt scared and shy at this new shame-exposed father. Her own shame rose up, too, at having questioned his love for her.

Leo held up a sign that said Roselore's Mummy. They ran into each other's arms as if they'd been apart for months. Rudie cried a little against his shoulder, then moved her head back. His pale freckled cheeks were wet, his grin as wide as hers. This man had known Agnes in some deep way before he'd introduced her to Rudie. He'd brought Rudie together with the creative soul of her project. A catalyst of a man. A connector. Leo took her hand and led her through the crowd.

"Have you seen her yet? Has anybody seen them?"

"No, but soon. We have only half an hour before we meet them at the hotel. Then they'll bring us together."

After twice bumping into people's suitcases, once with her thigh, once with her bag, Rudie caught her toe on the side of a garbage can with three holes in the top for sorting trash. She stumbled onto one knee and the lid went flying.

"Keep going," Leo laughed, his brown eyes flashing. He was wearing a Canada Goose coat she hadn't seen before and a camel turtleneck. He hadn't shaved and curly russet hairs shadowed his chin. He looked new to her and not because they were about to become parents together, but because the interview with Agnes had given her a key to part of him that he had hidden from her. She played with the name Lenny in her mind, practised saying it to the back of his head as he pulled her by the hand running through the airport.

"Don't mention money," he said as he opened the door to a cab. "The agency will pay."

"I wasn't. I wouldn't have." They chatted for a few moments more before noticing the cab driver sitting still, eyes straight ahead.

Leo leaned on the back of the front seat. "Did we forget to tell you where to go?"

"To the hotel," Rudie yelled helpfully. She couldn't remember which hotel. She unzipped her purse. Leo turned back to her.

"You were just there, Leo!"

"I wasn't. I've been here waiting for you."

"Oh."

He scrolled around his phone while she sifted through receipts in her wallet. "All those reminders to each other –"

"The Sheraton!" they said in unison. The cab driver touched the brim of his Greek fisherman's cap and swung the car neatly onto the road.

—

At the hotel, there was an equally panicked moment as Leo and Rudie rifled through Rudie's papers looking for the room number. For a moment, Rudie lost the ability to read or even register marks on a paper. She swallowed several times, her throat dry, but she was afraid to drink in case she forgot how to do that, too. Finally, Leo asked at the desk, where a tall receptionist with a man bun and a gentle voice said, "You must be so thrilled. I will lead you to them. We've seen the children. They're –" He, too, looked about to cry. He steered them through doors and down a hall and through another door as Rudie fought off envy that this young man had seen Roselore before she had. So had Ann, though, and many other people in Roselore's two years of life, so Rudie choked down that feeling and forced herself not to muscle aside the hotel receptionist and run headlong down the carpeted hall, opening every door until she found her daughter, scooped her into her arms and sprinted off into the Ottawa night.

Leo's hand kept her from floating to the ceiling. They stopped talking as they reached the end of the hall and the young man stepped back, smiling as he gestured them into a meeting room.

The sounds struck her first, more specifically, the voice, a loud, rasping child's voice naming the objects around her: "Chair! Boot! Coat!" The child had dark brown curls held away from her face with a pink headband and she wore a long-sleeved blue dress.

Ann Hepner spotted them at the door. She held her hand out to the child who spun in circles watching her skirt twirl out.

The child swatted at her and wouldn't look up. Tears streamed down Rudie's cheeks. The child had no idea – well, maybe some idea. Ann had promised preparation in Haiti and on the airplane – but right this moment the child pirouetted, suspended in a bubble between what was and what would be.

So were Rudie and Leo, but this moment belonged to Roselore.

Ann stood aside and said, "Give her time."

Rudie didn't know who she meant. Then something kicked in and Rudie took off her boots, then walked over to Roselore with an exaggerated tiptoe. The child raised her chin and met her eyes with what Rudie told herself was recognition. The girl looked away, then, not at Ann nor Leo, but at someone who was no longer there.

Rudie squatted. "Yes, it's me, Roselore. Here I am." Without hesitation, she took her daughter's hand.

ACKNOWLEDGEMENTS

Immense gratitude to Krista Foss, Canisia Lubrin, John Miller, Elizabeth Ruth and Emily Schultz. A special acknowledgement to the Canada Council for the Arts, the Ontario Arts Council and the Banff Writing Studio. Deep appreciation for Noelle Allen, Jennifer Hale, Ashley Hisson and the staff at Wolsak & Wynn. Hat tip to the Harwood Museum of Art in Taos, New Mexico, and the Big Top Restaurant in Hamilton, Ontario. Profound love for my dear ones, Raven Cooper-Hill and Isis Cooper-Hill, and to Daniel Hill, thank you.

Agnes Martin was one of the most significant abstract painters of the twentieth century. Born in Macklin, Saskatchewan, in 1912, she spent the last twenty-six years of her life in New Mexico. Her minimalist work consists of pale washes and pencilled grids on square canvases and is internationally renowned. The Harwood Museum in Taos, New Mexico, exhibits seven of Martin's paintings, donated by the artist, in an octagonal room. She died in Taos in 2004. Agnes Martin did not receive recognition for her work until she was nearly fifty.

SALLY COOPER is a Hamilton-based novelist, essayist and screenwriter. She is the author of the acclaimed novels *Love Object* and *Tell Everything* (Dundurn) and the linked story collection *Smells Like Heaven* (ARP). She has published widely in such places as *Electric Literature*, *The Millions* and *TNQ: The New Quarterly*. She is represented by Samantha Haywood at Transatlantic Agency.